Ten years ago, the passion was ignited...
And it's only gotten hotter with time!

Blaze

**Join the editors in celebrating
a decade of wonderful authors,
irresistible stories...and great sex!**

**Look for all six
Special 10th Anniversary Collectors' Editions
from The Original Sexy Six authors.**

Check out:

THE BRADDOCK BOYS: TRAVIS
and *THE PLEASURE PRINCIPLE*
by Kimberly Raye

HOTSHOT and *GOING FOR IT*
by Jo Leigh

UNDENIABLE PLEASURES and *YOU SEXY THING!*
by Tori Carrington

COWBOYS LIKE US and *NOTORIOUS*
by Vicki Lewis Thompson

TOO HOT TO TOUCH and *EXPOSED*
by Julie Leto

EXTRA INNINGS and *IN HIS WILDEST DREAMS*
by Debbi Rawlins

Harlequin Blaze—
Celebrating 10 years of red-hot reads!

Dear Reader,

Ten years ago, I was living in Houston, Blaze was a flash on the cover of Harlequin Temptation, and Birgit Davis-Todd was my editor. She asked me if I would like to write the second book of the brand-new line, Harlequin Blaze. I quickly said yes!

Today, twenty-three (and counting!) Blaze books later, I live in Utah, I've been married and widowed, and I spend far too much time wrangling three dogs and six cats, all of whom are spoiled rotten. Thankfully, Birgit is still my editor, I still enjoy the challenge and thrill of writing for the most innovative category books on the market, and I'm proud and pleased to offer *Hotshot* as my tenth anniversary milestone book.

I've never been in the armed services, but I've always respected and admired those who are. As I'm writing this note, my nephew is getting ready to serve his tour of duty in Afghanistan, so the issues in the book were quite personal. Writing *Hotshot,* one of the Uniformly Hot! series, was a challenge and a privilege, and the men and women who advised me on the U.S. Air Force were incredibly helpful and gracious. To all of you who serve, or who have loved ones who serve, thank you. Writing the book changed me in the best possible way, and I hope I did you justice.

Yours truly,

Jo Leigh

Jo Leigh

HOTSHOT
GOING FOR IT

Harlequin®

TORONTO NEW YORK LONDON
AMSTERDAM PARIS SYDNEY HAMBURG
STOCKHOLM ATHENS TOKYO MILAN MADRID
PRAGUE WARSAW BUDAPEST AUCKLAND

ISBN-13: 978-0-373-79632-8

HOTSHOT
Copyright © 2011 by Harlequin Books S.A.

The publisher acknowledges the
copyright holder of the individual works
as follows:

HOTSHOT
Copyright © 2011 by Jolie Kramer

GOING FOR IT
Copyright © 2001 by Jolie Kramer

Recycling programs
for this product may
not exist in your area.

Printed in U.S.A.

CONTENTS

ABOUT THE AUTHOR

Jo Leigh has written more than forty novels for Harlequin and Silhouette. She's thrilled that she can write mysteries, suspense and comedies all under the Blaze banner, especially because the heart of each and every book is the love story.

A triple RITA® Award finalist, Jo lives in Utah where she's at work on her next book. You can come chat with Jo at her website at www.joleigh.com, follow her on Twitter @jo_leigh and don't forget to check out her daily blog!

Books by Jo Leigh

HOTSHOT

My deepest thanks to Muna, Jill and Debbi,
and to the Blaze team.
It's been one hell of a ride!

1

CAPTAIN SARA WESTON was on hold. Still. She left the confines of her temporary office, nothing more than a motel conference room swallowed by her charts and files, to get more legroom in the hallway. Pacing while on hold had become such a large part of her day she'd decided two weeks ago to fill the time with some useful exercise. She doubted any amount of walking would ease the tension in her shoulders or make her any less furious.

This was the third call in as many days to the public affairs office at Fort George Mead, where she'd been put off, transferred, hung up on, stalled and once, infuriatingly laughed at. She had a situation here and, by God, today she was going to have her solution or heads would roll.

In exactly one week, the Why We Serve college and job fair's western tour would begin. The bookings were set, logistics getting squared away, staff assigned, and motels allotted. The slide shows had been honed to appeal to specific audiences; the talks, with one notable exception, had been rehearsed and finessed.

Today, the notable exception would be handled. If she had to go all the way to the general of the air force, she would. She needed a flyer. An air force pilot who'd seen action, who could talk to kids, who had a story worth telling. An active-duty air force flyboy who wasn't on assignment, who could be in San Diego in twenty-four hours.

"Captain?"

"If you transfer me one more time…"

"Captain, I'm sorry, but if you want to speak to Captain Alonzo, I'll have to transfer you."

Sara held the phone away from her ear as she deeply inhaled. She was not going to lose her cool, not yet, that was for damn sure. She brought her cell back into range. "You do realize I've been playing this game for three days? That I've been transferred twice already on this call alone?"

"Yes, ma'am, I do realize that, and I apologize for the inconvenience. Captain Alonzo was inadvertently delayed. He's en route as we speak and I'm sure he'll be available in moments. I'll transfer you now."

Turning at the end of the hallway, she listened to yet another phone ring, and as she walked she unclenched her jaw, moved her neck, rolled her shoulders. She'd been in the service long enough to know that channels were channels and snafus were standard operating procedure. And that she was far less likely to achieve her objective if she told Captain Alonzo exactly what he could do with his inadvertent delay.

At the other end of the hallway, where her offices and the civilian world met, she saw Master Sergeant Mike O'Malley, his back ramrod-straight, his uniform impeccable, his scowl firmly in place, and she felt instantly better.

O'Malley looked like a pit bull and bit like one too, but Sara couldn't imagine what she'd do without him.

He was in charge of logistics, but equally as important, the old goat held the keys to her personal sanity. No one listened like O'Malley, and if she didn't get connected to Captain Fred Alonzo in about ten seconds, O'Malley was going to need to talk her down before she went postal.

She turned her attention to the phone when she heard a man's voice. Alonzo's voice. Finally.

"Captain Weston. Sorry for the delay."

Just as she opened her mouth she looked up again, and there was someone with O'Malley, blocking him. A man. She could only see his back.

The air left her lungs, her mission left her head, and as she lowered and closed her cell phone, all she could think was, *What the hell is he doing here?* He couldn't possibly be here. Not here. He was in Bagram, Afghanistan, attached to the 455th Expeditionary Fighter Squadron. It made no sense that he'd be standing talking to O'Malley in a Victoria Inn off the 405 Freeway in San Diego.

But she knew it was him. Lucas Carnes. No other man on the planet stood just that way, had that exact lanky build, and no one on this planet held his head just so.

Yet, it was a full-body slam when he turned and she saw his face.

Son of a bitch.

SEEING SARA WAS A roundhouse punch to the gut. It took everything Luke had to stay solid, to remember he'd planned to smile, act casual. He needed this gig, and Sara could find a way to derail the whole operation before it got started.

He smiled, but for the life of him he couldn't make it feel natural. All this time he'd figured the hard part would be the talking. But looking at her, seeing her face, damn near crippled him. It had been seven years since they'd last set eyes on each other, seven years since… God, she was a beauty.

The first step was forced, but then he needed to be closer, to see the little things. The hint of red in hair that looked so dark a man might think it was black. The Cupid's-bow mouth she toned down with her lipstick but that came out to play after she'd been thoroughly kissed. The way she'd smile so quickly sometimes that if you weren't watching, you'd miss it. He doubted he'd see that today. But he didn't care. He was in the same country as Sara, the same state, the same city. The same hallway.

Her shoulders in her starched uniform straightened, and that little tie tab never looked better on any woman in the service. He looked at her face, ignoring her eyes for the moment. Her mouth was tight, which he expected, but he knew those lips in all their permutations. Grinning, frowning. Opened wide, breath held as she was about to come.

Up an inch, and there it was, the little dent on the end of her perfect nose. She'd hated that thing, sworn she was gonna get it fixed one day, but he never used to miss a chance to kiss that very spot.

He could feel her impatience so he took a fortifying breath and faced her squarely.

"What the hell is this?" she asked, her voice as dark and cold as a mountain at midnight.

He pulled himself into a sharp salute, years of practice and routine helping him keep his expression neutral. "Captain Lucas Carnes reporting for duty, ma'am."

Her eyebrows, dark chevrons he'd traced with his tongue more than once, rose. "What?"

He lowered his hand. "You needed one replacement fighter pilot for your dog-and-pony show. I'm your man."

For a long moment she didn't say anything. But she

spoke volumes. Her nostrils flared with banked anger, her cheeks flushed with it, her hands, he had no doubt, were curled into tight fists. "Orders?" she said, icy and so controlled.

He got his orders out of his kit and handed them to her, knowing that if she wanted him gone, he'd be gone. But he also knew she was desperate, and that if she didn't take him, she'd be short a fighter pilot for the tour. She couldn't have changed so much that she wouldn't put her assignment before her personal feelings.

Her hands trembled. Not a lot, but enough to make her snap the papers down and give him a glare that singed. "Why are you here, Carnes?"

So she was going with his last name. Not Luke, not even Lucas. He'd never even hoped that she'd call him Solo even though everyone else did. It was tradition, after all, for a pilot to be known by his call sign, but Sara didn't see him as a fighter pilot. Just a jerk.

"I'm here to do my best," he said, meaning it. "To make your job easier. With luck, to inspire some young people to consider the air force as a viable and valuable career."

"See Master Sergeant O'Malley for your room assignment," she said, as if he'd never spoken. She turned in dismissal. After two steps, she paused, glanced over her shoulder. "If I were you, I wouldn't unpack."

He didn't respond. She needed some adjustment time. And truthfully, so did he.

He'd been so damn sure. The opportunity had opened before him like a gift. He couldn't remember exactly when he'd heard about this tour and Sara's assignment. No surprise there. He'd always known where she was stationed, if not the details. Two months ago, he'd figured he might as well take his leave in California. Why not? It was about as far from Afghanistan as a man could get.

Then he'd gotten the news that her pilot had been hurt. Hell, he knew Captain Wiley. They'd been in training together at Sheppard. Luke was sorry about the accident, but he'd jumped all over the temporary duty assignment.

Now that he was here, though, Luke had to wonder. It might end up a holy disaster. If she shot him down, so be it. He deserved nothing less. What he didn't know, not for certain, was whether his being here would make things worse. That, he'd never forgive himself for. He'd done enough damage. More than enough.

He went to find O'Malley, deciding it would be wise to heed her advice and not expect a goddamn thing.

SARA LEANED AGAINST the motel-room door. There was no denying seeing Luke had shaken her to her core. He had no business walking into her work, into her life. It made no sense.

Luke would rather have his arm cut off than be sidelined by a recruitment tour. Even before he'd become the air force pilot poster boy, she'd never known him to miss an opportunity to fly. By the time he was fifteen, he'd been addicted to flying, taking up his dad's private plane to skim the treelines of Santa Rosa. At Berkeley, even with his heavy class load and ROTC, he'd still made time to fly, racking up his hours in anything from crop dusters to Cessnas.

The only other thing he'd pursued with the same dogged tenacity had been her.

She grabbed a bottle of water from her minifridge and collapsed into her chair. Seven years since they'd broken up, and the bastard still haunted her. Seven years since he'd dumped her, scraped her off his life as if she were something unpleasant on his shoe. So much time had passed, and yet what persisted, what kept cropping up in her life over and over again, wasn't the way it ended, but the way it had been for the five years before that. She'd thought they'd be together forever, and he'd walked away without a backward glance.

She didn't want to think about that. Or anything but sending him away.

His orders told her nothing. It was a standard TDY, that's all, but there was wiggle room. She did have recourse. First, she could declare him unfit for this duty. Not every officer was equipped to handle public speaking, and she could build a solid case that he would be detrimental to the mission, despite his exemplary record. But it would mean she'd have to find the perfect candidate first, and dammit, *dammit,* she'd hung up on Alonzo.

Snapping her cell open, she redialed his number, not in the least surprised when it went to voice mail. She made up some crap about being cut off, but figured the way her day was going he wasn't about to call her anytime soon.

Okay, strategy two: according to Air Force Instruction 36-2909, if professional judgment and common sense indicate that a relationship may reasonably result in a degradation of morale, good order, discipline or unit cohesion, a commander or supervisor should take corrective action. In this particular case, she was the supervisor and Luke Carnes couldn't help but degrade good order and morale. The problem wasn't in the principal of taking action, it was in the details. She'd have to admit, on record, that she and Luke had been lovers. That she'd never truly gotten over him.

She moaned as her head hit her cupped hands. Luke wouldn't be sent away—she would. To a psychiatric ward. No right-minded adult held on to a college relationship for this long. The very notion was ludicrous.

But really, the fact was she didn't love him, hadn't

for a long time. If she felt anything it was anger, disappointment, an acute sense of betrayal. Not wanting to work with him was completely understandable. He was her worst memory, and no one should have that shoved in her face on a daily basis. It didn't help that he was still the most gorgeous guy she'd ever seen. God, what those green eyes could do to her—

Sara winced. She straightened her shoulders and collected her thoughts. It was too soon to make a decision. She needed to speak to Alonzo, find out if he had someone waiting in the wings. Right now though, she would put the Luke situation aside. She had a tour to prepare, and half the time she needed to do it in.

THE DINER WAS RIGHT NEXT to the motel. Despite the great restaurants downtown, Luke was too tired and hungry to foray. With a magazine tucked under his arm, he went inside and decided right then that he'd have himself a nice slice of that apple pie in the case. When he managed to look past that to the dining area, he saw O'Malley sitting in a booth with Sara. Her back was to Luke, and he didn't even think about it, he just walked.

O'Malley caught his eye but there was no welcoming smile to go with it. By the time Luke got to the booth, a less-determined man would have had second thoughts. He wasn't sure if the scowl on O'Malley's face was because Sara had filled him in or if he always looked like that. It didn't matter. The two of them hadn't been served yet; his timing was perfect.

"Mind if I join you?" Luke kept his gaze on the sergeant, but he could feel Sara tense.

"Take a seat," O'Malley said brusquely. The tension Luke had sensed from Sara a few seconds ago? That had been nothing. Especially when the older man made no move to make room.

Sara tried to wait him out, but Luke maintained his presence. Finally, she shifted over and he sat, surprised the vinyl seat hadn't frozen over solid.

He dared a glance and got her profile. Her mouth was a thin rigid line, but that was the only outward sign of her annoyance.

Before he could even think of an opening line, a waitress arrived, a pretty girl whose white spiky hair sported a swath of jet black right down the middle. She smiled at Luke. "You want a menu?"

"No, thanks. I'll have what she's having."

He looked at Sara in time to see her head jerk in his direction. The glare was there, but only for a moment. Her eyes calmed along with her lips as her gaze moved to the waitress. "I'll have the liver and onions."

Shit. Stupid move on his part. He despised liver, and, of course, Sara knew that. The smell alone made him sick.

O'Malley ordered a cheeseburger. At least Luke would be able to wash away some of the liver with a large chocolate shake, although the damn organ meat would haunt his nightmares. Score: Sara–1, Luke–0. He would have given himself a point for showing up, but if she got rid of him by morning, that wouldn't be a win at all.

The waitress offered him a flirtatious smile, and he returned it. Habit. One he had to break, and quick.

"You with the 455th?" O'Malley asked, even before the waitress turned.

Luke nodded.

"You know Master Sergeant Tobias?"

This grin, Luke could afford. "Who doesn't? Meanest

son of a bitch in Camp Cunningham, and that's saying something."

The scowl twitched in what Luke realized was a smile. "Good to know he's still raising hell. He owes me twenty bucks. I should get on that."

"You been in the Sandbox?"

"Oh-three to oh-seven. Tangoed with an IED, they sent me back."

Luke nodded again. He wouldn't ask the details. He'd heard O'Malley's story a hundred times, more or less. The man was lucky. He was still walking and still in uniform.

"What brought you here?" O'Malley asked, sending what could have been a questioning look at Sara.

Luke kept his focus on O'Malley, but he knew Sara had wanted this explanation since the hallway. "I have some time before I need to be at Eglin for flight training. They sent me here first."

"Eglin?" O'Malley looked at him as if he was lying, but Luke wasn't going to assume anything about the older airman. "The F-35 Lightning II?"

"Yep. Eventually."

"You ever done a recruitment tour?" O'Malley asked. Evidently he was in charge of interrogation as well as logistics.

"Nope."

"Public speaking?"

"Nope."

O'Malley's scowl deepened. "You're gonna face auditoriums full of snot-nosed kids who think what we do is bullshit."

Luke shrugged. "I have no idea why they thought I'd be good for this detail."

Sara made a noise that couldn't be mistaken for anything other than disgust. "Probably figured if you could charm the panties off a general's daughter, you could handle a hundred teenagers."

So she'd heard about that. "In my defense, I wasn't aware she was a general's daughter."

"Yeah?" she said, meeting his gaze with an anger that had simmered for years. "All it'll take is one encounter, hotshot, with one of these students. I guarantee I'll be front and center at your court martial."

"So it's safe for me to unpack?"

Sara's eyes narrowed. "I assume all you've got is an economy-size box of condoms and your copy of *Top Gun,* so it shouldn't be a problem."

Luke turned away, only to be face to face with O'Malley. The master sergeant didn't give away a thing. Luke knew guys like him, old-guard soldiers who pretty much ran the service. They never said much because they didn't have to. If you wanted something done, they were the bottom line. So when they didn't exactly stick to protocol or forgot a salute here or there, it never got mentioned.

Luke was damn sure O'Malley wouldn't say a word to him about the general's daughter or Sara's anger, but he could screw up Luke's life in a day. At this point, Luke was frankly more concerned with Sara.

He didn't begrudge her the anger, or the insult. But he knew, now, that the apology he owed her wasn't going to be accepted anytime soon. Of course she hated him, and he was pouring gasoline on that fire by stepping onto her turf. She had no reason to believe he was sorry for his behavior. He'd barely come to accept it himself.

He wasn't the man he used to be. Even though he didn't understand much about the man he was now, he knew without doubt what he'd left behind in Afghanistan—the part of himself too narcissistic to care about a young woman's heart. But Sara would have to see that for herself. She might never see it, and even if she did, it probably wouldn't make a difference. Still, he would try.

The food arrived. When Luke looked back, Sara had been facing the window. He watched as she settled herself, brought herself under control. She'd found indifference again, and the longer he was here, the stronger that would become. Indifference would make his job harder because Sara was strong and stubborn. Her patience stretched like taffy, but once it snapped, it snapped for good.

2

It was 0500 hours. At 0700 Sara would call Alonzo. If she didn't get him then, she'd call hourly until she did.

She fought a yawn, pissed at herself for being in the office so early, pissed at her head for keeping her up most of the night and pissed at Luke for everything. Following her to dinner. It was just like him to be so arrogant. Talking to O'Malley as if they were war buddies. O'Malley wouldn't be caught dead hanging out with a man like Luke Carnes. O'Malley had standards.

Her headache, courtesy of sleep deprivation, continued to distract her, which added injury to insult. She'd like to know what military genius had thought it was a good idea to send Luke "Solo" Carnes on a goodwill tour. Didn't they know their audiences would be primarily men? If the tour had been to modeling schools, sure, no better speaker could be found, but this was an important effort. The air force needed serious candidates who could envision more to life than instant gratification. Who could realize that service had rewards that went infinitely deeper.

In her opinion, the country would be better off by far with mandatory service for all young people. If not in the military, then something like it. Kids needed discipline, whether they thought so or not. Needed a purpose bigger than their egos. Which was exactly why Luke was unfit for this assignment. Nothing existed that was larger than his ego.

Solo. She knew damn well he'd come up with that call sign himself, not that she could prove it. If he'd been tagged by his buddies, it would have been Skywalker or Narcissus—no, that was too intellectual. Ego. That's what anyone who'd been alone with him for more than five minutes would call him.

Solo. Not because he was a lone wolf, which he was. Oh, no. In honor of his beloved *Star Wars.* How many times had she watched that damn movie back in college? How many times had he stopped whatever he was doing—whatever *they'd* been doing—when Han Solo muttered some arrogant nonsense. Luke had always identified with Solo, always. A hero. A babe magnet. A cocky SOB with attitude to spare.

Damn it, why was he here? Why couldn't she just ignore him? Why did thinking about him hurt so much?

Out of the corner of her eye she spotted a shadow, then O'Malley was in her doorway, looking like he did every morning, spit-shined shoes, shirt so starched it could stand up on its own, face that made grown men tremble.

She jerked her head for him to enter, and when he did, she saw he wanted to have a chat. She knew that because he'd brought bribes. A mocha-raspberry latte, which she shouldn't drink, and an apple fritter, which she shouldn't even think of eating. She took both.

He perched himself on the edge of her credenza, eschewing the two ugly, uncomfortable guest chairs, plain black coffee in his to-go mug. "Start talking,'" he said.

She took a bite of fritter to forestall the inevitable. He hadn't pressed her after dinner, but he knew her too well to let it go. She'd never told him about Luke. Why would she? He was ancient history. It wasn't as if she thought about him often, she really didn't. When she did, though, the pain was like being slugged on a bad bruise.

"I knew him in high school and college."

"That sure as hell doesn't explain last night."

"I'm allowed to be bitchy."

O'Malley sipped his coffee, his dark, hooded eyes eternally patient.

"We had a thing. He was an ass. He's still an ass. I don't want him on my team."

"A thing?"

Sara winced, but covered it quickly. "I swear, you're as bad as a thirteen-year-old girl. In fact, you *are* a thirteen-year-old girl."

He didn't even blink. He simply sat and stared at her like some ancient tortoise. Waiting, always waiting for her to spill her guts.

"Tell you what," she said. "When you tell me about your first love affair, I'll reciprocate." She pushed away the fritter, her appetite gone, along with her good humor.

"So it goes all the way back, huh?" He frowned as he took another sip of coffee, eyed the pastry. When he looked at her again, she watched his curiosity turn to concern.

"Yes. A long way back. A lifetime ago. It's not a big deal. I'm surprised he's here, that's all."

"Right," O'Malley said. "You know, if you don't want him here, I can—"

She held up her hand. "No. It's fine." She cleared her throat, met the sergeant's gaze. "I appreciate it, but I don't need your help. If Carnes is right for the tour, he stays. If he's not, he goes, and you won't have to work any of your mojo, either way."

"Mojo? Me? I'm just the logistics guy."

"Seriously. Don't screw around with this."

"I never screw around, Captain. I just ride a desk, and now it's time for me to get to work."

"I'll handle this," she said, as he walked out the door, but even she could hear the wobble in her voice.

"Never doubted it," he said from the hallway.

She sat back in her chair, stared at her coffee. She couldn't believe she'd let her guard down in front of O'Malley. He already thought he was her big brother, and she didn't want his sympathy or his interference.

She hated that Luke had this kind of influence over her. The way it had ended between them had shattered her. Because she'd still loved him. He'd said goodbye seven years ago, but the way she was feeling, it might as well have been seven minutes.

He had been the love of her life, and if she wasn't careful, if she didn't get her act together, he could shatter her all over again.

She tried to take a sip of coffee. Her hand shook so badly she spilled the damn thing on her reports.

LUKE HADN'T SLEPT WELL. That wasn't unusual, sadly; hadn't been for a while. So he did what he always did—a hundred push-ups by the side of the bed, then a hundred sit-ups, followed by a run. The streets were unfamiliar, but he was able to get his bearings. A park wasn't far from the motel, and it had a walking path, so he tuned into his muscles and his breathing, forgot about the nightmare that had woken him at six. Finally, he walked back to his room. The shower had to be cold or he'd find himself leaning against the wall, head dipped, eyes closed. Not today.

Instead of the diner, he decided to try a coffee shop

he'd seen on his run. It wasn't a chain, wasn't a trendy coffeehouse. Just a place a guy could get some eggs and, he hoped, a good cup of coffee.

He hadn't yet gotten used to being around so many civilians. It was a culture shock to come back to ordinary lives, to safe streets and access to everything.

The waitress looked as if she'd walked across the scarred linoleum floor a million times. She didn't spare a glance his way when she put down his menu and filled his cup. Good. He wasn't in a cordial mood.

He didn't get a newspaper, hadn't brought his magazine. As he drank his coffee, then ate his breakfast, he steadied himself for the day. It wouldn't be easy for Sara to find a replacement, no matter how much she wanted him gone. The odds of staying were in his favor. He would give his role his full attention. That meant he had to play catch-up, figure out what he was gonna say to the students. Not the truth, not all of it, at least. Some things were better left alone. Some things couldn't be understood without the experience. No one could hope to imagine ejecting from a jet into enemy territory. Being certain every breath was your last.

He reached for his toast and latched on to a different memory, infinitely better. Another breakfast, this one in a dorm room. He'd brought coffee and donuts; Sara had made instant oatmeal. Her roommate, Nancy something, had left for an early class.

It had still been new, the freedom of living on campus. They'd already been seeing each other for a year, but that had been high school and sneaking around. College meant all they had to find was privacy. She'd frowned at the donuts, afraid of the Freshman Fifteen, but she really liked donuts. He'd fed one to her, bite by bite, captivated by her lips, her teeth, the way she looked at him. He'd been hard from the moment they were alone, but he didn't touch himself. Not during the oatmeal or the coffee or her leaning forward in her V-necked shirt.

She'd known he could see all the way down to her nipples. Hard pink buds. Hard for him, like he'd been hard for her. Talking about something, anything that wasn't the hot ache. Knowing that after the food was gone, they'd still be hungry. That they'd strip each other bare and touch anything they pleased.

Shit. He was hard now, and his eggs were cold, and only a fool would think about something that sweet when the woman involved disliked him so very, very much.

He finished breakfast, paid his tab. Took his time going back to the motel. When he let himself think of Sara, it was as she was now. In charge and no-nonsense. Wanting him gone.

But he shoved all that away when he walked into the motel. It wasn't difficult to find the rehearsal room. It was early, and he was alone. A large table dominated the space, but a podium with a stand-up screen mounted behind it filled the far end. Military posters lined the walls, a whiteboard was covered with bullet points more appropriate for actors than airmen. There was a good hour he could use to look through the material he found in neat stacks on the back tables, and he wanted to read them all.

Not five minutes had passed when the door behind him opened. Sara stared at him, then shut the door and turned the lock. When she looked at him again, he saw none of her anger, but that didn't mean she wasn't furious. This was Sara in armor, prepared to get the job done. He didn't know if she wanted a fight or not. She wouldn't get one.

"What are you doing here, Luke?"

"I told you."

She walked to the end of the long elliptical table. She didn't sit. "No way this is a coincidence. Not possible."

His thoughts went first to lies, but he checked himself. He'd promised. "You're right," he said. "I heard about Wiley, realized I'd have the time to fill in before I report to Eglin."

"Why?" There was nothing in her voice that even hinted that she was pleading, but it was there in her eyes. A flash, then it was gone. A stranger wouldn't have noticed.

"I owe you."

She looked at a poster tacked up on the side wall, an F-15 Strike Eagle at takeoff. "You don't owe me a thing."

"You need a fighter pilot. Your choices are limited."

"Not this limited." She looked at him again, completely in control, more beautiful than she'd ever been. The years had brought out the elegance of her bone structure, her fierceness. "I haven't even begun to call vets."

"I'll do the job well, Captain. I won't embarrass you or the service."

She stared at him, no doubt trying to find an answer in the way he sat, the inflection of his words. If he could have, if he thought for a second she'd have believed him, he'd spell it all out for her, the business in Afghanistan, how he'd seen so clearly how wrong he'd been seven years ago.

"I know you'd be good at this," she said. "And that's my dilemma. This duty means a lot to me. I intend to have an extraordinary success rate."

"You will, with me or without me."

"Quit trying to act as if this is some noble gesture, would you? I'm not buying it. I just need to know what you want. If you can't tell me, I'm going to have to make those calls, because I have a job to do, and I'm not going to let whatever games you have planned derail me."

He hated feeling so damn uncertain. He'd come here for a second chance, not to make a bad situation worse. He would, of course, step away if she asked him to. Yet he couldn't help taking one last shot. "Will you believe me if I give you my word?" he asked. "If I swear to you, on my wings, that I'm not here to screw with you? There's no game, Sara. I want to help. I was a jackass, I know that. But it was a long time ago. When I saw you needed help and I was in a position to do something about your predicament, I didn't hesitate."

Sara pulled out the chair to her right and sat down. Once more she looked away, staring at anything that wasn't him. Her lips pressed together, then relaxed; there was the slightest tick at the edge of her eye. When she finally looked back, it was with utter indifference. "You understand why I'm having trouble here."

He kept his gaze steady as his chest imploded. "Of course." He paused, hoping for—what?—that she'd forget? Let bygones be bygones? "I'll find a reason I shouldn't be on this assignment, one the brass will buy."

She let the words hang for so long that he pushed the brochures together and abandoned his last flicker of hope.

"Not right now," she said.

He paused.

"I don't have a replacement. It might take a few days."

"In the meantime?"

She stood, lifted the plastic chair with both hands and placed it under the table. "Do your job."

Luke nodded. He figured if she continued her search, eventually she'd find someone else. He knew they wanted active-duty personnel for this gig, but if push came to shove, there were a lot of ex-pilots out there itching to tell their stories. Anxious enough to drop whatever they were doing and take the stage. He'd hoped to have more time for his campaign, but this was right. As it should be. He'd leave and she'd go back to her life. She was better off without him.

She left without another word, leaving the door open behind her, and he listened to the sound of her heels disappear.

IT WAS TWO HOURS AFTER the lunch she should have taken, and Sara hadn't begun her search for Luke's replacement. She'd finished her status reports, revised two budgets, gone over the slide show with Sergeant Tritter and teleconferenced with her boss, Colonel Graves, and the public affairs liaison from the University of California, Los Angeles.

She would check in at the conference room, make sure everyone was playing nicely, then she'd have an hour or so to make some calls.

It troubled her that she was leaning toward letting Luke stay. The thing was, he'd sworn on his wings. If he'd said anything else, even sworn on his mother's life, she'd have doubted him, but his wings were everything to Luke. He was a born pilot, designed as perfectly for the desert war as his precious F-15 was.

Now that she'd settled from the initial shock of his appearance, she had to admit he was a perfect fit. He might not have done any formal recruitment, but she'd seen his power when he got on the subject of flying the fast movers. He'd known how to keep an audience interested, whether they were a haphazard group of students in his dorm, or a gaggle of fawning women poolside. The man could mesmerize, without hyperbole, anyone—and he managed to do it without sugarcoating.

She could only imagine how much more strength his message would have now that his knowledge was practical instead of theoretical.

The door to the conference room was shut and when she slipped inside it was dark except for the brilliant images on the screen and the spotlight on the speaker. They'd be using much more sophisticated equipment to display their media when they were on the tour, but for the rehearsals, this was fine. Timing was critical. Images, sound and speech were all important weapons in the recruitment arsenal.

She'd put together a program designed to inspire, not just the mind but the spirit. Honor, duty, camaraderie, responsibility, all of them were targeted. They had to be, because she had been adamant from the start that these talks be truthful. The air force wanted the best and the brightest, and it was her job to reach that audience.

Captain Terri Van Linn had the podium, and she had almost as much charisma as Luke. The looks, the smile, the job. Well, not quite. Van Linn was an investigator for the OSI, the air force equivalent of the navy's now-famous NCIS. The woman was a brazen redhead, small in stature, large in appeal. Men fell all over themselves with Van Linn, and when she was onstage, they listened. Van Linn knew it too. Which was fine with Sara. The more men who paid attention, the better the recruitment numbers.

Sara moved to the table as quietly as possible. The only available seat was next to Luke. She considered standing at the back, but that would look bad. Great, how was this supposed to work out when she could barely sit next to him? Biting the bullet, she took the seat. He spared her a glance, his attention fixed on Van Linn. Her talk was nearing its end, which was good, as Sara wanted an update on today's rehearsals.

Of course, since there was no way Luke could have come up with any kind of a speech, now would be a good time to throw him behind the podium to field questions.

Her other speakers were all there: George Tritter, the photographer; Danny Franks, the electronic system security specialist, better known as a hacker; Captain Rick Hanover, combat rescue operator and Captain Nora Pearson, a drone operator who used computer tech to guide unmanned aircraft into battle.

They'd each been subjected to the gauntlet of hostile questions from their fellows, and they'd all, eventually, passed with flying colors. Luke was in an unenviable position—he was an unknown quantity replacing a valuable and well-liked officer who had been particularly qualified for the job. The questions would be brutal. It should be interesting.

Captain Van Linn finished to the applause of her fellows, then the room lights went on. Hanover had turned toward the podium when Sara stopped him. "I'd like Captain Carnes to take the stage."

Luke didn't hesitate. It didn't seem to matter that he had no idea what she'd ask him to do, or that he'd had so little prep time. He got behind the podium, appearing completely at ease.

"I'm finishing my master's in computer science," she said, throwing him into the deep end of the pond without preamble. "Why should I join the air force when I can get a job that pays seven times as much right out of the gate?"

Luke didn't even blink. "You shouldn't. If it's only about the money, the armed services are the last place you should go. You have to know what it is you want out of life. Accumulating wealth is a viable goal. In my experience, however, money isn't the best foundation for real satisfaction.

"To join the service, particularly the air force, you'd have to want a lot more than a big bank account. A master's degree in computer science can lead to all kinds of challenges in this branch of the military. You could end up at NASA working on cutting-edge technology for manned space flight. Or designing the next generation of unmanned aircraft or underwater vehicles."

Sara let out a resigned sigh. He was just as sharp as she'd feared. In under a minute, he already understood the challenge, answered frankly, and hit the bull's-eye. She sat back as he continued to list several other computer-related fields that would entice a tech-minded college student, and by the time he was finished, she noticed that every person in the room was leaning forward, actively listening, reeled in like spring trout.

The questions came at him rapid-fire after that, the group fully engaged in tripping Luke up. Even when he didn't know the answer, the sly bastard used his ignorance to his advantage. Sara didn't participate again, but she watched and learned. The first hint of trouble came a couple of minutes later, when she noticed her heart rate had accelerated.

She, too, was leaning forward, and instead of actually hearing the questions and Luke's answers, she'd been thinking about the past. About the day she'd become aware that Luke was something special.

It had been her first day as a senior in high school, in a political science class. She'd transferred from Chula Vista, and she hadn't met many people on campus. Didn't know the teachers yet. He'd sat two rows in front of her, to her left.

Luke had disagreed with something the teacher said, and the two of them had gotten into it as if they were the only people in the overcrowded classroom. Luke had the confidence of someone years older, and his arguments had been sound. The teacher, she thought his name was Linus, had been engaged, not threatened, and when he'd made valid points, Luke had acquiesced charmingly. Effortlessly.

She had sat very much as she was sitting now, leaning on her elbows, caught up in his words, his presence. She'd felt things that day, in the pit of her stomach. Adrenaline. Intensity. Attraction.

She hated that he could make her feel like this, given all she'd been through, but his appeal was undeniable. All she had to do was glance around the room. This wasn't a true test though, and she'd have to fix that. Soon. Especially because she couldn't trust her own objectivity, not yet.

She stood, realized a beat too late that Luke was still talking. To cover, she pulled out her cell and flipped it open, then made her exit as quickly as possible.

Her step slowed in the hallway. Whatever else was true about her, she placed the service and her responsibilities before anything else in her life. She hadn't joined the air force for the college tuition or for her résumé. Having Luke on this tour was going to test her. But it wouldn't break her.

The past was just that, and she was tougher than her memories. She would make it work for her, instead of against her. This was an opportunity to wipe the slate clean once and for all. For too many years, she'd held on to something that had never been real. It was time to let it go. Long overdue. By the end of the tour, Luke would be safely in the box of idle remembrances, along with her Air Force Barbie and her first trip to Disneyland. If she survived.

3

INSTEAD OF A RUN, Luke decided to start the day in the motel's exercise room. He'd checked it out the night before, after he'd survived what he expected was the first of many tests. Then he'd called in a pizza and holed up, reading brochures and manuals.

He'd woken early again this morning, fixed himself a cup of weak-ass coffee in the tiny complimentary pot, and made it to the weight room without seeing anyone. There were a couple of treadmills, a mounted TV that worked, two stationary bikes and Sara.

Her back was to him, and she wore earbuds connected to an MP3 player pinned to her waist. As she ran her easy pace, her ponytail swung from side to side, and it was as if he'd been transported to the gym at Berkeley. He'd stood behind her then, not often, but when he could, to watch, to admire.

Sara was tall, five-nine to his six feet, and most of her was long, gorgeous legs. Firm, shapely, he'd loved looking at them, often wished he could ask her to wear more skirts, shorter skirts, but he'd known she wouldn't have appreciated the suggestion. She had acquiesced though to some of his wishes, far more daring, and Luke had learned early to pick his battles. No, the win in the clothing department had belonged to lingerie, incredibly skimpy lingerie.

So he'd taken his pleasure checking out her legs in the school gym, at the pool, on the hiking trails. He knew the feel of her skin after a run, that slight sheen of sweat that clung to her.

Sometimes she'd worn tank shirts, snug ones, and he'd loved that, despite the sports bras. He'd never complained about those either.

Her arms were toned, now even more than in senior year. She'd been a hell of an athlete, had taken her body seriously, but not as seriously as he had. He'd mapped her like his private island, combing over every inch. Learned her secrets, made discoveries that had surprised them both. How she trembled when he licked the contours of her hip bone, blew his warm breath over the wet stripe.

Christ, he was doing it again. Letting himself get carried away. It was inappropriate, and he'd better get himself in check before he ruined everything.

Grateful for his jockstrap, he closed the door behind him with enough force that she'd hear his entry. She didn't turn, but her posture changed.

He went to the second treadmill, keeping his attention where it belonged. He knew the unit, so he programmed a run that would work him hard, but nothing brutal. He hadn't brought his iPod, which he realized was a tactical error, but he could watch the news without bothering Sara too much.

He flipped the channel to a twenty-four-hour cable show, then started his workout. He hadn't looked at her once. It didn't take him long, however, to realize he could see her reflection in the television monitor even through the news footage. He could see her clearly. It also became obvious that Sara had been able to watch him as he'd stood behind her, checking out her ass. She'd seen him open and close the door. Adjust himself.

Great. He'd probably given her yet another reason to kick his ass to the curb.

SARA KEPT ON RUNNING. She'd been at it for forty minutes, and was almost certain that her increased heart rate was from the exercise, not from the little show Luke had put on behind her. Idiot. He hadn't even bothered to check out the rest of the room. His gaze had settled on her southern half, and with two minor exceptions, stayed there.

She should have jumped off the treadmill immediately, but the screen had gone dark, and his reflection had been vivid enough to see the look on his face.

Something had kept her running even as her thoughts stuttered. There was no way to be sure, but she could have sworn he'd looked... She barely knew what to call it. A mixture of hunger and sadness? Wistful with a dose of "I'd still hit that"?

She was confused, not just about his expression, but about her reaction. It wasn't funny anymore. The first time she'd seen him, she'd been shocked, angry, and yet she'd felt the old pull. They'd been together for five years. They'd made love so often she'd asked her doctor if something was wrong with them. After she'd been assured it was perfectly normal to do it two or three times a day, they'd dedicated themselves to reaching a new personal best.

Dammit, thoughts like those were why having Luke around was dangerous. It was her responsibility to stop, this instant. She was almost thirty years old, for God's sake, in control of her life and her body.

She bit down on her lower lip and focused on her

breathing, on lengthening her stride. She would not look. She wouldn't. Not at him, not at his reflection.

But she did. She looked at the TV, a glance, that was all, and he was looking at her. Her right foot hit the edge of the treadmill, just enough to throw her off.

Luke caught her stumbling backwards. She hit the hardness of his chest instead of the floor. His right hand gripped her upper arm, his left spanned her hip. He wasn't pulling her flush against him; he didn't have to.

Every sense she had went into overdrive. He smelled of soap and the pillow in her dorm room. His breath on the sweat of her neck was hot as a Santa Ana wind. His cock pressed into the side of her butt, not fully hard yet, but on its way.

She didn't have her feet under her yet. Luke took a step back, distancing himself, stabilizing her. It helped. Not enough, though. Little fires sparked through her body in all the wrong places. Her lips parted without her permission as he turned her around to face him.

Sara met his gaze and realized they weren't far enough apart. Not by a mile. His pupils had taken over his eyes, his breathing was even quicker than a moment ago. Rolling forward to the balls of her feet didn't improve her balance at all.

Luke made a sound. Not a word, more of a click at the back of his throat. That's when she realized they weren't touching. Wait, no, his breath, she could still feel it whisper by her ear. But the persistence of memory tightened the skin of her arm where he'd gripped her, warmed his handprint on her hip.

Did he still taste the same? No matter what he'd eaten or had to drink, underneath she had always found Luke. Weirdly, the flavor that came to her most often in her dreams and right this second, was his flavor after a sip of beer. It shouldn't have been appealing, she barely liked beer herself, but God…it had turned her on. Would it now? Would she melt against him if he took a swig of Dos XX and pulled her into a kiss?

His fingers brushed the skin of her arm, not the same place, and the shiver rippled up and down and deep inside. He was off balance too, leaning, breathing. Her eyes fluttered as her head tilted slightly to her left.

A crash, shattering glass, lots of it, from the outside corridor broke the spell, propelled her back a step, then two and three. She came back to the man he was now, not the boy he'd once been. She didn't know this man, didn't want to.

"I'm good," she said, turning her face so he wouldn't see the heat redden her cheeks.

"Right," he said, then he cleared his throat. As she passed him, she glanced down meaning to avoid his gaze. What she saw was the evidence that no matter what, there was still something happening between them. Something hard and hot, and she'd have to be so much more careful.

Pros:
1. He's a charismatic speaker.
2. He'll be perfect in any media setting.
3. He'll be the most successful recruiter on the tour.
4. He'll make me look good professionally.
5. He's here, now.

Cons:
1. He's Luke.

SARA PUT DOWN HER PEN and took a sip of her watery soda. She'd meant to bring a real glass, but she hadn't and now she was stuck with the thin plastic thing that came with the room and the ice from the hallway. It was early, there were restaurants and bars within easy walking distance, but she didn't want to run into Luke.

She'd seen him during the course of the day: after her shower, after she'd put on her uniform. It had been fine. But she wasn't stupid. For whatever reason, and for the life of her the only one she could come up with was masochism, she still felt drawn to Luke physically. It would be foolish in the extreme to ignore the incomprehensible fact. But it was also a fact that she'd had no luck at all finding a replacement. Not that she'd killed herself looking, and what did that say about her? She'd have to turn to retired pilots tomorrow if she couldn't come to a satisfactory decision tonight. Her boss did not want a retired pilot on the tour.

She skipped a few lines on her yellow legal pad and started a new list.

Code of Personal Conduct:
1. Never go out of my way either to avoid or seek him out.
2. Don't laugh at his jokes unless someone else does first.
3. Don't be alone with him. Unless it's job related. Maybe.
4. Don't drive with him.
5. Don't dine with him.
6. Don't

She pulled the paper off the pad and crumpled it into a ball. Screw this. Screw this whole thing. Luke Carnes wasn't an infectious disease, although now that she thought about it, he was a lot like malaria. He kept recurring, even when she thought she'd been fully cured.

What she needed was to be immunized. Numbed to any reaction at all.

The point was, she was giving him way too much power over her thoughts and actions. Everything nonprofessional that could happen between them had happened. Past tense. It meant nothing now. So she'd been hurt. Well, boo-friggin'-hoo. People got their hearts broken every day. Only the weak stayed broken.

If Luke were right for the job, he'd stay. He was part of her team, she would treat him as such. It was incredibly simple, and all she'd required was a little time to adjust and now things were in their proper perspective. The stumble in the gym had been a wake-up call, nothing more.

After tossing her note in the trash, she made sure her uniform was presentable, then applied fresh lipstick. In her briefcase she found the public relations newsletter she'd been meaning to read, and she grabbed it along with her purse. It was after eight, and she was hungry.

With renewed vigor, she walked to the diner and one quick look told her Luke wasn't there. Good. Excellent. How absurd that she'd thought, for even a moment, to avoid him.

She slid into a booth, glad she didn't have to eat liver again. She didn't hate it, no, but she didn't particularly like it. Another thing she'd never do again.

She was a captain. Even without her rank, she was proud of who she was, and how she conducted herself. That he—that any man—could rattle her made her a little sick to her stomach.

"What can I get you, Captain?"

She smiled up at the older waitress, impressed by her savvy. The woman recognized rank designations on sight, and not only air force insignia. Sara had noticed that on two occasions when the waitress had addressed both army officers and marines. "Was your family in the service?"

Bonnie—according to her name tag—shook her head. "From San Diego."

Sara glanced at her own right shoulder epaulet. "Smart."

"I always thought so," Bonnie said, sharing a wry smile.

"I'd like the chef's salad with oil and vinegar on the side, please, and a large lemonade."

"You got it, Captain."

Sara opened up her newsletter, grinning at the woman's ingenuity. No reason Sara couldn't be equally clever in her own situation. Just as Luke knew a great deal about her, she knew a great deal about him. What she had to do was use that knowledge to her advantage. She would capitalize on his strengths, downplay his weaknesses.

Luke was at his best playing to an audience. The team itself was good, but there weren't enough of them to use as an accurate gauge. The tour was almost upon them, and she had to get him up to speed, and fast. So she would give him an audience. No visuals to interest a crowd, no auditorium to set expectations. Just Luke. Yes. She'd take him out for a test drive. See exactly what he had under the hood.

AFTER ANOTHER poor night's sleep, Luke had made it into the office two hours early and had heard all the revised talks by two o'clock. As the critiques progressed, he'd realized how greatly he'd underestimated his role. An extemporaneous talk in a group setting was one thing; a recruitment speech with targeted goals, another. Everyone on the team had better skills, had had time to work out the details. He would mostly be shooting from the hip. No question he did that well, but—apples and oranges.

What he had to do now that he was alone in the conference room while the rest of the team was at dinner, before he even knew precisely what to study, was narrow his focus. The reason Sara needed a fighter pilot was to talk about being a fighter pilot. Sounded simple enough, but he'd already gone off on unnecessary tangents. The speech had to be streamlined, tailored, a laser beam highlighting not merely the good parts, but also the difficulties, the dangers, the odds.

Thank God for Wiley's notes. They were a tremendous asset, but Luke couldn't use most of the speech as written. Not that it wasn't accurate or even that he thought he could do better. It just wasn't him. He wasn't Wiley and it would be a mistake to try to be.

He'd worked through lunch and planned on working until midnight. He wasn't writing anything as organized as a rough draft, not yet. This was the first cull, that's all; what he could keep from Wiley's material, what had to go, what he'd use to replace the missing parts. He could do this. If he could keep his mind off Sara.

He'd gotten used to thinking about her way before he'd arrived in San Diego. Ever since he'd joined up with Alf, his weapons system officer, back in the F-15. Civilians didn't get what it was like for a pilot and his WSO. In any two-man jet, especially in war, a bond formed, one that everyone who flew understood was as important as the fuel or the engines. He and Alf had become a team, and even though it had started out all about the flying, the hundreds of hours they spent together had turned them into brothers. Alf was better at the bonding thing than Luke. He'd made it easy for Luke to talk about the important stuff, the stuff that wasn't jets.

Weirdly, once Luke had started, he'd had a hard time shutting up, and most of the conversations had been about Sara. Even before that night in Khwaran Ghar. Alf had been the one who'd pointed out that Luke had been saving up stories for her. It hadn't mattered that they'd broken up years before. Luke had somehow figured that one day he'd be able to take out all the tales, the funny ones and the frightening ones—and especially the proud ones—and lay them out before her like a string of pearls. Alf had also pointed out that Luke's ego was way the hell out of control.

At least Luke understood that part now. The humiliating truth had hit him with the power of a mortar shell. It was no coincidence that every fighter pilot he knew thought they were God's gift. You needed to be this side of overconfident to fly into combat. But there had to be a balance.

The fact that he'd been willing to do whatever it took to fly the fast-movers had gotten him through training. Holding life and death in his hands had been a towering lesson in responsibility. But he'd only discovered bone-deep fear last year.

After the crash, when he was safe once again, the pendulum had swung the other way, too far. He'd blamed himself for every damn thing. It had slowly come back near center, but he wasn't *there* yet. The sweet spot kept eluding him. All he knew for sure was that Sara's forgiveness wasn't mandatory. His apology was.

If he hoped for more, it was that she might help him find the final piece of his puzzle, that she would help him make sense of who he was now, because he didn't have a clue.

But he couldn't apologize if she sent him packing,

so it was back to the books, back to making his talk the best it could be. He could do this.

IT WAS EIGHT-THIRTY when Sara got to the conference room and saw the light bleeding under the door. This after leaving multiple messages for Luke on his room-phone voice mail and his cell.

She opened the conference room door ready to read him the riot act until she saw Luke with his head bowed over a notebook, papers spread out in a fan before him. He was completely focused on what he was writing. Even from the door she could see the tension in his neck, in how he held himself. She never thought of Luke like this. Even when he should have been tense, during finals, before important games, he'd always been loose and easy, his confidence as infuriating as it was enviable.

His posture changed and he turned to face her, still gripping his pen tightly. He didn't smile. In fact, if anything he seemed more tense. "Hey."

"I've been trying to reach you."

His slow blink was followed by a glance to a pile of papers. He huffed a sigh as he uncovered his cell phone. "Shit. No bars."

"I see," she said, stepping inside. "Working on your speech?"

He nodded. "I'm trying to get it into shape. I thought it would be easier."

The admission caught her off guard. In the years she'd known Luke, he'd never made a statement like it. There had been plenty of times she'd suspected…known he was having trouble. He'd simply brushed it off, made a joke, changed the subject. This was different and unsettling.

"Every word counts," he said. "There's a science to this. I'm going to have to lean on your expertise, I know that." He pushed a tired hand through his short hair. "I'm trying to narrow down the field. Separate what matters to me from what would matter to a civilian."

"That's right," she said. This wasn't the moment to think about her personal reaction. She focused on the speech, the job. The rest of the evening. "But it's also important to trust your instincts. If they weren't important, we would have hired speech writers. The personal stories are what capture the imagination."

He nodded slowly, putting his pen down. "You were trying to reach me?"

She'd planned a test for him tonight, and now, seeing him grapple with such sincerity, she wondered if it was the right move. But yes, it was, because tonight would be about his instincts, and they both had to find out what he did with them. The real question was, should she clue him in?

"We have somewhere to go," she said, deciding to let it play. "I'd like you to put that aside for now. Come with me."

He raised his eyebrows in surprise. "Sure. Where to?"

"You'll find out," she said.

His gaze met hers, and again she saw his uncertainty, and again she hadn't expected it.

LUKE SAT IN THE BACKSEAT of a rental van. It was white, utilitarian and crammed with boxes. O'Malley drove, Sara sat shotgun. Neither one of them so much as glanced his way.

He wanted to know what was going on, where they were headed, what the assignment was, but he'd been in the service too long to be impatient. At least as far as assignments went.

The more pressing issue seemed to be his inability to

sit still. He'd been fine for the first fifteen minutes, and then his gaze had caught on Sara's right shoulder. She'd rolled it, as if she were trying to release some tension. He ended up stretching his own neck, but it didn't do much good. Because after that, he couldn't get his mind off Sara.

He wanted to touch her. Her shoulder would do, but what called to him was the nape of her neck. It was a beautiful neck, and it didn't surprise him that he remembered the feel of her skin. Or at least thought he did. It would only take a few seconds to confirm, his cool palm on that perfect expanse of warm flesh.

Which would result in him being sent home with a large black mark on his record and a huge lost opportunity.

So he sat and stared and tried to think of other things. Such as the fact that she hadn't told him to bring his gear. Wherever they were going, it wasn't to the airport. And they weren't traveling south, so they weren't going to knock him out and drag him across the Mexican border. Good to know.

That was all he could glean from the trip so far. It was only natural, then, that his mind went back to Sara's neck. He forced himself to look out his window. At the freeway. A freeway like all the other Southern California freeways, and he wasn't familiar enough with the area for the signs to mean anything.

The soft dark hairs that floated just underneath her neat twist pulled him back. It was long, her neck. He used to be able to fit his whole palm against it when he pulled her into a kiss. Sensitive, too. He loved to skim his fingertips down that delicate skin and feel goose bumps and shivers. So responsive. Vocal, too, when she could be.

Her hand came up, touched the very spot he was staring at, and his breath held. The move only lasted a second, but damn, it took him a long while to exhale. She didn't know, couldn't know. She'd had an itch, that's all. Nothing to do with him.

Oh, Jesus, he had to stop. He was deep in boresight, unable to see the big picture, and that could get a man in trouble. They could pull off the freeway any second now, and he didn't want to step out of the van with his cock at quarter-staff.

He did the only thing he could. He closed his eyes and went through his pre-flight checklist. Slowly. And again.

Finally, when they did exit the freeway, he had his wits about him, and he realized they must be very close to the beach in a touristy section of town. Despite the fact that it was past 10:00 p.m. the well-lit, wide boulevard was congested with slow cars and tanned people. The sidewalk patios had few empty tables, and when he lowered his window a little, music spilled out of the many bars like snapshots of sound.

Curiosity pressed hard against his patience, and he was about to ask what the hell was going on when O'Malley pulled up in front of yet another restaurant bedecked with a large patio. It was a place called Lefty's, and Luke saw that it wasn't a restaurant exactly. It was a coffeehouse, open twenty-four hours a day. They served food along with coffee and other soft drinks, and they had open-mike nights from 6:00 p.m. to 11:30 p.m. seven nights a week.

"This is us," Sara said, the first words he'd heard from her since they'd gotten into the van.

"We're going to a coffeehouse?"

"That's right." She opened her door, which let in a warm breeze and the scent of the ocean.

"What are we supposed to do here?"

Sara looked at him with the beginning of a smile at the corner of her lips. "Order coffee."

He hadn't expected that, couldn't make sense of it, and while he had a smart-ass response on the tip of his tongue, he held back. If there was one thing he'd been trained to do, even more than keeping his thoughts to himself while in uniform, it was to keep his eyes open. His life depended on his observational skills, absorbing the sky around him and the land below, always assuming there was someone or something out to kill him.

No one here, thankfully, would want him dead, but the woman leading him into the coffeehouse might want him disappeared. Especially now that he'd confessed he was having trouble with his speech. But a café? He couldn't even fathom a guess. Instead, he inhaled deeply the moment he stepped inside. Coffee. Real American coffee that always made him feel like home, whether it was in Kabul or on a transport flight. Just under that, suntan lotion. Not the thick sunblock they sold at the BX, but the kind that smelled like surfboards and beautiful women.

He smiled, taking real pleasure in the moment. He was grateful to be right here, right now, no matter what happened next.

She led him to a table for four. O'Malley would join them soon. Luke took the seat next to Sara after a brief internal debate. He wanted to look at her, of course, but she was facing the stage and he figured he'd better, too.

The comic behind the mike moved stiffly, spoke too fast and wasn't very funny. Although the place was pretty full, few people paid much attention to him, with the exception of one rowdy group of kids Luke suspected were the comic's buddies. It wasn't a hostile audience, though. No heckling, no one tried to drown him out with loud talking. That would have been difficult, though, as there were speakers hooked up all the way out to the patio.

Luke checked the counter. It was big and there were a lot of people behind it, more than just the baristas. Sandwiches and chips were for sale; bagels, muffins, salads. But the coffee was the star, and they made every concoction he could imagine. He thought of getting the two of them drinks, and then it occurred to him that he didn't know what kind of coffee Sara liked. It used to be some hazelnut thing, but now? He had no idea.

O'Malley joined them before Luke could ask her. He took the seat on the other side of Sara, barely giving Luke a glance. "You seen him?"

Sara shook her head. "He's here."

The sergeant didn't respond, but Luke's suspicion that the two of them were close was reconfirmed. He'd watched O'Malley watch Sara the other night. While Luke and the old guy had talked, O'Malley had kept checking in on her. He'd been cagey, but that kind of silent communication took time and trust. Tonight on the ride, the silence between the two of them had been comfortable.

A brief nod from Sara made Luke look past the tables. A gray-haired man was heading for them, and Luke knew instantly that he was ex-military. No question about it. He was older than O'Malley.

"Captain," he said, as he sat down across from Sara. "Sergeant."

"Thank you for this, Chief," Sara said.

The man gave Luke a once-over, but there was nothing to read in his expression, although Luke gathered he'd been a chief master sergeant at one time. His attention went back to Sara. "You want the usual?"

"Decaf for me," Sara said.

"Hell with that," said O'Malley, with enough emphasis that it made Luke grin.

Sara gave a brief nod in Luke's direction. "He'll have water."

"I figured." Chief left as abruptly as he'd arrived.

"So you gonna tell me what the hell's going on?" Luke asked. Enough was enough. He'd wanted a damn coffee.

"Pay attention."

The chief hadn't gone behind the counter. He'd walked up the few steps to the stage and took his place behind the mike. He must have been up there a lot, given that the crowd quieted straight off.

"Tonight we're doing something different. You can stay, you can go. Same as always. I'd appreciate it if you stayed."

That was it. He left the stage bare but for a microphone and a spotlight.

Luke's guts tightened. He turned to Sara.

"You're up, Captain. Tell these fine people about being a fighter pilot, and what an honor it is to serve in the United States Air Force."

4

LUKE MADE HIS way through the tables to the stairs the
same way he'd made it to the cockpit the first time he'd
ever flown an F-15: trying like hell not to vomit. He kept
his back straight, his gaze forward, and told himself he
could ace this. So he'd been blindsided. It wasn't the first
time. He was good at improvising. Nobody was as quick
on their feet. Nobody. All he had to do was find someone
in the crowd who seemed interested. Just one person. One
woman. As long as that woman wasn't Sara.

He surveyed the room. People were curious, but curiosity wouldn't last long. He wondered if there was anyone
in those chairs who'd seriously considered a life in the
military. Most people were biased one way or another
before they reached high school, based on family, friends,
schools, the State of the Union. However, most people had
no idea what opportunities were available in the military.
So that would be his primary goal. Keep their curiosity
piqued, then tell them things they didn't know.

"Ladies and gentlemen, I'm Captain Luke Carnes.
I'm an active-duty fighter pilot for the United States Air
Force. I've just returned from my fourth tour in Afghani-
stan. I've killed people. I've saved lives. I've been shot

at, cursed at, been given boneheaded orders and faced impossible situations that scared the living crap out of me, including standing in front of you right now."

There was a smattering of laughter, polite, primarily female. A-OK.

"I'm preparing to do a recruitment tour, along with a lot of other fine officers and airmen, focusing on university students and those who might be looking for a career change. I suppose it doesn't matter who I'm addressing, though, because the only story I have to tell is my own."

Just saying those words calmed his heartbeat and settled his stomach. "Since I was seven I wanted to be a pilot. I wanted to be a fighter pilot when my dad took me to see the Thunderbirds at an air show. At fifteen I got my pilot's license. I was first in line to join the ROTC in high school. There was nothing in my life that I wanted more than to strap on an F-15 Strike Eagle.

"My goal had nothing to do with serving my country, with honor, with duty or my fellow citizens. I became a fighter pilot because it was the coolest damn job on the planet. And because it was my first-class ticket to the hottest women."

Even more laughter of the feminine kind, but he didn't want to reach only the ladies. He wanted airmen of all stripes.

Luke latched on to a pretty blonde sipping a big old iced coffee who hadn't stopped staring at him, despite the fact that her boyfriend kept nudging her to get her attention.

"What I didn't know," he continued, "about life, about what was important, about myself, was a lot. I had a great family and they supported me and taught me things I'll always be grateful for, but I learned who I am and what I'm made of because I enlisted in the U.S. Air Force for all the wrong reasons. I am the luckiest son of a bitch in the world."

His gaze shifted to the boyfriend, who was paying attention now.

"A pilot I met when I was in training told me that there was only one real path to finding satisfaction in life, and that was to focus my efforts and my strengths on a cause that was bigger than myself. Because my ego was a whole lot larger than my good sense, that lesson didn't sink in for a long, long time.

"Let me go back a bit. To when I got into Fighter Pilot Training. I was designated, by real pilots, as Boner-5. My fellow classmates were Boners-1,-2,-3,-4, all the way up to Boner-8. At least, we started out at eight. That's because the washout rate was so high, nobody bothered to find out newbie's real names. Man, we were hot shit, ready to take on the world and fly the fast movers. One through eight.

"To give you some perspective—Air Force Pilot Training receives fifteen thousand applications per year. There are two thousand admissions per year. One thousand-one hundred airmen graduate from flight school each year. Fifty pilots are accepted at Seymour-Johnson Air Force Base in North Carolina for Fighter Pilot Training on the F-15 Strike Eagle. The average number of pilots who graduate from Fighter Pilot Training is eight. My class graduated five pilots. Of those five pilots, one became Top Gun. It wasn't me."

SARA LEANED BACK in her chair as she tried to process what she'd heard. She'd been surprised at the motel, hearing his vulnerability, seeing it, but his words on stage had shocked her.

Who was this guy? What had happened to the Luke

who'd had the world at his fingertips, who never lost his cool? Not during finals, not in ROTC, certainly not in bed. She couldn't remember a single time that Luke had truly been humble. He'd been scared when he'd tried to kiss her for the first time. But by the third kiss, he'd mastered the course, and hadn't looked back.

This made no sense. She felt off balance.

He'd just admitted in front of God and everyone that he'd joined the air force to meet women. He'd confessed and she was sitting right here. She'd been sure of that, but she'd never in a million years expected to hear it from him. Not at Lefty's on open-mike night.

"You okay?"

O'Malley's voice snapped her back to the room. "Yeah. Fine." She threw him a smile, briefly remembered that she'd have to watch herself more in front of O'Malley, nearly forgot to resent the fact, then went back to staring at the man on the stage. This imposter wearing a Luke suit.

If anything, she'd have thought becoming a pilot would have made him worse. How could he have become this guy? She couldn't wrap her brain around it.

But she'd seen him in the conference room. He'd had no idea about tonight. The way he'd gripped his pen! As if the next word was the most important thing he'd ever write.

She should be looking at the crowd. He was still talking, although Sara didn't think she could stand it if he said one more terrific thing. Dammit, she hated him. She had every reason in the world to hate him. He'd treated her horribly. Dumped her after five years of pretending to love her. No one could change this much in seven years. It wasn't possible.

She turned in her seat, facing the crowd instead of

Luke. Some of them had left already. Not as many as she'd expected. But people had laughed when it was called for, paid attention. There was even a small crowd gathered at the back of the room. Okay, so maybe a crowd was an exaggeration, but these folks were listening.

Many were women, which she'd anticipated. It didn't matter, though. Because, by and large, the faces watching Luke were attentive and interested in more than his body. That's what she needed. Someone who would keep them looking, keep their cell phones in their pockets. Get them engaged and imagining new possibilities.

She'd had a lot of experience in public relations. Listened to so many recruitment speeches, she could recite the basics in her sleep. The only thing that really got to an audience was when the speaker told the truth. She knew that for a fact. She'd chosen her speakers based on their ability to connect. There'd been dozens of candidates for the positions, but the six who'd made it had been those who'd bared their souls. Each one of them had shared from the heart.

That's what Luke was doing. But where had he gotten that heart?

Not a soul in the audience had any doubt that he was a hotshot fighter jock, even though he wasn't in the flight suit he'd wear on the tour. Central casting could not have done better. He looked like a hero. And real heroes didn't lie about what counted.

She glanced at the stage. At how it appeared he was speaking to one person. Her gaze followed his, and found a beautiful girl at the end. Okay, that was better. That, at least, made sense.

Despite what she'd heard, Sara wasn't yet willing to say Luke was a different man, but she would concede that differences existed. He'd asked for help, seemed dedicated to making the job more important than himself. It could be it was all bullshit. In fact, that was a much more logical conclusion. He could have planned his speech, knowing he'd have to appear to be humble, appear to be earnest.

But why? Why come at all if he was just going to lie?

Whether he was lying or telling the honest-to-goodness truth, it was working. He had the crowd, and if he could get the crowd in here, with no notice and not nearly enough time to prepare, he would be one hell of an effective speaker. Fine. It meant she'd have to rearrange her head, but she could do that. She was a professional.

O'Malley leaned over closer. "What was that nod about?"

"I believe we have a recruiter, Sergeant."

"Lotta women gonna be joining up, that's for sure."

She looked at O'Malley. "You have a problem with that?"

"What do you think?"

She smiled as she turned back to watch Luke. O'Malley thought women should run the world, no joke. He'd been raised by a single mother and five older sisters. No wonder she got along with him so well.

Luke loved women, but he didn't understand them. Which didn't matter, not for her purposes. He understood the job and that's all she required from him. She might never uncover the truth about what had changed him—if he'd really changed—but who cared? What counted was that the tour could move forward confidently with a full roster of speakers.

Even if he'd miraculously turned into a saint, it didn't change the past. Nothing could.

LUKE HAD TALKED FOR twenty-two minutes and answered three questions. Then he'd been met by a few people at the foot of the stairs. Which would be great on the tour, not so great now. It was late and Sara was exhausted.

"Want me to do it?" O'Malley asked.

"Do what?"

"Extract him?"

"I was thinking about having another cup of decaf, but I suppose you should."

O'Malley gave her a look and mumbled something she knew was unflattering, not to mention disrespectful, as he entered the fray.

She concentrated on her coffee, which was down to the dregs, and didn't look up until the two men were standing next to the table. She grabbed her purse from the back of her chair and stood; her gaze met Luke's when she looked up.

"Captain," he said.

"You ready?"

"Actually, I'd like to get a cup of coffee and make a pit stop before we go."

His voice sounded calm, his look easy, but then his jaw twitched. Nervous? Playing her? She closed her eyes, knowing she had to let go of motive and deal with actions. "Go," she said. No matter what, he deserved a few minutes alone.

When he walked past, a chair from the next table made him shift closer and the back of his hand brushed against hers. It wasn't intentional, and with a wipe against her service pants, it was gone. Sara decided to get Luke his coffee so they could get on the road.

When he returned, he accepted his cup with a nod, sipped it, smiled. "Thanks."

"Let's go."

O'Malley went to the parking lot via the back door as she and Luke walked toward the curb.

"Listen, Sara," Luke said, and Sara paused to look at him. He seemed shaken, but that could be adrenaline.

"I know I messed up there, too many numbers, not enough about what it takes to get into the flight program. I haven't had the chance to put it in order."

She cleared her throat as she regrouped. "Luke, you did a great job. This was a difficult room, and you made it yours."

He ran a hand through his dark hair, leaving a cowlick sticking up in the front. "The other speakers are really good. I can be, too."

She blinked, felt her own frustration that she wasn't prepared to deal with this Luke. First though, she had to know one thing. "The things you said up there, were they what you were working on back at the motel?"

"Oh, hell, no," he said, the last word buried in a laugh. "I was scared to death, and just started talking." He glanced away. "I don't remember half of it, but I won't let that happen again. I swear."

If this was acting, it was far beyond anything she could catch. She felt his anxiousness, his need to please her, his fear that she would make him leave. When her hand went to his arm, it was a jolt for both of them. "You did well. I mean it. I was watching the crowd, and you had them."

"I don't care about them," he said, looking at her hand, then her eyes. "I won't let you down. There are four more days, and I don't care if I have to work 24/7, I'll nail this. Your tour will be a success, Sara."

She should have taken her hand back, because the contact wasn't helping, but she couldn't. Whatever else might be true, he had come here for her. She believed that now, and if it came back to bite her in the ass, so be it.

Of course, believing him made everything more complicated. How she'd been treating him, for one thing. If he'd been a stranger, would she have thrown him into the pit like this? Shanghaied him into a public performance where he could have crashed and burned?

No. She would have bent over backwards to do anything she could to help. Now, she released him, embarrassed that she'd acted so unprofessionally. Damn it, she had to reassess everything. Where was O'Malley?

"Sara?"

She met his gaze again, that same concern was there, so evident in his eyes. Luke had never wanted to be anything less than the best. When it mattered to him, he would go to any lengths to be number one. That could work in his favor, and her own. "You're part of the team now, Solo. We'll make it happen, and you won't have to get on a stage again until you're prepared. I'll do whatever it takes to make sure of that. If there's something you need to talk over, you come to me, okay? I'm good at this stuff, and I can help you hone your strengths."

He stepped closer, and for the first time that night he seemed relaxed. Pleased. It was his hand now, on the back of her arm. "Thanks."

"No problem."

"So we're…?"

"We're on the same team. I wasn't prepared for that, given our history, but I believe you told me the truth. You came here to help. You're helping."

He nodded, searching her face, her eyes. She let him look. It was her turn to pitch in, to show him she was capable of being the kind of leader he could count on.

It would be easier if the feel of his hand didn't make her knees weak. But that was her problem, not his. "Never thought I'd hear you admit you didn't make Top Gun."

"Yeah, that surprised me, too. It was a hard pill to swallow. Still is, sometimes."

"I'll bet you were runner-up."

He grinned. "You'd be right."

Where was he? If O'Malley was doing this on purpose...

"Look, about tonight," she started, but when he casually leaned into her personal space the way he used to, she almost choked. "If it seemed unfair throwing you out there..." She shifted closer to the curb, pretended she was searching for O'Malley. "I had to see if you had the right instincts for a live tour."

"Of course," he said. "I needed to know that, too."

When she looked at him, he smiled. She couldn't help smiling back.

The van swerved into the loading zone, and the two of them took their seats. During the quiet ride Sara thought about Luke, and how he'd become a whole different kind of problem than she'd ever anticipated.

DESPITE THE DECAF, Sara's mind had still refused to settle forty-five minutes after she'd gone to bed. It was late, and she had an early-morning meeting, but she couldn't seem to slow down. She adjusted her position until it felt right and concentrated on her breathing. She had a go-to-sleep routine, flexing and releasing her muscles from her toes to her head, which had always worked for her. It hadn't tonight. Yet.

The tour would start in four days and there was so much to do, so many details dangling that she should, by all rights, be thinking about nothing else. Instead, big surprise, her thoughts kept returning to Luke. How he'd looked at her in the gym, how he'd walked across the stage at Lefty's. How it had almost felt like old times waiting for the van.

Her eyes closed as she sighed, tired of her confusion.

It didn't seem to matter how many times she told herself their relationship was strictly professional, he still ran through her like a low-frequency sound wave.

Four times she'd caught herself remembering details from their first date, then pulled back, turned her thoughts to anything but Luke. The fifth time, she'd given in. She wasn't sure why that memory was so insistent. Because they'd been so young, perhaps? Because it had been so simple? They'd both been sixteen. Five months separated their birthdays, and she'd enjoyed teasing him about her being older. Only kids joked about that.

He'd worn jeans, Air Jordans and an Eminem T-shirt. She'd snuck a spritz of Romance perfume from the mall and after a dozen changes, finally went with the pink shirt that made her boobs look bigger.

They'd been terrified in the third row of the Multiplex. *Galaxy Quest* was on the screen, not that she'd paid any attention. All her senses were tuned in to the boy next to her. She'd felt him shaking when he'd placed his arm on the back of her seat. Who was she kidding? She was the one who'd been shaking so hard her teeth had chattered.

He'd tried to kiss her three times. The first one turned into a cough. The second, she worried she might be sick. The third time, he'd put them both out of their misery and kissed her full on the mouth, as if he'd done it a hundred times before. And even though she'd practiced her first kiss over and over again, on her pillow, on the back of her hand, on the inside above her elbow, the real thing had been like fireworks, like an earthquake. Neither one of them had so much as thought about parting their lips.

They'd walked out of that movie boyfriend and girlfriend. She'd been madly in love, as only a sixteen-year-old can be. He'd told her she was the prettiest girl in school. He'd asked her if maybe, one day, she might like to go flying with him. If his dad said it was okay. When they'd reached her front porch, it seemed as if he'd grown a foot and aged a year.

A couple of months later, they'd moved way past kissing. He'd wanted everything, every way, everywhere. She hadn't had a problem with that. Even when the *where* had been dangerously stupid.

It surprised her that her hand, the one he'd brushed at Lefty's, was on her stomach. Low. Moving down. She whipped it up, away, over the covers.

Nothing good could come of letting that train of thought get to the end of the line.

Which pretty much guaranteed it would take a house falling on her head to stop it.

Her hand slipped beneath the covers, all the way. She tensed even before her finger touched her clit. Behind closed eyes were images from the past, sounds, one after another as real as the room, as her heartbeat.

At the debate, senior year. In a broom closet. One door away from a room full of people. Professors. Her parents. His parents. A crying child. Luke behind her, lifting her skirt, pulling down her panties. His right hand over her mouth, his cock hard and slamming into her as she braced against the door.

The sound of his panting in her ear, his moan when he came so loud she was certain they'd be caught.

She'd had to bite the back of her own hand when he spun her around and finished her with his mouth.

When she came in her motel-room bed.

5

WITH TWO DAYS UNTIL the start of the tour, Luke had been working his ass off, they all had. They'd thrown in the towel at nine-thirty with orders to get some dinner and some sleep.

Luke pushed open his motel-room door and headed for the shower, a private shower with lots of water at the perfect temperature, something he'd never take for granted. He groaned as the heat hit the back of his neck.

For a couple of minutes, his mind was blissfully quiet, filled with nothing but steam. Then he started thinking again. Jesus.

He'd always been a simple guy. The opposite of deep. He liked flying and women so he'd built his life around those two things. Unapologetically. A second layer, which he'd had to concede when he went into flight training, turned out to be his competitive streak, his pride and satisfaction in service to his country and his strong affection for well brewed beer. It should have been a damn-near perfect life.

Then his F-15 had slammed into a mountain in Khwaran Ghar, Afghanistan, and his world had spun into an unrecoverable dive.

Turns out there was a third, and now possibly a fourth layer to him. Before the crash, things had been right on track. He planned on living a long life emulating his personal hero, test pilot Chuck Yeager. Instead, Luke had screwed the pooch. Evidently, there was no going back. And even more evidently, he had no idea how to move forward.

He grabbed the soap, and thought of Sara.

They hadn't had a minute alone. Not when the team rehearsed until their throats were dry and tempers were on edge. Still, Luke thought about her every spare moment. On his run, in his bed, in his dreams. Since the night she'd tested him at Lefty's, things had been better between them, at least more friendly.

He kept going back to the way she'd touched him. The way she'd spoken to him as if he wasn't the enemy. She'd smiled and meant it. While he was grateful as hell, he didn't understand it. He hadn't apologized yet.

The shift in her attitude had bewildered him. Sara thought his rambling talk had been okay. He barely remembered a word.

What he didn't know was whether he still needed to say he was sorry, or if apologizing would reopen a wound that had already healed.

It was too big a question for this late at night, and what he really wanted was to go to bed.

With Sara.

Shit.

Hadn't she'd told him to feel free to come talk to her if there was anything she could help with? Time to test the waters.

SARA PUT DOWN THE LATEST logistics memo when she heard knocking on her door. Had to be O'Malley. He knew she'd still be working at ten-forty.

She opened the door and stared, astonished. "Luke?"

"Hey," he said, holding up a six-pack of bottled soda. "Thought you might be hungry."

"It's late."

He nodded. "Time stopped having any meaning days ago. So, pizza?" He lifted the soda again, then realized his mistake with a laugh. "Jeez, I'm punchy."

The very ends of his hair were damp, his plain white T-shirt looked as worn and comfortable as his low-slung jeans. It had been a long time since she'd seen him in jeans. She ran a self-conscious hand down her hair, wishing she'd done more than drop her cap and let it fall.

"Is this too weird?" Luke's gaze met hers, and there was that disconcerting uncertainty right there, out in the open. She wondered if he realized how transparent he was, that she could see the chinks in his armor.

"It is," he said, taking a step back.

"What?" She'd been staring. Still was. "No. Sorry. I'm dead on my feet."

"Should I go?" he asked, although he didn't move.

"What kind of pizza?

"Half veg, half pepperoni."

That had been their regular order. She never had been able to give up her beloved pepperoni, even though it was terrible for her. She stepped back, knowing it was a bad idea.

He passed her closely, and she let herself look at him, his broad shoulders tapering to his slim hips. He stalled when he tried to put the box on the table as it was already covered with notebooks and file folders. Sara scrambled, keeping her piles in order as she transferred them to the counter by the sink. She would have put them on the bed, but she hadn't finished reading that lot piled there.

She turned around to find he hadn't put the box or the

drinks down. Luke abruptly lifted his gaze. He'd been staring at her legs. God, she was in her shorts, the really short shorts. Barefoot. T-shirt, oversize and bulky, but oh, crap, she'd taken off her bra. From the look on Luke's face, he'd just realized the same thing.

He got busy with the meal. Pizza box open, napkins and little packets of cheese and dried red pepper flakes on the open lid, two sodas lifted from the six-pack then placed carefully in front of each chair.

After she took her seat and Luke settled across the table from her, the déjà vu was so strong it made her dizzy. It hadn't been a round table in college, but a storage chest. The dorm rooms had been tiny. No one had thought twice about eating and studying while on the floor. Or doing other things.

It was safer to focus on the food, and not the man. She hadn't even realized how hungry she was. Luke was right, the days had blended together. It seemed like weeks since they'd stood outside Lefty's.

She sneaked a peek at him. When he peeked back, she shifted her gaze. So high school. *Them* in high school. In the cafeteria. Her with Tricia and Susie, him with his football buddies, stealing furtive looks.

"You forgot the pepper and cheese," he said. "I got you extra."

"Thanks," she murmured, amazed he remembered so much.

"Your hair's long."

She touched the ends. "It's for the cap," she said. "Pinning it up is easier."

"It looks good."

She waved her slice and gave him a *pfft*. "It looks like hell."

He only smiled, his gaze flicking to her breasts. Then

he leaned back, totally at ease, as if he owned the damn room. This was more like the old Luke, the one she'd known so well. The guy she'd loved beyond reason.

Sara grew conscious of the need to breathe, to blink. To step the hell away from the edge of the cliff.

LUKE CAUGHT THE SECOND her interest turned to alarm, and he cursed himself. Too soon, too much. It didn't help that his cock ached against his fly.

He smiled with as much nonchalance as he could fake. "Hanover told me that when he did a couple of college talks the students asked really embarrassing questions. Like how we handle bathroom breaks on a mission and—" Rick had been asked if it was creepy, jerking off in a barracks where everyone could hear "—stuff."

Her eyes were no longer wide and startled. Good, that was good, only, she didn't seem interested, either. The flush had vanished, leaving her skin pale from too much work and not enough sleep. Her pupils had contracted, and to his disappointment, her nipples, which had been poking through her faded shirt, had, too.

He knew exactly how to fix that.

The memory of her in his mouth made him bite back a moan, a reason to pull himself together. He grabbed his soda and drank, just to have something to do with his hands.

"He was only trying to get a rise out of the new guy," Sara said. "When it comes to hazing, you boys never grow up."

Luke had to think for a second to figure out the context of her comment. Hanover. Hazing. Finally back on track, he said, "No, that wasn't hazing. Hazing was when they dosed my salmon with half a bottle of habanero sauce during my welcome dinner."

She laughed as she got herself another piece of pizza. "Did you eat it?"

"Every damn bite. Thought I was gonna die, but I ate it."

"I'm sure everyone appreciated your team spirit," she said. "I've been on a lot of college tours, and you'll get some smart-asses in the audience, and some anti-war protesters too. But you'll handle it."

"You seem pretty sure about that."

She chewed for a minute, swallowed. "You may be new to public speaking, but you're still you."

He wasn't, though. How did Sara not see it? She'd known him better than anyone, even better than Alf. It bothered him, when maybe it shouldn't. He expected too much from her and now he was flying blind, no stabilizers, no command center to guide him home.

Luke stared at the pizza crust in his hand, worried that if he stayed, he'd do something irrevocably stupid. "I've been meaning to ask," he said, "how did you end up with O'Malley?"

She didn't answer right away. When he looked at her, he found her brows lowered and her head tilted just so. Just as she always had done when she didn't quite understand.

Then her head straightened and she smiled. "O'Malley's something else. He volunteered for this tour. Astonished the hell out of me. He was running logistics at Randolph. O'Malley knows everyone. Everything."

"He knows you," Luke said, hoping she wouldn't hear the jealousy in his voice.

"He does. I'm not even sure how we became friends. Proximity, at first. We kept bumping into each other. Something ridiculous made us both laugh, a slip of the

tongue by a colonel, and we ended up having lunch together a couple of times a month."

"So you got your gossip from the horse's mouth?"

She took a hit of soda, eyed a third slice of pizza. "He's
actually completely discreet. The only reason I know he
knows everything is because other people started bugging
me for gossip. I asked him about that, naturally."

"Brave."

"I knew him by then. He was tickled. Said his spy
network only reached half the world. That the trick was
never letting on which half. I don't think he was kidding.
I've seen him go into private meetings with generals."

"Probably didn't salute them, either. I don't personally
care, but I bet it rankles some officers a great deal."

"That might be a safe bet."

"Well, he scares the crap out of me."

She laughed. Luke's chest tightened.

"I think that's the point." She gave in to piece number
three, and that made him stupidly happy for no reason at
all.

"He's on this tour because of me, though," she said.
"He doesn't have a family. I think he enjoys looking out
for me."

Luke nodded, felt that damn stirring low in his belly
again.

"It's late." Her eyes had darkened. The edge of her
teeth skimmed her upper lip.

"I should let you get some rest," he said, making no
move, hoping like hell she'd ask him to stay.

"You need some yourself. It's been a brutal schedule.
But you've really stepped up to the plate. I appreciate it."

Reluctantly, he stood.

She got up, too, and she was close. He could reach out

and touch her shoulder, her waist. For God's sake, the bed was right there.

Her gaze went to his arm and his muscles flexed. He hadn't meant to show off or anything, or maybe he had. If he stepped a little closer, he'd catch her scent. He brushed the back of his hand against her arm as he reached for the pizza box. He froze right there. Still touching.

His hand turned slowly until his fingers wrapped around the impossibly delicate circle of her wrist. He forgot how to breathe again as his body gave in to the pull.

He kissed her.

No thought, just movement, just pressure. Taste, dammit, the taste of her and he was gone, past Mach II, into the stratosphere. Jesus.

She moaned, something high and needy, and he stepped closer until he was pressed against her, and there was the scent of her. Of Sara and pizza, the way it used to be when things were simple. They were lovers on a single bed, with tomato sauce on the T-shirt he threw to the floor, they tasted like heat and beer and cheese and Sara, her long legs wrapped around his waist as she rose up to meet his thrusts.

Her fingernails dug into his shoulder, her tongue chased his, and he never wanted to stop, not for anything in the world.

Until she stilled. Completely. Tongue, breath, hand, body. Froze as cold as ice.

He stepped back. Left the mess on the table as it was. Hurried to the door.

"Luke."

He paused, his hand on the knob.

"That was…"

He couldn't look at her. He hadn't meant to do that, but that was no excuse.

"Next time," she said, "eat with one of your team members."

SARA STARED AT THE CLOSED DOOR, the ghost of Luke's touch making her shiver. He'd done a nice thing, bringing her dinner. The conversation had been easy, and they were both so tired. That was it, of course. If she hadn't been so exhausted, if it hadn't been so familiar.

It would have been so simple to take the next step. As easy as breathing. Now it was the memory of Luke's body that heated her, from her lips to her thighs. There had been too many pizzas connected with too many kisses, and she couldn't separate them. One touch brought back a hundred others, perfectly preserved in overwhelming detail. His laugh, his words, how he'd said her name mingled with other nights, other rooms, and it was all too much.

She had to get rid of the pizza box. The soda could stay, but not the food, not the smell. She opened her window first, wishing there was more of a breeze. Then she gathered his napkin and his crust, threw her trash on top of the congealed cheese, shut the box and grabbed her keycard.

Shy of a jog, she reached the motel's back exit, pushing against the metal bar hard with her side. She realized she was barefoot and braless as she went off the path to the big trash bin and threw the box so it banged against the side, certain its disappearance would quell her circling thoughts.

Stubbing her toe helped more. She hopped, cursing, until she was inside again. Leaning on the beige hallway wall she looked at her foot. No real damage. Only pain.

She was Luke's supervisor. His boss. He was a part of her team, no more, nothing more. There had to be distance, physical distance because he still unnerved her. The way she wanted him bypassed her logic and reason. Which didn't mean she had to succumb.

He wasn't her boyfriend, he was her colleague, and every time she saw him that had to be the very first thought. Her only motive.

She might not be able to do anything about their strange alchemy, but she could control her own actions. And if she couldn't repress the old memories, she had to stop new ones before they got started.

LUKE RAN A HAND OVER his face. He'd had a lousy night's sleep after leaving Sara's room, and he'd paid for it all day.

He'd been such an idiot. Too much, too soon. Of course she'd told him to go. What had he been *thinking?*

He'd wanted the pizza to be a kind of peace offering. Get them to a place where they could talk. Just talk.

So then he had to go and kiss her.

He closed his eyes, and he was back there again, holding her, tasting her.

One more deep breath, one more internal reboot, but just like every time he'd tried to stop thinking about Sara, about how he'd messed up, it didn't work. He should have known. Sara had been nice to him for a couple of days and he thought he could march into her room with a pizza. Moron. He'd thought about her so much for so long, and she hadn't thought of him once. Not until he'd crashed her party.

He wished like hell he was already at Eglin, learning the intricacies of his new jet. He would be able to breathe there. He could forget about Sara, move on.

His gaze locked on the papers in front of him. He

finally had the talk part down. Most of it was memorized, and he knew enough now to fill in appropriately where his memory failed. It was the question-and-answer crap that had him up at 10:00 p.m. Again. When he wasn't thinking about Sara, his head swam with job descriptions, qualifications, options for new recruits.

The college kids were the problem. He wasn't worried about the job fairs, but students had those damn hormones going on. All that confusion about what came next. Unless kids had changed a hell of a lot since his day. But then, he'd known forever that the air force was going to be his life.

Luke stretched his neck, rolled his shoulders. It wasn't enough. He got up from the conference table and arched his back. The room felt different now that most of the boxes had been loaded into trucks, but the Victoria Inn would continue to be home base until they'd finished the rotation of venues in the Greater San Diego Area. In fifteen days they'd go on to L.A. and that would last two and a half weeks, then they'd finish up in the Bay Area. Two days after the last speaking engagement, he would report to Florida.

The empty room closed in around him. He wasn't used to this much time sitting on his ass. What he needed was to get the hell out of here. City air would clean out his lungs, help him get back on track. Yeah, he knew it was full of smog, but there wasn't any sand for miles, it wasn't a hundred and twenty degrees and it was, by God, the good old U.S. of A.

He turned off the overhead light and went toward the lobby.

"Hey, Solo."

His head jerked up at the feminine voice, even though it wasn't Sara's. Terri Van Linn stood at the front desk, her smile as friendly as always, but instead of her uniform, she wore snug jeans and a shirt that showed off everything important.

"Heading out?" she asked.

"Thought I'd walk a bit before I hit the books again."

"Want company?"

Instinctively he wanted to say no. He'd gotten a couple of confusing vibes from her in the past. But she was a colleague, one of those people Sara had told him to eat with. "I'm not heading anywhere special."

"Just where I wanted to go."

They met at the front entrance, and he held the door for her. She smiled up at him. He returned it. As she passed him, he glanced back to find Sara staring at him with big wounded eyes. Even from across the room, he could tell she was jumping to the wrong conclusion.

Shit.

6

"SOLO?"

He turned away from Sara—a remarkably hard thing to do—and faced Van Linn. He'd tell her he forgot something, that he had a phone call to make.

But something made him glance back to the hallway. Sara had gone.

He should go to her room, explain...what? It was just a walk. Van Linn was on the team. And she was waiting.

He stepped outside.

"You okay?" Terri asked.

He glanced behind him again. Whatever he did next would be wrong. "I'm fine," he said. "It feels good to get out of that conference room."

Committing to the course took longer than it should have, but halfway down the street he started to relax. The September night felt good on his skin. It was the kind of night that made fall seem far away. He guided Terri to the right, toward the park, which he knew was well-lit and well-traveled.

"I hear you're getting in on the ground floor with the F-35," Van Linn said.

His surprise must have shown because there was a

hint of smugness in her upturned face. "It's good to know that gossip has no borders. Yeah, I'll be in one of the first units at Eglin, then I'm moving on to Hill."

"I've got friends in Hell."

He'd heard the nickname for the Utah base his first week in basic. He'd also heard from a lot of folks that life was pretty sweet in "Hell" if a pilot got the job done. "I wonder how long it's going to take until I hear all the Hell jokes," he said. "I'm guessing a week."

She laughed, the sound oddly throaty for such a petite woman. Terri came up to about his shoulder. She was a redhead, although he doubted she'd been born that way, despite the smattering of freckles across her nose and cheeks. All her features were diminutive, but he knew from seeing her in the gym and at the pool that she packed a lot of muscle in a surprisingly curvy body.

She was hot, a fact none of the men on the team had missed, although nothing had been said. At one point he'd wondered if she and Hanover had something going on. There'd been a vibe there. But then, Van Linn was a woman who liked to tease. She used that borderline flirting in her speech, used it particularly well during the question-and-answer sessions. She must be an excellent investigator—she played people, especially men, with skill and strength.

"Guy I know who's been at Hill the longest, he's pretty high on the place," she said. "It's easy to get around, the base has good morale and there's not much crime. Relatively speaking."

"It could be in the armpit of any state in the Union and I wouldn't care. I just want to get rated and start flying."

"Yeah. You flyboys, you do love your toys." Her voice was different out here, breathier than when she was practicing her talk and lower than during meals or meetings.

He wondered if she'd come along on this walk because she was looking to get laid. Of course, it was equally possible she was catching a cold. "I suppose in your line of work, you've got a toy or two of your own," he said, then hoped it didn't sound too flirty.

"You referring to my Sig Sauer? That, my friend, is no toy."

"No, ma'am. No disrespect intended."

She nodded. "Okay. I will admit that I love my Porsche to pieces. I wouldn't think of taking it on the job."

"Yeah, I get it. I don't fly my Cessna in combat, so I can see we're on the same page."

At the stoplight, he realized how close she stood, a definite breach of his personal space. It wouldn't take much for him to accept the invitation. While he now understood the situation completely, he found himself unsure of his next step. He didn't want to hurt her feelings or piss her off. He did have to work with her.

Weird. He was back to scratch in the air, but his reflexes with females since last year were still off. He used to be able to read a woman like a menu. At least where sex was concerned. Despite everything, females were fifty percent mystery. But his instincts in situations like this had been honed over a lot of years and a lot of personal experience.

Van Linn was a very beautiful woman: strong, charismatic and arrogant. He could see where other women might not like her, but men? Yeah, she could have her pick.

Back in the day, he wouldn't have hesitated making a night of it. He'd have stepped close, touched her just the right way. He'd have been a perfect gentleman until the bedroom door was closed and locked. They'd have sparred, neither of them figurative lightweights, and who knows which one of them would have ended up on top? None of it was appealing. Not because he was tired, either.

He stepped away. Not enough to make things awkward. Just a bit. Maybe he would have been up for it if last night hadn't happened, but probably not. The only woman he wanted in bed was Sara.

If Alf could hear him now, he'd laugh his ass off. Solo turning down a beautiful woman like Van Linn? Never.

"Solo?"

He started, aware the light had turned green and Van Linn was in the crosswalk. He caught up to her. "Sorry."

"You looked miles away."

"Thinking about an old buddy."

"A buddy or a lady friend?" she asked teasingly.

"Nah. My WSO when I was flying the Eagle."

"Is he still in the Sandbox?"

"Nope. He's home in Iowa. With his family."

"Well, good for him. What about you? Where's your home?"

He told her his story for a while, listened to hers. The dance continued as they hit the park, her moving in, him sliding away. Then they were under the trees, away from the lights, and he guessed this part of the park wasn't as popular at night, because they were alone.

She touched his arm. "We're gonna get real busy real soon."

He nodded. "I hope I can keep up."

"I have a feeling you could keep up with about anything," she said, moving just that little bit closer.

He met her gaze through the shadows. "This is new territory for me, Terri, and I made a promise that I'd keep my nose buried in the books. Which is a shame, but true nonetheless."

She stilled, then lifted her hand from his arm. "Fair enough," she said, her voice a little tighter. She hadn't expected this, didn't like it, that was obvious from the narrowing of her eyes. "You know what? Now that you mention those books, I've got some things I want to read up on before it gets too late. So I'll see you in the morning."

"I'll walk back with you."

"I can take care of myself."

"I never doubted it," he said, taken aback at her reaction.

"In the morning, then."

As he watched her leave, he replayed the conversation in his head, and he thought he'd been okay. Nice, in fact.

Well, that was just great. He couldn't even tell when he was being an ass.

SARA STARED AT THE motel-room wall, watching as the lights from passing cars flashed between the blackout curtains. She needed to sleep. Tomorrow would be a killer day, and she had to be up at dawn. But every time she closed her eyes, she saw Luke and Van Linn at the motel exit.

She shouldn't care. She'd like to think that if she hadn't let him in last night, she wouldn't have minded, but that wasn't true. Last night had just made her more honest.

Luke wasn't breaking any rules, not even his word. Van Linn was fair game. Sara suspected that two of the other speakers were more than colleagues. Both were officers, and it didn't interfere with the job, so she ignored it. As she should ignore Luke and Van Linn. He was just another team member.

One who still had so much power over her it wasn't even funny.

She turned over in bed, tucked her arm under her pillow and sighed. The day had been a struggle. Thoughts of Luke had intruded at the most inconvenient moments. She'd told herself the bit about being his supervisor, but it had only worked marginally. She had too many feelings, that's all. Way the hell too many and she didn't know how to shut them off.

There had to be some way to do that, right? She'd never let a man interfere with the job, not once, not even when she'd been in the giddy first stages of what she'd hoped was love.

It hadn't been love that time, or any other time. Wrong. It had been love once.

But that had been long ago, and how could just the *memory* of love have so much power? It made no sense.

She'd have to get tougher. Harden herself, be unforgiving. It couldn't matter that he was with Van Linn. That everyone thought she was so hot. That she and Luke were so alike.

Sara kicked her blankets off, suffocating in the stupid motel room even with the window open.

How could he be with Van Linn less than twenty-four hours after he'd…

Sara squeezed her eyes shut, thought about tomorrow night's official start. Everything could go wrong. The sound system had been flaky, half the speakers were first-timers and they could freeze in front of the audience. The simulators could break, but then no one was probably going to show up except for the students who were earning credits. It would be a disaster, Colonel Graves would pull her from the assignment, and she'd end up filing back at Randolph.

She could always leave the air force. O'Malley would get her decent letters of recommendation, and she could

find a job in some city. Someplace with real weather.
Snow would be good. Somewhere in Utah, maybe. Near
Hill.

She moaned and knocked her fists against her temples.
A lobotomy was the only solution, but there was no time.
She was going to see him tomorrow. And the next day.

God, she needed to sleep.

LUKE KICKED THE COVERS OFF his bed. It was late. Tomorrow was show day, and he had to sleep. First thing,
though, he would have to make it clear to Van Linn that
he'd meant no offense. That he'd been flattered. End
things right there, get back to business.

He also had to make sure Sara hadn't misunderstood
what she'd seen. Suddenly, talking to Van Linn seemed
like nothing. Most likely, Terri hadn't left because she
was insulted, but because all she'd wanted was a jump,
and if that wasn't on the table, she wasn't interested.

Damn, he should have clued in on that straight away.
How many times had he done the same thing? Not that he
did it anymore. That was what he wanted Sara to know.
But he couldn't come out and just say that to her. He'd
have to think of how to tell her in a roundabout way.

He groaned and turned over again. This *thinking* thing
was full of crap. It had been so easy before. If he thought
about stuff, it was about flying, sports or sex. All this
business about regrets and consequences was like learning Chinese. His brain didn't work that way.

It hadn't up until last year. Until he'd lost his plane.

All he wanted was to be himself again. And the only
thing that would get him there was making things right
with Sara.

He closed his eyes and reached for his cock. A quick
jerk-off would relax him, and he wouldn't worry or

ponder or wonder or plan. He would be the old Luke, the mindless hotshot who was so full of himself he didn't have room for anyone else.

THE DAY HAD STARTED with too much caffeine after four hours of sleep. They were in a university auditorium, the first of many, and while the seats were empty now, they wouldn't be in five hours and twelve minutes.

Sara looked up at the two big screens on either side of the stage. They should have images screaming across them, some simultaneous, some individual, but they remained blank because of a gremlin in the equipment. Which was fine. This was the rehearsal, the appropriate time for glitches to be ironed out. She had expected snafus. There was no reason for the headache or for her to clench her fists. Her reaction pissed her off more than the actual problem.

Why couldn't she be more like O'Malley? Nothing ruffled him. He'd told her when they'd first met that the secret to good management and planning was to anticipate possible screwups since they were inevitable. She'd done just that as best she could, but there were always a few impossible to predict.

Sara left the auditorium for the parking lot her team had taken over. Their trucks were at the periphery, several of them empty. Four of the simulators were in place. They looked like what they were—the biggest, baddest, most technically advanced computer games in the world. The truck-size generator rumbled loud and low, a constant irritant. O'Malley was directing the unloading of the final two flight sims, and there were teenagers gathered around the barriers watching everything. Some were taking pictures with their cell phones. Some, she noticed unhappily, were smoking. She supposed there was nothing she could do about that. But if one of them dared light up around her equipment…

Someone came up beside her and before she could turn her head, an open hand was in front of her, waist-high. On the broad palm were two pills.

"You're supposed to be rehearsing," she said, every muscle in her body tensing. She would not let it show. "Not playing Nurse Nancy."

"I'm on a break. Thought I'd get some air."

She met Luke's gaze and instantly wanted to look away. She didn't. Luke was part of her team. That's all. Nothing else, and what he did with his free time was—

He was just part of her team.

His gaze was on her, and it was as if he was studying her, tallying up her weaknesses. "They're not symbolic," he said, nodding at his palm. "They're just aspirin." Then he lifted his other hand, which held a bottle of water. "*This* is symbolic."

She couldn't resist an eye roll, but she took the two pills and popped them in her mouth. Drank them down, and gave him his bottle back. "Thanks."

"I don't think I recognize that big blue one," he said.

He was talking about their newest simulator. It was the one she was most troubled about. She was under no illusions about what these sims were here to do. They were war games. Two from the point of view of pilots, both jet and helo, one as a search-and-rescue specialist, one driving a Hummer into an ambush and one as a first-person shooter. The new one simulated a drone pilot. These machines were built to recruit gamers. Millions had gone into making them realistic down to the last detail.

"They never really get it right," Luke said. "Damn close, but there's a difference. It's not the fault of the machines, though. There's no way to simulate being so afraid you're sure you're going to die."

"You? Afraid?"

He snorted softly. "Oh, yeah."

She looked at him again. "Hard to imagine."

"There are scary things out there," he said, meeting her gaze, only this time he looked away quickly. "That's the part of this that has me worried. I feel like I should tell them, but telling someone isn't enough." He nodded toward the machines. "Sitting in a box can't hope to do it justice."

Sara knew Luke as well as she'd ever known another human being. She'd been sure, absolutely certain, she'd seen every emotion play on his face. Seeing such humility in his eyes was still new. And confusing. She reached out to him, catching herself seconds before contact. She drew her arm back and took a step away, hoping he hadn't noticed.

All she could see was his profile. So handsome he took her breath away. His lips parted as he blinked, and then his mouth closed again.

"Tell them that," she said, leaning in so he could hear her. "Tell the students what you've just said. Hearing it from you will make a difference."

The right corner of his mouth lifted. "No, it won't."

"It might."

He turned to face her. "I'll do my best."

She swallowed, her mouth dry. "I know."

He stepped away and she made herself look at the trucks, at anything. He would make a difference on the stage. No one could make a person believe in the impossible like Luke Carnes.

His footsteps faded a lot quicker than her confusion.

He was vulnerable, and he continued to show it. She didn't know what to do with that information.

But he was Van Linn's problem now. Let him get comfort from the redhead.

Sara's stomach turned at the thought, or maybe it was the headache that made her feel sick. "Crap," she said. She had no time for this now, then she jumped when she felt someone at her back.

It was O'Malley.

"What's got your panties in a bunch?"

She laughed. She couldn't help it. O'Malley's expression didn't change, all except one bushy eyebrow. Let him wonder. "Are those machines gonna be ready anytime soon, Master Sergeant?"

"They'll be ready when they're scheduled to be ready, Captain."

"Good," she said. Then she left him standing in the parking lot. It didn't hit her until she reached the auditorium that he'd seen her with Luke. No way O'Malley didn't know what was going on by now. She supposed she'd better incorporate the master sergeant's snooping into the plan. As soon as she had one.

7

Luke had been correct in his assessment of how the night would go. The talk was easy, once he'd decided to completely ignore the size of the audience. Especially after he'd locked on to one person, this time a girl who'd reminded him of Sara when they'd been at Berkeley. It was the questions and answers that had been tricky, but he thought he'd done all right. He kept bringing the subject back to service, not politics. He was looking to motivate those who were searching for something to matter, some way to make a difference.

The crowd that had gathered around him afterwards had been interesting. The flight suit had gotten its fair share of attention, the subject of *Top Gun* had worn out its welcome quickly, but there had also been a few phone numbers slipped his way. That's where he'd fumbled. Not critically, but it hit him yet again that what had once been the simplest part of his life was now the most difficult. Much better were those half-dozen people who'd stuck it out to the end to ask the real questions. He had given them cards for the local recruiters and hoped for the best.

Now, though, he was done with his part, and thank God, because he was exhausted. The speakers—including

Van Linn, who had been avoiding him since their walk—
were sprawled out in the front row of seats, watching as
O'Malley coordinated tonight's portion of the packing.
Luke kept looking around for Sara, but she must have
been outside with the simulators and trucks.

He wanted to see her, to get his performance-eval. Just
to see her.

"Listen up, people."

He lifted his head to find Sara standing between the
seats and the stage. She looked great, as if she hadn't been
worrying about every single thing that had gone on for
the last twelve hours. She'd freshened her lipstick, and he
got stuck right there. On her lips, shiny and inviting, and
all he wanted to do was kiss the gloss off. He liked her
lips naked, liked *her* naked, hair wild on the pillow. That
moment when the kisses sparked a blaze. He pictured,
so clearly, her eyes with her pupils blown so dark they
seemed otherworldly. All for him. Jesus.

"Evaluations will begin tomorrow morning, eight hundred sharp, conference room. You will now report to the
minibus." Her lips twitched slightly. "To be transported
to the Tin Shack, where I will buy the first round."

The team groaned at her teasing, then hustled to the
exit. He glanced back in time to see Sara turn to a scowl-
ing O'Malley. Even knowing the story of how the two
of them had become friends, watching them together
seemed completely illogical.

"What's so funny?"

Luke grinned at Hanover. "Just thinking my first drink
will be the most expensive Scotch in the joint."

"I've been to the Tin Shack," Hanover said. "The most
expensive Scotch is the only Scotch. Do yourself a favor
and stick to beer. And not the tap swill."

"Duly noted."

THE SPEAKERS HAD DONE a terrific job, and they deserved not only some R & R but some attaboys. She deserved some privacy to get her thoughts in order, which was why she'd driven her own rental.

Sara was pleased with the turnout and the retention. Overall, the night had gone well. Better than expected. She'd seen the recruiters' cards go into pockets and purses; more importantly she'd seen that several, maybe more than several, people in the audience had been engrossed. Their minds had opened to the possibility that they could be part of the air force. That was huge. That was success. She would concentrate on that, and on the team who pulled it off.

She would even compliment Van Linn. The captain had done an exemplary job.

The bar wasn't far from the college, and she landed a decent parking space. She straightened her jacket after she closed the car door, then wondered if it would be more appropriate to leave her jacket behind. No, she was good.

The minibus hadn't arrived as far as she could tell, which would give her an opportunity to speak to the bartender. She'd pay for the first round, but only the first round. And she'd make sure the evening didn't get out of hand, because no one would benefit from hangovers.

Despite the music being awfully loud, she was able to make her arrangements and take a moment to look around. She'd been there before because the Tin Shack catered to a military clientele. There were uniforms of all sorts, some air force, but mostly navy.

She caught the entrance of her group, pleased to see them looking happy. Of course, her gaze settled on Luke. He'd been magnetic tonight, even better than she'd imagined. She'd been right to have him speak last. And yes, she would give him his due because he was a part of the night's success.

The group joined her at the end of the bar. It was a tight fit, but no one seemed to mind. "Order up," she said, loudly enough to be heard over the country music. "Beer or wine is fine. More than one, you're on your own. But remember, it's a school night."

As a group, they scowled at her, but they didn't really mind. She saw a handful of marines vacate a table near the pool room and she managed to snag it ahead of a small group of navy pilots.

Slowly, the team joined her, Luke and Van Linn trailing the pack. It was a good thing that Sara had her game face on, because she felt angry heat bubble up, but as they walked, she noticed that Van Linn wasn't wearing that seductive smile from the night before. In fact, she seemed pissed off. Trouble in paradise?

Luke seemed…puzzled. Terri stopped; so did he. Luke went from parade rest to attention, and then Terri left him behind. Even when the OSI officer made it to the table, there was an air of irritation about her.

It occurred to Sara that she'd forgotten to get herself a beer, which would make it difficult to raise a toast. She'd improvise, but first she had to forget the Luke/Terri thing and focus.

By the time Luke arrived at the table, she'd pulled it together. "Congratulations," she said. "You were all fantastic tonight. Each of you brought your A game to the stage, and it made a difference." She met each gaze as she moved from speaker to speaker. "I know *you* made the difference tonight. The air force will change because some of those kids will enlist, and it'll be due to your sincerity, your professionalism and your determination.

Thank you for all the hard work and thank you for being the kind of examples that stir others to service."

There was a lifting of bottles and chilled glasses, a "Hear, hear" that sounded loud even in that crowd, and dammit, she wished she had a drink.

Not everyone had a seat, but the group huddled. She wondered if they'd have the same camaraderie by the conclusion of the tour. A flash told her that Tritter had brought his camera, and that was a good thing, too. He'd been busy tonight. After his talk, he'd taken photos of the evening, some of which would be included in future presentations, press releases and media kits.

Luke had disappeared, but then Danny Franks caught her attention, and they got into a discussion about how to handle the technical questions that had come after his presentation. He wanted to impress the tech heads, but he didn't want to alienate the rest of the audience. The two of them stepped back without disengaging from the group too much so Sara could keep a weather eye out.

A hand on her shoulder startled her. It was Luke. Something in her flared, and it wasn't anger. He handed her a beer, smiled, then went back to the others.

She managed to finish her talk with Franks. When he left, Luke took his place.

"Congratulations," he said. "You put together a hell of a program."

"Thanks. And thanks for the beer."

"No sweat."

"You and Van Linn have a falling-out?" She hadn't meant to lead with that, but it was a valid question. They were part of the team, and she needed her team strong.

His lips thinned and his gaze darted away, but he said nothing.

"I wasn't implying anything. I just need to know if there are any problems."

"We should speak," he said. "Privately."

"Privately?" she asked, keeping her voice steady. "Really?"

He nodded. "I'd rather not discuss it here. And it should be soon."

If another member of the team had said those words, she would have agreed immediately. "Fine. We shouldn't be here long. Meet me at the diner twenty minutes after we get back to the motel."

LUKE WALKED INTO the restaurant ten minutes late. It hadn't been his fault, he'd been unable to extract himself from the group discussion that had begun during the ride. Sara was already sipping coffee. When he joined her, she pointedly looked at her watch.

"Apologies," he said. "Couldn't be helped."

"Fine," she said, and it hurt because her tone was all business, as if they hadn't laughed, hadn't felt the heat between them. "What's the problem?"

"I didn't pursue anything with Van Linn. I was just going for a walk."

Sara took in a breath, let it go as she studied the empty space beside him. "That's your business, Luke. As long as it doesn't interfere—"

"It was her idea. Joining me."

The fingers holding her cup tightened, were pale with the effort. When he looked up again, he had no idea what she was thinking and that was crazy. It was Sara. How could he not read Sara? "She asked to come with me. I said sure. It was only a walk."

"Was this why you wanted to talk? Because, honestly, it's fine."

He leaned forward, resting on his arms. "Is it?" he asked.

She blushed, held her breath.

Luke sat back quickly, cursing his thoughtlessness. She'd staked out the boundaries of this conversation with her first word, and he'd had to push. It was all he could do not to uncurl her fingers from the cup, bring her hand to his lips… He cleared his throat. "Captain Van Linn came on to me. It was subtle, but the invitation was clear. I begged off. I'm pretty sure I wasn't a jerk about it. It bothered her, though. I could tell by the way she left. As if I'd embarrassed her." Just like he'd embarrassed Sara.

A waitress arrived, and Luke ordered coffee. Sara didn't say a word, didn't even look at the woman.

Once they were alone again, Sara's blush had gone, leaving her pale skin perfect.

"She avoided me all morning," he said, "but things were fine at the auditorium. I thought we were cool. We aren't. At least, she's not cool with me."

Sara leaned in. Not by much. It made him feel fractionally better. He had made her smile over pizza. Made her laugh out loud. "It was…awkward," he confessed. "She told me to stay away from her."

"It's hard to believe," Sara said.

"That I turned her down?"

"That you were awkward."

He laughed. What the hell else was there to do? "I was. It was."

Sara smiled, but it was sympathetic, not gloating. He hadn't realized until then that he expected her to enjoy his uncertainty.

"You think she might cause trouble for you?"

He shrugged. "I have no idea what she'll do, I mean that. I can't read her." He couldn't read Sara, either. She seemed soft again, the way she'd been the other night. Not only her voice or her eyes, nothing he could point to and say: 'That's it. That's the way it feels when we're right with each other.'

"I appreciate you telling me," she said. "I'll keep it in mind."

The waitress startled him, he'd been so focused on Sara. The coffee helped him relax even more. He had given her the full story. The facts, at least, but not the reason. "The thing is, I don't care if she spends the next few weeks glaring at me. My conscience is clear, but I worry about how it could affect the team or the tour."

Sara frowned briefly. "You think she's that angry? She'd risk the tour?"

"I don't know the woman." He picked up his spoon to give himself a reason to avert his gaze. "But I know the type. Big ego, used to getting what they want. Going after it at all costs, acting like a child when they don't get it. Someone like that doesn't always think about consequences." He finally looked at her. "She might regret it like hell later, but the damage will be done."

Sara's face didn't reveal a thing. She looked as if he hadn't just given his own confession, as if he was nothing more than a member of the team. "I'll keep it in mind."

"I don't want to make any trouble for you, Sara." Screw it. He touched her cold hand. She didn't pull away, just stared at him, her face paler now. When she said, "I'd better go," it surprised him. He'd been sure she'd meant to say something else.

Out the window, across the parking lot, he saw Franks and Pearson headed toward the restaurant. Shit. He cleared his throat, pulled back his hand. "The show was great tonight. You know that, right?"

"Right." She blinked. "You all did a wonderful job." She hesitated, put two dollar bills on the table, then stood.

"You made it happen," he said. "Your fingerprints are all over this carnival, and you've outdone yourself. We had them. They listened. You should be proud."

She smiled, a real smile, licked her bottom lip, and then her gaze flicked to the window and sharpened with awareness. Her eyes tracked the other two team members. "Thank you, Luke." She met his gaze, and they had one tiny moment before she was gone.

SHE'D WALKED TO THE coffee shop, and was glad of it as she headed back to the motel. It wasn't a long walk, no more than a block and a half, but she needed to think before she got to her room. It was late, she was achingly tired, but if she didn't get herself squared away, she'd never get any rest.

He'd turned Van Linn down. *Why?* Sara had made it blatantly clear that nothing was going to happen between herself and Luke. He knew damn well that she was off-limits. No matter what else was true about Van Linn, the woman was gorgeous and single and she'd offered herself up for the taking, and yet Luke had said no.

Sara hadn't even considered that possibility. The vulnerability, the weird level of honesty, of humility, none of that meshed with the man she'd thought she knew better than anyone. He had changed, which didn't make sense to her. It wasn't as simple as him getting older and wiser. If she could believe the evidence, he'd practically become someone else.

People didn't do that. Men, especially men as good-looking and self-assured as Luke, couldn't alter the basics. For God's sake, he was still a fighter pilot. A warrior. A man who could charm the panties off a three-star general's daughter. In the general's house. Luke still made Sara's knees weak and her body ache. He knocked her for a loop any time they were close.

And then tonight. Jesus, he'd been talking about himself, not just Van Linn. Two months ago, if someone had told Sara Luke would be sitting across a table from her saying all that stuff, she would've laughed in their faces. Yet, tonight he'd had her. Not with his confession, but with his compliments. She believed him. There was no doubt in her mind that he meant every word he'd said about her. It shouldn't matter, not any more than any other compliment, and she'd received several tonight. But his words got to her. They made her feel warm and proud.

She quickened her pace as the enormity of the problem hit her. If she tried to unravel the truth about Luke, or if she continued to let her guard down, there was every reason to believe she'd lose herself in the process. She couldn't dare take a step down that path. Not even one.

LUKE STARED AT THE rippling water, debating a late swim in the closed pool. After four days of tension, four nights of inspirational talks, questions, challenges, too many guys trying to out-man him with a handshake and far too many young women looking for a fantasy, he wanted out. He was tired. He wanted a goddamned good night's sleep. He wanted Sara. But she was busy, or trying to avoid him. He couldn't tell which.

The only bright spot ahead was that he would be in the air in a couple of days. They had time off, not much, but he was going to make the most of it. He'd found a plane to rent, a Cessna, and he'd booked that sucker for a whole afternoon.

He missed the sky like a lover. That's where he got it together, up there, and it didn't matter if he was crawling along in a biplane or stealing all the speed at Mach II. Even when it was crap, and even when death was all he could smell, when the heat sucked the marrow from his bones, he could get okay at takeoff. He could think, he could relax, and he could let the annoying voice of his WSO wash over him because he knew Alf so well that Luke could tell unerringly when to tune in. Now he had to listen so damn carefully.

He shouldn't have come on this tour. It served him right, and he had to be here, but dammit, he wished it could be different. Yeah, wishing had worked out so well for him in the past.

He'd been naive as hell to think there was any kind of redemption. It was what it was.

He glanced up at the sturdy pound of shoes, and he wasn't surprised to see Mike O'Malley coming his way. They hadn't talked much; O'Malley saved all his conversation for Sara.

"What are you doing up past your bedtime, flyboy? Thought a princess like you'd need all your beauty sleep."

"It's my night to give one up for the needy. You'll get the card in the mail when it's your turn to receive."

"Oh, you're breaking me up with that cutting, sophisticated humor." O'Malley halted a few feet away, staring straight at Luke.

"What?"

"I didn't say anything." O'Malley's mouth hardly moved, nothing about him moved that wasn't essential.

"You're going to, though."

"I might."

"If it's about leaving Sara alone, I already got the message."

Nothing. The bastard just kept staring at him. Luke wondered how long he could keep from blinking. "Look,

I'm sure she told you about what an asshole I was to her after college. I was, okay? I admit it."

"No question about it," O'Malley said. "Not that I was going to mention it."

Luke thought about jumping into the pool right now. He had another uniform ready in his room. The shoes might be an issue, though. "Fine. What were you going to mention?"

"You showing up here out of nowhere. Your connection with Captain Weston. The timing was too neat, and it felt wrong."

"Fair enough," Luke said, wanting the man to get to the point, knowing he would take his sweet time.

"I asked a few questions. Put in a few calls."

Luke's gut tightened. This guy knew everything, according to Sara. Knew where all the bodies were buried. "And?"

"I got some unexpected information. Things I shouldn't have seen. Classified reports."

A chill ran down Luke's spine. He didn't have to ask what O'Malley was talking about. "Why the hell bother to call anything classified? You're a goddamn master sergeant, not the fucking CIA."

"The system isn't perfect. There are still people involved."

Luke nodded as the water shimmered. "People suck."

"I've been in this air force a long time, son. I've seen my share and then some. Fortunately, my ears work better than my mouth. Understand?"

He wouldn't tell Sara. Good. Sara didn't need to know. It bothered Luke, though, that O'Malley knew. What had happened wouldn't be a secret forever, he knew that, but here, on this tour, he'd wanted things kept quiet. God forbid Sara should find out what had really gone down.

The investigators had said it hadn't been pilot error. It had been made very, very clear that it had been a technical glitch. The investigators were wrong. He should have felt it. Should have been able to get back to base.

Luke met O'Malley's gaze for a second before he looked into the pool again. "From what Sara's told me about you, I know you can be discreet."

"You being on this tour has made her question things. She's smart as a whip, and she knows a lot of people, too."

"Yeah. Well. There's nothing I can do about that."

"You could make a preemptive strike. What you did was first-rate, Captain, and it's yours alone to tell it."

The silence was awkward and painful. Finally, Luke turned to face him.

O'Malley saluted. It was the first time Luke had seen the sergeant do so when not in public. The salute held, sharp as a blade, full of respect.

Luke acknowledged, swallowing past the lump in his throat. Then he turned tail and left.

8

IT WAS TOO EARLY on a Friday morning to deal with television producers. Sara shut her cell phone, then her eyes. She should have taken control of the situation, and she hadn't. What kind of a public relations professional couldn't make a glorified production assistant bend to her will?

A bad one. That's what kind. Sara thought about calling Kathleen Freeman back, but the woman had insisted. It was Sara's own fault. It had been stupid to participate in the Q & A last night, and she'd only done it because Pearson had been ill.

Now if she wanted the publicity they would get from the popular San Diego show, it meant traveling with and talking to Luke Carnes for the better part of the day. Checking the time, she realized they'd have to leave soon.

She called his room, and when he didn't answer, she rang his cell.

He sounded out of breath as he answered, "Solo."

"I need you to be in your flight suit and ready to go in twenty."

"Flight suit? A talk?"

"A television show. *San Diego Today.* They had a cancellation, and we're the replacement."

"Who's 'we'?"

Sara thought about the day to come, the opportunities for things to go wrong, and she hardened her voice. "The clock is ticking, Solo."

"I'll meet you in the lobby."

She studied her timetable. Everything had to be rescheduled, and she called her support staff. When she met Luke in the lobby, she felt sure that things would run smoothly in her absence. She wasn't nearly as certain about spending the day with Luke.

He looked ridiculously hot in that damn flight suit. She always imagined him striding out of a billowing white cloud, helmet under his arm, cocky and sure and one-hundred-percent hero. There was a reason the show's producer had asked for Luke. Who wouldn't?

He waited for her at the exit, and they didn't speak as they got in the car. In theory, the studio was about forty minutes from the motel. With Southern California traffic, it could take hours. It didn't have to be weird or tense. If he were any other member of the team, they'd have been able to talk, to while away the time pleasantly. Simple.

"TV, huh?" He buckled his seat belt. "I've never been on television."

"You'll be great."

"That depends. What's the format of the show?"

She pulled out of the parking lot and headed toward the 405 Freeway. "Question and answers. Two hosts—one male, one female. They get good ratings, although it's daytime and not our target audience."

"So why are we doing this?"

"It's good PR, that's why."

"So why just me?"

She looked at him as she braked for a light. "Not just you."

He smiled. She merged onto the freeway. So far, so good. It would be fine as long as it didn't get personal.

They drove along in silence for a couple of miles, and while the quiet wasn't unpleasant, exactly, there was a bit of tension. Which was normal. Television appearance and all.

"Any suggestions?" His voice was calm, easy.

"About...?"

"How to handle the questions."

"Don't screw up."

He chuckled, and that helped.

"Seriously," Sara said. "Do what you always do. Pretend the cameras aren't there. Listen to the question. They'll try to get you to say something provocative, but so do the students. You've been handling them well."

"They're so young," he said. "So sure of everything."

She glanced at him, not quite as surprised at this contemplative change of subject as she would have been a few days ago. "They want to matter. They haven't given up yet."

His nod was slow. "I knew what I was going to be when I was seven. When kids who are twenty, twenty-one, tell me they don't know what they want to do with their lives, it throws me. That's probably the most difficult thing, knowing how to respond to that."

"You were lucky," she said. "Most people have no clue and they end up boxed into the wrong careers for all the wrong reasons." She slowed down with the traffic, kept her eyes on the road as they came to a dead stop.

"Right." Luke shifted so he was angled more toward her. "They want money or fame and to be noticed. They've been told their whole lives that they could do anything, everything. But that's not true, is it? Even if you work really hard, do the right thing, give it your best shot, there are no guarantees. You could still end up poor, unloved, unappreciated."

It was alternate-universe Luke, or maybe a Luke from a far-distant future. He'd always been the embodiment of the American dream. He worked hard, he did the right thing and reaped his rewards.

Luke had passed all the outward tests: bravery, courage, honor, sacrifice. She'd never thought he would have any real perspective, though. How could he, living in the center of the dream as he was?

When she glanced at him again, he met her gaze with a look she wasn't able to decipher. Not even a guess.

"I went down in Afghanistan," he said. "The plane crashed in the Khwaran Ghar mountains. The investigators determined that it was a technical glitch, not pilot error."

She felt hit. Slammed. Devastated for him even as pieces of the puzzle started to fit together. Knowing him, he'd waited until the last second to eject. He was incapable of not trying everything possible and impossible to save his plane. She knew of Khwaran Ghar, that the mountains there were surrounded by Taliban cells. "Crashed. Not shot down?"

"No. They haven't shot one of us down in years. A software malfunction."

"Jesus. I'm sorry." It would have been horrible for any pilot to lose an F-15, but she knew no matter what the official cause of the problem, Luke would blame himself. It was his superhero complex. A good pilot would have figured out a way to get back to base at the very least. A great pilot would have seen the problem before they took off.

"You want to talk about it?"

"No," he said. "Not here. I wanted you to know, though, because the information's out there. O'Malley heard about it."

"I hadn't. I would have thought—"

"It was classified. It is classified. I have no idea who he heard it from. I guess it doesn't matter."

"It matters."

"Traffic's moving."

Sara started as she looked at what was actually in front of her. She eased off the brake. "You—"

"Look, Sara. I don't really want to talk about it right now. I only told you because I didn't want you to hear from someone else."

She nodded, took a breath. He'd let her off the hook. There was probably something she should've said now. Something comforting. But she had no idea what. As much as she liked the idea of treating Luke as if he were any other member of the team, he wasn't. He hadn't just been her lover, he'd been her friend. She still hated what he'd done to her. Doubted she'd ever forgive him. But she was also attracted to him, and if the way her heart ached for him right now was any indication, she still cared.

There were lines that couldn't be crossed. Lines that shouldn't. She had no idea where any of them were.

LUKE KNEW SARA HAD BEEN RATTLED by his confession. Not that she wasn't the epitome of class and purpose at the studio, but she had tells: quick-as-a-blink sidelong glances, a stumble over a cable. Nothing anyone who didn't know her as well as Luke would notice.

He wasn't at his dashing best himself. Thank God he could fake it so well. The producer, Kathleen, was a good-looking woman who seemed shrewd and interested. She'd stood next to him while a makeup man had put an uncomfortable amount of gunk on his face and neck. Sara was being treated to the same procedure by a makeup woman, and Luke didn't think that was an accident. Not from the way Kathleen stared.

He had no business complaining. His face had bought him a million excuses, hundreds of open doors. After all, he was the luckiest son of a bitch on earth, right?

Finally, the makeup and the questions stopped, and Kathleen led them to the green room. There were two couches, a flat-screen television on the wall, and a strange assortment of snacks on a large square coffee table. Packaged Danish, cookies, a few apples, tiny boxes of raisins, as if the show was hosting schoolchildren. At least there was bottled water along with store-brand sodas. He grabbed a water and settled on the farthest couch. Sara sat in the other.

"Leanne will let you know when it's ten minutes. Then she'll bring you to the set," Kathleen said.

"You received the video?" Sara asked.

"After we spoke." The woman looked at Sara for perhaps the first time. "We can't use the whole thing, of course, but it'll be impressive."

"Good."

Then they were alone. Sara still wasn't back to normal, and he needed to do something about that. "I want to claw my face off. How do women do it?"

"This is television makeup, you dope. Not daywear."

"Still gives me the creeps."

"Just don't touch yourself."

He arched a brow.

She rolled her eyes.

It was better. Between them. Not by much, but some. "You ever been on TV before?"

"Yes. Not a talk show, though. News briefs, that kind of thing."

"Of course. You'd be really good at that."

She seemed surprised. "Why?"

"You're gorgeous and strong. You look like you can handle anything."

She took her own bottle of water, drank a little, looked up at the monitor. "I can't. Not *anything*."

"Yeah, well, that's probably not a bad thing."

"What about you?"

He smiled, pulling on his flyboy act a few minutes early. "My ego's too big to get in the way of feelings."

"So some things never change, huh?"

He glanced at a magazine on the table, then back at her, deciding right then that since the line had been crossed into personal territory, he was going to stay there. "Do you still see Nicky?"

Sara's eyes widened and her lips curled up in unconscious pleasure. "Yeah. We're still close."

"What's she up to?"

Sara took a package of cookies from the table, fruit-filled something-or-other, and fiddled with opening it before she leaned back on the couch. "She's married. He's a nice guy, an artist from Glasgow. They live in New York above her gallery."

"Nicky was pre-law, right? She'd gotten into one of the Ivy League law programs."

Chewing on her very small nibble of cookie, Sara nodded. "Harvard. She went, passed the bar, got a great job, but she wasn't very happy. She saved every nickel she could, and when she had enough to keep her afloat, she quit. Went to Europe, fell in love with modern art and Donnan."

"I'd never have guessed. She always seemed so sure of herself, I mean, about the law."

"I don't think she changed," Sara said. "The law wasn't what she imagined. She still convinces juries to see things her way, only they're called art collectors."

"When did she get married? I remember a wager between you two."

"We swore we wouldn't do anything permanent until we hit thirty. She paid up three years ago. They're trying for a kid now."

Luke drank some water, thinking about Nicky and her rotation of college boyfriends. She was great. Beautiful, although not in Sara's league, strong, determined. Smart as hell, too. It was difficult to imagine her as a wife or a mother. But then, it was difficult for him to imagine that of anyone in his age range. He'd never given it any thought. The idea wasn't on his radar. Despite her bet with Nicky, the same wasn't true for Sara. She'd wanted to be married. Had she been tempted? The thought made him tense so quickly, so deeply, he couldn't pretend he was anything but jealous.

A fake cough let him cover his mouth, hell, half his face, but he had the feeling that if she'd been watching him, she'd have seen it. He had no idea if she'd recognized the flush for what it was.

"What about you?" she asked, and there was a bit of a wobble in her voice. Could have been a reaction, yeah, but it could have been the thin ice they were both skating on. "You didn't have close friends back then. Has that changed?"

"Yeah," he said, grateful they'd both skimmed right

over the fact that for years she'd been his best and only real friend. "I've made a few."

"Fighter pilots, I bet."

"Yep. And one weapons system operator. Alf."

"For the TV puppet?"

Luke grinned. "Annoying Little Fucker."

"Ah," she said. "You boys are so cute about your pet names. It's endearing, really."

The reflex to stomp all over those fighting words was cut short by her bark of laughter.

"Oh, God," she said, shaking her head. "Like shooting fish in a barrel."

"Fine. Make fun. Get me all worked up just before a big TV interview." Right, as if he hadn't screwed her up by telling her about the crash. She'd respected his request and hadn't brought it up again, but he knew she was shaken for him. Funny, spilling should've bothered him more, but he was always better when he was with Sara.

She held up her hand. "Sorry, sorry. Sometimes I forget what a delicate flower you are. I'll be more careful."

"Jesus," he said, giving in to his own laughter. "Ruthless woman."

"I am," she said. "But I'll stop now. Promise. Tell me about this Alf."

"Little guy. Red hair, big eyes, farmboy down to his—"

Leanne stuck her head in the door. "We'll be ready for you in ten minutes. I'll be right outside."

Luke stood up and met Sara's gaze as she rose to walk with him to the door. Just as he was about to grasp the knob, he said, "I'll tell you about him another time."

Sara rested her hand on his arm.

He inhaled sharply, shocked her touch could still fry his whole electrical system.

"I'd like that," she said.

He met her gaze, and it was as if she could see through him. His barriers, hard-fought but tenuous, dissolved in an instant and he was back there. Hurtling through space strapped to a scrap of metal. Landing so hard he'd thought that was it, that he'd never catch his breath again.

Then the real bad stuff began.

It was a wave of sense memories, a big one, so large he hadn't expected it, wasn't prepared for it. Before he could think, he pulled her into his arms and kissed her. Just held on to her as if she was the last thing holding him up, the only thing that could save him.

She kissed him back. He didn't know if it was pity or surprise or what, and he didn't care. It was Sara in his arms and on his tongue, filling him with heat and blood.

When she drew away from him, it was gentle and she didn't seem mad. Not even a little. "You ready?" she asked.

He used the strength in her eyes to give him a jump start. "Let's do this thing."

Now that the interview was over, all Sara wanted was to get out of the studio. What she mostly wanted to do was get back to the motel and hide in her room until she could figure out what the hell she was supposed to do about that kiss. But that wasn't gonna happen, not yet.

"Thank you," Kathleen said, shaking Sara's hand. "It was even better than I'd hoped for."

"I'm glad. We appreciate the opportunity to get the word out."

"I would imagine it's getting harder and harder to get people to join."

Sara didn't care for the implication, but she was used to it. "True, but once people hear the scope of opportunities, quite a few come to see the service as a privilege and an opportunity."

"Oh. Sure," the woman said, and the dismissal couldn't have been more obvious. Kathleen turned and shook Luke's hand with much more enthusiasm. "You ever think about turning in your wings, you'd make a great anchorman."

"No thanks. I'm one of those suckers who really do think it's a privilege and an opportunity."

Sara smiled at the censure in his voice, but more so at the blaze in his eyes. She'd thought she'd lost him for a few minutes there, but he'd taken his seat in front of the cameras and made magic. She'd held her own, she supposed, but she doubted anyone had given her a second glance.

Kathleen laughed as she dropped his hand.

Sara and Luke were out the door and in the parking lot before there was time for a breath.

"Do you happen to have, like, a million baby wipes in the car?" he asked.

She chuckled, and breathed a sigh of relief. He'd opted for ignoring the whole kissing business. Excellent. "No, but I'm sure there's going to be a washroom at the restaurant."

"Food. That's a great idea. You know any place to eat around here?"

"Not a clue," she said, beeping the car locks. "We'll find something."

"It's on the expense account, right?"

"Yes," she said, knowing where this was headed.

He opened his door. "Let's go crazy and find a place that uses real napkins."

She got behind the wheel and buckled up. "It's the taxpayers' money, hotshot."

"I'm a taxpayer, and I'm starving."

"Fine. We'll go inside instead of using the drive-through."

"Hey."

She grinned, and punched it out of the lot.

9

AFTER GETTING BACK TO THE MOTEL, Sara had to scramble to catch up with her day, returning phone calls mostly, but also going over tomorrow's agenda. She knew O'Malley had taken over, so she wasn't worried, exactly. It was a matter of concentration. She was having a difficult time not thinking about the crash. And the kiss. She wanted to know more about both, but he hadn't offered, and she hadn't figured out how to ask.

She'd just finished a tour of the sims set up in the basketball court at the University of San Diego and was heading up the back stairs of the auditorium stage. The presentation was about to start, which meant it was time to give her mini pep talk. At the entrance, where the curtains kept the speakers hidden, Sara slowed. Terri Van Linn was speaking, and something about the tone of her voice made Sara pause to listen while keeping out of sight.

"Did she even mention it to anyone?"

Silence.

"I didn't think so," Van Linn said, sounding accusatory and bitter. "I only heard about it because a friend of mine called to ask why I wasn't on the show. Why none of us were."

Sara glanced behind the edge of the door. The team, minus Luke, had gathered on the other side, waiting for the crowd to settle.

"I'm sure the captain had her reasons," Hanover said. "What does it matter?"

"It matters," Van Linn said, "because they have a history."

"So what?" Danny Franks sounded tense, but he always got nervous before he got on stage. "And how the hell do you know?"

"I know a lot of things."

Van Linn's head turned, and Sara ducked back.

"Why don't you just tell her you'd like to be on the next television show?" Nora Pearson's voice seemed calm, reasonable. "I'm sure she'll be happy to include you."

"You really don't care that Carnes is taking over? For God's sake, it's like he's a fucking movie star." Van Linn was pacing as she talked, and Sara pressed herself closer to the wall. "I didn't sign up to be one of the Pips to his Gladys Knight."

Hanover laughed. "If it pisses you off, say something. Personally, I don't give a rat's ass."

"You don't give a rat's ass about anything, Hanover," Van Linn said. "And don't think I don't know about you."

"What's that supposed to mean?"

Sara coughed loudly before she entered. "It's almost show time," she said, making her voice as normal as she could. "Everybody ready?"

Silence again. Her gaze shifted from person to person, and when she finally looked at Van Linn, there was a smile on the OSI's face. All traces of vitriol gone. "Everybody's here but Captain Carnes."

"Nope, I'm here." He came around the door, handsome and dashing. No wonder people got jealous. "Just had to make a late pit stop. Sorry."

Hanover hit him on the back. Interestingly, Pearson put her body in between Luke and Van Linn. Sara thought about telling them all about *San Diego Today,* but kept her mouth shut. She'd anticipated some tension between Van Linn and Luke, but something private, definitely not a blatant attempt to draw the rest of the team into her personal grudge. And evidently, Van Linn had no qualms about inferring that Sara was playing favorites. How the hell did she know about their past? Sara didn't like that one bit.

She'd have to think this through carefully. The tour had barely begun, and while the team had ignored Van Linn on this round, Sara couldn't count on them doing the same down the line.

"Good luck, everyone," she said. "Keep doing exactly what you've been doing. You're terrific."

"Thanks," Tritter said, as he lifted his camera. "We'll have to be extra terrific with this crowd. There are protesters out there, so be prepared."

"Where?" Sara asked.

"Outside the front entrance last time I checked," he said. "Standing on the grass in a clump. There weren't many."

"Thanks. I'll see what I can do about keeping them outside."

"Don't sweat it," Luke said. "We'll be fine."

She smiled, and for an instant she wondered if the smile was warranted. Her gaze returned to Van Linn, and sure enough, the woman was watching. Sara didn't change her expression one iota as she faced the group. "I'm not worried at all," she said. Then she left the stage.

Protesters, she could handle. A diva in the mix, especially an investigator with a vendetta against Luke, could be a problem.

LUKE GOT OUT OF THE MINIBUS first, wanting more than anything on earth to be in his room. The protesters had made things interesting, which had helped him, personally. It had kept him on task, made him sharp. The team had dealt with the situation well, and he'd be shocked if a good number of the students in the audience didn't take the next step with a recruiter.

Everything had been fine, in fact, until later. Until he'd seen Sara. She'd put on a great act, but he knew her too well to believe it. Something had her worried, and he hoped like hell it wasn't that business at the TV studio. He shouldn't have kissed her, he knew that. But she'd seemed to understand. Maybe he gave her too much credit.

Nope. He'd have known hours ago if she'd been upset. It was something else. The protesters? Why, though? She'd expected them. He had; they all had. Protests were inevitable. It was a messy war. Sara was too savvy to let protesters, especially such well-behaved protesters, get to her, and yet, he'd seen the way she held herself. O'Malley had noticed it, too, although the two men hadn't spoken about it.

He nodded to Pearson's "Good night," but kept on walking. He wanted out of his flight suit. Strange after wanting to live in the damn thing for so many years. It used to make him feel invincible.

He took out his keycard, but even as the little dot on the lock turned green, he paused. Sara wouldn't be back yet. When Luke had left, she'd been in the middle of an interview for the *San Diego Union Tribune*.

He dipped his card again, and went inside, but instead

of heading to the shower he went to his dresser and got out his swim trunks. He could stand to burn off some energy. He was tired, but he was also restless and he needed to sleep. If he didn't burn it off, he'd dream, and while his dreams of late had mostly been decent, some had woken him up in the early hours, sweating, shaken. It had been a year since the crash, but there was no expiration date on memories.

The pool, which was closed for the night, was empty. He climbed over the fence and dropped quietly onto the grass. After tossing his towel, he dove in.

The first dozen laps were useless. He could still think, still breathe. So he pushed harder, swam faster, barely coming up to snatch air before his face was in the water again. Over and over, his legs pumping, his hands pulling him, counting the strokes before the turn, then doing it again and again until everything burned. His muscles, his lungs.

He stopped as a stitch hit him hard on the left. He made it to the shallow end where he could stand, his fist digging into the pain. It took a while to settle, to feel the burn become an exhausted ache. Finally, when he got out of the pool, he figured he was safe. No dreams tonight, just nothing. Which was all he wanted.

He dripped his way down the hall, tugging at the small towel he'd put around his neck. As he turned the corner by the elevator, O'Malley nearly walked straight into him. They both halted, inches apart, before the master sergeant stepped aside.

"Did you talk to Sara?" Luke said, surprising himself as much as O'Malley.

"About what?"

"You know what I'm talking about. Something's eating at her."

O'Malley shifted. "No. She finished the interview before I could get to her."

"Huh."

"If you're so concerned, go talk to her."

Luke shook his head.

"If you don't, that means I'll have to. I'm not in a sympathetic mood," O'Malley said, then grunted.

Luke doubted O'Malley would be anything less than sympathetic when it came to Sara, but he nodded. He'd go to her. They'd crossed a barrier today, and he thought he might be welcome. As a friend, at least.

Luke continued down the hall as he pondered his opening salvo. Screw it. He didn't need anything but the truth that he was worried about her. If she told him to get lost, so be it.

Sara opened her door a crack. Her eyes widened at him, then narrowed. "What's wrong?"

"Can I come in?"

She glanced behind her, and for a moment Luke thought she wasn't alone, but she was, as he saw when she stepped aside to let him in.

"What's this about, Solo?"

He'd never hated his call sign, but he did now. It was how she'd said it. No particular nuance. Nothing. She shut the door behind him, but he stalled. She wasn't in uniform. Very much not in uniform.

She circled around him, pulling her really short, really shiny kimono robe tight. It was a deep red—scarlet. Underneath, her nightgown was the same color, and even through the two layers of silky material, he could make out her nipples. Erect and familiar and off-limits. "Well?" she asked. "What's wrong?"

"You seemed worried. Tonight, I mean."

"What?"

He shrugged as if he wasn't getting hard underneath his wet trunks. Why the hell hadn't he changed before he came here? "I wanted to make sure you were okay, but I can see now's not a good time, so—" He turned toward the door.

"Why did you think I was worried?"

He stopped. "I know you."

Behind him, she sighed. He closed his eyes tightly, because he knew that sound, too. He'd been right. She was anxious, and he cursed himself. He'd let his guard down, let her see how damaged he really was, and she'd—

"Van Linn."

That made him spin back to face her. "What?

A flush had come to Sara's cheeks. "I overheard something. She was upset because I didn't tell the team about the TV show."

"Why would she care?"

"Ostensibly because she wasn't invited, although I don't think that's the real reason. What bothers me is that she was doing her best to get everyone else upset about it, too."

"It didn't occur to her that the decision hadn't been yours?"

Sara blinked at him. "How did you know?"

"If it had been, you'd have brought anyone but me." Wow. He'd hit that bull's eye. Her flush deepened, but Sara was Sara, and she didn't look away.

"You're wrong. I would have sent you with someone else."

"Same difference."

She snorted, delicately. "Not really."

"Well, I kind of figured Van Linn wasn't finished."

Sara nodded as she went to the little round table and sat on a squat motel chair. "I thought the trouble would stay between the two of you. I didn't consider a larger canvas."

"It all comes down to feeling slighted," he said. "By me, by not getting on TV. But the team is sharp as hell. They're gonna see right through her. It's not as if she's the first officer who thinks they've gotten the short stick."

"She's OSI, Luke, and she has access to a lot of things. Like personnel records. As much as I hate to admit it, she can make trouble. She already knows about our past."

He didn't think, he just sat down in the other ugly chair. "Results are all that matters. The mission is being accomplished. I'd be willing to bet good money that the recruitment numbers are up considerably in San Diego."

She nodded, glancing at him, then away. "They are."

"See? No problem."

"It's not that simple. You know the schedule. It's brutal. I don't want dissension in the ranks to screw things up."

"It's the air force. There's always dissension in the ranks."

Her smile was welcome, even though it wasn't real yet. "True. But I have to be careful. I can't afford to show favoritism."

"You haven't."

"Not intentionally, no," she said. "But you being singled out to appear on camera is going to happen again. You're a fighter pilot, you're gorgeous, and you're a natural charmer. It's only logical."

He pushed aside the compliments even as they settled warmly in his chest.

Sara shook her head. "Van Linn's used to being the belle of the ball. She's almost as good as you on that stage."

"And when it's appropriate, I'm sure you'll put her to good use."

"I'm not entirely certain I can be unbiased," Sara said, studying the texture of the table.

"If anything, you'll put the others first. Like I said. I know you. You're good at this."

Her gaze shifted to the wall, but his was on her chest. Her nipples. Shit. They were so *there*. He looked up, hoping Sara wouldn't notice his distraction. He would not stare, not again.

"I'm good because the team is good," she said, and he breathed a sigh of relief. He hadn't made any weird sounds or blushed bright red.

"The team is fantastic," Sara continued. "I want to keep it that way."

He should probably say something now, but he was having a lot of trouble thinking. "I can talk to her, if you think it'll help."

That made her laugh, and it wasn't *with* him, which was almost as embarrassing as the wood that was now painfully obvious in his trunks. "No, thanks."

He shrugged. "You could sic O'Malley on her."

Bingo. Her smile hit her eyes. "That would be mean."

"I know."

She shook her head. "As fun as that sounds, morale is my pervue."

He put his hand over hers. In his defense, it was a very small table. God, he was a putz. "You're going to do the right thing," he said, hoping the rasp in his voice didn't give him away.

Her gaze was on their hands, and he couldn't read her at all. Who was he kidding? When it came to the two of them, he was lost.

Her head lifted. There were still smile lines fanning slightly at the edges of her eyes. No anger. In fact... Oh, man.

Her pupils were huge. He used to know what to do in this situation, especially with Sara. But the rules were different here. He'd just gotten used to them being friends, then that kiss had happened, but it was all too soon. He hadn't apologized yet. And she'd just finished telling him she was worried about playing favorites.

Still, his cock got harder and want blossomed in his chest.

Sara's lips parted on an "Oh." It was less than a word, more than a breath.

He stood to leave, because he had to. Because even the new boundaries had blurred. But Sara stood, too, and they were next to each other, inches apart.

Her eyes were filled with everything they shouldn't want. If he looked to his left, just moved his gaze an inch or two, he would see the door, the right thing to do next. But her "Oh," still echoed down his body, and any resolve he'd once had was paper-thin.

Sara leaned forward in a world gone slow.

Luke blinked and when he could see again her lips had parted

He broke.

SARA FOUND HERSELF pushed against the wall next to her bed, not clear how she'd gotten there. Very clear that Luke had pressed his full weight against her, pinned her. As if she'd try to move, as if she'd try to *run off* when his *taste…* Dear *God…*

She gripped Luke's hair with one hand, pulling until the angle felt right. Luke made a small satisfied sound in the back of his throat as he sucked on her tongue, then nipped her bottom lip.

"This is insane," she said, her voice ragged, tearing her mouth away for a second, barely enough time to breathe before his mouth took hers again. Luke's kiss was greedy, demanding, but Sara felt greedy, too.

Her hand went to his bare chest, and she couldn't stop the comparisons even though her thoughts were as ragged as her breathing. Her fingers knew the places that were smooth, right there, just below his shoulder, but if she moved down closer to his arm, he would flinch not because he was ticklish there, but he *was* ticklish half an inch to the left. She couldn't help it, she tested him with just enough pressure, her fingers skimming over the muscle, and there was the flinch, the hitch in his breath.

He pulled back, all of him, her mouth left open with an unfinished kiss, her fingers still tingling with the feel of his cringe, to tug open her kimono, to bend and capture the tip of her nipple between his teeth. The satin nightie rubbed against the sensitive nub he pressed with his tongue. Even with her eyes closed, especially with her eyes closed, she could see the round wet circle he made, and she held him there, glad his hair was longer now. When he groaned she could feel the vibration through the material and into the places he used to know so well.

He stopped again and went to his knees. Their eyes met and he held her gaze as he touched the sides of her panties and drew them down until they pooled on her feet.

Luke didn't even blink as he lifted the hem of her nightie, watching her, breathing so hard he trembled with each inhale.

With what looked like pain he lowered his head, then leaned forward to place a gentle kiss on her warm skin. His forehead came to rest against her belly, and she felt the incremental slowing of his shuddering breath as he calmed himself; waves of warmth made her own pulse quicken as she petted his hair.

Her head hit the back wall when his fingers skimmed her inner thighs, asking her with a gentle touch to part. One foot rose, slipping out of her panties, and she stepped down again. Far enough that she felt his breath inside her.

Then, it was more than breath. Tongue, teasing with gentle licks and tiny pokes. Thumbs spreading her open. He'd loved the taste of her. He'd told her so and made her blush, made her fidget, made her come to terms with the truth of it. She'd had no idea it had ever been an issue; she'd thought it was somehow a favor, not a treat.

He'd shown her how very wrong she'd been.

When he found her clit, she had to grasp his hair with her other hand. She tried not to do anything but hold on, but God, what he did, how he *knew*. She moaned as her head rocked to the side, and before it was even possible, she could feel her orgasm start to build.

He felt it, too. He always had, and he never made her wait, never teased her along, because he also knew that he could make her come again. And again.

He braced her thigh with his arm when her knees wobbled, but he didn't let up, not for a second, and she had to be quiet, she couldn't cry out. Then his fingers pushed inside her, two fingers, deep and hard and fast, and she bit down on the fleshy part of her palm as she completely came apart.

LUKE FELT HER COME, heard it, tasted it and, shit, he was so close that if he touched himself even once, he'd be done for. If she touched him...

He pulled back, stood up. Looked at her. He'd dreamed of seeing her this way. Seeing that flush on her cheeks, how she could hardly stand, the rise and fall of her chest, and Christ, the wet silk clinging to her nipple—

Cock straining in his trunks, he pressed himself

against her hip. He came so hard he saw spots behind his eyes.

When he could breathe again, when he opened his eyes, she had lost the post-orgasmic haze. She smiled, but it disappeared quickly.

"Please," he whispered, "don't regret this."

"I won't," she said, stepping to the side, toward her bed. She closed her robe, tightened the sash. "I wanted you. I have feelings for you." Now, she blushed, looked away, then back. "Problem is, I don't know what they are."

He nodded, backed up further. "Tomorrow afternoon I've rented a plane. O'Malley knew a guy... It doesn't matter. I'm taking off at eleven. Maybe you want to come?" He swallowed hard. "There are things to say. Things I need to say."

"I don't know. Maybe."

"Fine," he said. "That's...good." He headed for the door, hoping she'd stop him, knowing she wouldn't. Halfway through the door, he paused. "I have feelings for you, too. I know exactly what they are."

10

SLEEPILY, SARA REALIZED the buzzing she was hearing wasn't from a broken microphone, but her cell. Whoever had woken her up was going to die, and no jury would convict when she explained that it was her day off. The first in more than a month. She thought about letting it go to voicemail, but it could be something important, so she reached for the phone and hit talk. "Weston."

"Get up."

It was O'Malley. Something had to have gone wrong for him to risk life and limb. "What time is it?"

"Time to get up. I'm taking you to breakfast, so haul your ass up and get dressed."

"I was up till 2:00 a.m. I don't want to go to breakfast."

"Tough. I'll meet you at your car in thirty."

She gave him the finger, but he couldn't see her so it wasn't very effective. "Fine." She tossed the phone on the night table, groaning as she sat up. Her eyes felt gritty and she wanted coffee and it was disgustingly early.

Her gaze traveled to the wall; her hand curled with the memory of Luke's soft, short hair.

She considered going back to sleep. It had been so hard to find it last night. Her brain had tripped over itself with questions and rebuttals and decisions made in stone that turned to tissue in minutes. She'd painted her toenails, for God's sake, while listening to a heavy-metal station. But O'Malley didn't believe in random acts of kindness, so he wanted to talk to her. He probably already knew she'd been with Luke. She wouldn't put it past him. She didn't know how he knew half of what he did.

She sighed. If O'Malley wanted to talk about Luke, she'd tell him to mind his own business. Or she'd listen to him. She couldn't decide which until she'd had coffee. Then she'd have another decision to make. Luke. Flying. God, she really craved more sleep, more oblivion. But she'd already agreed to meet O'Malley. So shower and sundress, blush, mascara, lip gloss. Her cell went in her purse, her feet went in her sandals, and she was out the door.

O'Malley wore his civvies, too, but he shouldn't have bothered. He still looked every inch the master sergeant. The man probably slept at attention.

He took the keys right from her hand and got in behind the wheel. She didn't bother arguing. Or speaking. But she pouted for all she was worth.

The coffee came in a to-go cup and her breakfast was a lousy egg-and-cheese sandwich from a drive-through. Even after driving through San Diego for half an hour, he still hadn't said anything. If she could have gotten the keys back from the son of a bitch, she'd have left him in the middle of the lot where they'd finally parked. It helped a bit that the parking lot in question was at Black's Beach, which was pretty and not as crowded as she'd imagined it would be on a warm Saturday morning.

She tossed her empty cup and wrapper into a trash can right before they hit the sand, then slipped off her sandals and stuck them in her bag. O'Malley didn't take off his shoes. No surprise there. She couldn't imagine him barefoot, could hardly imagine him at the beach at all, despite the evidence. They walked in silence until they were alone. "He ran into me last night."

She contemplated not responding. Giving him a dose of his own— Oh, who was she kidding? "So this is about Luke?"

O'Malley nodded. "He dripped all over the carpet."

"Why?"

"Because he'd just been swimming."

"No," she said, and her temper was right there, ready to rip. "Why did he run into you? Why are you telling me this? Out for breakfast, my ass."

"He was worried about you. Thought you were unhappy."

"So he went to your room?"

O'Malley gave her a sharp, brief stare. "Not in my room. In the hallway. I told him to go talk to you, not me."

"Ah, so you're wondering how that turned out."

He grunted. "Just making sure I made the right call."

"Huh," she said, which was better than admitting she didn't know the answer.

"I gave him points for noticing," O'Malley said.

"Meaning, you'd noticed, too."

He barely nodded. Like some kind of secret sign, something you'd get from a monk in a monastery, or as the covert signal that the bomb was about to be detonated.

"It was nothing. Van Linn was pissy that I hadn't announced the TV appearance."

"Van Linn's a prima donna. Of course she was pissy."

Sara felt the sun on her face. If they were to walk for long, she was in for a sunburn as she'd forgotten to bring sunscreen. "She could make trouble."

O'Malley's irritated sigh was louder than the surf.

Sara ignored it. "And you didn't think it was the protesters, either."

"Nope."

"So you figured it was something to do with Luke, and that Luke thought he'd done something to make me worried."

"Yep."

"You're infuriating."

"Thanks."

She shook her head. Definitely not how she'd pictured the day. Or her life. "Luke was great yesterday. On the drive, on the show. It should have been awkward, but it wasn't."

"And that's a problem," he said. Didn't ask.

"Yeah," she said. It didn't seem wise to be pissy herself. She had no intention of telling O'Malley what had happened in the green room, and no way in hell would she hint at what happened in her room, but she still trusted the sergeant's judgment a hell of a lot more than she trusted her own right now. "I had a very good hate going on, and he's messing with it."

"Because way back when, he dumped you like yesterday's trash."

A sharp pain stabbed through her. As she'd discovered last night, having sex and feeling betrayed were not mutually exclusive. "Please, don't bother to sugarcoat it. Really."

Another stare from O'Malley's piercing eyes, not quite as brief.

"It wasn't just that he dumped me," she said. "It was when and how."

"You were in love with him."

She was tempted to tell O'Malley to butt out, but she wouldn't. "I was. Deeply. Stupidly."

"You believed he was in love with you."

"Yep," she said.

He slowed, waited for a group of teenage girls to run past them into the water. "You two never hashed it out?"

Sara tensed at the question. "Considering he dropped the bomb on me the day after we graduated, then left the day after that, no, we didn't hash it out."

"What was that, six years ago?"

"Seven. And you already knew that." Her heart felt heavy, as if the weight of Luke's betrayal had continued to grow despite her ignoring it. "He said he was sorry. That he loved me. That he just couldn't do it anymore. *It* being *me.*"

"Harsh," O'Malley said, and his voice had gotten softer, his pace slower.

She quickened her own, embarrassed about what had happened back then and what had happened last night. "Nothing's ever hurt like that before or since."

He halted. "It was cruel. Unforgivable."

She nodded as she turned to her friend. "Yes." Then she met O'Malley's inscrutable gaze.

"I don't know about relationships," he said. "Never been in one that took, myself. But I know about people. Not regular folks. I'm talking about men in war."

He held up his hand as she opened her mouth, cutting her off before she could start.

"I said *men* and I meant *men,* because when it comes to romance, women confuse the hell out of me. Just shut up for a minute. I've seen men change. From the ground up. Be one kind of man before the fighting, and a different kind after. I don't know Solo. He still could be a class-one prick. But I know you. You liking him now doesn't necessarily mean you're being an idiot."

"It's not just the breakup," she said. "It's the current situation. I'm the supervisor on this gig. I have no business liking anyone."

O'Malley's brow furrowed. "There's nothing in the regs say two captains can't see each other on their own time."

Sara pushed her hair back behind her shoulders. "When he first got here I almost sent him packing because you and I both know there's enough rope in those regulations to strangle a captain who isn't smart."

"Then nothing to worry about, right?"

She snorted, and it wasn't particularly dainty.

"You have a window of opportunity," O'Malley said. "Don't screw it up."

Her gaze went to the ocean, past the breakers to the blue-gray horizon. "You think I should talk to Luke. You think we should hash it out, that I won't be able to see him clearly until we get straight about what happened."

"I don't think much of anything," O'Malley said, and she could hear a smile in his voice. One she liked to think he reserved just for her. "But I'm damn sure the woman you are today can handle the truth."

"Tell me one thing, then," she said, as she looked up at him. "This change thing. Is it for keeps?"

O'Malley nodded. "In my experience, it goes to the core. If I didn't believe that, I wouldn't be walking on a goddamn beach."

LUKE SURVEYED THE CESSNA he'd rented. It was a beauty, just as he'd known it would be. Although he'd never met the owner, Bill Benedict was an ex-fighter pilot, so of course he'd care about his plane. They were a breed, fighter jocks, and Luke wore his membership proudly.

Luke headed to the tail of the plane, figuring he'd take his own walk-around before Benedict arrived, already instinctively gauging the wind and what it would feel like at one hundred forty-five knots. Brushing the metal alloy with his hand relaxed him. It wasn't quite the rush of an F-15, but it was a solid reminder of who Luke was at heart, who he would always be. As he inspected the tail, a flicker of pale blue in the distance caught his eye. His hand dropped. "Sara."

She smiled at him as she approached. Somehow she was here, her dark hair fluttering across her almost-bare shoulders. Her dress swirled around her legs, flattened at her stomach, curved around her breasts, and he could hardly breathe.

He'd given up hoping at ten-thirty. Even so, he'd kept checking his cell as he drove to the airfield.

She walked toward him, a white tote clutched tightly in her hand. Her toenails were painted pink. "I'm here. Still want me to be?"

"Always," he said.

She was a foot away from him now, and he could see a hint of the sun on her nose and cheeks, caution in her eyes. "O'Malley dropped me off."

Luke's chest tightened as it hit him why he'd asked her here, what he was getting himself into. He grasped blindly at the idea of changing his mind when a silver-haired man drove up in a red Corvette convertible. Benedict. Too late.

Now that he was committed to the flight, Luke wanted this part over with quickly. He shook hands with the retired captain, introduced Sara, got straight to business. Bill wanted to talk about the war, and if Luke had been alone he'd have been happy to oblige, but he cut things short. Sara covered for his abrupt demeanor with her thanks when Benedict handed her a small cooler filled with iced bottles of water and sandwiches, a present from Mrs. Benedict.

Finally, it was done; Luke had given the man his check and Sara was belted in the passenger seat. Luke climbed into the cockpit and for the first time ever, it wasn't an unmitigated pleasure. He'd wanted to talk to her in the safest place he could imagine. Where he couldn't run away, where he couldn't avoid the conversation with touches or so much as a kiss. Where she could have her say, uninterrupted.

As soon as they were in the air, fear got the better of him. He'd rather face a sky full of bogies at the moment. His fear wasn't because he had to confess the worst behavior of his life, but because Sara liked him now. They'd laughed together, they'd talked and, sweet God almighty, tasting her last night had been the best thing that had happened to him in years. Bringing up the past would remind her what a sorry excuse for a man he'd been and probably still was, and that would just about kill him.

"I'll bet you're excited about the F-35," she said, and from the rush of her words, it occurred to him that she was nervous, too.

That didn't prevent him from jumping all over the excuse to delay. "Hell, yeah. It's a beauty. It's got amazing stealth capabilities plus the speed and strength of a born fighter. I've been talking to some of the test pilots, and they say she's a sweet ride with hardly any gremlins at all. Better takeoff and landing, real flexibility, although it's too fast for tight work, but…" He shook his head. "What I meant to say is, yes, I'm excited about the new jet."

She laughed, and that was better than flying. Better

than almost anything. Jesus. He wanted to touch her, take her hand in his, stay up in the blue for as long as he could just like this. But that was his selfishness talking. He'd sworn to stop being that self-centered ass. It was time to pay up. He looked at her and said goodbye to her smile.

SARA WATCHED HIM GATHER his courage. A deep breath, a slight flush on his cheeks, his hands tightening on the controls. She was pretty sure about the topic, but not sure at all what it would be like to hear the words.

"A lot of things changed for me when I was in Afghanistan," he said. "After—" He shook his head, took another breath, tried again. "I had a lot of time to think."

His shoulder twitched. This was hard for him, and it was an amazing contrast to see him stumbling when she'd seen him sweep up entire audiences with his poise and polish.

"You're what I thought about," he said. "Not the whole time because there were things to do, but after… When it mattered. It was you."

She tried to make sense of what he'd said but gave it up after a few seconds. "I don't understand."

His Adam's apple rose and fell. Twice, he looked out his side window, and twice he struggled to meet her eyes. Finally, Luke cleared his throat. "My behavior after graduation was unconscionable. Unbelievably cruel. You didn't deserve any of it. I'm also sorry it took years, fuck-ing *years* for me to even get that it was a despicable thing to do."

She inhaled as her whole body trembled. Even being near him every day for these past weeks, she hadn't re-alized how desperately she'd wanted to hear the words. She'd thought it would feel good, that she'd feel better.

"I don't have any kind of excuse," he said, and his

voice sounded farther away. "Nothing. I wanted the perks, that's all. I wanted to be free, to have all the women, to fly the fastest planes. I wanted to be everything I imagined a fighter pilot should be. I believed..." He looked away then. Banked the plane, turned it around, and he didn't speak again until it was flying straight once more. "I believed I *deserved* it all. That—I don't know—that I was some kind of special... The rules didn't apply to me. I knew you figured we would be together after college. That we'd get married. But when it came down to the wire, I chose something else."

Another blow, even though he'd admitted being a selfish bastard on stage, in front of all those people way back at Lefty's. She'd heard this before, so why did it feel as if she'd just been struck? She fought the tears burning in her eyes, the urge to weep like a child. But she had to ask. "When did you know?" Her throat was so tight, tighter than her fisted hands.

He didn't answer for a long while. "The beginning of senior year."

Another breath filled her lungs. Somehow, her heart kept on beating. "I thought you loved me."

"I did."

She winced.

He nodded, his face drawn and paler than it had been just minutes ago. "The closer we got to graduation, when I was accepted into flight school, I started going over what that meant. What it could mean to be a free agent. I knew it would hurt you. That *we* were part of your dreams. I should have warned you, given you time to adjust. How I handled it was vicious and cowardly."

His voice broke on the last word. "I know it's too little too late, but I am truly sorry. You were more than great. You were the best part. I didn't know how great at the time. I didn't deserve your friendship, let alone your love. I'm ashamed of what I did, and I wish I had a way to make things right, but I don't."

Sara wanted to be back at the motel. She never should have come with him. The sky was his territory, not hers, and if she'd had a parachute, she'd have leaped out the door.

God, he'd known at the beginning of senior year. She hadn't been prepared for that.

All she could do was turn away. She shut her eyes, willed the tears back. If she were going to cry, it would not be in front of him. Memories came at her fast and furious, the nights she'd sobbed herself to sleep, feeling like an empty shell for days, for weeks. How everything had reminded her of Luke and how she'd loved him and how wrong she'd been. How *stupid*.

She gripped the bottom of her seat, struggled to breathe. If this was hashing it out, she wanted no part of it. Because it felt too much like being shattered. Again.

Slowly, other thoughts came to her, and with them, a measure of reason. There was no doubt Luke meant what he said. He was sorry, and while that mattered, it wasn't at all what she'd imagined. She'd thought...

So many things, depending on what was going on in the rest of her life. At first she'd wanted him to suffer, to feel every moment of her pain. Later, she'd practiced being cold and cutting when he'd beg to have her back. She'd been rehearsing this moment all these years, trying on every emotion she had until at last she'd come to indifference. Although, now it was obvious she'd never been indifferent for a second.

Mostly, though, she'd thought his apology would mean it was over. That once he'd said it, admitted how horrible he'd been, she'd finally be able to begin her new life. That

Hotshot

Luke and all he'd meant to her would disappear without a trace as she moved on. But that was years ago when the pain had been fresh. It should have been better now. Instead, here he was. Again. As always, in her heart.

"Sara?"

"I'm not ready yet," she said.

"Okay. No problem. Just…the wind is getting pretty bad, so I'll put her down. Get you back to the motel. I promise."

She nodded. Stared at the sky and concentrated on breathing, in and out, aware that the buffeting she felt had nothing to do with the wind.

11

NOT A WORD HAD BEEN SAID all the way back to the motel. Luke made up scenario after scenario, imagining what was going on in Sara's head. Her expression gave him no clues. She looked stoic, blank, as if she were pondering about something that didn't touch her, a purely intellectual query.

He'd seen her first reaction, though. How she'd flinched as if he'd slapped her. He hadn't been prepared for the "when" question, and he still wasn't sure he had been right to answer her honestly. He'd told himself he didn't want to ruin her year, so he'd kept his mouth shut. He hadn't believed that, even at the time.

The fear that made his stomach churn as they headed to the motel entrance was that she had gone back to hate. A deeper hatred, now that she knew what he was really like. A hate strong enough to make him repellant, to make her ashamed that she'd wanted him then, that she'd touched him last night.

He should have told her on day one. Hell, he should never have come down here, except on leave. He could have sent her a letter, kept everything distant and vague. He'd have been better off, and so would she. But then he would have missed pizza in her room. Kissing her. The scent of her. The proof of her softness, and how they fit together.

As they walked down the hall to her room, it came to him—he was in love with Sara. He had been since long before the crash and he was right now. Today.

Alf had hinted, but Luke hadn't listened, hadn't believed it. Luke had never stopped loving her, and being with her for these last five weeks had proved it. He loved her, and he'd just ruined any chance he had of winning her back.

As if there had ever been a chance. He'd lost this round seven years ago. Nothing he could do at this stage would make her love him again.

They were at her room, and she got her keycard out of her purse. He wasn't sure why he was even waiting. All he'd get now was a door slammed in his face, but if she wanted that, he'd give it to her. He'd give her anything.

She looked at him again as if she was seeing the bastard he was for the first time. He wanted to tell her something that would change things, but those words didn't exist. "Are you okay?" he asked.

She nodded before she turned and opened the door.

He still didn't move. Even when she stepped back, holding the door open.

"It's okay," she said. "Come in."

"Are you sure?"

"I need you to."

He kept his distance, not wanting to do or say the wrong thing.

She walked inside and put her purse on the table. "I don't know what to do," she said, turning to face him.

"You don't have to do anything."

"I waited such a long time," she said, as if she hadn't

heard him. "Even when I thought I'd gotten over you, I hadn't. You've been in my head since I was sixteen."

"I didn't know leaving would hurt you that badly," he said. No, *honesty*. He'd promised. "Wait, that's not true. Of course I did. I ignored it. I'm good at that."

"Oh, I believe you," she said, "but what's got me stuck is that I had no idea. I was utterly convinced you loved me. How is that possible? You knew for a year that we were over, and I never got a hint. You have feelings. You had them back then, I know you did. That's why it was so painful. You loved me and then turned it off like a light switch, and I didn't see it. I thought I knew you, and I missed the biggest thing of all."

He could tell she didn't mean this to hurt, but it did. That he'd treated her, of all people, with such callous disregard made him the lowest thing crawling on this earth. What she was asking for now was a way to understand. She wanted closure. An ending. "Sara, you weren't wrong. I did love you, all through senior year, but it wasn't love the way you mean it. It was completely selfish. I loved you like a kid loves a favorite toy, until he gets a newer, shinier toy. All that's on me, my fault."

She nodded, and it was as if he could watch her put the pieces together, stuff him into a box she could finally throw away. "That makes sense," she said, leaning against the table, her hands braced behind her. "Everything came to you effortlessly. Friendship, attention, success, popularity. You still do that, you attract like a magnet. You had no reason to think it wouldn't continue. That it wouldn't keep getting better."

"It didn't."

"What do you mean?"

He started to tell her that he'd never loved anyone else. All that time, and all that playing around, and nothing had come close to the experience of being with her. But he was here to make amends. Nothing else. Not to muddy the waters, or make it easier on himself.

"Luke?"

"It got different, not better," he said. "Just, I'm sorry for the pain I've caused. I would rather cut off my own arm than hurt you again."

Sara smiled. A little smile. "I believe that, too," she said, pushing up off the table. "You did a horrible thing. I doubt you'll ever really know why it was so awful. I loved you unreservedly, and you made me doubt everything."

She sighed. "But I also appreciate what you've done by coming here. You've given it your best and it's made a difference in the tour and in my career. I should have said something yesterday at lunch. You were great during the interview. Generous as hell. I never would have guessed. I know you meant it when you said you'd come to help. You have. Helped."

"It's not enough," he said.

The look she gave him made his heart seize. "No. It's not."

"Right," he said, going toward the door. "I'll leave you alone."

"There's one more thing."

He steeled himself. "Okay." At least if she had questions, he knew all he had to do was tell her the truth.

"Thank you for the apology."

The fact that he loved her cascaded through him, filling him with regret as deep as the sky was wide. Karma was a bitch.

EIGHT DAYS HAD PASSED since that flight in the Cessna, and Sara was finally feeling like herself again. It had helped that she'd been incredibly busy. The move to Los

Angeles the day before plus the additional job-fair booking had meant long hours with not enough sleep. Today was no different. It was 1820 hours when she dragged herself into the motel, and she'd been up since 0500 and had worked through lunch.

Unfortunately, she couldn't go directly to her room. Or to dinner. Her crew had been spread out all over the place today, most of them at the job fair, where Van Linn was the featured speaker, some at tomorrow's junior college site, and a few here at the motel, finishing the unpacking. Each team leader had agreed to meet in the lobby at 1830 hours to give their status reports. Sara was tempted to go sit in one of the big leather guest chairs, but she was afraid she'd fall asleep in an instant.

Her plan was to finish the check-in, grab a yogurt, an apple and some aspirin, take a swim, then sleep like the dead until the alarm woke her at 0600 tomorrow. It was tempting to skip the swim, but she had to make sure she didn't lie awake in bed, thinking about Luke.

She'd done enough of that. He'd been on her mind every spare moment. When she had dealt with him, it had been strictly professional. She'd replayed last Saturday's conversation dozens of times, cried so hard she'd had to fake a late-summer cold, and faced some painful truths, not only about Luke, but about herself.

Despite everything, she still cared about him, probably loved him on some level, and she'd given up beating herself up for it. Her attraction to him was alive and kicking if her dreams were anything to go by and she'd quit denying that as well, although she hadn't acted on it. But she hadn't eliminated the possibility.

For the last three nights, instead of thinking about the end of their relationship, she'd been remembering the rest of it. For five years they'd been a couple, and those years, except for the last few weeks, had been the best of her life.

She saw Senior Airmen Boyd from the motel crew, and he'd brought along Sergeant Wilson. Sara returned their salutes, and then the final team leader came in from the back entrance. They appeared as exhausted as she felt, so she made it quick. Seven minutes, to be exact. Finally, she was alone and wondering if yogurt and fruit was going to cut it.

"Hey."

She heard Luke's voice behind her. She turned around and saw him standing beside the motel entrance. He lifted a large brown bag. "I come bearing food."

"What kind?"

"Chinese. Didn't have time to try samples, but it smelled great. I took the liberty of ordering dinner for you and O'Malley."

Nice. Considerate. Either she was too tired to be worried that a meal was breaching the professional distance of the past week, or that boundary had reached its natural end. The way her stomach was grumbling, she didn't care which. "What did you get?"

"Most of the menu." He held up another bag, equally large, that she hadn't noticed in his other hand.

"Wow. Okay. Great. I have no idea where O'Malley is. Probably still with the trucks."

"I caught him outside. He should have things wrapped up in ten. Said we should gather in the conference room."

She nodded, reminding her of the headache she'd had since this afternoon. "Why don't you go set up? I'll join you in a minute."

"Great. Two questions, though. Where's the conference room and do you still like Dr. Pepper?"

She gestured toward the hallway on her right. "Three doors down. It's unlocked. And yeah, I still do."

He smiled at her and she managed to return it with a tired lift of her lips. As he passed her, her gaze moved down his back and paused at his butt. Yeah, the attraction was there, all right, and it wasn't out of the realm of possibility that something could be done about it. But not tonight. Her head hurt, her stomach rumbled and she was determined to swim and sleep. First, though, she needed to freshen up, then eat.

LUKE HAD PUT THE BOXES in the middle of the table along with the chopsticks, paper plates, fortune cookies, napkins and the waxy bags that held the fried stuff. Their sodas were in cans, which were cold, but he'd also brought an ice bucket and some plastic glasses. The room smelled fantastic.

O'Malley had taken the seat closest to the door and made himself at home. The sergeant worked his way through each box, piling food on his plate in concentric circles. So mesmerizing was his methodology and attention to detail, Luke didn't hear the door open again, and when he finally glanced up, he caught Sara's tired grin.

"This," she said, "is awesome."

How she managed to look so beautiful after the heat and pressure of the day was a mystery he'd probably never figure out. "Glad to be of service," Luke said. "Dig in."

She took a seat next to O'Malley and grabbed a plate. Luke put together his own dinner, but he couldn't help noticing that her tastes in Chinese hadn't changed much. Broccoli beef, chicken and mushrooms, lots of veg, fried rice, no noodles. But she must have been really hungry because she also had fried shrimp, an egg roll and three crab Rangoon.

"Excellent initiative, Solo," O'Malley said, and Luke noticed that he was eating in the same circular pattern.

"It's appreciated," Sara said.

They were quiet for a long time. Luke darted glances at Sara, but she wasn't glancing back. She was looking at her can of Dr. Pepper. She'd relaxed into her chair, her chopsticks held easily in her long, slender hand. But there was a difference in how she'd spoken to him, how she sat. He'd been studying her for eight days. Discreetly, because he didn't want to make her uncomfortable. None of the words they'd spoken to each other since that Saturday had been like Sara's brief thanks just now.

Something shifted in him, relaxed. Not completely, because he still didn't know what it meant, but the pressure in his chest wasn't quite so bad. Of course, her tone could mean she'd decided not to care at all. After a week of being polite and distant and in the dark, he would prefer to know.

"Something bothering you, Captain?"

He looked at O'Malley. "Not a thing."

"Good. 'Cause that dumpling's gonna fall in about two seconds."

Luke hadn't realized. He shoved the food in his mouth, trying to recall when he'd picked it up.

Sara pointed her chopsticks in his direction. "Have you checked out the workout room and the pool?"

"Not yet," he said.

"I was assured they would meet our requirements. For the price per room, they should."

"I'll have a look before I turn in," he said. "In fact, I think a swim before bed would be just the ticket. I'm stuffed."

"Hmm," she said. "Me, too. And yet, I have enough room for my fortune cookie." She plucked one from the pile. The restaurant had thrown in a large handful, considering the sheer volume of his order. The crack of the cookie was loud enough to say the cookies weren't fresh and she pulled out the slip of paper.

Her lips turned down a bit.

"What?" he asked.

"'Use your head, but live in your heart.'"

Luke chose one for himself, unwrapped and broke it. He read it.

"Well?" O'Malley said.

"'There's a good chance of a romantic encounter soon.'" He stuffed half the cookie in his mouth, and stared at the wall behind O'Malley.

The old man picked up a cookie and grunted as he read the strip of paper. "'Your winsome smile will be your sure protection.'"

Luke laughed, covering his mouth quickly so he didn't spray the table with cookie fragments. Sara's laughter was louder, and Luke hadn't even realized how much he'd longed to hear it. O'Malley kept eating.

FROM HER VANTAGE POINT in a darkened section of the fenced-in swimming-pool area, Sara watched Luke exit through the back door of the motel, stride past the gate with the closed sign, then plant himself between the fence and a tree. He eyed the chain link, paying particular attention to the pointed wire that ran along the top.

He continued his walk around the perimeter to the next tree, then flung his towel over to the grass on her side of the fence. Barefoot, shadowed and stunning, he began to climb.

Watching him changed her chemistry. He didn't have to be near enough to smell or touch. All it took was looking at him for her hormones to go crazy.

She'd finally and truly accepted his apology, and not just the words, but the intent. What he'd done to her had been selfish and cruel, but he'd gone to a lot of trouble to get this TDY and he'd come with the express objective of making amends.

The dichotomy had given her pause. She'd done things she wasn't proud of when she was in college and after—some very disturbing and humiliating. She wasn't above thoughtlessness or cruelty and she knew it. Joining the service had helped her become less of an ass, actually. The breadth of humanity she had to deal with was a great teacher. You either got patient or petty.

O'Malley had been right. Luke had grown a conscience. Maybe as a result of his crash, maybe as a by-product of growing up. Whatever the catalyst, his actions proved that he was no longer a class-one prick.

She didn't quite know what to do with her conclusions. Could they be friends? Friends with benefits? Were they already friends? Was friendship too risky altogether?

She watched him swing his leg over the top of the wobbling fence, all smooth grace and strength. The benefits package was sounding better and better.

Luke did it for her. Always had. Since day one, he was what she meant when she talked about her ideal lover. They'd done it, in her dreams. Not just against the wall, although against the wall had been hot as hell. No, they'd all but broken the bed in last night's dream, waking her panting and sweaty.

He dropped to the grass with the agility of a cat, then rose slowly, as if he were in enemy territory. She laughed as she walked toward him. So superspy. Jeez.

He spun to face her, his wide shoulders back, his chest muscled with perfect definition. Even his legs were strong and chiseled. She tilted her head to the gate. "It wasn't locked, Sherlock."

His grin changed him again, and it was a good smile, self-aware but not self-conscious. "I should have checked."

She tossed her towel and her little bag on a plastic chair, conscious of her own body now. She was in shape. She worked at it. And right now, all those salads seemed like less of a punishment. She'd almost put on her one-piece suit. She'd known he was going to be at the pool, he'd said so at dinner, and she'd chosen the bikini, not a butt-floss postage-stamp number, but it didn't hide much.

As she walked to the edge of the pool, there was no way he wasn't scoping her out, top to bottom, and she didn't mean her feet. She'd known he would. The truth of Luke Carnes was written in her skin, lodged forever in the places that were tender. What had become clear was that she was just as much a part of Luke. Even as he devoured her with his gaze, there was fear in his darkened eyes. Hope, too, but mostly fear.

She dove into the deep cool water. She stayed under, gliding to the other side of the pool. Waiting.

There it was. The wave of his entry swept over her, the gentle buffeting welcome. When she turned, one hand gripping the pool's edge, it was to see him rise, wet hair plastered like a brown helmet. He bent back and dunked his head again, and when he stood he wore a grin so wide it made her glad to be alive.

He made his way over to her side. "This," he said, "is also awesome."

She chuckled. "Yes, it is."

"Headache gone?"

Of course, he'd known. "I hadn't eaten much before dinner."

"I should have gotten you water."

"The soda was fine."

It was quiet, just crickets and the lap of water. Well, quiet for the city. There was always a distant sound of cars, but that was L.A.

"Is this okay?" he asked.

So interesting. The old Luke would have assumed it was okay between them given the fact she was at the pool. It was far more considerate and far less cocky of him to ask her. To put her comfort first.

"It's fine," she said. "I've spent enough time being angry. I'm glad you're here. Glad we talked. I think we can be friends now."

"Friends?" he said, and his forehead creased in a frown that disappeared in a flash. "That sounds great."

"It does," she agreed, then she pushed off the wall and let the water take her.

She'd forgiven him. That was major, that was spectacular. Friendship was the best he could have hoped for. Not what he'd wanted, but that was fine. He'd adjust. He'd adjusted to hard things before, so this wasn't going to be so bad. He'd been an idiot to think for a minute he could have more of her.

Friendship. Excellent.

Of course it was excellent, it was Sara. With her hair down, her body sleek and perfect in that stunning bikini, not hating his guts. He was the luckiest son of a bitch in the world. He'd kissed her. He'd tasted her. So what if he didn't get to do it again. They would be *friends*.

He pushed off the wall and caught up to her, swimming in tandem, and he couldn't keep his eyes off her. Until he took in a mouthful of water and had to stop or choke. Smooth.

She turned toward him, swam faster. Beauty to the rescue.

He captured her arm in the air, quickly stepped in and scooped her up by her naked waist. She blinked at him, coughed, wiped her eyes with her free hand.

Pulling her closer, he smoothed back her wet hair, wanting to see the whole of her face, needing to read her eyes, but the lights weren't enough for that. The only things he knew for sure were that her gasps matched his own and that they had nothing to do with swimming. That his hard cock pressed against her hip was an unmistakable confession. In about one second his fate would be sealed. Sara was about to kick him in the nuts—or kiss him.

12

SHE KISSED HIM. Hard. Fast. Then she shoved him away and got out of the pool. Sara grabbed her towel and her bag from the plastic chair, then gave him a look. He was a smart guy and he'd seen the look before. Not for a long while, granted, but there were some things a person would never forget. She headed for the gate, trusting he would follow. Even though they weren't in uniform and it was late and dark, the things she wanted to do were definitely not for public consumption.

Friends with benefits. Temporary. End date set in stone. A win/win situation.

Suddenly Luke was behind her, rushing her through the pool's gate as if they were being chased. He came close, very close, almost stepping on her heels during the sprint to the back entrance of the motel and all the way to her room.

Her shaking fingers slid the key card into the slot, then they were inside and he had her against the door, pressing against her with the cold wet of his trunks and the hard length beneath. Her cry was swallowed by his kiss. She let go of everything except the man in the room and the need to be naked.

As his tongue explored, he stripped off her top. It plopped by the door. A freezing hand on her breast made her hiss.

His erection pulsed against the dip beside her hip bone. It felt deliciously hot right there where he pressed. "Bed," he said, his voice as swollen as his cock.

"Wet," she whispered, then ran her tongue over his lower lip.

His fingers, not as cold as before, traveled down her side to the crease between her torso and thigh, then underneath her bikini bottoms and inside her. "Yes. Very."

"Not what I meant," she said, as giddy from his slow, two-finger exploration as she was from the dance of their noses touching, how their lips brushed in a simmering tease. "Dripping here," she whispered. "Puddles. We need towels."

"No, no, no." He stretched the words, curling her toes, and still she pushed his chest, forcing his fingers out, his body away. She glanced at herself in the mirrored closet, almost naked, her nipples as hard as her want. *Oh, shit,* she thought. "Yes, yes, yes," she said, her gaze back on him, on his very dark green eyes, on how his nostrils flared, and why that should be so sexy. "I'm not sleeping on wet sheets."

"One of us will have to."

Rolling her eyes at him didn't ruin the mood at all. "You are such a guy. I have to at least dry my hair."

"Really? It looks so sexy dripping."

"The sooner you get the towel, the sooner we can skip the ridiculous sexual innuendos and have the actual sex."

"Right." He stepped back, shook his head, spraying her face with droplets. "I'm all over it."

Flipping on the bathroom light, she watched him, her

gaze roaming, especially after he tossed her one of her bath towels, then stripped off his trunks and kicked them in the tub.

His *ass*. She had to take a moment. Really, it was just too much. Firm, high and pale, she moaned at the little dimples not only above but actually on the sides of his cheeks. Holy crap, he was breathtaking.

"You're not drying your hair," he said as he turned around.

Sara blinked. Something was different. She knew his penis. Really knew his penis. She could have drawn it freehand and they could have used it to identify his body. It had the shape she had learned intimately, but it seemed bigger. Not porn bigger, just bigger. Of course, this was only the sight portion. Taste and touch would tell the truth.

"Hair. Dripping," he said. He glanced at her big makeup case sitting on the counter by the sink. "Uh, condoms?"

"What, you don't have any on you?"

He looked down at his very naked body. "Not enough pockets."

She smiled and nodded, wet cold drops landing in inconvenient places. "Second level, far right," she said. The box of condoms was small and unopened. More a just-in-case kind of precaution than a must-have.

Luke found it, his shout one of triumph as he walked toward her. Each step caused things to move. Side to side, up and down. Mesmerizing.

He tossed the condoms onto the bed, took the towel out of her hand and moved behind her. She stood still as he dried her. Each time the towel went forward, she got a little poke in the butt or a brush of his chest on her back. God.

It wouldn't be good to come from drying her hair. Not when there were so many things yet to do, even if it did feel amazing to brush her bare backside with the underside of his cock.

Another swipe that made him hiss, and screw it, her hair was dry enough. After running the towel down her body in what was less than a half-hearted effort, he abandoned the damn thing so he could pull her into his arms. The feel of her against him, a whole lot of skin on skin, firm little nipples on his chest, was electric. Cold spots warmed, warm places heated. As appealing as it was to stand together, they'd done that last week, in a night that would live forever in his memories, but this time there was a bed only a few steps away. The bed opened up vistas, whole remembered worlds.

He walked backward, awkward with her so tight against him, until his legs hit the mattress. It was simply a matter of tilting, then gravity did the rest.

His left arm got trapped, not that he cared, but her right arm was under his body, and that wouldn't do. So he rolled them over until she was more or less beneath him.

Thank God she'd left one of the bedside lights on when she'd gone to the pool. Watching her, seeing the proof of her, was necessary. *Sara.* It was Sara, and he could taste her, rub against her. It wasn't enough.

"Want you so much," he said, his hands reading her textures, her curves, the mole she'd had forever, the bump from the horseback-riding thing. He'd mapped her body in his mind too many times to count during those long days hiding in caves, scared to make a sound, to breathe in case the enemy was on the next ridge. He'd watched until his eyes watered with fatigue, slept in snatches only to wake with a start ten minutes later. And he'd pictured this woman.

Sometimes from when they'd first met, more often as she'd been in college. In the absurd single bed of her dorm, lights on, lights off, it didn't matter, because each had its own wonders.

He pulled away from a kiss, not wanting to pause, but wanting to see. Her eyebrows, the length of her lashes, the almond shape of her eyes. Good that her pupils were so large and so dark, because he'd need days, not hours, to make sure the colors hadn't changed. "I used to think your eyes were brown," he said, running his fingertips slowly down her temple.

"They *are* brown."

"They are a hundred browns," he said. "Some there aren't even words for."

She smiled, letting out a breath that brushed the side of his mouth.

He used his pinkie to touch the slight indent just above her lips. "You know what this is called?"

She shook her head.

"Technically, it's the philtrum. I call it very, very lickable." He turned to the perfect angle, and did exactly that with the tip of his tongue. Even though the cleft wasn't deep, it tasted like Sara. So did the little dip on the end of her nose. He toured her face with infinite patience, wanting to memorize so many things at once. The feel of her right eyebrow as he slowly traced it with his lips, so long remembered, now reawakened as if he'd never done this before. Jesus, it was…

She laughed. "Luke, it tickles."

"Bad tickle or good tickle?"

"A bit of both," she said, after a moment.

"I'll stop," he promised, but he didn't say when. He

couldn't, although he did move on more quickly than he'd intended to the enticing shell of her ear.

That made her shiver, as he'd known it would. So sensitive, especially when he nipped the lobe, then sucked that bit between his teeth. There it was, the long low moan that made his balls tighten even as his body wondered what the hell he was waiting for.

Everything changed when her hand curled around him. Thankfully, she didn't move it, because he was beyond ready. He'd imagined her hand there so often that having the real thing still seemed impossible. He lifted himself just enough so he could look down, see for himself that it was Sara's hand. "Damn," he whispered, before he met her curious gaze. Of course she didn't understand. How could she?

Then her hand moved and his brain just stopped.

SARA KNEW HE WOULD COME if she didn't do something drastic. One more pump, and she released him. Lifted her hand to his jaw and waited for his disappointed moan. "You'll live," she whispered. "Besides, I want you inside me. And I want it to last."

Luke moaned again. It started off broken and petulant, then, amusingly, his voice rose into a happier range.

"Or, we could just continue with my hand," she said.

"No. No, your plan is much better. Terrific plan. I just need a minute. Maybe two. With you not moving at all."

"I'm not doing a thing," she said, trying hard not to laugh.

"You're breathing. Against me. With your chest."

She did laugh then, couldn't help it. "If you can suggest an alternative…"

He caught her in a kiss. "Oh, go ahead, breathe, touch me, lie there looking gorgeous. It's too late." He bucked against her, his hard cock painting a needy trail across her thigh. "I want you too much for any kind of self-control."

Sara kissed him back, amazed that they were teasing each other already. She'd anticipated the heat. That had been sizzling since he'd arrived, but she'd thought the days of playful back and forth were gone forever. "It's all right," she said, wrapping her leg over his hip. "We have time."

His brow furrowed at that and his hand on her arm tightened. "We have now," he said, and then he kissed her again, diving into her, stealing her breath, stealing all thoughts but one.

"Please," she whispered, as she pushed herself against him.

He reached across the bed for the box he'd tossed there earlier. He used his teeth to rip it open, then did the same for the silver packet. He came back to her in a fever, his gaze all over her face, his thighs trembling as he settled himself between her legs.

At the touch of his fingers on his cock, he hissed, his head went back and he held very still for a long moment. Moving more slowly, he rolled the rubber down.

He arched over her, his hands coming to rest on either side of her shoulders. "Sara," he said, staring into her eyes.

She reached between them, using touch alone to find his erection, to bring him to her sex. "Please," she said, again.

He thrust inside her.

It was everything she could do to keep her eyes open as the sensation swept her away. Nothing had ever felt like this. He fitted her perfectly, he was made for her, and she'd missed him so much.

"God," he said, his voice cracking into a moan as he filled her completely.

Time stretched as they moved together, as they fell back into a rhythm they'd rehearsed for years. Nothing was forgotten, no kiss, no touch, not even the way he nuzzled the curve of her neck as he said her name over and over again.

When she came, he swallowed her cries, and when she could think again, she realized he'd come, too.

Everything about the moment was incredibly right. She could feel Luke all around her, the old familiar blending with the exciting new man she was learning. The sound of his quick sated breathing, the way he covered her with his body, careful not to crush her, all of it was like a balm for the wounded spirit of the girl he'd left behind. She clung to him for safety and comfort, reveling in the moment because she was no longer that lovestruck young thing. Luke wasn't meant for love. As soon as he left her room, it would all be over. It had to be. Sara had already paid dearly for the hopeless romanticism of her youth. She wouldn't make that mistake again.

13

JOB FAIRS WERE DIFFERENT, especially the fairs that were tailored to the junior-college crowd. No speeches, just answering questions. Luke felt like a poodle at a dog show as he smiled and kept on smiling even as he was asked the same questions over and over again. Mostly by impossibly young women with shining eyes. What did he fly? Was it like the jet in *Top Gun?* It didn't seem to matter that *Top Gun* was years old, it was the standard for civilians, hell for fighter pilots. Jeez.

He wished his head didn't hurt from lack of sleep, that his back didn't ache from being overly enthusiastic last night. He wasn't complaining though. The last four nights he'd spent with Sara had been gifts. Mostly in her room, once in his. She was at the end of the hall. Easier to sneak out at three in the morning. Tonight he was going to have to cool it. They'd been stealing time, snatching a couple of late hours a night, and it was starting to affect them both. It would be horrible to go to sleep without making love to Sara, but he'd survive.

He shut his eyes, wondering how many aspirin he would have to take before he overdosed.

"You look like crap on a cracker."

Luke opened his eyes to Rick Hanover's self-satisfied grin. "Screw you, too."

"What's your problem? Not getting enough sleep?"

Luke tried not to react. Tritter and Hanover had asked him to go for drinks last night. He'd gone because that was the plan. Nothing suspicious, no obvious changes in behavior. Pearson and Van Linn had joined them at the bar, and even though it hadn't been the most comfortable few hours of Luke's life, it had been a smart move. "I only had a couple of drinks and left at midnight. Don't know about you, but I had plenty of sleep."

Hanover grinned.

"Go away. You're making my headache worse."

"I will when there's something to do that's more distracting than pissing you off."

Luke snorted. "Flyers. Go pass out flyers. There's tons of them."

"I said more distracting."

"We're surrounded by gorgeous co-eds. What's wrong with you?"

"Already taken care of, my man. Got myself all signed up for a conjugal." Hanover rubbed his hands together.

"No wonder you're so insufferable. Go brag to someone else, would you?"

"Can't. At least not here. You and me are the only two who're getting any. I don't want the others to get jealous."

Luke froze where he stood, adrenaline spiking through his body. "What?"

Hanover gave him a puzzled shrug. "You know."

"No, I don't."

"Dude, you and the captain? At the pool."

Shit. He'd kissed her. In public. What the hell had he done? "Does anyone else know?"

"Not that I know of. Maybe."

"What about…?"

Hanover leaned closer, kept his voice down. "Don't worry about Van Linn. She's hot, but she's crazy. She complains about everything. No one takes her seriously."

This was not okay. Van Linn was unpredictable, although Sara had been giving Van Linn most of the choice interviews as well as a lot of attention. Luke played back last night's drinks with Van Linn. She hadn't acted any differently. Still, he and Sara would have to be more careful.

Someone tugged on the sleeve of his flight suit. He turned to face a young Asian teenager who smiled at him with what looked like all the courage she could muster. She was accompanied by two older women. Mother and aunt? He had no idea, but he'd better focus, and right now, because he had a feeling this conversation wasn't going to be about *Top Gun.* "How can I help you?" he asked.

The girl glanced behind her, but only for a second before she met his gaze squarely. "I want to be a fighter pilot. My family doesn't think I can hack it."

Luke nodded before he launched the discussion. He'd call Sara as soon as could, but in the meantime, he'd help this young lady find the path to her dreams.

SARA WINCED AT THE NOISE LEVEL in the convention center. Normally it wouldn't bother her, she was used to the constant buzz of job fairs, but her head hurt and oh, yeah, her boss had shown up at 0600 this morning, before she'd even had her first cup of coffee.

Of all the days for a surprise visit, why did it have to be today? Sara hadn't slept more than three hours and she looked as if she hadn't slept for a week.

She liked Colonel Graves. He was an easy man to work for and with. He expected results, didn't micromanage, and he believed in the power of potential, which was something rare in her military experience. She'd noticed shortly after her first encounter with him that he started quite a few sentences with, "Given the chance…" Which is what he did. What she liked to believe she did.

The important thing was that Graves had given *her* a chance, and she wanted to feel worthy of it, which she most definitely did not at the moment. Although she didn't regret a single minute she'd spent with Luke the past four nights, she truly was going to have to be more sensible before she crashed and burned. It wasn't as if they had to make up for the past seven years in a few days. Her head ached, her eyes stung, and every step seemed half a beat behind.

It didn't surprise her that the colonel had found Luke before she'd made it past the navy booth, with the coast guard display still to go. But she hadn't seen Luke since his pre-dawn streak out of her room and it would've been nice to give him a heads-up.

She slowed her hurried pace, taking a hard look at what was happening at the air force booth. Two of the speakers were greeting visitors, handing out pamphlets. Two were behind the desk, manned with clipboards, and Hanover was talking earnestly to a thirtysomething man in a well-cut suit who was filling out paperwork. Luke was also speaking to a potential recruit. The girl was tall and slender, sported a dark bob and very large breasts. It didn't appear that she'd taken the term *job fair* too seriously, unless she was trying to get work as a call girl. Her low-cut top and high hem almost met in the middle. The smile she offered Luke was a blatant invitation, her body canted so far toward him, a strong wind would send her toppling from her ridiculous heels.

Sara wasn't surprised. Everyone gravitated toward

Luke, flirted with him to some degree. Even the ones with boyfriends, and men who weren't remotely interested *that way*. It was that damn charisma, and she knew it far too well. She'd had a moment's pause just this morning as Luke had kissed her goodbye. She was allowing herself to be dazzled when she should be more cautious than ever.

But Colonel Graves was getting his first live view of Luke in action. Sara had learned a thing or two about the colonel, and while his expression remained neutral, she could tell by his right eyebrow he was very pleased. Why wouldn't he be?

How lucky for the air force that Luke had fallen early and hard for flying. It was, she knew, his only true love. And she was fine with that, she reminded herself. Friends with benefits. That's all they were.

She walked up to the colonel and waited.

"Solo Carnes?" Graves said, keeping his voice low.

"That's right, sir."

"I'm looking forward to seeing him do his talk. He looks great on the videos."

"He is great. The whole team is. Honestly, I'm not surprised that our numbers are so good. These people are fantastic representatives."

Graves, who was a nice-looking man, especially with his thick salt-and-pepper hair, smiled at her. Great smile, still fighting-trim. If Sara could have managed it, she'd have put him on the team first thing, although Graves's appeal was more in his quiet power than in whatever combination of voodoo and allure Luke had. "You've put together an impressive tour, Captain. As I knew you would."

"Thank you, sir."

"I'm going to check out the competition, but please extend my invitation to the team to join me tonight for dinner. I've got O'Malley setting things up, and he's planning on the whole group."

"I'd be surprised if anyone had to beg out, but I'll let him know."

"Excellent." Graves nodded at Luke's salute as he circled back to the navy team.

Luke turned his head a bit more and smiled at Sara, and from the brief look he gave her, she could tell he wished they were alone. She held her breath as she smiled back, still finding it hard to believe that he was in her life again. In her bed.

LUKE TOOK HIS SEAT to the right of Colonel Graves, as requested. He'd stayed at the job fair until the end, then come straight here to the Border Grill for Mexican food. Luke didn't like these kinds of dinners around big tables. The team had to spread out, and there was no way to address the group as a whole without shouting.

Sara had taken a seat on the opposite side of the table. He hadn't talked to her about Van Linn yet, and that bothered him. He'd called her twice, but she'd been glued to the colonel's side the entire afternoon. He'd even tried to get her alone before dinner, but there were too many people and too many chances to be overheard. At least he got to look at her. The problem was that he also had to look at Van Linn, a seat away from Sara.

The redhead had been all smiles for the colonel, but there was something about the way she looked at him that made the small hairs on the back of his neck stand up. Luke couldn't be certain if he was assuming the worst or if Van Linn was planning some way to take him down. It had to make her mad that he was sitting next to Graves. Especially after Van Linn had somehow managed to hitch a ride to the restaurant with Graves and Sara.

The menus arrived, and ordering grabbed the attention of everyone at the table but the colonel. He turned to Luke. "I've been impressed with your skills on the tour, Captain. Especially given the short time you had to prepare."

"Thank you, Colonel. I'm glad I could make a difference."

Graves nodded. "It's important. We need bright young minds. From what I've seen on the videos, you're striking a chord with the students."

"The air force is my life," Luke said. "Aside from my family, it's been my biggest and best influence. It's not hard to recruit when I believe every word of the message."

Graves placed his hand on Luke's shoulder. "I see that in you, son. It was like that for me. I knew right off I was going to be air force, same as my dad and my grandfather. I've never been sorry. I know you'd rather be flying, but this is an important mission as well. I'm glad to have you on our team. Keep up the good work, Captain."

"I'll do my best, sir."

The colonel turned to Captain Pearson on his left, and Luke relaxed. He'd never had a problem with the brass. Impatience, yes, but the chain of command was ingrained in him as firmly as the alphabet. He'd known for a long time that he'd keep flying as long as they'd allow him in the cockpit. He didn't want to pilot airliners or private jets. That would bore the crap out of him. He was living the life he chose, and not many people got to do that.

He glanced at Sara, caught her looking back. She seemed tired. His fault. Hard to feel too badly though. Him. Sara. Again. Jesus.

His gaze shifted to the right. Straight into Van Linn's glare.

DESPITE YET ANOTHER NIGHT of not enough sleep, in this instance courtesy of her boss, plus another long day of meeting with Graves, Sara felt wide awake and more excited than she'd been since getting this assignment.

She glanced at her watch. Almost 1500 hours. Luke might not have left yet for his turn at the radio station. She hadn't spoken to him at all during Graves's visit, and now that the colonel was en route to the airport, Sara could finally tell Luke all her good news.

She called his number from her cell, and he answered on the second ring.

"Carnes."

"Hey, stranger," she said.

"Hey," he said back, his voice soft.

"Are you here?"

"Nope. On the way to the station."

"Dammit."

"My thoughts exactly."

"I should wait and tell you in person."

"Tell me what?"

Sara grinned as she spun around in her terrible office chair. "I can't wait. I had this idea, and I've been putting some things together to pitch it to Graves, but it wasn't ready yet. I only had the outline. I didn't know he was coming, so I was thinking I'd write the proposal up, submit it a week before the end of the tour."

Luke laughed.

"What?"

"Nothing. Go on." He sounded strained, reminding Sara that he was in a car with Pearson and Franks, and that he couldn't freely respond the way he might like to.

"I am," she said. "So the project is for a comprehensive study of what works and doesn't work on a recruitment tour. There hasn't been one done in years, not even after the big Department of Defense speakers' initiative in 2006. I want to go into speaker selection, audio/visual opportunities, venues, online coordination, everything. Historical precedence, new decisions and approaches and real-world results. We're just beginning to understand social media tools—" She paused, took a breath. "The bottom line is, he said yes."

"Really? To the whole project?"

"No. To me putting together the proposal. But he's very much in favor of the project, and he gave me his word he'll make it a priority."

Luke cleared his throat. "That's fantastic. I'm so pleased for you."

"Pleased, huh?" She glanced at her closed office door, then grinned. "It's really a pity you're off doing public service announcements, flyboy, because if you were here, I swear I'd drag you into a closet and do every manner of evil things to your body."

He coughed. "It sounds to me like that's an idea worth saving."

"I don't know. It's gonna be a while till you get back. I don't know if I can wait. I might have to take matters into my own hands."

"I'm sure you'll find I'm more qualified for the job."

"Are you blushing? You'd better not be blushing. I mean it. You're in uniform, Captain."

"I'm incredibly aware of the restrictions, thank you. More so now than ever."

She grinned. "I can't wait for tonight. Although, God, if I don't get some decent sleep I'm going to collapse. So it'll have to be a quickie."

"Sounds good," he said. "I'm anxious to speak to you. On several matters, actually. But for now, you have my congratulations. Well done. Very well done."

"Thanks. Kick ass on the radio." Sara disconnected and let her head fall back. What a day. What a week. But now was no time to slack off. The colonel had given her some points to cover and she had to get them all down on paper while they were still fresh in her mind.

Two hours later a knock made her look up, and while she hoped it was Luke, it was Van Linn who entered. The captain was well put together, as always. Even though her work at OSI didn't require a uniform, she'd worn hers for the duration of the tour. But her air of authority didn't depend on wardrobe. Van Linn was cocky and cunning, and Sara sensed that this was not a social call. "What can I do for you, Captain?" she asked, setting her pen down.

Van Linn stared at her for a long, uncomfortable moment, her green eyes hard. "I'm here to give you a heads-up."

"Oh?"

"You've put together a good tour. The numbers are impressive. I'm glad I've been a part of it."

The silent *but* hung between them. Her cell buzzed. A glance told her it was Luke. Sara didn't make a move.

"However," Van Linn said, "I've been disappointed and upset at the day-to-day management." She didn't sit, and Sara didn't offer.

"How so?" Sara leaned forward in her chair, folded her hands on the desk. She'd been expecting this discussion. It hadn't been Sara's decision to seat Luke next to Colonel Graves at dinner. Sara had gone out of her way to make Van Linn feel appreciated, but there was only so much she could do.

A hint of a smile touched Van Linn's lips, then the captain lifted a small notepad and began to read. "'On five separate occasions since Captain Lucas Carnes joined the recruitment tour under the supervision of Captain

Sara Weston, I observed Captain Carnes entering Captain Weston's motel room after hours. On four of those occasions, it was past midnight. Captain Weston, who was not a member of the speakers' team, accompanied Captain Carnes and only Captain Carnes to a television interview, without consulting the rest of the team. In addition, Captain Weston and Captain Carnes were observed kissing in the public pool in full view of all personnel and civilians.'"

The smile was back, not so small, and there was no effort to hide it. Sara's stomach had already tightened, but now it rolled with the shock of realizing this wasn't just about Luke, it was about the two of them. About their relationship. She'd been prepared for an argument about Luke, not about them kissing, not an already-written report and not a complaint about Sara's professional conduct.

Van Linn must have seen something in Sara's face, as a new smugness came to her voice as she continued reading. "'Captain Weston singled out Captain Carnes at Colonel Graves's team dinner, again without consultation with the rest of the speakers. Despite Captain Carnes joining the team as a last-minute replacement, he was immediately given priority in the speaking order, and in all Q & A sessions and at job fairs. As a result, professional judgment and common sense indicate that the relationship between Captain Weston and Captain Carnes has resulted in a degradation of morale, good order, discipline and unit cohesion, and are subject to action under the Uniform Code of Military Justice.'"

Van Linn had staked out their rooms? She was in OSI; it was conceivable she'd done more than that.

"How very thorough," Sara said, finally.

"It's my job to be observant. I'm very good at my job."

"Yes, I know. That's why I invited you on this tour."

How Sara made her voice sound so calm was a miracle. "Have you sent it in?"

"Not yet, no."

"Why not?"

Van Linn blinked slowly. "I'm trying to be fair, although the evidence doesn't lend itself to misinterpretation."

"I see."

"It's not just me," Van Linn said. "It's all of us, the whole team. You seem to have forgotten that we exist. Carnes doesn't outrank us, and he's not actually Tom Cruise. We're all supposed to be in this together." She took a step closer to the desk.

Sara knew this wasn't winnable. Van Linn was out for blood, whether from jealousy alone, or from a staggering need for the spotlight. In the end it didn't matter why. This wasn't about fairness.

There was a way to fight it, of course. Even Luke going to her room after midnight. He was the newest team member. He might have needed her help. Each incident had a perfectly plausible explanation, and she had considerable latitude as to how to use her staff. Every incident but one.

The kiss at the pool.

That was what was going to hang her. There was no explaining it away, especially if anyone else had seen it. Sara hadn't given it a thought at the time or since. She'd been too caught up with Luke, learning the new man, reacquainting herself with the taste and feel of him. But the irony that her one mistake with him, of all people, was going to hijack her career tasted as bitter as cyanide.

She wouldn't be court-martialed, most probably wouldn't even be disciplined. However, the complaint would become part of her record. The tour would continue to be a success, and that would stand on its own.

And her new project? Colonel Graves would assign it to someone else. He wouldn't be happy about it, but the integrity of his unit was more important than his relationship with Sara. She wouldn't get the big jobs, not the important ones. Because it was her personal reputation that would be questioned. And those who ranked above her wouldn't want to risk it.

"I understand your concerns," Sara said. "I'd appreciate a few days to give the matter my full attention."

Van Linn's eyes narrowed. "I'm writing this up tomorrow. I won't hold on to it for long."

"Understood."

Van Linn didn't salute. It wasn't necessary given their equivalent rank, but the manner in which she left felt like an insult. The door closed, and Sara didn't move. She played back the overheard conversation the evening of the television appearance. The rest of the speakers hadn't seemed to give a damn about Luke being on the show. But that wasn't necessarily true now.

She hated to think that her behavior had been a source of embarrassment to the service. Her face heated with the thought, nausea making her swallow hard. She loved her job, loved being in the air force. She'd found her place, and she'd given it everything she had.

God, today of all days... Colonel Graves had placed his faith in her... Damn. Her eyes stung. She blinked. Getting emotional wouldn't help.

She couldn't blame Luke. This was all her fault. Again. There was only one thing she could do that would fix this. The prospect literally would have brought her to her knees had she not been sitting. But she could see no other way around it.

She'd have to step down.

14

SARA LEFT HER OFFICE AT SEVEN. As the door clicked shut, she heard the too-familiar sound of Mike O'Malley half a hall away. She willed him to disappear, but the boot treads continued ever closer.

He was near enough that she could hear his annoyed mumble, but not the words.

"I'm not in the mood, O'Malley," she said, finally letting go of the door. Could've been worse, she supposed. It could've been Luke. She'd dodged his calls, then left him a message strongly urging him to go out to dinner with one of the other team members and that she'd see him later. After she'd pulled herself together. She didn't need to cry on his shoulder, but she did need to tell him to keep his distance.

"Who says I want something?" O'Malley asked.

She turned to face him. "You're here. Ergo, you want something."

"Ergo? Jeez. You look like hell."

"Thanks. You're a prince among men. Now go away."

"You haven't eaten. I know you missed lunch and I'm guessing you skipped breakfast, too."

"What are you, my mother?"

"Nope. But you're my friend and I want company at dinner, so as my friend, you're going to join me, and not piss and moan about it."

"O'Malley..."

"The sooner we get it over with, the sooner you can go sulk."

"Insufferable. I have no idea why I put up with you."

"It's 'cause I'm so classically handsome."

"Pfft."

"I knew you'd say that. We're just going to the diner."

"How come you never come to me with your problems?" she asked. "Why am I always the one who needs to whine?"

He eyed her without turning his head. Kept on walking.

"I hate it when you go all Yoda on me," she murmured.

When they reached the motel exit, O'Malley held open the door for her. "I didn't say a word."

"You're buying," she said, as she passed him.

"Wouldn't have it any other way."

By the time they were seated, she had accepted the fact that she was going to tell him everything. Almost everything. Some details would go with her to her grave, but O'Malley would get the gist because she needed a sounding board, and no one listened like Mike O'Malley.

He studied the menu. It was a rare thing, to have a night off that wasn't a weekend or a moving day. Tomorrow would be a long one, though, with a job fair in Culver City during the day, followed by a full presentation. She'd scheduled this night off months ago. It should have made her feel good that things were working so smoothly, but with the massive sword hanging over her head it was hard to be self-congratulatory.

"I'll have a chef's salad with ranch," O'Malley said. "Large chocolate milk."

Sara hadn't even noticed the waitress. The idea of food made her stomach tighten, but if she didn't order, O'Malley would grumble. "Grilled cheese on white, please. And chocolate milk sounds great."

The waitress left and her dinner companion stared. He wouldn't come right out with it, but of course he'd known something was up. He'd been looming ever since she'd made peace with Luke, but with the colonel's visit and all, he'd been too busy to corner her for a chat. Damn, he had to know about the pool kiss, too.

She met his gaze, opened her mouth and burst into tears.

O'Malley's eyes widened with panic, which made her laugh while she was still crying.

"So, uh…" O'Malley said, his voice higher than she'd ever heard it. "Are you, like, pregnant?"

She laughed and sobbed simultaneously, harder now. Her only option was to grab her purse and make a run for the ladies' room where she locked herself in a stall. The histrionics took a minute to control, which was several minutes shorter than the time it took to put herself back together. Pregnant. For God's sake. At least it was good to know that the inscrutable Master Sergeant O'Malley could be spectacularly wrong.

She tucked a loose hair behind her ear, and went out to face the brutal facts.

THE BANGING AT THE DOOR put Luke into motion before his feet hit the floor. He stumbled when he realized his flight suit wasn't waiting to be pulled on. Because this wasn't a war zone, and the banging wasn't bombs and he didn't have to do anything but open a motel-room door.

The damage was done, though, because the adrenaline rush guaranteed he wouldn't be going back to sleep anytime soon.

The second he was coherent enough, hope flared that it was Sara. Had to be. He'd waited up for her call, but he must have fallen asleep at some point.

Luke stumbled to the door, cursing when he recognized O'Malley. Then he got scared. "Is she okay?"

"Yes and no," the sergeant said. "We have to talk."

Luke ran a hand over his face, looked at his watch, at his bare chest. At least he still had his jeans on. "Goddamn, O'Malley, it's one-thirty in the morning." But he was already at his closet grabbing a non-uniform shirt.

"No need to get dressed. This won't take long." O'Malley had walked in. He waited by the table, arms crossed. Quiet. Intense.

Luke had the uneasy feeling that this had something to do with Van Linn. He pulled on the shirt, left it unbuttoned, and stood by the bottom of the bed.

O'Malley gripped the back of a chair and leaned over it. The look in his eyes could have curdled blood. "I need to know this, and you'd better not bullshit me, Captain, because I'll tell you right now I am one dangerous bastard. If you in any way lie, you won't see it coming, but trust me, you'll never know a decent day in the air force again."

"Fine," Luke said, pissed at the threat, but also real clear O'Malley wasn't kidding. "What?"

"Did you screw around with Terri Van Linn?"

"No."

"You sure? Not even a little bit?"

"O'Malley, I don't even know *how* to screw around a little bit."

"Flirting? Making promises she could misinterpret?"

Luke frowned. "What are you talking about? I thought this was about Sara."

"It is."

"Sara knows there is nothing between Van Linn and me. I told her everything. Terri and I went for a walk, early on. To the park. She invited herself. When I got the vibe she wanted something more I passed." He thought about bringing up the kiss at the pool and what Hanover had said, but reconsidered. "Why? What the hell's going on?"

O'Malley's shoulders relaxed, but he still looked serious. "I have to be sure. Van Linn's coming after Sara."

Luke tensed, and he was as awake as he'd ever been. "What does that mean?

"She's threatening to write up a formal complaint accusing Sara of professional improprieties and degradation of unit cohesion. It's all bullshit, but it won't look good on Sara's record."

"That's crazy. Sara would sooner shoot herself than put the tour in jeopardy."

O'Malley sighed as if he were just getting to the bad part. "Van Linn saw you two kissing in the pool. She might not have been the only one."

Luke sat down as all the air left his lungs. "So I heard."

The sergeant's eyes widened. Luke had gone from an ally to the enemy in a split second, and O'Malley looked as if he wanted to strangle him with his bare hands. "And you didn't tell Sara? You let her get blindsided?"

Luke felt like a goddamned curse. Like something biblical. He'd walked back into Sara's world and sent it straight into the toilet. "No, it wasn't like that. I heard it from Hanover before the dinner with Graves. I couldn't get to Sara."

O'Malley released the back of the chair, practically

throwing it across the room in his frustration. "You really are a selfish prick."

Luke stared back, guilt burning a hole in his gut. "You're right. I can be, but not when it comes to Sara. Not anymore. I left messages, I tried to see her. She ordered me to stay away until I heard from her. I thought it had something to do with Graves's visit."

O'Malley stared at him in that gargoyle way of his, assessing, measuring, and Luke wanted desperately to be sure that some small part of him hadn't avoided telling Sara what he'd heard. No, he'd dreaded telling her, hoped that it wouldn't put a damper on their new relationship, but he'd never imagined Sara would be Van Linn's target.

He kept his gaze even with O'Malley's. "Van Linn should've come after me. I swear to you I never would have done anything to put Sara's career in jeopardy. For God's sake, I—I wouldn't."

"Then you'd better fix it," O'Malley said. "Fast." He kicked the chair out of the way and left the room.

Clenching his fists, Luke watched the door close, his mind racing ahead. He had to get to Sara, and then he'd take care of Van Linn.

SARA HAD AVOIDED LUKE all day, and now that they were at the college auditorium, she couldn't put it off any longer. This morning, he'd knocked at her door at around two, then again at five. Of course she hadn't slept, and she figured if he was trying that hard to get to her, then O'Malley had paid him a visit.

Once she'd left her room, she'd been swamped. So had Luke. Still, he'd left message after message. She hadn't listened to one of them. She couldn't afford to. She wasn't going to speak to Luke until she'd made her final decision. Not that there were many options, but she couldn't risk getting sidetracked. Not today.

O'Malley had tried very hard last night to take the decision out of her hands, but she didn't want that. Well, not all of her wanted that. This was her mess. She was in charge, and if she couldn't handle it, then she didn't deserve to be in command. When it came right down to it, she hadn't needed advice, just a friend.

Her night had been interminable. She'd written enough lists to paper the walls and had paced what felt like the length of Santa Monica Boulevard.

Yet she always ended up back at the same place. She'd step down, walk away from the biggest success she'd ever had. What was she going to tell Graves? Probably the truth, although, God, she didn't want to. She could already imagine the expression on his face. He'd given her a chance, and what had she done with it? Allowed her ex-boyfriend to turn her into a confused, sloppy mess.

In her right mind, she'd never, never have dreamt of kissing anyone under her supervision, no matter what the circumstances. Not in public. God, no. It didn't matter that they weren't in uniform, that they were the same rank. It was a matter of propriety. Of dignity.

She'd been utterly reckless, and that's why she deserved to lose this battle. The rest of it didn't matter. She was in charge, and nothing should ever take precedence over that. Just because she wasn't on the front line and no lives were directly at stake, she had no right to do anything that would sully the reputation of the air force.

George Tritter brushed her shoulder as he hurried to get backstage. Everyone seemed on edge tonight. The job fair had been good, but long, and there had barely been time to grab a meal. Now the auditorium at Pierce

College was packed, and there was still one speaker to go—Luke.

Van Linn was on now, and while the woman's voice made Sara's skin crawl, she gave no hint of her discomfort as she looked for Luke. Sara had timed this down to the minute—she'd tell Luke not to worry, that she had everything under control. His only job was to concentrate on the talk and get on with the tour.

She hadn't planned on doing even that, but he'd been off his game at the job fair. He'd been distracted and jumpy, and she had to put an end to that. The only thing she could do was appeal to his professionalism.

Luke caught sight of her and froze where he was, hand just shy of running through his hair. When he exhaled, she could see his chest collapse with it, as if he'd been holding his breath all day.

The audio cues were such a part of her that she barely had to listen to know that Luke had seven minutes before he had to get on stage. Sara wanted to be gone by then. She had no desire to see Van Linn, to stretch things out.

Luke took hold of her arm the minute she was near enough, and pulled her away from the curtain, into a dim corner with no traffic.

Before he could speak, she held up her hand. "I'm stepping down. I'm not sure when I'll be leaving, but it'll be soon. I'm going to make an announcement to the team tomorrow and I know you'll want to defend me, but don't."

Even in the terrible light, she could see Luke's jaw tighten. "Damn it, Sara, I'm sorry I didn't warn you about Van Linn."

"You did. I didn't take it seriously enough."

Luke shook his head. "No, about her seeing us kiss at the pool."

Sara blinked. "What?"

"Hanover told me. Right before the dinner with Graves. I couldn't get to you with the colonel hovering, and it didn't occur to me—I thought *I* was her target, not you."

"You thought—you didn't tell me?" She saw the frustration in his face, but didn't care. "This is my command, Captain."

"I know that, and I swear it wasn't what you think." He leaned in and lowered his voice. "Please don't do anything rash. We'll talk about this later, but you need to know I'm going to speak to Van Linn tonight. This was all my fault, Sara, and I'm not about to let you take the fall."

She stared at Luke, trying to make sense of what he'd said. She already knew she'd let her feelings for him cloud her judgment, but how far off the rails had she gone? No matter what else, Luke should have warned her. A friend would have called. A lover would have broken down doors. Was it possible he had been manipulating her all along? She needed time to think, to sort this through because she didn't want to believe he'd fooled her again.

Luke's musical cue was seconds away. "It's my responsibility. Not yours. You have to get out there. Do your job."

They both looked at the stage, at Van Linn coming through the curtains. She saw the two of them standing close in the small space and she smiled.

Sara wanted to smash the woman's face, but she just smiled and nodded in return.

"Fine," Luke said, tugging her with him as he headed for the stage. "I swear, we'll figure this out. Just don't do anything until we talk."

"There's nothing to discuss."

He stopped, touched her cheek. "Please, Sara. Trust me. Just for a little while longer."

Sara closed her eyes and realized she'd leaned into his hand. God help her, his touch felt safe. It shouldn't but it did, and damn, she was tired.

The stage was empty, the music playing on a loop in Luke's absence. "Go," she whispered.

She didn't open her eyes until the sound of applause drowned out his footsteps. His voice rang loud and clear through the speakers, and Sara went down the stairs into the auditorium proper. She found a seat at the end of a row where she had a good view of both Luke and a large section of the audience.

They were so quiet. The particular kind of quiet where attention was being paid. By the end of his speech, right before the applause, ninety percent of the students would be leaning forward, looking up. Didn't matter that most of them had already decided the military wasn't for them and were here for other reasons.

She listened to Luke, for once not evaluating or making notes on improving and changing his talk. She put a lid on her doubts about his sincerity, about his motives. If she could, she wanted to hear his story as if she'd never heard it before, unbiased, as if she weren't his lover.

Minutes in, she was captivated by his passion, his eloquence, his humor. She looked around, and though it seemed outlandish, the fact was most of these people had fallen a little in love. Luke somehow made it feel as though each individual was in a private discussion with him, and every word was meant for that person alone. So much adoration from so many people, all in the blink of an eye. Not just when he was on stage, either. This was Luke's life.

He held back nothing, despite all the drama off stage.

There was no faking, no going through the motions. The idea of him leaving the tour was ridiculous. Luke was irreplaceable.

Oh. The whole picture suddenly came into sharp focus. Terri Van Linn's anger and frustration had nothing to do with Sara or Luke, not personally. Van Linn wanted what Luke had. She coveted his magnetism, not his relationship or Sara's management skills. The OSI officer was furious that no one leaned forward for her.

Van Linn was coming after her to weaken Luke. Clever woman, she must have realized Graves wouldn't kick the most popular speaker off the team. But she could still screw up his game by going after his lover.

Well, damn. Even if Sara did step down, it wouldn't address Van Linn's problem. Luke's resignation was the only thing that could, but that option was off the table. In the end though, if Van Linn sent in the complaint, this kiss would derail her career. Better to remove the threat entirely by resigning. That way, Luke's name would never come up and she could use her resignation to convince Van Linn to destroy the report.

The prospect made her ache. She loved the service, loved her job, but she'd acted inappropriately, and that was all on her. Luke had gone through enough during his time in the service. He didn't deserve a stain on his record. It didn't matter what their relationship was, or why he hadn't warned her about Van Linn. Sara would convince her to drop the complaint. That was all there was to it.

She went back to watching Luke. Whatever happened later, there was a good chance that this would be the last time she'd ever get to see him on stage, and she wasn't going to waste it.

He'd just said something funny which she hadn't

caught, but she found herself grinning along with everyone else. Whatever his magic was, it was infectious. Whether these kids knew it or not, Luke's very presence up there was a greater influence on their future decision than any combination of words and pictures and music.

Luke understood his gift. Understood the ease with which he could pull people in. It came as naturally to him as breathing.

And for the first time in seven years, Sara understood that for her, Luke had been and would always be *the one*. For Luke, she was and would always be one of many.

Nevertheless, she would put her career on the line. Because the other thing she understood was that being around Luke made her foolish. It didn't seem to be something she could control. Better that she leave him now, before he became far more than a friend with benefits.

LUKE SAW SARA LEAVE the auditorium. He'd just said something to the crowd. No idea what. "Sorry, lost my place. Anyone remember?"

A kid stood up. He was skinny, smiling, and had one hell of an impressive Afro. "You were saying that the food sucks, the hours suck, it's mostly waiting around, then waiting some more, following rules and taking orders, and doing all that while sitting inside a really big, sandy toaster oven where a lot of people would just as soon kill you as cross the street." The smattering of laughter was good; it helped get Luke in gear.

"Right," he said, grinning. "That was great. Maybe you should take it from here."

More laughter from the crowd, and he was back. Nothing else was in his head, just this, these kids.

"God, I miss it," he said, and he wasn't lying at all. "Because with all that crap and inconvenience, the mind-blowing insanity and real, honest to God, freeze-your-blood terror, there's a bond that I guarantee you have never experienced before in your life. Even if you play for a team that's tight, even if you have friends that mean everything to you, even if you think you know what it's like, it's not like that. The best description I've heard is a band of brothers, but that's because there aren't words in any language to convey the full truth."

He paused. "I mean what I'm about to say in a literal way. No bull. I mean it."

Another pause, but this one was for him to take a breath. "It is an honor and a privilege to be in this uniform." It was no use, he had to pause again, let the catch in his throat ease up. Images flashed through his head, of his unit, of his WSO, of his folks and the house where he'd grown up. And as always, of Sara. If this was his last time up on this stage, he wasn't going to waste it.

"There are two things in this world that I'm one-hundred-percent grateful for—that I'm allowed to serve, and that as a result of my service, I've learned what truly matters."

He walked to the very edge of the stage and he looked into the eyes of the boy who'd spoken, of the girl next to him, and on down the row. "Most people," he said, his voice a little shaky, "most people don't find out what matters their whole lives. They go from job to job, one relationship to another, and they wonder, what's it for? Why am I here? What can I do, I'm just one person? I don't have to ask any more. I know. You can know, too."

15

THE WHOLE TIME Luke was answering questions from the Pierce College kids, he tracked Van Linn. She was outside the auditorium fielding questions like the rest of the team, but her laughter carried across the grass. She was obviously enjoying her moment. But not for long.

Luke had come to his decision during the talk. His priority was clear. Absurdly simple. It was Sara. She'd become his priority after he'd survived the crash. She still was, and now that he'd fallen in love with her all over again, the stakes were even higher.

"I've heard it was better than sex."

Luke's attention jolted back to the young man standing to his right, the one with the big grin on his face. "That depends," Luke answered. "There are very few things that can match the thrill of strapping an F-15 between your legs, but better than sex?" He smiled. "Not if it's sex with the right person."

The small group around him laughed, which gave him an excellent exit strategy. "Everybody have recruiter cards?" When there was no response, he backed up. "Do yourselves a favor. Check it out. You've got nothing to lose. Everything to gain. Thanks for coming tonight."

He turned, found his target. There were two students still with her, both of them guys, no surprise. When Van Linn turned it on, she was one hell of a compelling woman. Why she'd become so insecure was something Luke couldn't guess at.

When Van Linn caught sight of him standing in the shadows, her smile became smug. He approached the trio, and something about him must have alarmed the students because they scrambled the second he reached her.

"Captain Van Linn. Just the woman I was looking for."

She faced him, legs shoulder width apart, hands on her hips with her elbows wide, chin jutting forward. She wanted this confrontation; she'd been looking forward to it.

"I didn't want to have to do this out here," he said, "but then again, I figure I'm better off having witnesses. You being so quick with reports."

"You brought this on yourself, Solo. So don't imagine you can intimidate me."

"Intimidate you? I wouldn't think of it. You're going to tear up that complaint of your own free will."

She inhaled, puffing up her chest. "Oh, please. Don't try that macho crap with me. I've made tougher men than you beg."

"You're a hell of a speaker. And I imagine you're terrific at your job. I really think it's in your best interest to let this thing go."

"Just like that."

"Before it gets out of hand." Luke saw from her viciously pleased reaction that he was going about this the wrong way. It could only be a fight if both people swung. "Look, Terri, I'm sorry we got our signals crossed. I never meant to hurt you in any way. But come on, this is between the two of us. It never had anything to do with Sara."

His tactical shift seemed to throw her. "Oh, don't flatter yourself. *I* don't think you're God's gift to the world. I'm just sick of you and your biggest fan hijacking this tour."

"Is that what you think's going on here?" He had to be missing something, because what the hell did that night in the park have to do with hijacking the tour? With Sara?

Out of the corner of his eye, he saw Hanover walk over to Tritter, Pearson and Franks. They were hanging around the minibus, and while they made no bones about staring at him and Van Linn, the four of them remained out of earshot. Luke looked back at her, determined to get to the bottom of this puzzle. "Whatever's going on between me and Sara has nothing to do with the tour."

She barked out a laugh. "You think screwing the CO isn't hurting the integrity of the mission?"

"I know Captain Weston has always put the tour first and foremost."

"You mean she's put *you* first and foremost."

"You want more stage time? Is that it?"

Whoa, he'd hit a hot spot. Van Linn's body went from confident to livid. It was obvious from the tightness of her jaw to the fury in her eyes. Suddenly, it all became clear. This whole mess was about power. Van Linn had been the diva of the show, then he'd come along and overshadowed her act. She couldn't handle sharing the limelight. No wonder she'd been so pissed off in the park. It hadn't been about sex at all. How had he not seen it? This was his old act, right down to the ego as big as the great outdoors.

"Hey, you want to be last speaker of the night?" he

said, keeping his voice low and unthreatening. "You want all the interviews? They're yours."

"Yeah, right," she said. "The damage is already done. Graves thinks you're the goddamn chosen one, and the rest of us are bit players. Weston did that. Since the moment you got here. What'd she do, bribe you into coming on the tour so she could get you into bed? Oh, man, she is going down. Don't think I can't do it, either. I know people, Carnes. Powerful people."

Luke was taken aback at the vehemence of her attack. Even at his most narcissistic, he'd never been willing to trash someone else's career. This was way bigger than wanting to be the star of this show. The woman needed help, and he might have been willing to give her a break if she hadn't gone after Sara. "You honestly think I'd let that happen."

She smiled. "You don't have a choice."

"I could leave the tour. Take away all your ammunition."

"Too little." She shrugged, certain of her triumph. "Too late."

"Have it your own way, then. Here's what's going to happen. First thing tomorrow morning, I'm putting in a call to my friend Colonel Graves. The one who personally asked me to sit next to him at dinner."

She blinked and he saw it. The tiny crack in her armor. She didn't know what was going to happen next, just that the game was about to change.

"I'm going to let him know I'm leaving the tour. He'll want to know why, and I plan to tell him."

"And risk your slot on the F-35? I don't think so."

Luke smiled. "I doubt it will come to that, but it's a risk I'm willing to take."

Van Linn looked at him with renewed confidence.

"You're crazy if you think I'm going to believe that. I know fighter pilots. There's nothing you wouldn't do to keep your ride."

Luke took in a deep breath, released it slowly. "You've never been in love, have you, Terri?"

She snorted. "Love. Isn't that precious." She smiled as if the battle was over. "I'm sending the complaint tonight."

He took a step closer to her, right into her personal space. "Don't for one minute think you'll come out of this smelling like a rose. What will Graves think about you when he realizes this whole mess comes down to petty jealousy? Does he seem like the kind of officer who's gonna let that slide? Did you know this recruitment tour is his pet project? To say he's invested in the outcome is an understatement. Yeah, he'll probably be delighted to see a formal complaint come through channels." Luke shook his head, but he never let go of her gaze. "Colonel Graves knows people, too, Captain Van Linn. Powerful people."

She stepped back. "I have proof, Carnes. Dates. Times. You made out in public, for Christ's sake. You know as well as I do that all it takes is the perception of favoritism and your captain is reassigned with a very black mark on her record. If Colonel Graves tries to hush this up, I'll go above his head."

He stared at her, surprised that she'd made it this far in the service without sabotaging her own career. The woman was so accustomed to having her way, she didn't know how to cope with losing. She hadn't even considered how this would look on her own record.

He hadn't wanted to use his trump card, but she'd left him no choice. "When you start going up the list above Graves's head, be sure to include the President of the

United States. He's the one who'll be pinning the Air Force Cross on my uniform in about three weeks."

That stopped her dead in her tracks. The AFC was the highest honor in the air force, awarded for extraordinary heroism. It might not be familiar to most civilians, but in the service, getting the AFC was a major damn deal. She might have connections, but he was a bona fide war hero, which meant he held all the cards.

Luke lowered his voice. "Don't do this, Terri. It's not worth it. You won't win."

She'd stiffened with panic. He could practically see her scramble to find another gambit to get out of this on top. When she looked over her shoulder to see the rest of her team, none of them willing to stand with her, the fight drained out of her. When she turned back to Luke, her lips trembled. "Fuck you, Carnes."

Luke bit back the easy reply. "I hope you find what you need," he said firmly. "I mean it. Anyway, there's a bus waiting for us."

SARA EYED THE COFFEE on her desk, far too buzzed up to drink any more. Instead, she went to the laser printer, picked up the letter she'd written and took it to her desk.

It was late, the minibus should have been back by now, but they could have been delayed. The team never left before all the students had their questions answered. After hearing most of Luke's speech, Sara had no doubt there would be a large post-show crowd.

She'd been tempted to go to the motel parking lot to wait, afraid that Luke would get to Van Linn first, but they were both on the bus and he wouldn't talk to her there. Besides, the driver had been given instructions to call Sara five minutes from time of arrival. Sara would meet Van Linn in the lobby and escort her back to the office.

Her gaze went to the letter addressed to Colonel Graves. It was her formal resignation request. If necessary, it would be her final solution.

Unfortunately, it wasn't enough for Sara to quit; she had to make sure Van Linn didn't send in the report. Luke's reputation was at stake. So before Sara brought out the letter, she would offer Van Linn the thing she wanted most—to be the star. She'd have the final speaker's slot, Sara would make sure she arranged some kind of television promo, and Tritter would do an in-depth video of Van Linn on the tour and on the job back at Andrews AFB. It would be Van Linn's wet dream, with the added benefit of getting to lord it over Luke and Sara for the duration of the tour.

If that wasn't enough, she was prepared to throw herself on her sword and beg. The letter was just humiliating enough to appease a woman like Terri Van Linn. Sara had admitted that she'd crossed the line with a member of her team. She hadn't mentioned Luke, and wouldn't, but she'd treated herself unmercifully. She still had another year to go on her service obligation, but the request would be granted, Graves would have no choice.

Her cell rang. The team was five minutes out.

LUKE SAT IN THE FRONT SEAT of the minibus, Van Linn in the back. The team had exchanged lots of meaningful looks, but no one spoke during the ride.

All Luke cared about was getting to Sara. He couldn't call her until he was alone, back at the motel. He would head straight for her room and hope he found her there.

Instead of winding him up, the confrontation with Van Linn had left him oddly calm. For the first time since the

crash, he felt whole again, fully himself. Not at all the
man he'd wanted so desperately to become. Probably for
the best, he thought with a wry smile. The old Luke was
far too much like Van Linn.

If the woman was crazy enough to pursue the complaint, he'd do what was necessary. If that meant losing
the F-35, so be it. It would hurt like hell, but not as much
as losing Sara. Though it was a distinct possibility he'd
already lost her. He would cross that bridge if he came
to it, but now he could be satisfied with the fact that he'd
done the right thing.

Alf would be proud, Luke thought. The little guy was
all about doing the right thing for the right reasons. He
didn't go for any of that ends-justify-the-means crap.
Nope, when Alf talked about honor, it was from the
ground up.

Annoying little... Luke rested his head against the window. They were almost at the motel, and he was so tired
he felt as though he could sleep for a week. But nothing
mattered except making sure Sara was okay.

SARA DUCKED BEHIND one of their half-ton trucks as Luke
headed for the motel. She dialed his cell, heard it ring just
before he got to the entrance.

"Hey," he said. "Where are you?"

"I'm finishing up some business. Meet me at my room
in ten?" She hadn't lied. Her business with Van Linn
could be over in a few minutes.

"I'll see you then," he said. He sounded exhausted.

Sara disconnected, wishing it was over already. She
waited until Van Linn got off the bus. Last. The woman
didn't look like someone who'd scored a coup. In fact,
she seemed wired, upset. She walked quickly, and Sara
followed, keeping just far enough back that Van Linn

wouldn't notice. As soon as Van Linn got in the elevator Sara took the stairs to the second floor. She waited until Van Linn was in her room, then followed.

At her knock, Van Linn ripped the door open immediately. She appeared taken aback to see Sara, but her expression hardened quickly. "I'm off the clock."

"I know. I won't take up much of your time, but I'd appreciate a word."

"Why?"

Sara blinked, confused. "I have a proposition for you. I think it would be better if we talked inside."

Van Linn gazed at her as if Sara was crazy. As if she hadn't instigated this whole fiasco. "What is it, Captain?"

"About your complaint—"

Van Linn gave a furious shake of her head. "Your errand boy took care of it."

Sara frowned. "You mean Luke?"

"I don't know what the hell I was thinking coming on this tour. I have more important things to do. A real job. This goddamn dog-and-pony show has been a waste from day one."

"Wait. What do you mean, he took care of it?" Sara asked, holding down her temper until she heard more.

"Huh. I guess he decided to swoop in and play the hero. Getting that medal must have gone to his head. I still don't believe for a second that he'd actually give up the F-35. No fighter pilot would." She tried to shut the door.

Sara prevented her. "What the hell are you talking about?"

Van Linn groaned, so furious she shook. "You won, okay? I'm leaving. The report won't go in, and you're going to come up with a damn good reason why. Just don't get in my way again. If you'd pulled this shit with

anyone except Carnes, you'd be looking for a new career."
She slammed the door in Sara's face.

Sara stood rooted to the spot. Van Linn's speech had
her reeling. Luke had offered to quit the F-35 program?
And what medal? No doubt he'd accumulated a few, but
which one had scared off Van Linn? What the hell was
going on here? This was still her command. She was in
charge, and she didn't need anyone to come to her rescue.
Not O'Malley and not Luke.

Sara realized she was still standing at Van Linn's door,
staring at it like a damn fool. She turned, only to stop
again when she saw Luke, two doors down, watching her.
How much had he heard? It didn't matter. She was still
angry.

On the other hand, *he'd offered to quit the F-35.*

16

LUKE WATCHED, WAITED, his heart pounding faster than it should. He'd been too late and too far away to hear what had gone down, but the moment Sara's uncertain gaze met his, a rush of dangerous emotions swept through him, threatening to throw him off course. He'd done what he'd needed to do to save her career, protect her from humiliation and disgrace. He loved her. Even if she kicked him to the curb. Even if she never smiled at him again.

"What the hell, Luke?"

He had to be careful now, as careful as he'd been in the mountains in Afghanistan. The wrong move could spell disaster. He couldn't kiss her, not yet, although, God, how he wanted to. "We'll talk," he said. "Not here."

She nodded, walked past him to the elevator, pressed the button. They stood maybe a foot apart, but Luke felt as if there was a vast chasm between them. It wasn't only confusion in her eyes, but anger. Understandable. Sara had told him to leave it, that she'd handle the situation. She most likely assumed he'd interfered because he believed he could do a better job of it. Completely logical, utterly wrong.

Sara was nothing short of amazing. She could handle anything in her path. But this was his fight.

They remained silent during the walk to her room. He tried not to look at her at all. She was in uniform, he wore his flight suit, they were in public. The lesson of the week had sunk in to what Alf called his unbelievably thick skull, and Luke wouldn't take Sara's nearness for granted again. The pull, though, was as strong as a riptide.

Once they arrived at her room, she checked that they were alone in the hallway at the same time he did, then opened the door. Like the fine officer she was, she held the door open for him, locked it carefully once he was inside.

When she turned to him, there was more going on in the arch of her brow, the small frown and the sadness in her eyes than he'd prepared for. Misgiving, confusion, indecision: he could read the litany of his failings in her sigh. Luke struggled for the words, where to begin. When she had to turn her gaze away, he realized words wouldn't cut it.

It was instinct, or maybe just plain need that made him pull Sara into his arms. That made him kiss her as if his life depended on it. She had to know this, first. That he loved her. More than he loved his wings, more than he'd ever loved himself.

Something must have gotten through because, after a terrifying moment, she melted against him, and there was nothing confusing now. Nothing but heat and yearning and honesty. Whatever happened, he had *this*. Sara in his arms, on his tongue, underneath his hands.

He'd never told her he loved her. Not in all the years they were together. He'd avoided the word as if it were a curse, a life sentence. A bigger damn fool had never been born.

Sara pulled back, shifted her hands to his chest. "Luke. Wait."

It hurt, but he stepped away.

"I don't even know…" she said, more to herself than him. She cleared her throat. "What happened? What did you do?"

"I couldn't let her hurt you," he said. "It was my fault. All of it. No way I was going to make you pay."

Sara's soft fingers went to his lips, at war with the steel in her gaze. "Tell me what happened. Not why."

Luke held her gaze. "I asked her to back off. Told her Graves wouldn't take kindly to an official complaint."

Sara crossed over to the bed. She removed her cap, undid her tab tie and the top button of her blouse. "I need specifics. You stepped way over the line tonight, we both know that. From the way Van Linn behaved, you had to have threatened her somehow. I'm trying to make sense of it. Why did you tell her you'd give up the F-35?"

"Because it was true. I didn't think it would come to that, but she had to understand. So I told her." He watched Sara rub the back of her neck. He wanted to take over, rub her neck, ease her pain, but the next move was hers.

"So you said you'd leave the tour, but that obviously didn't satisfy her," Sara said, studying him as she worked things out. "What did? What did you say?"

"I told her if she didn't tear up the report, I'd call Graves and cop to everything. That the tour was important to him, and that he thought I was important to its success. That she was acting out of jealousy, and I'd make sure Graves knew it"

"And?"

He sighed. He'd never been good with confessions.

"She threatened to go over Graves's head." He'd meant to tell Sara the next bit under very different circumstances. "What she didn't know, what no one knows, is that I'm being awarded the Air Force Cross. There'll be a lot of publicity around it. The ceremony is in three weeks, after the tour. She realized she couldn't fight that."

Sara stared at him, astonished. "The Air Force Cross? That's… Why the hell didn't you tell me? It's about the crash, isn't it? Oh, my God, what happened out there?"

He had no idea why it unnerved him to talk about it. Maybe because that had been his fault, too. Or maybe because it still hurt so much. But it was time. Not just because of the Van Linn situation, but because he needed her to know. Not about the medal; that was nothing. But about how the crash had changed everything. He needed her to help him make sense of it.

He sat next to her on the bed and took her hand in his.

SARA WAS STARTLED by the coldness of Luke's palm, the stark fear in his eyes. Van Linn and everything about her disappeared, leaving only Luke and what had happened to him in the Sandbox. She'd known it had changed him, but seeing his expression, the pallor of his skin, she got an inkling of just how bad it had been. "It's okay. Never mind. You don't have to tell me, Luke." She touched his face. "You don't."

He swallowed and leaned into her touch. He smiled a little, seemed more confident. He drew her hand away from his cheek, and squeezed it. "I want to," he said. "I'd never been so scared in my life." The quaver in his voice made her tear up, but she didn't want to cry. He needed her to be strong now.

"I didn't see it in time. I thought it was an engine problem. When I had figured it out, there was nothing I could do. I signaled, rode her down as far as I could, then ejected."

He smiled at her, a quick, embarrassed grin, then went back to studying their clasped hands. "So it was just me and Alf, in the mountains, middle of the night, surrounded by Taliban insurgents. Where we landed wasn't the best extraction site. We had to move into position. It was hairy, let me tell you. I could hear the enemy at night, hear them sneeze, hear them laugh. But the mountains bounced the sounds around, so it was hard to say where they were."

She brushed her thumb over a tiny patch of skin on the back of his palm.

"I dreamt about you. Crazy timing, but—" He looked up at her again, his pupils huge in his wide eyes.

She shifted closer to him, aching for how frightened he'd been. He'd changed, yes, but an admission like this still came hard to such a proud man.

"Sometimes I talked to you," he whispered. "Planned to talk to you, at least, tell you things I didn't want to tell anyone else. One day, I'd think, one day we'd get together. It wasn't until I was out there in a dark so deep it was like drowning that things got clear in my head. I'd screwed up. With you. I'd walked away from the best thing that had ever happened to me."

Sara's chest constricted and the tears broke through. She didn't dare move or look away. This wasn't like his apology. What he was offering her now was his soul.

"It took us a while to get out." His voice broke. The silence felt heavy, as if the dark memories had physical weight.

"You don't have to do this, Luke. I know it's painful."

His head dropped onto his chest and for a long moment he just breathed. Finally, he said, "The thing was,

I ejected fine. Alf had gone before me, and I knew how far I'd have to backtrack to find him. He was right where I assumed. But his chute—" He pressed his lips together for a few seconds. "His chute got caught weird on a rock. He didn't have the right traction to get himself out."

He stared at her, the tragedy written on his face hard to take. He was reliving his helplessness, and Sara had nothing to offer him. Maybe listening was all she was meant to do. God, she didn't know.

She gave him a watery smile. "But you got to him."

He blinked. Took a deep shuddering breath as he slowly shook his head. "I was too late."

All the air left Sara's lungs. Had she misunderstood? He'd talked about Alf as if… "Luke, I'm sorry, I'm confused." Her pulse quickened with a nameless fear. "Alf came home with you, didn't he?"

A small smile chased the haunted look from his eyes, but only for a second. "He did."

God, this was crazy. "I still don't…"

"His older brother had gone down in Iraq two years before. They never found his body. Alf was the last child. I gave him my word I'd get him home no matter what. He was a hell of a WSO. The best guy I knew. He shouldn't have died that way. I shouldn't have waited so long to eject."

So many thoughts collided in her head, so many unanswered questions. It was hard to think, hard to process everything he'd told her.

But now she understood about the medal. The Cross was the highest honor in the air force, awarded for extraordinary heroism in combat. When Luke said it was hairy, what he meant was that he'd had to engage the enemy. He'd fought his way out, carrying the body of his friend each step of the way.

She swiped the tears from her eyes so she could see him. She'd known Luke as a boy. Now she knew him as a man, forged by fire, strengthened by pain. God. "Luke…"

He put his free hand on her cheek, brushed his thumb across the track of her tears, comforting her.

"I talked to him the whole week. It kept me sane. I told him I was still in love with you," he said, and she forgot how to breathe. Then he gave a slight shrug. "I don't know if it was even true, not at the time. So much had happened. But I know now," he said, his eyes brimming with emotion. "I love you, Sara. More than I thought I was capable of. I was stupid and reckless with you once. Never again. You're the one for me. You've always been the one for me."

Sara kissed him. Her tears kept coming, wetting her cheeks and now his, but she didn't care. She ached for his loss, for his terror, but he loved her and that filled her heart with a stab of pure joy, because, God, it was as if all the dreams she'd never dared to dream had come true.

He pulled her close, his kisses sweet and hot and desperate. She moaned as he cupped her neck, as his fingers found the pins in her hair.

"Luke," she whispered as she shifted her lips, tasting his lips, his love.

"I love you," he said, again.

"Wait." She pulled back, and he followed, but she made him stop. Made him look at her. "I love you," she said. "You hear me? I love you."

He nodded, but his gaze skittered away. She'd known he wouldn't believe her. Because she knew him as he'd been. "Sweetie. Look at me."

He breathed in, shaking. He let go of her hair. The left half of her twist fell onto her shoulder. He still kept his palm on her neck. No pressure, just trembling as if the next minute would change the rest of their lives.

"Who you've become astonishes me," she said. "What you did for Alf makes me proud. *Why* you did it makes me love you more than I ever did before. You've always been the one, even when we weren't ready for each other. I'm ready for us now. I believe you are, too."

He swallowed hard. Closed his eyes and breathed deeply twice. When he looked at her again, his gaze was steady and a little damp. "I want you in every way possible," he said, his voice wrecked and gorgeous. "It's not going to be easy. You're going to Randolph and I'm going to end up at Hill, but I don't care. If it's too much, I'll get a transfer. I can fly anything. As long as you're with me, I don't care what."

She felt dizzy, and the only thing that could steady her was touching him. She pressed her hand to his chest, felt his heartbeat through his flight suit. "We'll figure it out," she said. "I have no doubt we can make it work."

He nodded. "Okay," he said, letting her nape go to capture her hand. "I want you tonight. I want you to hold me. To make love with me. I need to be inside you. I want to hold you as we fall asleep, wake up to you first thing in the morning. I want to make you happy for the rest of your life. Starting now."

Sara smiled as she reached for the zipper of his flight suit. "Duly noted. Now, kiss me, flyboy."

Epilogue

Eighteen months later...

THE F-35 WAS STILL IN TESTING, only at Edwards Air Force Base in California instead of Hill AFB in Utah. It was a chilly afternoon as mile upon mile of desert spread around the landing field.

Sara's gaze focused on a speck in the sky, a tiny blip that could have been anything, but she knew better. That was her man, in his jet, and he was coming in for a landing.

They hadn't seen each other in three weeks. She was still stationed at Randolph, about to start another road show, this time in the Midwest. Ten weeks of nonstop talks, job fairs, junior colleges, universities and radio spots. But this time, they were using her playbook.

Sadly, Luke wasn't one of her speakers. He'd been working with the new plane, taking it through its paces as the slow wheels of the Joint Strike Task Force rolled. But he was thrilled to be a member of the very elite team. They were lucky to have him.

Of course she wished she could see him more often. But there were benefits to him being a super pilot. He managed to come to her a lot more frequently than she got to him, and every time they saw each other it was an explosion.

She had loved him back in college, but that had been kid stuff, love with training wheels. Now they were... Well, there was a lot to be said for growing up, despite the difficulties. They had a trust between them that couldn't have come from anything but hard-fought battles and lessons painfully learned.

The speck was growing in the pale blue sky. The clouds were few and wispy, as if they didn't want to compete with the slick aerodynamics of the next-generation fighter jet. As Luke flew toward her, her heart rate climbed, the anticipation filled her with enough kinetic energy to light a building. She *missed* him.

They spoke every day, no matter what. They'd never gone three weeks without each other, even when he'd been in the classroom at Eglin, learning his jet from the inside out. Those visits had been odd, but good. Both of them working pretty much straight through, except for bedtime. But what bedtimes they were.

Now it looked like a plane. A small one, but getting larger as it traveled at supersonic speed, and it felt as if he was racing toward her. They had an entire weekend ahead of them in a sweet little motel just outside of Lancaster.

One minute, it was like something in a movie, something made of magic and metal, and the next the noise could drown out thunder. The very air shimmered in awe.

A perfect landing. Grinning like a lunatic, she watched his canopy until she could make out the man. She stepped away from the borrowed jeep, even though she knew she had to wait once more for Luke to come to her.

The moment the canopy went up, her heart surged and

so did her body, leaning, always leaning toward him. That never stopped.

He climbed out of his jet, whipped off his helmet, then paused until he spotted her. His smile made her fall in love all over again.

He wasn't walking slowly, it just felt that way. She maintained her dignity because she was in uniform. But watching him in that damn flight suit, with his helmet under this arm and his hungry grin made her want to leap into his arms and never let go. Unfortunately, they weren't alone. Not by a long shot. Each and every test flight of this new plane was monitored by dozen of people outside and in, on computers and cameras and satellites. It was a very big deal, and she was a guest, an outsider.

She didn't expect Luke to walk right past the first wave of support personnel, and certainly not the second. But he did. He ignored every call and every look except hers. Then his arm was around her and she was swept off her feet into a kiss that scorched the tarmac.

Finally, when the need for air became an issue, he let her down gently, but kept her attention with a look that made her tremble. "Marry me," he said.

Whatever had been on the tip of her tongue vanished along with her breath. "What?"

"Marry me. I don't know where we'll be, or what's gonna happen. What's more, I don't care. I love you, and I don't want to wait. Marry me, Sara. You're the goddamn love of my life, and I don't want to go another week without you being mine."

She gripped his arm so tight it had to hurt, but she was dizzy from his words and how he meant them. "Okay," she said, her voice as wobbly as her knees. "I don't think we can do it before next week—"

"There's a plane leaving tomorrow morning at 0600

taking us straight to Nellis. A car will meet us there and get us registered, and we'll get hitched on Sunday."

"Excuse me? When did you do all this? You've barely had time to sleep for the last three weeks."

His grin changed. "O'Malley might have had something to do with it."

Her mouth opened, but Luke brushed her cheek and she forgot about everything but him, and what they were about to do.

"He also gave me the name of a jeweler in Vegas," he said.

She touched his chest, anxious to find some privacy so they could really celebrate. "Don't you have to report in?"

He looked at the coterie of uniformed personnel and civilians waiting to get to work, then back to her. "Yeah." His kiss this time started out fierce, then gentled. "You wait right here, Sara Weston. I'm coming back for you. I will always come back for you."

* * * * *

GOING FOR IT

1

Dr. Jamie Talks Sex...and Manhattan Listens!

Darlene Whittaker took a deep drag of her cigarette outside the offices of WXNT Talk Radio and stared at the face on the billboard across the way. Dr. Jamie Hampton was the newest "It" girl in Manhattan, the topic of conversations from the Bowery to the Bronx. Beautiful, brilliant, radical Dr. Jamie.

Darlene hated the no-smoking laws in New York that had forced her outside and cursed the mayor and all the voters at least once a day. She missed her local bar, where she used to drink tequila shooters with beer chasers and go through about a half a pack a night. Damn, those were good times.

She was here on a hunch. The article had been her idea. It was also her idea to interview Dr. Jamie on the air. The good doctor hadn't wanted to, but her station manager Fred Holt had insisted. Holt was many things, but stupid wasn't one of them. The national exposure Dr. Jamie would get with the article was going to help get her syndicated, and that's where the big bucks were. Dr. Laura, Howard Stern, Delilah—they all made a fortune for four hours on the air, five days a week. Nice work if you could get it.

Unless, of course, Darlene's hunch was right, in which case the ensuing scandal would get Dr. Jamie a one-way ticket to obscurity, and Darlene about ten grand more per article.

She just wished she could be sure.

She focused on the billboard again. Even fifty feet wide Jamie still looked tiny. Didn't the woman know the waif look was dead? With that short dark hair and those huge dark eyes, she came across as Little Miss Innocent—which was the hook. Just like the sign said, she talked sex and Manhattan listened. Straight answers, no euphemisms, no giggling. She told women they could have sex like men, and the women were eating it up. She had the number-one show in her market, and she was the number-one topic around watercoolers and in lunchrooms.

Darlene snorted. She'd seen 'em come and go, and Dr. Jamie wasn't going to be around very long. She was like a pet rock or a lava lamp. A sparkler on the Fourth of July. The trick for Darlene was to catch the light while it flared and turn the sparkler into a Roman candle. Darlene would be the one to light the match, and Jamie would burn.

Jamie's eyes, almond-shaped, deep brown, with what had to be fake lashes, stared down from the billboard with all the innocence of a lamb before the slaughter. When Darlene was through with her, Jamie would be knocked off that perch of hers and she'd have to face life among the great unwashed. Hell, Darlene was doing her a favor. Toughening her up for real life. Especially life in New York City.

God bless research. If Darlene hadn't found Jamie's old roommate in college, if she hadn't gone all the way to Buffalo to do the interview in person, if Dianna Poplar hadn't dropped just enough hints about the sex doctor... this article would have been about as interesting as a night at the Laundromat. But a scandal—that changed everything. That sold magazines. And that meant the kind of money Darlene deserved. The kind that would get her out of her hideous apartment and into something decent.

That she was able to dethrone the current queen of New York was an extra bonus. The cherry on top. Jamie was so much like all the girls Darlene had gone to college with—beautiful, bright, successful without any effort. What had Jamie done, really, to deserve this job? Gotten her degree? Big deal. Darlene had a degree, and she wasn't about to go on the radio and say she was an expert on sex.

Jamie was a fraud. And Darlene was going to prove it.

The roar of a beefed-up motorcycle caught her attention, and she watched a guy on a Harley glide into a brilliantly lit parking space next to the Dumpster. She couldn't see much of him—just his leather jacket, the worn jeans, the boots and the black helmet. But as she stared, he got off the bike, took off his helmet and shook his hair free. It was longish, below his collar. Then, as if he sensed her watching him, he looked over. She was too far away to see the details of his face, but she knew who he was.

Chase Newman. The race-car driver. Another one of the beautiful people who showed up at all the right parties and were paraded on the pages of magazines like *Vanity Fair* with other gorgeous rich people. She happened to know that *People* had tried to dub him Sexiest Man Alive, and he'd told the magazine to go to hell. She had to give him credit.

He turned to lock up his bike, and the short hairs on the back of her neck rose. It was her own personal radar system. There was a story here. What, she didn't know yet. But the short hairs were never wrong.

She narrowed her gaze as she studied him. The way he moved, the way he stood, shouted confidence, sensuality, raw male energy. The kind of charisma that beguiled the most jaded hearts. Even she hadn't been immune. She'd met him at a fundraiser—some kid thing, or maybe pets. She'd wanted to do an article on him then, but she couldn't find a hook. If she could figure out a way to combine the Dr. Jamie story with a guy…especially a guy like Newman.

She'd seen it before, although not terribly often. Mostly there were wannabes, men who swaggered and flexed and flashed their money around for all to see. But when the real thing came along, everyone knew it. There were some men who commanded attention. Respect. Who made a person want to breathe the same air, or at the very least stand in their shadow. Who owned the room, and all the women in it. The ladies fell in love with a man like that after even the briefest exposure—like it was some kind of virus. She'd seen it a thousand times. Women falling all over themselves to be near a man with that kind of charisma. Believing some of it would rub off on them.

Oh, yeah. Chase Newman would be perfect to put into this piece, if only she could find a way. Something about Chase and this station niggled at the edge of her consciousness. What was it? As she reached for another cigarette, she glanced at her watch and swore. She'd better get inside. Dr. Jamie was waiting. She hurried inside to the smoke-free air of the most popular talk-show radio station in the five boroughs, New Jersey and parts of Connecticut, Massachusetts and Vermont.

"OKAY, BOYS AND GIRLS," Dr. Jamie Hampton said into the mike. Her favorite mug was filled with green tea, and her notes were stacked neatly in front of her. "With me now is Darlene Whittaker, from *Vanity Fair* magazine. She's going to interview me right here, right now, up close and personal. And a little later, you'll get your chance to ask me some questions, too." She turned to her guest, outfitted with fresh coffee and her own set of headphones. "So, Darlene. What can I tell you?"

"You're a lot younger than I thought you'd be."

God, she was tired of that comment. "Twenty-seven on my next birthday."

"Is the title real? Or does your first name happen to be 'Doctor'?"

Jamie laughed, already hating the woman. It wasn't Whittaker's looks. She'd dressed in Manhattan gothic, with horn-rimmed glasses, a head of curly, unkempt black hair, a black tunic over black jeans, and red lipstick so bright she probably stopped traffic. The look was too passé, but that wasn't it. The way Whittaker looked at her was another story. Something wicked was brewing inside the reporter. Something devious. "The title is real. I got my PhD in human sexuality at NYU."

"When?"

"Two years ago."

"At twenty-four?"

"Yep. I started college at sixteen, got my master's degree at twenty-one."

"Wow. That's some accomplishment. So, it was while you were a doctoral candidate that you started the radio show on campus?"

"Right. *The Sex Hour.* We broadcast from the campus radio station, and the show got pretty popular."

"Isn't it true that the reason you were so popular is that you're a female version of Howard Stern? Outrageous just for the sake of shocking your audience?"

"Well, I suppose that could be true if one considers the truth shocking."

"The truth?"

"I talk about sex. With all the weirdness that implies. Kinky sex, normal sex—whatever that is—solo sex, monogamous sex, safe sex. Sex on the beach, and in the kitchen."

"And the Woman's League of Decency has tried to shut you down because all you do is promote sex to teenagers."

"I wouldn't know about the Women's League of whatever, but I do know our demographics. Most of our listeners are in their twenties and thirties."

"The attempt to get you off the air has been in all the papers for the past six months. Don't you read the *Times?*"

"I skip over the boring articles."

Whittaker gave her a sarcastic smile. Damn Fred for making her do this. Sure, she wanted to be syndicated, but the show should speak for itself.

"When was the last time you talked about chastity?"

"Two days ago. I encouraged a caller to keep her knees together unless she was walking. Does that count?"

"But then tonight you taught a woman how to masturbate!"

"Someone had to."

"What are all the religious leaders going to say?"

"Thank you?" Jamie looked through the five-inch plate-glass window in front of the room, and met the gaze of her producer, Marcy Davis. Marcy's left brow arched as she fought a smile. Then Cujo, whose real name was Walter Weinstein, gave her the signal to go to commercial. "We've got Darlene Whittaker here from *Vanity Fair,* doing a live interview. This is Dr. Jamie, and we'll be right back."

She turned to her guest as she took off her headphones. "Having fun?"

Whittaker extracted her headphones from the forest of black hair. "Do I have time to go to the john?"

"Sure do. We've got a whole five minutes of commercials."

Whittaker crossed the room and struggled with the heavy soundproof door. Once she was out, Marcy walked in.

"So far, so good."

After checking to make sure no microphones were live, Jamie turned to her producer. Marcy was the best, and Jamie thanked the radio gods every day that Marcy had been the one to bring her over to WXNT. At forty-two, she bitched about being the old lady of the station, which was technically true, but no one cared except Marcy.

"You know," Marcy said, "I really like her sense of color. She's a summer, don't you think?"

Jamie put her finger to her lips. "She could be right outside the door."

"So what?" Marcy fell into the guest's chair. "This was a stupid idea."

"You won't get an argument from me."

"You're doing great. But I don't like that it's live. It's not fair."

"Since when did fair enter the picture? Either she'll write the truth or not. In the grand scheme of things, it doesn't really matter, does it?"

Marcy shook her head. "Of course it matters. This is

radio, sweetie—where numbers rule the day and the only thing you can count on is change. You need this article to be good, or at least provocative. A good scandal wouldn't hurt at all."

"Oh man, you're serious, aren't you?"

Marcy nodded, but something in the other room had captured her attention. Jamie knew what it was as soon as she glanced over. Ted Kagan, the DJ who came on after Jamie, was talking to Cujo. Ted was a sweetheart, and it didn't hurt that he was also deliciously gorgeous. Marcy hadn't ever said anything, but Jamie knew beyond a shadow of a doubt that her producer had the hots for him. And Jamie also knew that Marcy wouldn't do anything about it because Ted was thirty. As if that mattered. Love was love and, unless one of the participants was under eighteen, age didn't mean squat.

"Marcy?"

She didn't respond. Not for a few seconds, at least. Then she turned to look at Jamie. "What?"

"He's a doll, isn't he?"

Marcy's cheeks got pink. "Who?"

"Okay. Have it your way. But you do realize I'm an expert on relationships."

Marcy stood up. "Right. And let's see…your last relationship was when, exactly?"

"A person doesn't have to die to be a pathologist."

"Nice analogy, except that it has nothing to do with the subject at hand. I've known you over a year, missy, and I haven't seen you go on a date even once."

"I've been busy."

"Busy, my *ass*. You're a workaholic, and you know it."

Jamie relaxed. She could live with that diagnosis. "I know. And I'm trying to ease up. It's difficult."

"That's another load of garbage. Have you made any plans for your vacation?"

She shook her head.

"Well, if you don't, I will. I'm thinking Tahiti."

Jamie glanced at her panel. She donned her headphones and pressed her on-air button. "Welcome back to WXNT. I'm Dr. Jamie, and I'm being interviewed by Darlene Whittaker of *Vanity Fair* magazine. But first, are you tired of waking up with a sore back?"

Marcy sighed as she pulled open the booth door. It seemed to get heavier every day. Just as she got it open wide enough to walk through, Whittaker turned the hall corner and rushed past her without so much as a thanks. Rude, rude, rude. But then, so many people were these days.

She glanced in the production booth. Ted was still there. God, he was so yummy. Tall, slender, blond—he had the words "golden boy" written all over him. He was also one of the nicest men she'd ever met, and if she didn't stop dreaming about him, she'd have to shoot herself.

It didn't help that his divorce had come through two months ago, and that he was actually starting to show some interest in dating. She'd never survive watching him parade sweet young things through the office.

She really should ask him out. Just take the bull by the horns. Put it all out on the table. Jamie was always talking about how women let fear stop them from having fun. That they should have the same opportunities as men when it came to recreational sex. And that there was no point in beating around the bush. If she wanted to hop in the sack with Ted, she should simply walk up to him and ask. Go for it, as Jamie was so fond of saying.

Oh, please. She could barely look at the man without blushing like a twelve-year-old.

She sighed as she headed toward the production-booth door. The phones would start lighting up any second, and she wanted to get a real good mix on the line.

Ted was looking at a newspaper when she walked in, and he didn't even glance at her as she took her seat by the phone. The computer to her right was her link to Jamie. Once she got a caller, she'd type the name, age, location, and the gist of what he or she wanted to say. Most nights, the phones never stopped. Tonight was no exception, which was good. She needed to be too busy to think. She slid on her cordless phone receiver and pressed line one.

DARLENE KNEW SHE WAS losing ground. Dr. Jamie was a lot more poised than she should have been, especially at her age. Twenty-six, and already the top-rated DJ in New York. Shit. At twenty-six, Darlene had been in college, an English major with no boyfriends, no girlfriends and an eating disorder.

Of course, Jamie was prettier in person than in her publicity photos. Pouty lips, perky tits and, come on, couldn't she at least have one pimple to even the score? No. Pimples were for women like Darlene. In the article, she'd prob ably describe Jamie's skin as alabaster. Flawless. The *bitch*.

"If you don't mind, Darlene, I'm going to take a call."

Darlene nodded, wishing she'd had a chance to smoke during that last commercial.

"This is Lorraine from Queens." Jamie hit a button, and Darlene could hear a little static on the headphones.

"Dr. Jamie?"

"That's me. Do you have a question?"

"Yeah, well… Yeah."

"Go on. I don't bite."

"The other night, you were talking to Kelly from Point Washington about how she got seduced by this guy—"

"She *let* herself be seduced."

"Yeah, well, that's the part I wanted to talk about."

"The idea that no woman can be seduced unless she wants to be?"

"Yeah."

"Okay."

"I don't know. I mean, there's this guy at work. Steve. He is so gorgeous, and he's funny and sexy. You know what I'm talking about. He's one of those men who can have any woman he wants."

"No man can have any woman he wants."

"But, like, I've got a boyfriend, and I don't mean to say I did anything with Steve, but I sure thought about it. I don't like to admit it, but if he'd asked, I'd have said yes."

"Why? What is it about Steve that makes him so irresistible?"

"I don't know. He's really good-looking."

"So you'd have sex with all really good-looking men if they asked you?"

Lorraine laughed. "No."

"Then it must be something else."

"Okay. The way he looks at a person. It's like, uh… I don't know. It's like he sees right inside me."

"Great. He knows how to focus. Have you slept with every man who focused solely on you?"

"No. But that's mostly 'cause no one ever has. Not like Steve."

"I admit, being paid attention to is flattering, but it's no reason to drop your drawers. What else?"

"I don't know. I swear. It's just a combination of things, I guess. The way he walks and smiles. When he comes into my office, I can hardly breathe. It's like he's magic or something."

"He's not magic. He's just self-assured. He knows he can make women swoon, so he does."

"I'll say."

"Here's the thing, Lorraine. If you wanted to sleep with him, far be it from me to tell you what to do. Go for it. If you don't want to sleep with him, don't. But don't lie to yourself and say you were *seduced*. There's no such thing. Seduction is an excuse for behavior you know is inappropriate."

"It's a pretty damn good excuse."

Now it was Jamie who laughed. "Just be strong. Know you have a right to choose. Tell the truth to yourself and you'll be fine."

"So, you've never been seduced?"

"Nope. I haven't. Not even once."

Darlene got a little shiver, and said, "You don't think chemicals have anything to do with it? Pheromones? That a woman can get swept away?"

"No. Absolutely not. I do think there can be a chemical connection between people, and that attraction exists and can be very strong. But the idea that a woman is helpless to fall into a man's arms is ludicrous. Relationships, even brief ones, should be about making choices, and about honesty."

"And you don't think falling in love could just happen."

"No, I don't. I think that's one of the biggest myths in our culture. Lust can happen in an instant, although it doesn't have to be acted upon. Love only comes with time and work. It's a woman's choice whether she wants to have sex or not, whether she's married or not. It's your body. Respect it. Take care of it. Give it a treat now and again. And if you don't have anyone to help you, do it yourself, with or without help from toys. I'll bet there are a lot of married women out there right now who wish they'd listened. Who waited to see if the man who seduced them was actually a man they wanted to live with forever. Given the dismal marriage statistics, I'm willing to wager that for at least fifty percent of the women, they didn't look before they leaped."

Darlene felt those hairs stand on the back of her neck again. She had it. The perfect article. The perfect hook. "Let me get this straight. You're saying that no man, no matter who he is, can seduce a woman?"

"That's right. Not if a woman is honest."

"No amount of charm, charisma, sex appeal could have any effect?"

"Not if a woman doesn't want to be seduced. Have you ever looked up the word? I have. According to the dictionary, *seduce* means 'to induce to have sexual intercourse.' What I'm suggesting is the idea that no one can be induced. If it's forced, then it's rape. If it's consensual, it's not seduction. It's an excuse, nothing more. No woman can be seduced without her permission. Period."

Darlene closed her eyes for a second, just to calm herself. "How would you like to put your money where your mouth is?"

Jamie's brows came down. "What do you mean?"

"Exactly that. You say no woman can be seduced without her permission. I say fine. Prove it."

Jamie laughed a little. "There's no way to do that. Every woman has to come to that decision for herself."

"But there is a way to prove it." Darlene's heart hammered in her chest. This was so great. "Here's what I want to do. I'm going to set you up with a man who's seduced his fair share of women. More than his share. You two are going to spend time together. He's going to lay on the charm. And then we'll see what happens."

"I'll tell you exactly what will happen. Nothing."

"I don't think so."

"It's ridiculous. There's no way I can be seduced."

"You're on. I think you don't know what you're talking about. And we're going to see who's right."

"Hey, yeah, Dr. Jamie," Lorraine said, reminding Darlene that she was still on the line. "That would be so cool."

"What would be cool?"

"Well, like, for you to show us. To prove it."

Darlene held back her whoop of joy. This was even better than she could have hoped for. "Right. Walk the walk instead of just talking the talk."

"Hold on." Jamie looked at her with utter exasperation. Darlene didn't give an inch. Jamie turned back to the mike. "Lorraine, I wish you luck with your guy, and thanks for calling." She punched line two. "This is Dr. Jamie. Did you have a question?"

"Yeah," a deep baritone voice said. "I think you should do it. And I volunteer to be the guy. I could seduce you, baby. And it wouldn't take no two weeks."

Darlene leaned back. This was great. Just great. The article would write itself.

Jamie shook her head in disbelief as she pressed the next button. "How about line three. Pam from Chelsea?"

"Come on, Dr. Jamie. You could report every night. You know, give us an update. A blow-by-blow. Tell us what it's like out there in the real world. We could all learn something. You're always telling us to go for it. Now it's your turn."

"Thanks for sharing." She punched the next button so hard it almost broke. "Debbi from Yonkers. Do you have something else you'd like to talk about?"

"Uh, well, yeah."

Jamie's shoulders relaxed. "Great."

"I think, you know, that you shouldn't be the one to give the nightly reports. The guy should. Or you should do it together."

Jamie's head fell into her hands. But then she sat up again. "This is Dr. Jamie, and we're talking about sex. We'll be back after these commercials." Then she threw her headphones on the desk.

Dr. Jamie wasn't on such solid footing now. Darlene leaned back as she took off her own headphones. Her gaze went to the production booth and Marcy Davis. The woman wasn't looking so smug, either. The two of them were Barbie dolls, and Darlene wanted to make them squirm. Marcy turned to look at the door as a man walked into the other booth. Perfect. It was Chase Newman, the inspiration for this adventure.

He spoke to the board operator for a moment, then he turned so she could see his face. Good God, he was stunning. Fabulous jaw, dark brows over smoky, intense eyes. Just the right amount of five-o'-clock shadow. Now, *he* was an expert on sex. There was no question the man was a maestro in the bedroom. Those lips alone could send any woman over the edge.

She was a freakin' genius. This was *perfect*. Dr. Jamie didn't stand a chance. And wouldn't it be fun when all of New York watched her fall on her perky little ass. He just had to be willing to play along. Darlene would make sure he was willing.

JAMIE TRIED TO SMILE at Whittaker, but she couldn't. She wanted the reporter gone, the interview finished, her show over, and this nonsense dismissed. Where was Marcy? She should be riding to the rescue, dammit.

Whittaker did her a favor and left the room. At least Jamie could be grateful for that. But where was Marcy? Jamie's program was going up in smoke, and Marcy had decided to take a brief vacation. Jamie was going to have to kill her. In the meantime, though, she'd better get ready to sway this conversation another way. This was her show, dammit, not Darlene's.

Damn! Cujo's signal to her was desperate. She had no idea how long she'd been stewing. "Welcome back. This is Dr. Jamie Hampton, and we're here with Darlene Whittaker from *Vanity Fair.* Let's talk about *your* lives. Is there a question about your body you've always wanted to ask? How about sex? Come on, guys. Masturbation. Cross-dressing. G-spots. Don't be embarrassed."

All the lines were blinking, but according to Jamie's computer, Gabby Fisher was on line one. God bless her little neurotic heart. Gabby was a regular, and she wasn't shy about taking air time. She'd fill up a good ten minutes. Just as Jamie was about to press the button, Whittaker struggled through the door and hurried to her seat.

Jamie shoved the button down, terrified by the gleam in Whittaker's eyes. "Gabby, hi."

"Hi, Dr. Jamie."

"What can I do for you tonight?"

"I think it would be great to have you show us, you know, how to be strong with a man."

Jamie cursed silently. This wasn't going to go away. "You already know how to be strong. You don't need me to show you."

"I might know how," Gabby said, her voice dejected, "but it never works out that way. I guess I'm just not like you."

"You can be whatever you want to be, Gabby. You just

need to shift your beliefs about yourself. A stunt like this isn't going to show you anything."

Whittaker moved her chair closer to the desk. "Are you afraid, Dr. Jamie?"

"No, not at all. But my expertise is in helping others. This isn't about me."

"But don't you think it should be?"

"What, so all surgeons should remove their own gall-bladders, just for the experience?"

Gabby laughed.

Whittaker didn't. "I think you're hiding behind that title, Jamie. I think you don't want to put your money where your mouth is."

"You're right. In this instance, I don't."

Whittaker's gaze shifted to the window, then back again. "It would make a hell of an interesting experiment. I know your listeners would learn a lot. Show them first-hand what happens when a man is out for seduction. See what happens. Instead of talking about the experiment, go into the lab."

Jamie forced herself to keep calm—to not reach over and strangle the reporter. "I just don't believe this is the kind of thing one can demonstrate. It's not like baking a cake."

Whittaker smiled at her, then turned to the mike. "Well, audience, are we going to let her off the hook? I'll tell you something. My magazine wants this information. All the women in New York want this information. This could be the most important radio program ever. Or, Dr. Jamie, were you just blowing so much smoke?"

"I don't blow smoke. Ever."

"Then, that leaves only one option."

Damn her to hell and back. Marcy was going to pay for this. And so was Fred Holt.

Jamie leaned in to her mike. "I'll tell you all about options...right after these commercials."

She saw Cujo jump at the unexpected change in the schedule. But he was on top of things, and a second later Big Al's Furniture Mart announced a super, super, super sale.

She made sure her mute button was on, then turned to Whittaker. "What the hell are you doing?"

The reporter smiled so smugly that it was an invitation for a whack. "My job. Just like you're doing your job."

"You know this isn't the kind of thing one can demonstrate. You're talking about a publicity stunt."

"Not necessarily. It could be very educational. If any of it's true. Is it?"

"Yes, it is. But I don't intend to be anyone's guinea pig."

Whittaker shook her head. "Want to bet? If you don't do it, I'm going to smear you and your radio show into the dirt. I know that Independence Broadcasting is looking at buying your show for national syndication. And I know that one way or another, they're going to be influenced by this piece I'm writing. So the choice is yours. Play ball, or find yourself a new job."

"Why are you doing this?"

Whittaker smiled. "Because I can."

Jamie caught Cujo's hand signal out of the corner of her eye. She turned back to the mike, fuming. She wouldn't be blackmailed. Not by this witch. Marcy would tell Whittaker what she could do with her stupid idea. But right now, Jamie had to keep control of her broadcast. "Welcome back."

The production booth door opened. Fred Holt and Marcy walked in. Marcy looked panicked. Fred turned to face Jamie, his jaw set and his gaze filled with dollar signs. It didn't take a rocket scientist to get the gist. Fred wanted this to happen. He wanted his station to be number one and stay number one, and as far as he was concerned, Jamie was his ticket. But surely even Fred Holt could see this was a stupid prank. He wouldn't be manipulated by this crazy woman, would he?

Cujo flapped his arms at her, then pointed at the phone lines.

Dammit! "Gabby, you still there?"

"Yes, I'm still here. And I'm really glad you're going to do this, uh, thing. But maybe you could explain what it is you're going to do."

Whittaker leaned forward. "Here's what she's going to do. She's going to go out on a date. On a whole bunch of dates. Just like she was you or me. Only, she's gonna show us how it's supposed to be done. How a woman can't be seduced."

"Wait a minute. This has been fun, but come on. I don't even have a boyfriend right now so—"

Whittaker leaned into the mike. "That's not a problem."

Jamie's stomach turned. "What does that mean?"

"You'll see."

"Tell you what. Write whatever you want to in your magazine. I'm not playing."

"And disappoint all your loyal fans?"

"My fans are smart enough to realize that there is no such thing as seduction, so I've already won."

Darlene turned smugly toward the production booth. "Oh, really?"

Jamie didn't want to look, but she had to. Oh man. It was worse than she'd thought. Fred Holt had moved to the window. His face was very, very pink. His gaze nearly singed her eyebrows. This was no joke. Behind him, Marcy threw her hands into the air. So much for her help.

Jamie looked at the door. She could get up and walk out. That's all. Just walk out. But that would mean giving up her show. She loved her show. Her show was her whole life. The only thing she'd ever done for herself, by herself. And who was she kidding? She wanted syndication every bit as badly as Fred did. A national show would be the kind of achievement no one could deny—the money, the prestige, and proof she'd made the right life choice by turning her back on her parents' medical practice.

Jamie turned to the Wicked Witch of the West Side. "All right. I'll do it. But I'll pick the guy."

"Sorry. No can do. I pick the guy. You don't want to be accused of fraud, do you?"

"Whoa. No. No way. I'm not—"

Whittaker stood up and went to the door. This time, she opened it as if it weighed ounces instead of pounds. A man stood on the other side. He walked into the booth, which immediately shrank to half its size. Jamie swallowed, trying to figure out where all the air had gone.

He stepped into the light and everything stopped, including her heart. He was quite simply the most gorgeous guy she'd ever laid eyes on. He was sex on legs, the devil in blue jeans, trouble with a capital *T.* He was all that and a shot of Tabasco.

"Jamie Hampton," Whittaker said, leading him to the mike. "This is Chase Newman. The man who can't seduce you."

"Holy f—"

Cujo lunged for the button and, for the first time in a year and a half, there was a full twelve seconds when the five boroughs, New Jersey and parts of Connecticut, Massachusetts and Vermont heard nothing but dead air.

2

CHASE FOUGHT A SMILE. He was actually enjoying Jamie's reaction, the way her big brown eyes widened, the pink flush on her cheeks, how she nervously licked her lush upper lip. He'd seen her before when he'd come to the station, but they'd never spoken. In fact, she'd been frightened of him, moving to the far side of the hallway when he'd passed, sneaking looks at him, blushing, like now. The last time, about six months ago, he'd almost asked her why, but she'd ducked into the ladies' room.

He liked her show, even though her message was a bunch of garbage. It was a smart move on Fred's part to have hired her. The station hadn't had a major ratings winner in a long time. Not that he cared. This wasn't his thing anymore. His father had owned the station, and Chase had inherited it after the old man died. But he wasn't a part of it now. The only reason he came here was because they gave him a small office where he collected his business mail, and let him use Fred's secretary for some clerical work now and then. Not having a permanent residence, it was convenient.

He saw Cujo signal that the commercials were about to end. Jamie didn't look ready. Damn, she was a pretty thing. Innocent. At least she looked innocent, which all of New York knew wasn't true. But she sure seemed flustered as hell. She was known for her no-nonsense approach to matters of the body, for her unflinching answers to the most kinky questions. No one would mistake her for a silly female. Yet right now, she looked like a twelve-year-old with her underpants showing.

Darlene grabbed hold of him and pulled him toward one of the guest chairs. "Chase, why don't you sit down." The booth had been recarpeted since the last time he'd been in it. That had been years ago. Now, it seemed smaller, but like every other booth he'd seen—the thick carpet to mask sound, an oversize desk for the DJ and several mikes for group discussions. The console was computerized, a far cry from the equipment in place when his father had first started the station.

Darlene sat in the chair next to him. She gave him a set of headphones and found one for herself. Jamie just kept staring at him, and he wondered how long it would be before she blinked.

His attention went back to the other side of the glass where Cujo was waving wildly, trying to get Jamie's attention. Dead air was trouble. Chase decided to give her a break. He pressed the button to turn the guest mikes live.

Darlene caught on. "This is Darlene Whittaker from *Vanity Fair*. In case you've just tuned in, I'm interviewing Dr. Jamie for a feature article…"

Chase tuned her out as she explained the situation to the audience. He probably should have listened, given his role, but he was preoccupied. Jamie hadn't spoken yet. She'd run a hand through her short hair, making it a little messier than she'd probably intended, but he wasn't complaining. He liked seeing a preview of what she'd look like in his bed, hair tousled, cheeks flushed, trying to catch her breath.

There were two things that mattered to Chase. Racing and women. Not necessarily in that order. The pursuit of his two hobbies took equal amounts of time and energy. They were very similar, in fact. Both cars and women needed careful attention to make them purr. Truth be known, cars were the easier of the two. They never got emotionally involved.

"Chase, why don't you tell the listeners something about yourself."

He nodded, not taking his eyes off Jamie. "I drive cars. Sometimes, I live in New York."

"Yes, well, uh, you drive race cars, isn't that right? And didn't you win at Le Mans last year?"

"Yeah."

"And weren't you also dating Charlize Theron at that time?"

"Yeah."

"What happened?"

"She wanted a relationship."

"And what about you?"

"I was good in bed."

Darlene laughed, and Jamie's blush deepened.

He leaned over and took Jamie's right hand. It was fisted, and she tried to pull it away, but he didn't let her. "Jamie," he whispered, "what are you afraid of?"

She jerked her hand away, and in that act of defiance she seemed to gather her wits about her. She cleared her throat, moved her chair forward, adjusted her headphones. "Tell me, Mr. Newman. You seem to be a busy man with a full life. Why on earth would you want to do this?"

Good. She was back to her feisty self. "I don't have any plans for the next couple of weeks."

"You don't have any plans," she repeated. "Did you hear what Ms. Whittaker said? If we go through with this nonsense, we'll have to see each other every day. You'll have to come in to the studio and give progress reports." She shook her head. "You don't think this is completely nuts?"

"It's weird as hell, but I'm game," he said.

"There has to be more of a reason than your lack of a busy schedule."

"Why?"

"Because this is… It's absurd!"

"Is it?" Darlene asked. "Is it absurd when you tell Noelle from Brooklyn that she's not really in love with her boyfriend? Is it absurd when you teach Cindy from Queens that she's weak and spineless because she couldn't say no?"

"I never said she was spineless. Besides, that's different."

"Why? Because it's not your life on the line? Because your heart isn't at risk?"

Jamie turned her gaze to Darlene, and Chase was surprised the writer's hair didn't catch fire. This was not a mutual admiration society. These women were out for blood.

Maybe he'd been too hasty. What sounded like a laugh a few minutes ago was becoming complicated. He didn't do complicated. On the other hand, Jamie had that luscious mouth.

Darlene touched his shoulder. "Chase, have you ever seduced a woman?"

"Yep."

"How many?"

"All of them."

Darlene grinned. "So you think you can seduce Dr. Jamie?"

"Yep."

Jamie's eyes looked like they were ready to pop. "Are you serious? Every woman just falls into bed at the crook of your finger? Obviously that statement is a gross exaggeration."

"No, it's not."

"What, you're so fabulous, no woman can resist you?"

"No woman I'm paying attention to. I don't know all that much about the world, and I am, after all, only a guy who drives cars, but I do know what women want, and how to give it to them."

"Oh, please. That's the most arrogant crock of—"

"How long do you think it'll take Jamie to succumb?" Darlene asked, barely masking Jamie's curse.

He chuckled. "I don't know. It depends on how willing she is to play her part honestly."

"Explain that, please."

He turned from Darlene to Jamie. "She needs to walk into this with no prejudice. It has to be real—as if I asked her out and she said yes of her own free will."

"Jamie, how do you feel about that?"

"I think this joke has gone far enough." She lifted her cup with shaky fingers, then put it down again without taking a sip. "Why don't we hear from some listeners. Mr. Newman, thanks for being such a good sport, but you can go now."

"Not on your life," Darlene said, her tone as sharp as a knife blade. "There are only two ways this is going to end. Either you're going to come in here in two weeks, in front of Chase and all your listeners, and tell us you stayed strong, that he didn't seduce you, or you're going to admit you're a fraud."

"Ms. Whittaker, I invited you here as a courtesy. I agreed to be interviewed. I didn't sign up to be made a laughing stock."

"Oh, I'm not laughing. I'm dead-on serious. Because, Dr. Jamie, I don't believe you've ever been with a man like Chase. I don't think you've been with a real man. Because if you had, you would know that sometimes the mind takes a back seat to the body. You're just like the rest of us poor slobs, babe, and you know it. You're playing with your listeners' hearts, and their lives."

"I take what I say seriously. I've got a PhD in human sexuality. I've dedicated my life to this work."

"But you don't even date! You can't tell us you understand what we go through if you're safe inside your radio station. It's time to put up or shut up, Dr. Jamie."

Chase watched Jamie look through the window as she abruptly gave the station identification, not even trying to respond to Darlene's diatribe. Fred Holt stood with his nose practically pressed against the glass. He didn't look happy. The woman—what was her name?—the producer, was freaking out. She was yanking on Fred's coat sleeve. Chase's old buddy Cujo was grinning like the cat that ate the canary. Chase knew why, of course. Ratings. This little experiment would be a ratings monster. The Arbitrons would go through the roof.

He hadn't been involved with radio since he was a teenager, despite his father's wishes—but he knew the game. He knew what it took to be successful. His father had never understood that he found it all boring. He would never be at the mercy of numbers. Chase needed physical challenges. Excitement. The unexpected.

He turned to the lovely doctor. She still looked flushed, but the pink in her cheeks was fueled by anger now. She was trapped, and she didn't like it. It would be a challenge

to get through her defenses—to weaken her resolve. Of
course, he could do it. There was no doubt. Not because
he was Don Juan, but because women wanted to be seduced.

He understood the game, and he was an excellent
player—probably because he knew he had nothing to
lose. It was never going to develop into anything more
than some hot sex and some laughs.

This was a dumb stunt, and he shouldn't have agreed
to be part of it. He still wasn't certain he shouldn't back
out. But going for it would accomplish several things.
He'd have something to do while he waited for his next
race. He'd help the station, sort of a tip of his hat to his
dad. And he'd get Jamie into his bed.

Okay, so he didn't give a damn about the station, and
he'd never been bored a day in his life. The reason he'd
said yes was that he wanted to sleep with the sex doctor. His motive wasn't so different from Darlene's—he
wanted to show Jamie her theory was all wet.

He didn't listen to the radio often, but he did tune in
to Jamie's show whenever he had the chance. He liked
the sound of her voice, the way she laughed. In fact, after
he'd seen her the first time, the talk show had taken on
a whole new level of meaning. He'd never failed to get
turned on by Dr. Jamie. Something about her stirred him
up, made him hard. She was a fantasy, and soon she'd be
a reality.

Jamie threw her headphones on the desk as the second
commercial began. She didn't say a word as she yanked
open the heavy door. A moment later Chase saw her approach Fred. Man, she was one angry lady. Of course, he
couldn't hear the conversation, but he could read the
expressions and the gestures. Jamie didn't want to play.

"I've got her," Darlene said, her voice barely above a whisper.

Chase wondered if she realized she'd spoken aloud. "What do you want her for?"

She jerked around to stare at him. "What?"

"You've got her. But what for? What's the point?"

"Come on. You see her. Love guru? She's barely out of her teens and she's become the expert on love in New York? I'm sorry, but that's bull. If she's an expert, then I'm the Queen of England."

"Maybe she's gifted. People are, you know."

"Gifted? I'll tell you how she's gifted. She doesn't get embarrassed about body parts. She has this sweet little voice, and this angelic little face, and she talks like a biology teacher on steroids. That doesn't mean she knows a thing about love or relationships. She's a fraud, and I'm going to prove it."

He nodded. "Nothing personal, though, right? Just doing the noble thing to protect the innocent ears of Manhattan youth?"

"Laugh if you want, but you know what? I am doing the noble thing. A fraud is a fraud is a fraud. She may look great on billboards, but she's a menace on the airwaves."

"And you're going to stop her?"

"Damn straight."

"What if it doesn't work? What if she doesn't fall for my charms?"

Darlene's eyes narrowed. "You won't let that happen. I know some things about you, Chase. You didn't say yes for me. You want to prove her wrong just as much as I do."

He shrugged. "Maybe. Which means I probably shouldn't do it. I don't have anything against Jamie."

"Come on, Chase...
a marketing trick... She'll only...
comes along."

The doc...
whole de...
take her to...
And he held a...

Chase wasn't...
kid. And damn, sh...
was only radio. Just a s...
pulled. In the long run, it...

Despite what he'd said to...
Of course, he'd use all the weap...
Jamie said no, it would stay no.

He knew he sounded like an arrog...
didn't care about that. The truth was th...
wanted to be appreciated; to be admired...
were, not just what they looked like—althoug...
ignore that, either. Women wanted to be swept aw...
wanted a man to run the show. They wanted to ge...
and truly laid.

What the hell. It was all just a game, right?

JAMIE HELD IT TOGETHER just long enough to finish the
show. The moment she was off the air, she shot out of the
booth and found Marcy and Fred in Fred's office.

She walked in and planted a fist on her hip. "I'm not
doing this."

Marcy got to her feet, moving between her and Fred,
a human blockade. "I'll handle this, Jamie."

"There's nothing to handle. I refuse."

"Ladies, take a seat."

Marcy sat, and once Jamie caught a glimpse of the

s face, she sat down, too. It didn't
g to budge.

ny idea how many people have called
past hour? More than a thousand, and
mber we logged. Most people couldn't
e gotten calls from the *Post* and the CBS
of whom want to do stories on this."

sn't make it right, Fred." Jamie leaned for-
ng her hands on his desk. "I won't subject
his kind of humiliation. No job is worth that."

y? That's surprising coming from you. Didn't
me last week you'd do anything to get national
ation?"

didn't mean it literally, for God's sake. Fred, the
wants me to go out with that...that...man."

That man is going to save your butt," Fred said. "You
know that his father built this station—that Chase
imself could have owned the station, if he'd wanted to."

"So?"

"So you think he's going to let you fall on your fanny?
The man is his father's son. He's going to do what's right."

Jamie slid back in her chair and crossed her arms over
her chest. "Great. So not only am I going to be publicly
humiliated, I'm going to do exactly what I've been accused of. It's called fraud, Fred, and they have laws about
that."

"All you have to do is not sleep with him. You said
yourself, that was no problem."

"That's exactly my point. Nothing can possibly happen. You know that, and I know that. Don't you see? It's
not a contest. It's not even clever. It's just *that woman's*
idea of clever."

Behind her, a man cleared his throat, and she spun
around to see Chase at the door.

"Come on, Chase. This kid is a flash in the pan. She's a marketing trick. She'll only be around until the next fad comes along."

The door behind them opened. Jamie walked in, her whole demeanor spelling out her defeat. This stunt could take her to the top, could make her a household name. And he held all the cards.

Chase wasn't crazy about that. She seemed like a nice kid. And damn, she was pretty. But what the hell? It was only radio. Just a stunt, like all the other stunts he'd pulled. In the long run, it didn't matter.

Despite what he'd said to Darlene, he would play fair. Of course, he'd use all the weapons in his arsenal. But if Jamie said no, it would stay no.

He knew he sounded like an arrogant bastard. But he didn't care about that. The truth was the truth. Women wanted to be appreciated; to be admired for who they were, not just what they looked like—although he didn't ignore that, either. Women wanted to be swept away. They wanted a man to run the show. They wanted to get well and truly laid.

What the hell. It was all just a game, right?

JAMIE HELD IT TOGETHER just long enough to finish the show. The moment she was off the air, she shot out of the booth and found Marcy and Fred in Fred's office.

She walked in and planted a fist on her hip. "I'm not doing this."

Marcy got to her feet, moving between her and Fred, a human blockade. "I'll handle this, Jamie."

"There's nothing to handle. I refuse."

"Ladies, take a seat."

Marcy sat, and once Jamie caught a glimpse of the

expression on Fred's face, she sat down, too. It didn't mean she was going to budge.

"Do you have any idea how many people have called the station in the past hour? More than a thousand, and that's just the number we logged. Most people couldn't get through. I've gotten calls from the *Post* and the CBS affiliate, both of whom want to do stories on this."

"That doesn't make it right, Fred." Jamie leaned forward, putting her hands on his desk. "I won't subject myself to this kind of humiliation. No job is worth that."

"Really? That's surprising coming from you. Didn't you tell me last week you'd do anything to get national syndication?"

"I didn't mean it literally, for God's sake. Fred, the witch wants me to go out with that…that…man."

"That man is going to save your butt," Fred said. "You do know that his father built this station—that Chase himself could have owned the station, if he'd wanted to."

"So?"

"So you think he's going to let you fall on your fanny? The man is his father's son. He's going to do what's right."

Jamie slid back in her chair and crossed her arms over her chest. "Great. So not only am I going to be publicly humiliated, I'm going to do exactly what I've been accused of. It's called fraud, Fred, and they have laws about that."

"All you have to do is not sleep with him. You said yourself, that was no problem."

"That's exactly my point. Nothing can possibly happen. You know that, and I know that. Don't you see? It's not a contest. It's not even clever. It's just *that woman's* idea of clever."

Behind her, a man cleared his throat, and she spun around to see Chase at the door.

"Sorry to butt in, but I figure I have a stake in this, so I might as well hear what's going on."

"Come in, Chase." Fred waved him over to a straight-backed chair by his file cabinet, but Chase chose to sit in the leather wing chair by the bookcase. He sank down and opened the front of his jacket, revealing a plain white T-shirt. His knees spread wide in that totally masculine, completely arrogant manner of men who think they're God's gift.

"I was just telling Jamie about your ties to the station."

Chase nodded. Jamie didn't want to stare at him, but tearing her gaze away was proving a difficult task. Finally, she managed to turn in her seat so her back was to him.

"Hey, I don't care one way or another," Chase said. "If she doesn't want to do this…"

"Jamie can't do this." Marcy stood up and walked to the file cabinet. Jamie noted that from there she could see all three of the players. "It doesn't matter what that woman said. Jamie isn't a fraud. She has nothing to prove. Whittaker is just looking for cheap publicity."

"And you're not?" Chase asked. "Isn't that the whole point?"

Fred nodded. "I can't force you to do this. But I'll tell you this—we have a chance at syndication without it. A chance. But if you do this thing—if you go out with Chase and keep your legs crossed—we'll be syndicated before the end of the year. Guaranteed."

"I don't want it that badly."

"Is that so?" Fred asked. "You're young and you have a brilliant career ahead of you. Why blow it over something like this? You play along for a couple of weeks, Chase says whatever he has to, and that's it. Except that we have a hell of a lot of new listeners. Believe me, it'll be worth it once we're national. The rest of your life depends on your decision here. You can make the best of it, or you can walk. Wasn't it you who told me you don't believe in half measures? That you were going to get syndicated before you were thirty if it killed you?"

"Wait a minute." Marcy shook her head as if she could hardly believe what was happening. "This is nuts. Why don't we all just think it through? Who says we have to decide right now? By tomorrow, things will be much clearer and—"

Jamie stopped listening. She had a decision to make. She could walk out now and not look back. She'd find another radio gig. She was number one in her market, for God's sake. On the other hand, what if Darlene was right? That she had no business telling New York, let alone the nation, a thing about life or love. It wasn't as if she hadn't wondered—as if her own doubts hadn't made her contemplate quitting. Did she have any right to help all those callers? Wasn't it only appropriate that she should be tested by her own fire?

She wouldn't sleep with him. No amount of charisma was going to change that. So why not go along with it? She loved this job. She wanted to be syndicated. She wanted to prove to herself and her family that she'd made the right choice. And lord, she didn't want Darlene to win.

She put up her hand, stopping Marcy mid-sentence. "All right."

"What?" Marcy headed back to her chair. "Jamie—"

"I said, all right. I'll do it. But I'll only do it on the up-and-up." She turned her head so she could see Chase.

He looked at her with a curious smile. "You're sure about this?"

She nodded.

He stood. Walked slowly over to her. She almost

bolted. With each step he took, her heart beat faster and her thoughts grew fuzzier. He was so big. So imposing. So unbelievably handsome. The truth was, he scared the hell out of her.

He stopped, but only when he was very, very close. He took her hand and pulled her gently to her feet. His fingers went to the bottom of her chin, and he lifted her face, forcing her to meet his gaze.

"Are you sure?"

She nodded, even though she wasn't sure at all—especially now that she could see his eyes. They were dark, mysterious, and they saw too much. That was it, of course. Why he frightened her. It was the way he looked at her, as if he could see all her secrets.

Still holding her chin, he leaned forward, and she understood what his intention was seconds before his lips touched hers. She didn't jerk away. She didn't push him back. She just closed her eyes.

Soft at first, teasing. His breath, coffee with a hint of peppermint. His size, imposing, almost threatening. But his lips were tender, even as the kiss deepened.

Somewhere out there, she heard Marcy's voice. Then the sound of her own heart beating drowned out even that.

Her lips parted, and he slipped inside her. Still soft. Achingly soft. He found her tongue and touched it, letting her taste him, igniting a tingle that spread through her like molten lava. Before the heat dissipated, he was gone. His tongue, his lips, his fingers. All gone.

She heard him chuckle, then she opened her eyes. He hadn't moved away.

"I'll give you tonight," he whispered so that only she could hear. "But tomorrow, you're mine."

"We, uh, need to discuss this," she said, surprised at how slurred her words sounded. As if she were drunk.

"We will. Tomorrow." His gaze roamed over her from face to breasts, then back again. "And put on your good underwear." He winked, then he was out Fred's door.

"Jamie?"

As she came out of her daze, the sounds of the room became clear again and she turned to Marcy. "Yes?"

"Honey, you don't need to do this."

"Yes, I do."

"He's dangerous."

"I know."

Marcy shook her head. "It's a mistake."

"Probably. But don't worry. I'm not helpless here. I can take care of myself. You know, it's not all just talk. I do believe what I say on the air."

"I know."

Jamie smiled, although Marcy's doubt sat heavy in her chest. Who was she kidding? She knew books, not men. Definitely not men like Chase Newman.

She wasn't one to cuss. She'd always believed that if people tried, they could come up with better words, more exact words. But for the second time that night, all she could say was, "Holy f—"

3

CHASE SETTLED MORE COMFORTABLY into the black leather armchair and cradled the phone between his ear and shoulder. Rupert Davidson, his business manager, did like to talk. And talk. If Rupert wasn't so good with money, Chase would have fired him years ago. No, that wasn't true. Rupert had been part of his life for too long. He had been his father's closest friend, and he'd taken care of Chase and his mother after Jack had died. What everyone except Rupert knew was that he'd fallen in love with Chase's mother. Nothing would be done about it until after a proper mourning period, of course. Rupert would never disgrace Jack's memory.

Chase almost thought of Rupert as his stepfather, which he could have been if he'd only asked. But his mother couldn't or wouldn't urge him on, preferring the romanticism of an unrequited lover to anything real. It was an odd drama, played out over the years, one which he'd learned to accept.

"...I want to roll the CDs over. I've done some investigation about GF Labs, and it's risky, but I think it might be worth it—at least for a few hundred thousand."

"Do it." Chase looked at his coffee. It was on the

ebony-and-teak coffee table, out of his reach. He'd have to move to get it, and he'd just gotten comfortable. So what was more important? The way the chair molded perfectly to his back and shoulders? Or caffeine?

"Have you read the prospectus?"

"I don't need to. I have you."

"Dammit, son, don't you think it's time you accepted some of your responsibilities? Even one? You're thirty-one. You can't keep living like this forever."

Chase disagreed, but he didn't say so. He grabbed hold of the phone and leaned forward, bringing his coffee back with him. He tried to find the same position as before, but it was gone. He sipped the Kona blend, disappointed to find it was lukewarm. "Rupert, do we have to talk about this now? It's not even nine o'clock. I promise I'll call this afternoon, and we can fight all you want."

"I don't want to fight."

"Right. You just want me to do things your way."

"Not my way. The sensible way."

"Rupert, you're the most goddamn sensible man in New York."

"That's nothing to be ashamed of."

"I couldn't agree more." He liked Rupert, in his old-fashioned suits, with his antiquated sense of honor and obligation. He was refreshing, in an odd sort of way.

"How long are you here for this time?"

"A couple of weeks. Just till the racing season starts in Europe."

"You're going to see her, aren't you?"

"Yeah."

"And not just for an hour. She was hurt by that, Chase."

He closed his eyes, remembering the last visit with his mother. He loved her, but sometimes it wasn't easy to like her. To say she wasn't thrilled with his lifestyle was an understatement. She wanted him to be like her, like his father. To get married, have some kids. She'd told him he embarrassed her. That he was disgracing his father's name.

"I'll try, Rupert."

"Don't try. Do it. She's the only mother you'll ever have."

"Okay, Yoda. I promise."

"Yoda?"

"Never mind. You go ahead and put my money where you think best. I trust you, Rupert. You've never steered me wrong."

"Thank you, Chase. But I'm not crazy about doing so much without your input."

"I know about fast cars and women, old man. You have a question about either one, I'm the guy you come to."

"Amusing. Very amusing."

"You take care, Rupert. And, for God's sake, propose to my mother already, would you?" Chase smiled as he heard the sputtering on the other end of the line. He decided to do Rupert a favor and hung up.

Cars and women. He'd said that last night, hadn't he? It was true. He'd put restrictions on his life just like his mother had put restrictions on hers. No wonder they clashed. They were too much alike.

He got up and went to the window. He liked to watch Manhattan wake up. His suite was on the top floor of the Four Seasons hotel, and he stayed here every time he came to New York. They knew him here, and they made sure he was comfortable. It was easier this way. Maids, room service, desk clerks. That's what he was used to. He had a place just like it at the George V in Paris, and another at the Chateau Marmont in L.A.

His gaze moved to the park. He loved it there, with all

the kids on Rollerblades and the pigeons and the women with their strollers. Central Park always made him feel better, regardless of the season. Some of his favorite walks had been in the snow among the naked branches.

As he stared at the blanket of trees, ripe green at the height of summer, he thought about Jamie. He'd decided last night to call off the ridiculous stunt. He didn't need the aggravation, or the publicity. Sure Jamie was hot, but there were a million hot women in the city. He would call her today and tell her. She'd be relieved. He would be, too. Although, there was one thing he'd regret. He wanted to understand why she scared her so. Animals and children liked him. So what was she afraid of?

Such a paradox. The way she spoke was at complete odds with the way she looked. In fact, she was full of contradictions, and that certainly had its appeal. He enjoyed peeling back the layers. Not his own, mind you. But an interesting woman—that was something to be grateful for.

Those eyes of hers. One minute, radiating confidence enough to take on the world. The next, as frightened as those of a little mouse. Which was it? It occurred to him that he wanted to find out.

So okay, maybe he wouldn't call her. Maybe he'd go in person. She'd probably be up by now, right?

JAMIE STRUGGLED OUT of her dream and realized the banging she heard wasn't a demented jailer pounding on her cage, but someone knocking on her door. She glanced at the alarm clock on her nightstand. Eleven-fifteen. Odd, she never slept in. Her routine was to finish up her show at eleven, be home just after midnight, in bed by one and then up at nine the next morning.

Another round of knocking spurred her out of bed.

She padded across her wooden floor from the bedroom to the living room, then to the door with its five locks. Up on tiptoes, she looked through the peephole.

No one was there. That was weird. She undid each of the locks, poked her head outside the door. Nope. The hallway was empty. Had it been her nightmare? Her dream about being locked into something from which she couldn't escape had obvious connections to real life. She'd think about that later. Right now, her mind was on other urgent business. She closed the door and locked the dead bolt, then scurried to the bathroom.

Just as she was lifting her mouthwash to gargle, she heard the knocking again. She wiped her mouth with the back of her arm, then returned to the front door. This time when she looked through the peephole, the hallway wasn't empty.

Her heart thudded as she recognized the man standing at her door. Oh, God. What in heaven's name… He wasn't supposed to be here. She rocked back on her heels and ran her hand through her hair, which, thank you, made her look more like a porcupine than a person when she first got out of bed. To say nothing of her caked eye makeup, or the nightshirt that may have been snazzy back in 1994 but had gone straight downhill after that Laundromat incident in college.

She wouldn't answer. She didn't have to. He should have called. Because there was no time to shower, let alone buy a new outfit.

He knocked again. Then just as she thought he was leaving, she heard voices and she cringed. What if he knew she was here? That she was completely undone by his presence?

She lifted herself to peephole level again. Mr. Wojewodka, the super, stood next to Chase. He had out his

master key chain. The thing was monstrous, and when
hooked, it pulled his belt and his pants down a good inch.
Why was he searching through them now? Mr. Wojewodka was always harping on her to lock her doors, to
carry pepper spray, to call him if she was ever in trouble.
And now—

With a familiar squeal, the key entered the door. *He
was letting Chase into her apartment!*

She'd never make it to the bedroom. Was the living
room clean? No. Not important. Hiding was more important. Oh, God, the closest hiding place was the closet,
and she made it there in two seconds flat. After a few
more spent flailing about the knob, she pulled the door
closed behind her. She forced herself to stand perfectly
still, even though she was shaking with adrenaline, and
listen as the two men entered her living room.

"She's a good kid," Wojewodka said in his thick Polish
accent. "Gives me no trouble."

"Not even with her men friends?"

"What men friends? The girl is like a monk. She
doesn't see anyone, except her crazy brother."

"Really?"

Jamie rested her forehead on the cool wood of the
door as she plotted ways to kill her superintendent and
Chase Newman. If she couldn't kill them, she'd sue their
tails off. Talk about invasion of privacy! Or breaking and
entering. Yeah. That was worse. But she didn't think they
did any breaking. Just entering. Was entering against the
law? Had to be.

"I really appreciate this, Max," Chase said. "I didn't
like the idea of leaving this outside."

"I just hope she doesn't get mad at me."

"She won't."

Like hell. Jamie hadn't noticed Chase carrying anything. What was he leaving? She tried to see through the crack between the door and the frame, but that was useless. Maybe if she could get higher. She reached for the doorknob to get some balance, but even on tiptoes she couldn't see squat.

She gripped the knob with her hand as she flattened her feet, noticing something as she did so. A big, scary lump formed in her chest. The knob hadn't budged. She closed her eyes and said a short prayer, then she wiggled it. The knob didn't wiggle. It didn't do a damn thing.

Locked. How? Why? No, no, no. This wasn't funny. Wait. There had to be a way to unlock it, right? She ran her hand under the knob, over the wood, her movements growing faster as the repercussions hit her. *No, no, no, no.* This couldn't be happening. She'd be trapped. Better trapped than caught by Newman, though. The thought of how she'd look set her cheeks on fire.

Wait a minute. Maybe she should let him set her free. Then he'd have to explain what he was doing entering her apartment. But first, she'd have to explain what she was doing in her closet. Or would she? A person had a right to be in her own closet.

She lifted her hand to knock, then let it drop again.

"That's a big box," the super said.

"Yep."

"You gonna tell me what's in it?"

"Nope."

So Chase hadn't been putting on an act last night. He really did talk like Gary Cooper.

"I get it," Mr. Wojewodka said. "It's a surprise."

"Right."

Footsteps, followed by a *creak* of the front door. They were leaving. If she didn't do something now, she'd be locked in here for who knows how long—which would have been okay if only she hadn't decided to brush her teeth before taking care of her…other business in the bathroom this morning. Clenching her teeth and vowing revenge, she knocked on the closet door.

"Did you hear something?"

She didn't hear a response. Mr. Wojewodka must have shaken his head.

She knocked again, louder this time, cursing Chase, Darlene Whittaker, Fred Holt and everyone else connected to this malarky.

"Wait a minute." That was Chase's voice. "It's coming from the closet."

"Nah, couldn't be."

"Just hold on."

His boots sounded terribly loud on her floor. It was like listening to the firing squad take their positions. She wished like crazy that she'd at least had time to brush her hair.

He pulled on the door, unlocked it, pulled again—and this time the door swung open. She crossed her arms over her chest.

Chase looked at her with a completely calm face, as if finding her in the closet was the most normal thing in the world. But after a few seconds his head tilted slightly to the right. "Are you trying to tell me you're gay?"

"No, I'm not." She stepped around him, making sure they didn't touch. Wondering if anyone had ever died of embarrassment. Perhaps she would be the first.

"I mean, if you are gay, that's all right."

"I'm not gay," she said, not daring to look at him.

"Ah. So actually being in the closet wasn't symbolic or anything."

"No. I was…" She cast about for an explanation, any explanation. "I was looking for my cat."

"You got a cat?" Mr. Wojewodka asked.

She whirled around to find the building superintendent at the front door. Great. A witness to her humiliation. It would be all over the building by rush hour.

"Did I say cat? I meant hat. I was looking for my hat."

Mr. Wojewodka looked at Chase. Chase looked back.

"Which," she said, raising her voice, "is completely beside the point. Care to tell me why you broke into my apartment?"

"I didn't." Chase nodded at Max. "He was nice enough to let me in."

She frowned. "Why on earth would he do that?"

"Because I didn't want to leave that outside."

She turned to where he pointed—to a long, gold box perched on her couch. Flowers. It had to be. Because what else would be in a flower box?

Quelling her urge to race over and rip off the top of the box, she faced Chase again. "Sometimes when a person doesn't answer the door, there's a reason."

"Right. I should have figured you were locked in the closet."

"I wasn't."

His right brow rose.

"It doesn't matter where I was, or what I was doing. My home should be private." She marched over to the door and Max, her bare feet slapping on the hard wood. "Mr. Wojewodka, I'm surprised at you."

He had the decency to look embarrassed as he leaned toward her. "Do you know who he is?"

"Yes, I do. Do *you?*"

"Yeah, sure. He's the top-seeded race-car driver in America. In the world."

"And this makes him able to enter any apartment he wishes?"

"He was your friend. I did him a favor."

"He's not my friend."

"Right," Chase agreed. "I'm just supposed to seduce her. That's all."

Jamie winced. "About that…"

Chase moved over to the couch. It was a normal couch, but when he sat down it looked very small. She'd gotten it at an estate sale four years ago, along with the matching wing chair. She'd had them reupholstered in a cheery floral print, which Chase's presence also changed. She'd never realized the material was so feminine.

"About last night—" she continued.

"You don't have to apologize."

"What? I wasn't going to."

"Oh, okay." He smiled at her, and his teeth were slightly crooked, which for some reason made him even sexier. His eyes were perfect and so was his hair and his chest. The fact that his nose was a little crooked didn't detract from his face. On the contrary, like the small flaw of his teeth, it made him look more ruggedly handsome than if it had been straight.

"What do you mean, apologize?"

"Nothing. It doesn't matter."

"Yes, it does."

"I just figured, with you being in that bind and with me volunteering to help you out…"

"I wasn't the one who asked you to play this game. That was Whittaker, remember?"

He nodded. "She would have done it, you know."

"Done what?"

"She would have smeared your reputation, made sure there was plenty of bad press about you. She doesn't much care for you."

Jamie's hands fell to her sides. "Why? I never did anything to her."

"Don't tell me you don't get it. You're too smart to play dumb."

"Oh, you think she hates me because I'm successful? Because people listen to me?"

"That. And the other."

She wasn't about to ask what he meant. This whole conversation was going poorly, and the smart thing to do would be to stop right here, right now, and get Chase and his number-one fan the hell out of here.

She put her hands on her hips and opened her mouth to tell him to leave, but before the words came out, his gaze moved from her face to her chest. As he blatantly stared, his face changed. He smiled. Devilish, wicked, hungry. She felt her nipples harden and poke at her flimsy T-shirt.

"You're beautiful," he said, his voice low and seductive.

She turned away, crossing her arms once more. "Please leave. And take the box with you."

Max stepped outside the door, leaving her with Chase. She wanted him gone, too, even as his compliment swirled inside her head. He thought she was beautiful. It wasn't that she saw herself as ugly…but beautiful? That wasn't what mattered about her. She was smart, and she was ambitious, and she was able to talk to people. She'd never gone after beauty. Oh, she'd had compliments before, but as her mother was so fond of saying, beauty was the shallow refuge of incompetence.

He came up behind her, and her heart beat so hard she thought it might burst. When his hand touched her shoulder, her knees weakened and she forgot how to breathe.

It was nuts. Crazy. Why was she feeling like this? Chase was just a man. No big deal.

He turned her around until she faced him. Her arms were still covering her breasts, but from the way he looked at her, it was too little, too late. He'd seen her reaction. She closed her eyes.

"Jamie."

She shook her head. "Please, go."

"Jamie, look at me."

She didn't want to. But she couldn't help it. Her eyes opened to find him closer still, close enough for her to see the gold in his dark brown eyes.

"I was going to call it off," he whispered. "Then I started thinking about you. By the time I got here, I'd changed my mind."

"Why?"

He smiled, and her tummy got tight with a wave of desire. "There's something about you."

"What?"

He shook his head. "I don't know yet. I'll tell you when I find out."

"You don't have to. The hell with Whittaker and her magazine. I don't care what she says about me."

"Neither do I. But I do want to spend the next two weeks getting to know you, magazine or no magazine."

"I don't see why. You're a big-shot racing guy. You date movie stars. You live a different kind of life than me. Frankly, I'd bore you silly."

"You let me be the judge of that."

"What if I don't want to see you?"

He leaned forward until their lips almost touched, pausing for an instant, and then he captured her lower lip between his front teeth. A second later, he let her go, only to steal her breath with a kiss, his soft lips on hers, his tongue teasing her mouth open. Her eyes fluttered closed and her arms moved from her chest to his back. With gentle pressure, he rubbed his chest against hers, sweeping against her nipples. Pleasure and heat flowed from her breasts down to her stomach, and then lower still. She squeezed her thigh muscles, but the feeling didn't go away.

He did something terribly wicked with his tongue, thrusting it inside her, then pulling back, as if showing her what he wanted to do to her body. Goose bumps covered her flesh as vivid pictures came to mind. Him, naked— oh, lordy—thrusting into her, making her scream.

She whimpered. He moved his lips from her mouth to her ear. "I'm going to explore every inch of you, Jamie," he whispered, his hot breath making her shiver. "I'm going to know you better than you know yourself. And I'm going to give you pleasure you've never even dreamed of."

Then he stepped away, and, before she could catch her breath, she heard the front door close.

When she got it together enough to walk, she went to the couch and took off the top of the gold box. Two dozen red roses were flared beautifully, the long stems stripped of any thorns. She picked up the small card lying to the side of the flowers: "Dear Jamie, I dreamed about us. You had roses. See you tonight, Chase."

She picked up the box and brought it to her face so she could smell the flowers. His scent lingered, despite the sweet aroma of the gift. She could still feel his hard chest, his big hands, his soft, talented mouth.

Oh boy. She was in trouble. Bad trouble. She headed for the kitchen and a vase. Her first flowers, ever. And they were from a man who was from a completely foreign world, a man with enough experience to host his own radio sex show.

She put the box on the counter and stared out her window. The view from here sucked. It was just another building. And when she looked down, all she saw was a walkway where no one ever walked.

She couldn't let him into her life, not even for a moment. He was dangerous. He did scary things to her body. To her mind. Given even the slightest opportunity, he'd find out. Even if he never touched her down there, he'd know. He'd see it in her eyes, feel it when she trembled in his arms. And if he found out—the rest of the world would find out, and where would she be then?

No one had ever given her roses before. Because no one had ever been close enough before. She'd been busy with school, with the radio show. She'd never dreamed things would happen so quickly for her, or so publicly. But they had, and here she was.

Whittaker was right. She was a fraud. The honorable thing to do would be to quit. But that would kill her. She'd never loved anything the way she loved her show, loved its callers. And she knew she was helping. Honestly.

There was just the one problem, the one that could ruin everything if it ever got out. The fact that she was, at the ripe old age of twenty-six, a virgin.

4

JAMIE GOT TO THE STATION a little after five-thirty. Determined not to dig herself in deeper, she had spent the day trying to figure out a way to extricate herself from this mess without ending up fired. Unfortunately, all the ideas she'd come up with so far required either some form of magic or breaking several major laws.

She stopped at the reception desk, where the night guy, Geoffrey, smiled broadly as he gathered her mail. Over six foot five and thin as a rail, the twenty-year-old had neon-orange hair and more piercings than her aunt Emma's pin cushion. The pierced body parts were offset, of course, by tattoos ranging from the sublime (a perfect, tiny red heart at the base of his neck) to the ridiculous (Bart Simpson, bent over, pants down, eyes drawn on the buttocks).

She shifted her briefcase to her left hand as she took the unusually large stack of mail. "Thanks."

"My pleasure."

His tone made her pause. So did his grin, which had widened dangerously, exposing the braces on his molars.

"What?"

"Nothing." He arched his right brow. "Except that the

switchboard has been lit up all day. I swear, girlfriend, Mr. Holt has a major woody over this little stunt of yours. Brilliant." He crossed his arms over his Amazon.com T-shirt and idly fingered his nipple ring through the material. "And excuse the hell out of me, but could Chase Newman be more divine? I don't think so."

"Why don't *you* go out with him?"

He sighed. "If only."

She shook her head as she headed toward her office. File cabinets on both walls made the hallway narrow, and if someone had to find a file, all traffic came to a halt. Oddly enough, in her time here she'd only seen a file drawer open once or twice. She imagined they were filled with old ad logs and personnel files.

It wasn't until she neared her door that she heard her name from across the way. Elliot Wolf, the program manager, waved at her while he talked on the phone. Jamie sighed. Like the Energizer bunny, this nightmare kept on going and going and going....

"Sit," Elliot said, then to whomever was on the phone he added, "Tonight at the Palm II. *Ciao*."

She didn't want to sit. She didn't want to talk. She was cranky and getting crankier by the minute.

"So," he said, running a hand through his Brad Pitt hair, complete with dark roots. However, the likeness ended there. From the forehead down, Elliot looked eerily like a young Vincent Price, mustache and all. On the gaunt side, with a voice a little too high, he devoured scary movies like Raisinets, and his hobby, like Vincent's, was gourmet cooking.

"Elliot, I have work to do."

"I know. This'll just take a minute. Sit."

She obeyed, giving him a pained sigh in protest. She hated the chairs in his office. Leather and chrome, they tilted back, making it hard to get out of them again. But they looked chic, and Elliot loved chic. He'd decorated modern, with a very expensive, very ugly Chuck Close print dominating the room. He never had anything on his desk but his notebook computer, as clutter was one of his pet peeves. He had no such qualms about his secretary's desk.

"Here's the scoop." Elliot perched on the edge of the credenza. "We're running highlights of your shows for the next two weeks. Sound bites the other DJs will play before commercials. I'm working with Cujo on the reels. We've set up a separate phone line for people to call in their comments and suggestions. Holt is planning a major ad campaign, which means we need you and Newman for photos. Greg Gorman is going to do the shoot, but he only has two hours on Tuesday available, so if you have something scheduled at eleven, cancel it."

Jamie sat perfectly still, afraid that if she moved she'd throw up all over his Berber rug.

Either Elliot didn't see her distress or he chose to ignore it. "We've already heard from Independence. They love it. They want it. And dammit, Jamie, you'd better sweep Newman off his goddamn feet. I'm not kidding. We need this to happen."

With her education and résumé, she felt reasonably sure she could get a job at McDonald's. Because she certainly wasn't going to be working in radio much longer. What really got to her was that yesterday her world had been nothing but roses. Now, all she had were thorns.

"Why aren't you smiling?"

"There's nothing to smile about. I can't do this, Elliot. I mean it."

His pale face grew paler. "Don't do this to me, Jamie."

"I'm not doing it to you. I'm not doing it because it's

a terrible idea. There's no way in hell I'm going to let Chase, or any other man, seduce me. Not in two weeks or a hundred. So what's the point?"

"Publicity." He leaned forward, putting his hands together as if in prayer. "This is the best thing that's happened to this station since I came on board. Don't you get it? We all win with this. You get syndicated, I get a monster raise, Fred gets to be the big hero, and Marcy can name her own price."

Jamie couldn't look at the desperation in his eyes. "I never signed up for this. My personal life should be my own."

He leaned back. "In a perfect world. But, honey, this is radio. And opportunities like this don't fall in your lap very often."

She grunted. "Opportunities. Right."

"It is an opportunity. If you use it. You're smart, now be savvy. Milk this baby until it's dry."

"Is that it?"

He nodded. "Don't forget about Tuesday."

She hoisted herself out of the chair and headed toward his door. She stopped there, facing him head on. "No. You have pictures of me. I'll play along, but I won't help." She left the office.

"Jamie…"

She just kept walking.

CHASE LOCKED UP HIS BIKE, grabbed his helmet and walked into the radio station. It was almost eleven, and Jamie was nearly done with her show.

He wanted to see her. Except for racing, little excited him these days. Not even other women. One was much like another, and while his libido was always fully engaged, his interest rarely went beyond the bed. Jamie was interesting. He'd thought a lot about why, and the only thing he could come up with was that she wasn't at all what she appeared to be.

His last "girlfriend," for want of a more accurate description, had been exceptionally beautiful. A model, in fact, who had surprised him with her intelligence and curiosity. But for two weeks he'd watched her primp in front of any mirror she could find, anguish over the right dress, pour all of her energy onto the pages of *Vogue*. She'd wept when he'd said goodbye, but she'd made sure her mascara hadn't run.

Jamie was probably more of the same. Not that she was obsessed with her looks, though he felt pretty certain she was obsessed with her work. But, hell, this was only going to last a couple of weeks, and she did present a challenge.

He wanted to see what she'd do. And he wanted to sleep with her.

He'd tried a lot of things in his life, almost everything at least once. He wasn't into games, or sex that required a bunch of props. But something about Jamie made him want to pull out all the stops. That innocent act of hers fired him up. What would it be like to tie her to the bedpost and make love to her until she begged for mercy? That image had plagued him all day. Of course, he'd have to work up to that. She wasn't about to give in without a fight.

The receptionist's eyes widened as he walked into the office, but Chase was used to that. As celebrities went, he wasn't a real contender, but he did get great seats in restaurants and theaters, along with the occasional rabid fan. He smiled at the young man. He didn't get the whole piercing thing, though. What was the point? But to each his own.

"Mr. Newman."

"Chase."

The smile the young man flashed turned flirtatious. Chase wasn't interested personally, but like piercings, the flirting didn't bother him.

"She's got about ten minutes left of her show."

"Thanks. I'll just go on back." He headed down the hallway, and, as always, the ghost of his father floated on the walls, in the sound his boots made on the thin carpet. Chase tried hard not to remember too much. Not because the memories were painful but because they made him feel weak. He missed his father. He missed the sound of his voice, the way he looked in his dark suits.

A publicity poster of Jamie brought him back to the present. He studied her for a moment. Mostly her eyes. They were so damn big, almond shaped, framed with thick, dark lashes. Her nose, in comparison, was small, but her lips...ah, man, they were great. Just right. Plush and smooth... He hurried past the poster toward the booth.

He stopped at the production booth first. Cujo waved him in. Chase liked him, even though the guy was strange as hell—maybe because of it. Cujo was the ultimate techno-geek. His long blond hair was always unkempt, his chin most times in need of a shave. He lived in jeans and Metallica T-shirts, and he loved his job almost as much as he loved to smoke a joint at the end of the night.

"Uno momento." Cujo toggled some dimmers on the board, bringing up a commercial for cell phones. "How you doin', bro?"

Chase shook his hand. "Hanging in."

"That's what counts." Cujo nodded toward the broadcast booth. "You be careful in there. She's a mite prickly."

"Oh?"

"She told a caller to quit jerking off."

"And that's not her usual modus operandi?"

"Jamie? Hell, no. She believes everyone is worth saving. Man, she should meet a few of my friends. That'd change her tune."

Chase turned toward the window. Jamie sat behind the desk like the captain of a spaceship, her controls at her fingertips, the great, fuzzy mike inches from her mouth. She'd seen him. She didn't appear overjoyed. In fact, her scowl seemed downright unfriendly.

It was showtime.

"What did Jon say this morning?" Jamie said into the mike, ignoring Chase with due diligence, even when he sat down and put on his own set of headphones.

"He said he forgot that we had a date," said the caller. "He's the one that wanted to go out tonight."

Jamie turned a quarter of an inch in her chair. Away from him. "Gabby, we've talked about this before. Jon has a habit of forgetting dates."

"But why?"

"I don't know. But I do know you can't keep doing this."

"Doing what?"

"Depending on Jon for your happiness. Gabby, do you honestly believe he has your best interest at heart?"

Jamie shot Chase a quick glance. He leaned back in his chair, put his feet up on Jamie's desk and clamped his hands behind his neck. He closed his eyes, listening to Jamie's voice, letting his imagination run full throttle.

"But, Dr. Jamie, he said he loved me," Gabby said. She plucked another tissue from the box on the coffee table and wiped her eyes. Usually, Dr. Jamie understood. In the past few months, she'd been about the only one who understood.

"Does he show you?"

"Sure."

"How?"

"Well, he tells me I'm pretty and he likes my hair."

"I didn't ask if he told you he loved you. I asked if he shows you."

"I don't understand."

"That's right. I don't think you do. What matters is how he treats you, Gabby. If he puts your feelings ahead of his own. If he respects you and honors you, and he shows you kindness."

"He does."

"Does he?"

Gabby looked at the phone, then put it back to her ear. "Well, not all the time. But no one could do that."

"You don't think so?" Dr. Jamie sounded a little upset. "Tell me something, Gabby. Do you wait all day for Jon to call? For him to come over? Does life begin when he's there and fade when he's not?"

"Well, sure." Gabby looked over at the dining room table. She'd paid almost five dollars for the flowers in her mother's favorite vase. And she'd put out the company china. She'd bought him the knife he'd been looking at in his magazine, and she'd wrapped it real pretty with the bow-making machine she'd picked up at a garage sale two months ago. As of four o'clock this afternoon they'd been going together for two years. She remembered their first date like a photograph. Everything about it had been perfect. Her dress. His smile. The way he'd kissed her. But lately he hadn't seemed real excited to see her, not like in the beginning.

"I think that's a problem, Gabby. We'll talk more about it after the commercial."

Gabby heard the music that meant Dr. Jamie had to do

something during the break. Sometimes they chatted, just like real friends. But most times, Gabby went on hold. She suspected, although she'd never ask, that Dr. Jamie had to run to the little girls' room. She couldn't very well stop her show to do her business, could she?

Gabby had made Jon's favorite meal. Lamb chops. She'd even found the little booties that slipped over the bones. In the beginning, he'd gone on and on about what a good cook she was. He hadn't said that in a long time. Of course, they hardly ate any meals together. He was so busy at work. If he kept on going like this, he'd make himself sick.

She sniffed again, dabbed her eyes with her tissue.

"Gabby?"

"I'm here."

"Do you think it's fair that Jon should have to be responsible for your happiness?"

"He's not responsible. But I love him so much that when he's here, I'm happy."

"What would his reaction be if he called you for a date, but you were busy doing something that makes you feel good? That gives you pleasure? Something yours and yours alone?"

"Well, I don't know. I don't think he'd be very happy about it."

"I think he'd be relieved, Gabby, that you were taking care of yourself. That he didn't have to come up with some way to make your day. That the pressure was off him."

"It's not pressure to want your boyfriend to come home to his anniversary dinner."

"I know, Gabby. You're hurt and frustrated. When you talk to him, try to tell him what happened, but tell him in a way that doesn't blame him. Just talk about how you feel."

"I feel terrible."

"It'll get better. It would get better faster, though, if you'd go to counseling."

Gabby sniffed again. "I'll try."

"Okay. Thanks for calling."

"Bye."

The line went dead, and Gabby dropped the phone into her lap. The tears that had been under control while she'd talked to Dr. Jamie poured out now. Rivers of hurt, oceans of disappointment.

The dinner was ruined, and so was her life.

"WE'RE BACK, and we have time for one more caller." Jamie pressed line four, Audrey from Teaneck, who wanted to talk about Chase. Everyone, except for Gabby, poor thing, wanted to talk about Chase. About the bet. About seduction.

Obviously, Chase thought it was highly amusing.

He'd shown up just when she'd thought she was safe. And during the last commercial break, he'd told her he'd made dinner reservations.

"Um, hi, Dr. Jamie. Is, um, Chase there?"

He leaned in to the mike, all the while staring at her, smiling as if he had a secret, and, boy, was she going to find out what it was.

"I'm here."

"Hi, Chase. My husband thinks you're a shoo-in for the Budapest race."

"Thank him for me, although nothing's for sure."

"No? Then you think you won't be able to seduce Dr. Jamie?"

He laughed, and the sound rippled through Jamie. The

last thing on earth she wanted was to be turned on by Chase Newman. Unfortunately, her body wasn't getting the urgency of her message. When he looked at her, she went all smooshy inside. Oh, great. Now she was losing her mind. A *cum laude* PhD didn't use words like *smooshy.*

"I think it's going to be a hell of an interesting ride finding out."

"Me, too. We've got a pool started at the office. My money's on you."

"Why?"

"Because I've seen your picture. Honey, if I wasn't married…"

Jamie leaned in to her mike. "Now, come on, this isn't funny. Women have to take responsibility for every part of their lives."

"I know," Audrey said, "but I also think you're not accounting for sex appeal."

"I am. But I'm also accounting for reason. For judgment. For prioritizing. Women have to stop letting men make their decisions for them. We're not the weaker sex."

"I completely agree," Chase said. "You're not the weaker sex. In fact, you're strong as steel. But you also need a little romance."

"Romance and seduction are two different things."

"Not if you do it right."

"That might be true for the women you've gone out with. But, in my book, a woman doesn't let honeyed words and flattery alter the facts of a relationship. As I was saying to Gabby, it's the actions that count, not the flowers, not the compliments."

"Uh, Dr. Jamie?"

"Yes?" Damn, she'd forgotten Audrey was on the line.

"What are you going to do tonight?"

She looked at Chase. He winked at her, which thoroughly ticked her off. But she couldn't afford to tell him to leave. Not yet. "We're going to dinner."

"Where?"

"I don't think it's a good idea to say." Jamie cleared her throat. "We do need a certain amount of privacy."

"Besides," Chase said, "I didn't tell her."

"It sounds like you have the whole night planned," said Audrey.

"I do."

"You think tonight will be the night?"

"I hope so."

Jamie took a calming breath. This conversation was not going well. "It will not."

"Dr. Jamie? Is he as gorgeous as his pictures?"

Jamie closed her eyes. "He's very nice-looking."

"My friend Ellen said he has a butt to die for."

"I wouldn't know."

"I don't mean to be rude, Dr. Jamie, but with an attitude like that, you'll win this bet hands down...but it won't be fair."

"Thank you, Audrey. I'll take that under advisement. This is Dr. Jamie on WXNT. Ted Kagan is up next. Speak to you tomorrow."

She clicked off her board and swung around to face Chase. "You're getting a kick out of this, aren't you."

He nodded.

"Tell me. Is it the fact that I'm being humiliated, the fact that you're getting your own little fan club, or both?"

"Both."

"Wonderful."

Ted opened the door, his hands full of files for his show. Jamie nodded curtly and stowed all her gear to make room for him. Chase lifted the bundle of papers and articles out of her arms. It was such a courtly gesture.

"Jamie, honey," Ted said, "you need to move your behind."

She jumped out of the way, then led Chase to the door. As she reached for the handle, he again stepped in and did it for her.

"Are there things you have to do before we go?"

She thought about telling him she wasn't interested in dinner, but that would be a lie. She'd thought about what Elliot had said. The game was on, and she needed to be a savvy player. "I have to speak to Marcy and put my things in my office."

"Lead on, McDuff."

Marcy was in the production booth. She'd pinned her hair up, which made her neck look long and elegant. Her outfit added to the image, the dress hugged her curves but not too tightly. Everything about her looked polished. Jamie knew Marcy was putting on the dog for Ted, but she didn't think Marcy was aware of it.

"Great show." Marcy smiled at Chase. "And thank you for coming by. I wasn't sure you would."

"I almost didn't."

Jamie looked up. "What changed your mind?"

He met her gaze. "You."

"I don't understand."

He nodded. "My point exactly."

The all-too-familiar heat came to her cheeks and, needing something to do, she took her things from his hands. His response shouldn't have surprised her. He was following a typical male pattern—trying to disarm her, charm her. And the whole eye-contact business was right out of her textbooks. Eye contact was the first stage of the mating process, the first real evidence of interest.

What she didn't understand was why she was falling for it. This was a game to Chase, he was only here out of boredom. And yet, her insides fairly quivered when their eyes met.

"Jamie?" Marcy's brows had furrowed. "Are you all right?"

"Yeah, sure."

"I was saying that it would be great if you two figured out what you were going to do over the weekend. And I'd like you to call in. I'll figure out times tonight."

Jamie nodded, but inside her panic light had gone on. What was she going to do with him over the weekend? It couldn't be anything too private. The safest way to keep her secret intact was to avoid any situations that could lead to intimacy.

Chase took Marcy's hand and kissed the back. It could have been creepy, but it wasn't. It made Marcy giggle, which hardly ever happened. She even futzed with her hair. The man had the touch. Oh man, did he have the touch.

The hole Jamie had dug for herself suddenly got a lot deeper. *Damn, damn, damn.*

CHASE WATCHED HER FINGERS as she toyed with her spoon. She'd ordered tiramisu but so far she hadn't tasted it. Or her cappuccino. If she'd eaten four bites of her dinner, he'd be surprised. She was scared. And he was a bastard for enjoying it.

"I'd planned on going into private practice, but all that changed when I did the radio show at the university."

"You fell in love."

One side of her mouth quirked up. "I suppose you could say that."

"It's a good thing. Passion is important."

"What are you passionate about?"

"Racing."

"Why?"

He shifted in his chair and looked around for the waiter. "I like the speed."

"And the danger?"

He nodded. "Yeah."

"Have you always been an excitement junkie?"

"Pretty much."

"The need for adrenaline can be quite compelling. I read a study about people who need danger in their lives. The theory is it's chemical... What?"

"Where did you come from?"

"Huh?"

"Where were you born?"

"Minnesota."

"Brothers, sisters?"

"One brother, Kyle. He's a neurosurgeon at Cedar Sinai in L.A."

"Are your parents in the medical field?"

She nodded. "They're both gynecologists."

"That explains a lot."

"What do you mean?"

He shook his head. "Did they help you get through school so fast?"

"No. Well, maybe some of it had to do with my family. Mostly, I just liked school. I was good at it."

"I'll bet you were. When all the other kids were out getting sick on beer and pizza, you were in the dorm, studying the night away."

"Well, yes. I developed good habits early. I'm not ashamed of it."

"I wish I'd known you in college."

"Why?"

"I would have taught you a few things."

"What, like taking drugs or drinking? No, thanks."

He shook his head. "Nope. My curriculum would have been a whole lot more personal than that."

She cleared her throat and turned her spoon over. "My education was quite well-rounded, I assure you."

"Uh-huh."

"So what about you? Your parents? Your education?"

"My mother lives here in New York. She's very busy."

"And your father?"

"He died when he was thirty-five."

Sympathy changed her face. On most people, that look of sorrow and empathy would have been bull, but something told him Jamie wasn't shoveling. Of course, that's what made her good at her job. She cared about people. Or else she was a master at pretending.

"I'm sorry."

"Me, too." He caught the waiter's attention and asked for the check. Turning back, he nodded toward her dessert. "You going to eat that?"

"Oh." She took a bite. "It's good. Would you like some?"

He took her spoon from her fingers and brought it to his lips. He licked the remnants of her bite, tasting her along with the sweet concoction. She blushed again, which was the point.

JAMIE WISHED IT WASN'T SO HUMID, but she couldn't expect anything else in August. The rich folks were ensconced in the Hamptons by now, leaving the rest of the population to sweat it out. Still, this was her favorite time to be walking. Well after midnight, the streets weren't so crowded, the smells of the city weren't too overwhelming. And the Fifth Avenue windows were all still lit; the expensive trinkets and high-fashion clothes seemed like a private exhibition for her benefit alone.

Of course, her attention wasn't completely on the displays. They'd walked two blocks now, and at the corner of 44th and State, Chase had put his hand on the small of her back.

She'd tried to get him to talk about himself. That was one of her surest techniques. Most men found themselves utterly fascinating. But Chase kept bringing the subject back to her.

He leaned down, his lips close to her ear. "Tell me a secret."

The shiver went all the way down to her toes. "Pardon?"

"Tell me something you've never told another living soul. Something wicked."

"You go first."

He laughed, a deep, rumbling sound that swirled around her like a mist. "All right. When I was fourteen, I drove a car for the first time."

"That's wicked?"

"Considering it was a stolen limousine, yeah."

"You're kidding."

"Nope. It was a big old stretch limo. Belonged to my father. I decided I wanted to go for a ride. And ride I did."

"What happened?"

"They eventually got it out of the swimming pool, but the car never was the same after that."

She laughed, and it felt wonderful. For the first time since she'd agreed to this farce, she felt relaxed. Thank goodness for humor. She said that a lot on her show.

As her smile faded, her focus returned to his hand, which couldn't possibly be as hot as it felt. The warmth came from her mind, her imagination. Whatever caused it, the sensation intensified by degrees, and without giving him any warning, she stopped at a window. It was just a drugstore, and the displays were mostly paper goods, but it did the trick. Her back was Chase-free. And cold.

He came to her side. "Low on paper towels, are you?"

"No."

"Then, why did you stop?"

She shrugged. "It's getting late."

He touched her. "Come on."

She walked with him again. Just as it had warmed her back, his hand simmered on her arm. They didn't speak, but she felt him, felt his presence in a way that was new and scary as hell.

They turned a corner, and Chase moved closer to her. Something shifted, as if the air had become electrified. As if she'd forgotten how to breathe. He moved his hand to the back of her upper arm, guiding her steps, moving her away from the curb. Away from safety. From sanity.

His grip tightened, his pace quickened, and the next thing she knew, he'd pulled her into an alley. It was very dark, and she couldn't see his face. Fear jackhammered in her chest, and she tried to pull away. He pushed her against the wall, the brick rough on her back. He took her hands in his and pushed them against the rough wall, too, on either side of her head. The concrete scraped her flesh.

She couldn't escape, and she didn't understand, and her heart beat so fast and hard she wasn't sure she could take it. But something else was pulsing, too. Her breasts, and lower still.

The scent of baking bread snuck in between the dank smells of the alley, but when Chase pressed against her, it was his scent that took over. Masculine, slightly spicy, with a hint of sweat that made her insides clench.

He stole away her breath as he captured her lips. His kiss was as hard as the wall behind her, as hot as her flesh where he touched her, as scary as the dark recesses of the alley. His tongue thrust in her over and over, and his mouth widened and narrowed as he ravished her.

No one had kissed her like this before. It was a new thing, unique in its power to make her tremble. He invaded her mouth, took liberties with his tongue. Intimate, like sex itself, and she felt helpless to stop him.

And then his hips moved against hers with deliberate intent. He wanted to stir her into a frenzy, and, God help her, he was succeeding.

He pulled back, took his lips away, and she couldn't stop the tiny moan of disappointment. The only thing she could see was the outline of his head, his unruly hair. Not his eyes, though. She knew what she would have seen there—lust, and just a hint of cruelty.

"This is the first night," he whispered. "Before it's over, I'm going to have you in my bed. There are things I'm going to do to you. Things that will scare you, that will make your heart beat the way it is right now."

"No." She tried to push him away, but his hips ground into hers, keeping her still.

"I see the truth in your eyes. That untamed part of you is in there, and it's starving to death. I'm not going to let that happen. I didn't agree to this stunt because I was bored. I agreed because you wanted me to. Because you knew I wouldn't stop until I'd had you."

"I didn't—"

"Don't worry. I'm not going to take you against your will. I'm not even going to try to convince you. I'm going to wait until you beg me."

"I won't."

He let go of her right hand and cupped her between her legs, the intimacy shocking her. "You're on fire already," he said. "And we haven't even begun."

She closed her eyes, turned her head to the side, not willing to look at him even in the darkness. Because she *was* on fire.

CHASE LET HER GO for all the wrong reasons. Touching her was meant to shock her. He hadn't been prepared for a jolt of his own. It was all he could do not to take her, right here, right now.

He didn't like this. Not a bit. He never lost control. Not in a race, not with a woman. He steered the course— alone. He wasn't blind to his need to be in charge. It was all about power, and the illusion that the world didn't give one damn about him or his plans.

But with this one—this slip of a girl—something was going wrong. When he'd kissed her, it was bad enough. The taste of her, the way her shy tongue finally touched his, threatened his control in a way he'd never imagined. He felt almost…helpless.

And then when he'd touched her, felt her heat, imagined her naked up against that concrete wall in the middle of the city as he thrust into her over and over—

She gasped, and he realized he'd leaned forward again, his erection straining for release, pressing against her body as if she'd let him in.

"Chase," she murmured, her voice soft and trembling. "Please."

"See what you do to me?" he said, lowering his lips to the shell of her ear. "You want this as much as I do."

"No."

"Liar."

She didn't take the bait. Her chest rose and fell against

his, her breasts teasing him to the edge of his endurance. And then she moved her head, slowly, until her lips brushed his. He tasted her breath as she whispered, "No."

5

"WELL?"

Jamie didn't look up. Instead, she studied the commercial lineup for the evening as if it were a matter of life and death.

"I can wait here as long as you can. Longer. I don't have a show in ten minutes."

Jamie raised one brow, then let her gaze follow. "We had dinner."

"Where?"

"A restaurant."

"Ha, ha."

"Marcy, I don't want to talk about it. The whole thing is one big charade, and I'm counting the seconds until it's over."

"So something did happen last night."

Jamie gripped her papers tighter so her hands couldn't get to Marcy's throat. "Nothing happened. It was dinner. We chatted. We walked. He went home. I went home. The end."

"He didn't make a move on you?"

Jamie looked at her papers again, trying to find where she'd left off. "No."

"Liar."

"Hey."

"Honey, I took a lot of cockamamy courses at NYU. One of them was on body language. And you are not telling me the truth."

"Okay. Fine. Have it your way. He kissed me."

"That's better." Marcy slid her right hip onto Jamie's desk and leaned forward. "Details, please."

"There are no details. He kissed me. And he said he wouldn't do anything I didn't want him to."

Marcy leaned back and gave her a quick once-over. "Is that why you're dressed like somebody's aunt Fanny?"

"I'm not." She looked down at her dress. It was a little on the baggy side, but so what?

"And I suppose it's a coincidence that you didn't have time to put on makeup. Or do something with your hair?"

"I happen to think I look fine this way."

"You lie like a rug. You're putting up defenses, my friend. And the only reason to put up defenses is because you think he's got a shot."

"A shot at what? Seduction? Please, Marcy, do you think I'd abandon my beliefs so easily?"

Marcy shrugged. "Personally, I don't think he can seduce you—but not because of your beliefs. I've thought a lot about you, Dr. Jamie, and your lack of male companionship."

Jamie's heart thudded in her chest. "I've been busy."

"Or scared."

"Marcy, we haven't known each other long enough for you to make such an assumption."

"Maybe not. But I'll tell you my theory, anyway. I think you were hurt badly—probably in college, but maybe high school—by someone you loved a great deal.

And I think you're scared to care again because you think it was maybe your fault."

Jamie started to tell Marcy that she was way off, but she swallowed her rebuttal in a muffled sort of grunt.

"I knew it." Marcy stood and smoothed down her already smooth, gray slacks. "You're not the only relationship maven at this station."

Jamie nodded. "I don't like to talk about it. I hope you understand."

Marcy's victory smile faded. "Of course. Oh, hon, I'm sorry. I didn't realize."

The lie lodged in her chest, right next to her heart, making it hard to breath. She gathered her papers together. "It's all right."

Marcy didn't stop her as she left the office and headed for the booth. Thank God. She couldn't have kept up the charade for another second.

This was just swell. A whole new layer of torture. She hated lying, and she was terrible at it. But Marcy's explanation was so much better than the truth. In fact, that story was probably going to save both their jobs. She'd have to refine it, give it the details that made a story believable…and stick to it until the day she died.

She pushed open the booth door, relieved that Chase wasn't there. He hadn't spoken to her since last night. In fact, he'd left her right after the incident in the alley.

The thought conjured the image of his body pressed against hers—and her armload of paperwork fell all over the floor. She bent to gather her things, remembering the heat of his erection, the strength in his hands. The confusion when he'd led her from the alley, hailed a cab, put her in the back seat and closed the door. The yearning to take back her "no" and make it a "maybe." She hadn't gathered her wits until long after he'd paid the driver. In fact, she wondered if she'd ever have her wits about her again.

"Anybody home?"

Jamie grabbed the last newspaper clipping and stood up to find Fred Holt standing just inside the door. "Hello, Fred."

"Hello, my beauty. I have a surprise for you."

She groaned inwardly. Just a few days ago, his announcement would have filled her with anticipation. Today, dread washed over her like a bucket of cold water. "What now?"

"What now? Jamie, you're the talk of the town." He stepped closer and threw a folded newspaper on the empty desk. She recognized immediately that it was the *Post,* arguably the most notorious paper in New York.

"Go ahead." He nodded. "Check out the headline."

All things considered, she'd rather not. It couldn't be good, not with the way her luck had turned.

Fred couldn't wait any longer. He retrieved the paper himself and opened it so they could both see the oversize type of the headline.

The Sexpert And The Playboy!

Will He Seduce Her? Or Will She Just Say No!

She read with mounting horror that in offices all across Manhattan, bets were being wagered, sports pools formed, sides taken. Someone claiming to be an ex-lover of Chase's was quoted as saying Jamie didn't stand a chance: Chase could seduce any woman in any country in any language. He'd leave Jamie broken and heartsick as he sailed off to his next race.

But that wasn't the worst of it. Somehow, they'd gotten hold of Dianna Poplar, one of her college roommates.

Dianna and she hadn't known each other well, mostly
because Dianna had majored in sex, drugs and rock and
roll. But now, Jamie read that Dianna "…had been like
her sister." Dianna said Jamie was so smart and clever,
but she didn't date much. The inference was that perhaps
Jamie didn't have to worry about being seduced by Chase
because she was more interested in someone like Dianna.

Jamie wobbled over to her chair and sat down.

"Isn't it great?" Fred kept holding up the paper as if she
was next to him. "You're a household name. Everyone in
the city is talking about you. *People* magazine called. So
did *Cosmo.* This is brilliant. We're all gonna be rich."

If reporters had gotten to Dianna, they could get to
other people who'd known Jamie in college—people
who'd tell the world that she'd been a bookworm and a
social outcast. That she'd never had one single date, let
alone a lover. Maybe it wouldn't be so terrible to have the
world think she was gay. At least she'd have had some
experience. Her cover was going to be blown any second,
and the potential for humiliation was expanding expo-
nentially.

Fred closed the paper. "What's wrong?"

"Oh, nothing."

"That's good. We wouldn't want anything spoiling this.
It's our ticket, Jamie. Our big hairy multimillion-dollar
ticket."

"Right."

"You're on the air in two minutes."

She nodded, tried to put her papers in some kind of
order, even though she couldn't focus. When she looked
up, Fred was gone, Cujo was giving her the count, and
in five, four, three, two—

"This is Dr. Jamie Hampton. And we're talking about
sex."

MARCY TYPED IN the information for the tenth caller, then turned the phones over to Alexis, one of the new interns. Jamie didn't sound too good. Who could blame her? It was lousy that she'd been caught up in this, but that was radio for you. Marcy had been involved in a lot of stunts in her day, but this one was the craziest. But she'd bet the farm that it was going to be the most lucrative stunt she'd ever seen. She was due for national syndication. She'd been in radio for eighteen years, working her way up the slippery ladder. Jamie was her ticket.

Jamie was also her friend. And Marcy had a feeling this wasn't a completely awful thing for her. Jamie needed to get out there, to live life instead of just talking about it on the airwaves.

Chase wasn't a complete unknown, although he was at most an acquaintance. What she did know about him made her feel secure that he wouldn't hurt Jamie—not in the traditional sense, at least. He was a heartbreaker, there was no denying that—but this was only for two weeks, and surely nothing that terrible could happen so quickly.

She just hoped Chase would prime the pump for Jamie. Let her see that she could risk her heart again. Poor thing. Her college sweetheart really must have done a number on her.

But then, who hadn't had a sweetheart that did a number? She'd had hers—a charming, devilishly handsome man who'd stolen her heart at the age of twenty-two. She'd leaped into the marriage bed, only to realize her husband already had a lover—Scotch. For six tumultuous years she'd hung on to his falling star, but she'd had to leave before he hit bottom. She simply wasn't able to take it.

Marcy chased away her memories, walked over to the window and focused on the show.

Going For It

JAMIE PUT DOWN her empty teacup and concentrated on her caller's question. "Can you be a little more specific?"

"Yeah," Bev from Lincoln Heights said in her thick New York accent. "I'm just, you know, curious about this G-spot thing. Is that for real? My boyfriend—he said it was a bunch of bull."

"Oh, it's real. First, so you know, it was named after Dr. Ernst Grafenburg, a German gynecologist, who discovered it. The G-spot is about two inches along the inner upper wall of the vagina between the back of the pubic bone and the front of the cervix. There's a bundle of nerve endings there that may be more sensitive than the rest of the vagina. Although, this isn't true for all women. But it's worth exploring."

"Uh, how?"

"Have your boyfriend insert his finger inside you, palm facing up. When he's in all the way, have him rub the flat of his fingertip in a "come here" motion. You'll know right away if your G-spot is sensitive."

"What's supposed to happen?"

"Nothing's *supposed* to happen. But you may feel stronger sensations and climax sooner. So I suggest you go for it."

Bev laughed a little, which was normal. In fact, the whole conversation had been normal. Jamie relaxed as she finished off her tea.

"Did *you* go for it?" Bev asked.

"Pardon me?"

"Does Chase Newman know where your G-spot is?"

The second his name was out there, Jamie's body filled with heat. It wasn't embarrassment and it wasn't arousal, but it was something real close to both. "Not from personal experience, no."

"So what happened on your date?"

"We talked," Jamie said, trying to keep the anxiety from her voice. "We found out a few things about each other."

"What'd you find out?"

Think, Jamie. What had he said? "Um, he doesn't have a house. He lives in hotels."

"Cool. Why?"

"Because he travels so much."

"So did you go back to his hotel?"

"No, I didn't. Get your mind out of the gutter, missy."

Bev laughed. "But he's so gorgeous."

"Be that as it may, sex is not something that's going to happen. Not by accident or by design. No seduction, remember?"

"Yeah. Well, when is he coming back to the show?"

"I don't know. But I do know it's time for us to take a break. This is Dr. Jamie, and we're talking about sex."

She took off her headphones, pressed the mute button and leaned back in her chair. "The Sexpert and the Playboy"? God, she'd never live that down. The name would stick with her and make it virtually impossible for anyone in her field to take her seriously. A private practice would be a joke. Marvelous. She'd lose her radio show if anyone found out the truth, and now she didn't even have a backup plan. Maybe she could be a waitress. They made pretty decent money.

"Hey, kiddo."

She looked up as Marcy's voice came over the intercom. "Yeah?"

"You okay?"

"No."

"Can I do anything to help?"

"Shoot me."

"Other than that?"

Jamie shook her head. "No, wait. Tea. I have no tea."

"Coming right up. And Jamie?"

"Huh?"

"Cheer up. It's just radio. No big deal."

"Uh-huh."

Marcy gave her a perky little thumbs-up before she headed out the production booth door. Jamie let her head drop, and it hit her desk with a resounding *thunk*.

"Ow," she whispered. Was it possible to feel worse than this? To be more screwed? Wait. It wasn't smart to think that way. The gods always knew when she figured she was at bottom, and then they opened up a trap door.

The last thing she needed was a new low. Maybe Chase had grown bored with her. She'd expected him to be here. To discombobulate her with his slow smiles and his heat. She should be thankful, right? Only, she wasn't so much thankful as disappointed. Which made her certifiable. Completely whacko.

"Jamie?"

She lifted her head from the desk.

Cujo smiled at her from the other room. "We're almost on."

She adjusted her headphones, and pasted a smile on her face. Just then, Ted and Marcy walked into the production booth. Ted had his hand on the small of her back. Marcy was laughing about something. Then Ted moved away and Marcy turned to the window. She waggled here eyebrows and mouthed, *Oh my God!*

Jamie's smile became real, and, a second later, she was on the line with Ellen from Old Westbury.

"I've got one for you, Dr. Jamie."

"Shoot."

"What's the difference between a golf ball and a G-spot?"

"What?"

"A man will spend half an hour looking for a golf ball."

Jamie laughed. "Ellen, that was great. Just what I needed. Thank you."

"Sure thing, Dr. Jamie. Oh, and one more thing."

"Yes?"

"When you see Chase, give him a big old kiss from me, okay?"

Jamie shook her head. This Chase business wasn't going away. She was cursed. Cursed!

THE SOUND OF HER FOOTSTEPS brought him out of his meditation. He'd learned the Zen practice years ago from a Tibetan monk he'd met in Italy. At first he'd just meditated before a race to clear his mind, but slowly the ritual had become a habit, and he always made time in his day for the deep relaxation.

But tonight's session, attempted while leaning against Jamie's door, hadn't been relaxing at all. Jamie had seen to that. No matter how hard he'd tried to clear her image from his mind, she'd lingered. Her full lips, the way her skin felt under his palm, her wide, almond-shaped eyes. He'd actually become aroused, and that was one hell of a surprise because in his thoughts she was fully clothed.

"What in the world?"

He looked up. She stood a few feet from him, her arms loaded down with a grocery bag and her purse. He'd surprised her, and that made those eyes of hers widen so that she reminded him of those *anime* cartoons. Hoisting himself up, he took a moment to appreciate the rest of her face. Especially her lips. He liked them parted like that, ripe and ready for kissing.

"What are you doing here?"

"Waiting for you." He lifted the grocery bag from her arms. "What did you buy?"

"Dinner." She added, "For myself."

He looked at the vegetables, the small package of chicken breasts. "I can make it stretch."

She blinked at him for a moment, then got her key out of her purse. Once she'd opened the door, he slipped inside quickly, not giving her a chance to tell him to leave. From there, he went right to her kitchen. It was small, but then this was Manhattan. Only the rich or those in rent-controlled apartments had the luxury of space.

"Excuse me, but I don't recall inviting you to dinner."

"That's okay. I like to cook. Maybe you could open a bottle of wine or something."

"But—"

He put down the groceries and opened the fridge while she sputtered. It was cute sputtering, and he resisted the smile that tugged at his lips.

"Are you listening to me?" she demanded.

He spied a bottle of chardonnay and pulled that out. Then he opened cupboards until he found the wineglasses. "Here," he said, handing them to her. "Do you have any linguini?"

She nodded. "In the cupboard. Hey, wait a minute."

He crossed the kitchen and opened the pantry door. The linguini was on the top shelf, and so was the olive oil. He took both. Only when he was at the stove did he turn to Jamie. "Yes?"

"I want you to stop this. I'm not a child. This is my apartment, and I say who comes in here."

He walked slowly over to her, plucked the bottle and the glasses from her fingers and put them on the counter. "I'm sorry," he whispered as he pulled her into his arms. "Can you ever forgive me?"

He bent down, gently brushing his lips with hers, amazed once more how the slightest touch made him a little bit crazy. He licked her lips, tasting her on the outside before he dipped inside and tasted her there, too. The hell with dinner. He would dine on Jamie, until he'd sampled every inch. Then he'd go back for seconds.

She tried to push him away, but only for a moment. Once the kiss deepened, she surrendered. In fact, she sort of went limp on him. He took her hands and wrapped them around his neck. She got the hint and splayed her fingers, massaging him just enough to make his eyes close. He left her lips, but only to bring his mouth to her ear. "Say it tonight, Jamie. Say you want me."

The whispered entreaty didn't have the desired effect. She let go of his neck and stepped away, turning so her back was to him. "I'm tired."

"All the more reason for me to make you dinner. You're in charge of the wine, and then you have to step aside. I need some elbow room."

She faced him again wearing a cynical frown. "Oh, *please.*"

"What? You don't think I can cook?"

"I think you know how to make spaghetti. You don't even have a house, and the last I heard the Four Seasons doesn't have kitchens in the suites."

He didn't answer her. The food would be the proof. He got busy, first with a pot of water to boil, then with making the sauce. The wine forgotten, Jamie watched him. He focused on the preparations, using the knife like an old friend. He'd learned his skills years ago from a French chef. She'd schooled him in many techniques, not the least of which was how to please a woman with his lips and his tongue. Jamie would get the full benefit of his education. Tonight, she would eat well. And later tonight? If he had anything to do with it, she would learn his other secrets firsthand.

When the vegetables were ready, he pulled out another pot and put it on the stove. Still, he didn't look at her. Not until the last of the spices had been added to the gently simmering sauce. When he finally turned to her, she blushed. Her cheeks turned a soft pink and she wouldn't meet his gaze. Her thoughts hadn't been on pasta. But what had she been thinking? Had she wondered what his hands would be like on her flesh? How he'd treat her like the rarest delicacy?

He approached her slowly, not wishing to scare her off. She stepped back, but she didn't bolt. An extraordinary beauty, she did her best to disguise herself. But her baggy clothes weren't disguise enough. He knew what lay beneath—the gentle curve of her waist, the slight roundness of her belly...

Reaching up, he touched her chin with the length of his finger and raised her head. Her gaze darted away, but he wasn't in any rush.

Finally, she looked right at him. The blush on her cheeks deepened.

"What are you afraid of?"

She didn't answer, although her mouth opened slightly as if she wanted to tell him.

"It's all right. You can tell me."

"There's nothing to tell."

"No?"

She looked away again.

He moved closer to her, close enough that the hem of her dress brushed his jeans. "Just to set your mind at ease, I do know."

"Know what?

"Where your G-spot is. Among other mysterious female secrets."

Her gaze snapped back. "You listened?"

"I did. And I hate to say it, but I don't think you're trying very hard."

"Please don't tell me you're taking this seriously."

He nodded. "Of course I am."

"I already said it wouldn't happen."

"That's it, then? You're not even going to give it a chance? See what could happen between us?"

She moved away, grabbing the wine bottle as she crossed the kitchen. "Your water's boiling."

He turned to the stove, but not before his gaze was caught by a vase filled with his roses. They were on her coffee table, and they still looked as fresh as they had when he'd brought them. He smiled, then added the pasta to the water. After that, he stirred the sauce and adjusted the flame. She was at the counter struggling with the cork.

He could have taken it from her, but he didn't. Instead, he watched her try to yank out the cork. She didn't have the right leverage, which made the task twice as difficult as it could have been.

She was a stubborn little thing, though, and despite her stance, she succeeded, and the cork popped loudly in the small room. He brought her the glasses, and she poured his glass and her own, but hers she filled to the rim.

His guess was that she figured the liquor would calm her nerves. Doubtful. But it would loosen her up a bit, and for that he was grateful.

She was a puzzle, this one. He tried to think of a woman like her and he came up blank. She was a beauty who behaved as if she wasn't. A sophisticate who blushed at the first hint of impropriety. There had to be a key to Jamie. A clue that would make all the pieces fit.

He couldn't imagine a more entertaining project.

"Jamie?"

"Hmm?"

"You've told me a lot about your past, but not enough, not nearly enough…"

"I've already told you everything that's important. I really have a boring little life."

"I don't believe that for a moment." He sipped his wine, then leaned back against the counter and made himself comfortable.

"It's true." She picked up the big wooden spoon and stirred the pasta, then the sauce.

"No sale. Come on. I want to hear about all the men in your life."

She picked up her wineglass, brought it to her lips and drank—didn't sip—until half the glass was gone.

His brows lifted. He'd pitched and scored. All this mystery was about a man. Was he in her past, or in her present?

"Excuse me." Jamie put her glass down and headed toward the hallway.

He watched her until she'd entered the bathroom and closed the door. Interesting. Of course, he'd figured it was something along those lines that made her so shy.

Now, all he had to do was find out what the man who broke her heart was like, and be the opposite. Piece of cake.

6

JAMIE PUT DOWN THE LID and sat on the toilet. "Oh God," she whispered. It sounded good so she said it again and again until it was one long word. *OhGodOhGodOhGod...* What was she supposed to do now?

Maybe if she sat in here long enough, he'd go home. Even as she thought it, she knew it wasn't going to happen. Chase wasn't the type to tiptoe out the door. He was in her face, and he wanted answers.

She hadn't had time to make up her past. Her ex-lover didn't even have a name yet. Steve? Frank? Buddy? Alonzo? Her head dropped to her hands and she moaned, the small bathroom bouncing the sound right back at her. She sounded pitiful. She *was* pitiful.

The fact was, she had two weeks to get through, and she'd better get a grip or she was going to lose it, big time.

What if she'd called herself for advice? What would she say?

First, she'd ask herself if she was out of her mind for getting into such a ridiculous situation. But then, she'd probably ask what she wanted the outcome to be. Did she, in fact, want to win this bet or did some part of her want to be seduced by Chase?

Okay. Point one—she wanted to win, and not just because she didn't want her secret blown. She wanted to get closer to her listeners. She wanted them to trust her and feel comfortable asking her the most intimate questions. She wanted to help women see their part in the seduction scenario.

Then she'd ask herself if she was doing everything she could to win the bet. That would be a big no. In fact, she hadn't taken the initiative once. She'd let herself be buffeted about like a leaf in a gale. Every time he touched her, her resolve weakened a notch. He'd kept her off guard, which was how things got out of hand.

Point two—it was time to go on the offensive.

So then she'd ask about the, uh, situation. The one where she'd lose everything she cared about if the truth were to get out that she was indeed the phoniest of the phonies. That she knew about sex like fish knew about bicycles. However, she'd remind herself, the whole point of the game was to avoid being compromised, so what the heck was the problem?

Could she keep saying no to him? Yes. Of course. How ludicrous. No way she was going to succumb. Even though, oh God, she kinda sorta wanted to.

The confession made her moan. How was this possible? The bet, although embarrassing, should have been a no-brainer. She didn't believe in seduction, and therefore it wasn't going to happen.

But when he kissed her... She moaned again as her traitorous body reacted to the thought. "Reacted" was putting it mildly. Just thinking about his mouth on hers put every nerve ending in every erogenous zone on full alert.

Tough. It wasn't going to happen, couldn't happen, so she'd better get used to it. According to everything she knew about sexual intimacy, kissing didn't happen right away. Lots of things happened before getting that close. Eye contact. Light touches. Mirroring behavior. Asking the right questions. And sex? Please. That was the last step. She knew the road, which meant she didn't have to walk down it, right? She counseled a lot of women to watch for the signs, to keep one step ahead. She'd simply take her own advice.

Point three—no woman can be seduced. Period. No ifs, ands or buts. If she didn't make eye contact, or touch him, or mirror his behavior or ask intimate questions, she'd be fine. Because no amount of sexual chemistry was equal to the power of self-determination. She was stronger than her hormones. She was stronger than Chase. He didn't stand a chance. So what was she worried about?

A soft rap on the door made her jump.

"Jamie? You okay?"

"I'm fine," she said, trying to sound normal as her heart pounded in her chest.

"Okay. Just thought I'd tell you dinner is ready."

"Great. That's…that's great. I'll be right there."

Silence as the seconds ticked by. "All right," he said finally.

She rolled her eyes. *Way to take charge, Jamie.* Next time, she must remember to call Dr. Ruth.

MARCY FOUND AN EMPTY BOOTH at the back of the diner. It wasn't the most elegant of restaurants, but it served good food at decent prices, and they were open until two in the morning. She'd been coming here for several years, and not just because of the food or the fact that it was across the street from the station. She never felt awkward here eating alone. No one bothered her. She could read as she ate, sometimes the paper, sometimes a novel. It was nice, quiet and safe.

She grabbed a menu, but before she could open it she heard Jamie's voice. Surprised, she looked up, then realized she was listening to the radio behind the counter. Fred was running lots of clips through all the programs. A "Best of…" series.

"What are you so afraid of?" Jamie asked.

"I don't know," came a soft response.

"What's the worst thing that could happen?"

"He'll laugh at me."

"And?"

"I'll be humiliated."

"Have you ever been humiliated before?"

A sigh. "Yes."

"Did you survive?"

"Yeah."

"So, in other words, if you ask him to sit with you at lunch, he can say yes, he can say no, or he can laugh at you. Now, the odds are that third thing won't happen. But let's say he says no. What would that mean?"

"That he doesn't like me?"

"Maybe. Or maybe it means he has other plans for lunch."

"Oh."

"Or maybe it means he's seeing someone else, and because he finds you attractive it wouldn't be a good idea to sit with you at lunch. Or maybe it means he's gay. Or he's got crabs. Or a hundred other things, none of which have anything to do with you."

"Okay. I get it."

"Do you?" Jamie asked. "Do you see that fear is stopping it all? Stopping your life? That you'll survive even if it is awful, and, more than that, you'll have pride in yourself for taking a chance, for risking your heart. So, you go for it, girl. You ask him to eat lunch with you. He might just say yes."

"That was Dr. Jamie, and she talks about sex weeknights…"

Marcy tuned out Barry Leland's voice. He was on the air now and probably irritated as hell that he had to promote Jamie's show.

She looked at the familiar menu and decided to stick with her usual Santa Fe chicken salad. She really should try something new, but not tonight. Not with the blue funk that had her wrapped in its fuzzy arms.

It wasn't that anything was wrong so much as that not much was right. Dee, who worked here six nights a week and almost always waited on Marcy, came over and smiled as she got out her order pad. "Santa Fe salad, right?"

Marcy nodded. God, she was so predictable.

"Iced tea?"

"No. I'd like a beer. Whatever you have on tap."

"You got it." Dee finished writing, then stuck the pencil behind her ear. Her hair was so short, it was almost a buzz cut, but on her, it worked. "That's something about Dr. Jamie, huh?"

"Yes. It is…something."

"I've seen that guy. He's a tall drink of water. I sure as hell wouldn't kick him out of bed for eating crackers, if you know what I mean."

Marcy grinned. "I do indeed."

"Not that he'd want an old broad like me."

"You're not so old."

Dee shrugged. "Going on fifty. But it beats the hell out of the alternative, eh?"

"You bet."

The waitress headed toward the kitchen, and Marcy's gaze went to the door as a man walked in—only it wasn't just any man, it was Ted. Her pulse kicked up and her cheeks heated. She'd invite him to sit with her. He was a coworker, right? People ate with coworkers.

She smiled as he looked her way. He smiled back, but then he turned to a woman behind him. A beautiful blonde with arched eyebrows and pale pink lips. Ted touched her upper arm, leading her to a table. A table far too close to Marcy's. What was he doing here so late?

Something broke inside her. A last hope, perhaps? She had no idea who the blonde was. But by the way Ted touched her, Marcy guessed she wasn't his kid sister.

There was no reason for her chest to hurt. For her appetite to disappear. For a wave of sadness to make her want to cry. Ted wasn't her boyfriend. He didn't even know she was interested in him. Why? Because she was a big, fat chicken.

What was it Jamie had said? Fear can stop it all. Is that what her life was about? Hiding from fear?

Her answer came a few minutes later when Dee brought her salad. A lifetime of Santa Fe salad when there was a banquet being served? Is that all she was worth?

She looked over at Ted's table. He glanced her way and smiled. Only she didn't do the usual blush-and-turn. This time, she held his gaze. Just held it with her own.

He didn't turn away. On the contrary, his right brow lifted a hair, and his smile changed from an impersonal greeting to a question.

Marcy's heart beat so fast that she hardly remembered how to breathe. Finally, after what seemed like forever, she lowered her lashes and broke the connection.

She managed to shove a few bites of food into her

mouth while she tried to get a grip. Eye contact. She'd heard Jamie talk about it again and again, but she never dreamed it could work.

One more bite, then she dared another look. Ted's gaze met her own, and there it was again. A connection. A silent Q & A session. A moment.

He was the one to turn away this time. But he didn't want to. She could tell. *He didn't want to.* This was major. This was unbelievable.

"Thanks, Jamie," she whispered. "I owe you."

HE'D FOUND HER CANDLES. She kept a basket by the book-shelf in the living room where she stashed an eclectic collection of candles, from beeswax to scented votives. Most had been given to her as gifts, a few she'd bought herself, but she'd never placed them all over the dining room, and she'd never turned off the lights and lit them all at once.

It didn't feel like her apartment. It didn't smell like her apartment, either. The scent of Italian spices made her tummy growl. The scent of the candles made her giddy. The scent of Chase Newman did several other things, none of which she cared to focus on.

Chase stood between the kitchen and the dining room. He'd also found her place mats and silver, and the table looked sinfully elegant. Candles, of course, were the centerpiece.

"Welcome back."

"You did all this."

He nodded. "I had some time on my hands."

"Sorry."

"It's all right." He headed toward her, lit by soft, flickering lights. "Are you?"

"Am I?"

"All right?"

"I don't know," she said, which wasn't smart. But she couldn't help it. Her pep talk in the bathroom was fading like a bad dream.

"My linguini will fix everything," he said, his voice low and intimate as he held out her wineglass. "But first, you need to relax."

"I'm fine," she said, lying through her clenched teeth. She took the wine, thinking it might be a good idea to drink as much as she could as fast as she could.

He had other plans. Starting with a walk around her, a steadying hand keeping her from moving. Once he was behind her, he put his hands on her shoulders. She nearly dropped her glass.

His hands covered most of her shoulders, they were so large. The first wave of sensation was all about her own size, her fragility. How it would feel to have those hands caress her body. A shiver raced through her, and then he started massaging her, kneading her neck muscles.

He was surprisingly gentle. His thumbs found her pressure points, and she could feel herself melting. As if his magic fingers weren't enough, his warm breath whispered against her neck—her name, so soft it was hardly there. Then his lips were behind her ear, nuzzling as he continued working the tension from her body.

This was all new to her. No one had ever touched her exactly like this, or whispered her name in such a way. His shivery kisses made her want to weep for all she'd missed out on.

She'd thought it would be wonderful. Honestly, she'd fantasized about a man like Chase, a moment like this. But her fantasies had been woefully inadequate. No imagining could equal the feel of his hands running down her arms, the erotic web he wove with his breath, his lips, his hips rubbing against her bottom.

He slipped her wineglass from her hand and put it somewhere. She'd forgotten all about it. Her intoxication didn't need liquor, it seemed. Just Chase nibbling on her earlobe.

It wasn't fair. All these new sensations, and she couldn't let herself enjoy them. Well, not as much as if she were really going to make love with him. This was all about a bet, a wager, a game. He wasn't touching her this way because he wanted *her*. If it hadn't been for Darlene Whittaker, Chase wouldn't have asked her out in the first place. She must remember that…

His hands moved down her arms again, and then they were on her stomach, and she gasped when he didn't stop there. He moved his hands up just under her breasts, and then his thumbs, those wicked thumbs, rubbed her just below her nipples.

A hiss of breath hit her neck, and she had to squeeze her legs together tightly. She put her hands on his hands, meaning to pull them away, but then she seemed to lose her strength, to say nothing of her determination.

He teased her, but only until she whimpered. Then his thumbs touched the rigid nubs. Rubbed small circles, not too hard, just right. Behind her, he moved his hips, letting her feel his hard length straining against his jeans. That was new, too. She knew so much about men in general, and so little about a man.

He cupped her breasts, so small in his big hands. But his moan let her know he liked what he felt, that she was right for him.

"Jamie," he whispered. Then he turned her around and his lips came down on hers.

The kiss was different, hungrier. His tongue thrust

between her teeth, taking all he wanted, his hands on her back and then lower until he cupped her buttocks and pulled her tight against his heat.

She wasn't equipped to fight a man like Chase. He was too sophisticated, too devilishly handsome. His hands...they could make her do anything. The fact that he didn't really want her so much as he wanted to win the bet couldn't compete with the way his taste, his lips, his hands squeezing her flesh made her woozy with desire.

It would be her job. Her career. Unless she could convince him to keep her secret. But either way, she just couldn't fight him any longer. He'd won on day two. A TKO of the first magnitude.

She broke the kiss, raised her gaze to his.

He didn't seem surprised. He smiled, making her heart flutter. But then he did something that changed the whole game. He chuckled. It was very soft, and if she hadn't been watching him so intently, she would have missed it.

He'd known exactly what would happen. That with a touch here, a word there, he could make her melt. He was almost right. Almost.

She still tingled from head to toe. Her nipples were still hard and the throbbing between her legs was enough to make her yearn for release. But there was just enough sanity left in her to see what was happening. To understand that she was in the game—whether as a pawn or a queen was up to her.

The easiest thing in the world would be to surrender. To let go of her ideals and blame biology. But surrendering wasn't her style. She'd fought hard and long for everything she had in her life. Including her job. Her place in the world.

Was she going to lose it all to this cocky bastard?

"What's that smile for?" he asked, his voice gruff with the lust she still felt in his hands, in his body.

She moved her hands down his chest, brushing lightly with her fingertips. *Come on, girl. You know how to do this.* She knew how to exploit a situation for her own benefit. Hadn't she done that with the radio show? With school? Of course she had. So why couldn't she do the same thing with Chase? Turn the tables. Be the seductor instead of the seductee. She could hold all the cards, every last one. And Chase wouldn't know what hit him.

Her fingers moved down to his belt where she lingered for a moment, teasing the buckle as if she were going to undo it. His breath caught. She gave him a suggestively raised brow. Then she purposely stepped away.

Wait for it... Wait... There.

He let out a frustrated moan, chalking one up for her side.

Take that, Chuckles.

HE'D HAD HER. So what the hell just happened? A moment ago she'd been putty in his hands.

"Did you say dinner was ready?"

He nodded. Watched her get her wine, take a sip, smile at him over the rim of the glass as if she knew a secret. Then she walked to the table, running one hand down her backside, showing him the shape of the curves he'd only begun to discover for himself.

The real problem here was physical. It wasn't the first time he'd been left dangling, so to speak, but it hadn't happened for years. Women didn't turn him down. Not women he went after in high gear.

The feel of her hard nipples, the way she fit into his hands...

What the hell——?

"Chase? Would you like me to serve you?"

"Sure." As long as it was her on a platter. The pasta held no appeal. Nothing did, except finishing what he'd started.

She busied herself with the plates, gave them both generous portions, but she didn't dig in. Instead, she ran the tip of her finger over the rim of her nearly empty wineglass and looked at him from under her dark lashes.

She was coming on to him, right? The fingers, the glances, the subtle smile, the flush in her cheeks. She wanted him. But if that was the case, why was he over here, and why did she have her clothes on?

"It smells wonderful. I was wrong. You do know how to cook. I should have guessed."

He needed to move. To go sit down. To pick up where he'd left off. Only, something was screwy.

He understood women, almost as well as he understood cars. They were predictable in their unpredictability. They wanted to succumb, to be swept away. When Jamie had leaned back in his arms it had told him everything he needed to know. Only, he had on his clothes, too.

"I'll be right back." He took an uncomfortable walk to the bathroom and shut the door behind him. Once he was alone, he leaned against the wall and willed himself to calm the hell down. The pressure eased a bit, which let him think more clearly.

Okay, so maybe Jamie wasn't the pushover he'd imagined. Maybe she'd take a little more work. Which made sense. Hell, look what she did for a living. He'd figured she wasn't very experienced. A hundred small things told him that. The way she blushed, her tentative kisses, the way she trembled in his arms. All signs of a woman who hadn't had any in a while.

He'd been with women like her before. Shy women

who'd had inadequate lovers, who ate up the attention and longed to be set free.

But none of them had stopped midway through the first lap. Certainly not after they'd found his belt. Dammit, that was usually a sure sign.

He splashed some cold water on his face as he tried to assess the situation. There was only one pertinent question—did he honestly believe he could seduce Jamie? Could he shake her down from her intellectual pedestal? Could he make her surrender?

Yes.

Why?

Because of the wager? No. It was a stupid bet, and the only intelligent thing to do was bow out. He knew without a doubt, though, that if he called off the bet, he'd lose his only hope of getting her into bed. She'd run and hide, just the way she used to at the station before all this started. He used to wonder why he frightened her, and the last couple of days had shown him why.

So the bottom line was simple. Screw the bet, and get Jamie Hampton into his bed. That was the game. That was the goal. Like winning at Le Mans.

He looked at his reflection. Why not? What else did he have to do that was anywhere close to this fascinating? Good for her, knocking him off balance. That made things…interesting.

Dammit, he wanted to win.

What was the expression? *Live hard, die young, leave a good-looking corpse?* Hell of a motto, but then he didn't have much choice in the matter, did he? After all, he had the Newman curse.

That was his ultimate strength—the knowledge that he'd only be around for a few more years. No one else knew, and he wouldn't say a word. He'd just go at thirty-five, as had his father and his father before him.

The doctor he'd talked to said it was a coincidence, but the doctor didn't know about Chase's great-grandfather. Dead at thirty-four. A heart attack, out of the blue. His mother knew, and in those first years after his father died, she'd warned him not to repeat his father's mistake. Not ever to leave a wife and child behind.

At least Chase had some warning. And he'd taken it seriously. He did live fast, as fast as he knew how. He'd been all over the world, been with women from Africa to Istanbul. He'd tried everything at least once, daring himself to go further, deeper, and to risk more. And he'd never let anyone get too close.

His mother had nearly gone insane at the death of his father. No way would Chase leave behind a grieving widow, or a son who would have to face the same destiny.

He lived for the moment, never for the future, never in the past. And, right now, his moment was in the dining room. If she wanted to roll up her sleeves and fight, so be it. In fact, he liked that she wasn't going to be easy. Too damn much in his life had been.

He had no doubt he'd win. But now, getting there was going to be a lot more fun.

Grabbing a towel from the rack, he wiped his face and hands, then headed back to the dining room. At the far corner of the table sat Dr. Jamie, his worthy opponent. Her dark eyes flashed with a seductive welcome.

But he had her number. Oh, yeah. *Baby, the flag is up.*

7

JAMIE WATCHED HIM EAT. Of course, he watched right back. It was like staring into a mirror. Well, not quite. But he would take a bite, she would take a bite. He'd sip his wine, she'd do the same. She echoed every gesture, paused with every pause. She was Ginger to his Fred; dancers with no music.

When he didn't react, she decided to crank it up a notch. Carefully, she put her fork down on the side of her plate, then made the *mmm* sound of appreciation, only real low and deep and sexy. Then, feeling quite foolish, but daring, too, she licked her upper lip, taking her own sweet time.

Nothing changed. His expression was exactly the same as— Hold on. Oh, my. He'd put his fork in his mouth, only he'd forgotten to pick up any food on it. And yet, he didn't seem to notice as he proceeded to chew and swallow.

Excellent.

She picked up her wineglass and took a tiny, quick lick of the rim before she sipped the chardonnay. As she'd anticipated, Chase's gaze was fixed on her mouth, on her tongue. Such a bad boy.

Next, she reached across the table to get the pepper

mill, even though she had no desire for pepper. But she knew that when she stretched, her dress molded against her breasts. She didn't even have to look this time to sense where his gaze had wandered. Heck, this was like shooting fish in a barrel.

He cleared his throat and shifted his gaze. She'd see about that.

"These candles are really beautiful, aren't they."

His grunt sounded sort of like "Yes."

"I think the flickering light is so soothing. You know what one of my favorite things is?"

"I wouldn't even hazard a guess."

She smiled, although she didn't give him any teeth. "I love slipping into a nice, hot, wet…bubble bath."

No comment, except for the bobbing Adam's apple.

She sighed as she ran two fingers lazily up her arm. "I light my private candles and fill the tub with rose-scented bubble bath, then I sink down until my whole body is under the water, and my head rests on my bath pillow."

She took another sip of wine, giving him time to fine-tune his mental picture. "I close my eyes and let the water and the roses soothe away all my worries. All that's left to do is wash. I don't like to use a cloth or anything. I just get my hands all soapy. Of course, I start with my toes—the summer can be so harsh on bare feet. And then I work my way up to my ankles." She paused, milking the moment. "Then I move my hands to my legs and knees."

He swallowed again, his eyes slightly glassy.

"I lean back to wash my thighs, of course. Because I need to be comfortable and completely relaxed when I…"

Chase couldn't help it. He leaned forward, waiting for her to finish the sentence. And waiting. Dammit. What was she doing to him?

She took another sip of wine, then put the glass down.

He let out his breath, sure she'd go on, begging her to go on.

She twirled some pasta on her fork and brought it to her mouth. Opening her lips, the food slipped inside, and then her lips closed on the fork—and he had to look away before he started crying.

This wasn't amusing. She was doing it on purpose. All of it. He'd thought she was innocent. A babe in the woods. What a laugh. She was more like the big, bad wolf.

He took a deep breath and loosened the stranglehold he had on his glass before it shattered. He also wanted to loosen his pants before they burst at the seams, but that was a no-go because he was afraid to touch himself anywhere in the vicinity of his fly. A stiff breeze would probably push him over the edge, and on the list of tricks to impress your date, coming at the dinner table was below everything with the possible exception of choking and turning blue in the face.

There was only one other time in his life when he'd been in this much trouble. He'd been fifteen and, like most guys his age, he'd been a virgin. A hopeful virgin. He'd spent the summer at his friend Jeff's place, and Jeff had a cousin. Her name was Eve. She liked to tease him and, at seventeen, she was already a master.

One day she left the bathroom door open, just a tad. Just enough for him to peek inside. He hit the mother lode—Eve, who was built like a brick house, was taking off her bathing suit.

Years later, he realized she actually had been putting on a show for him, and that the door wasn't left open accidentally. At the time, he thought he'd died and gone to heaven.

Eve was the most gorgeous creature on the planet. Blonde, tall, with legs that went on for about a mile, she was the picture of feminine perfection in his eyes, a veritable Miss July, sprung fully formed from the pages of *Playboy* magazine.

His fifteen-year-old hormones went into overdrive. But before he could move away, Eve yanked open the door. She had somehow put a towel around her good parts, and she was furious.

He begged her not to tell. He didn't want to be banished to his parents' incredibly boring apartment back in Manhattan. He wanted to be with Jeff, and the pool and the goddess who had him by the T-shirt.

He'd begged, and she'd finally agreed to keep his secret, but only if he'd submit to being her slave for the rest of his stay.

The torture had been exquisite.

She'd made him rub lotion on her body, fetch drinks, give her massages, make her bed. And he'd had the erection that wouldn't die. It went on for days. Eve had wanted him to take off his clothes for her, but at that he put his foot down. It was bad enough that he had to wear two pairs of jockey shorts under his bathing suit just so he wouldn't give Jeff's mother a stroke, but there was no way he was going to show Eve his predicament in all its glory.

Of course, if he'd been just a bit older, he would have understood that her request wasn't the cruel trick he'd imagined, but a wicked introduction to the wonders of sex. Damn. He could have had a really great summer. Instead, it was full of pain and anguish and sweet suffering. Like tonight.

He wondered where Eve was now. She was probably a dentist or an island despot.

But because there was a great deal of humor in the universe, he'd found himself another Eve. He was older now. Wiser. He knew perfectly well that Jamie was intentionally torturing him. That every move she made was meant to torment him. He was wise to the woman, no doubt about that. Unfortunately, his penis caught none of the nuances and, frankly, misunderstood the entire scenario.

"Chase?"

"Yeah?"

"Where have you been? I've been talking to you and you haven't heard a word I've said."

He smiled, although it was definitely not one of his best efforts.

"And you've hardly eaten a thing."

"I'm not very hungry."

"Did you have dinner before you came over?"

He shook his head.

"Then, you must be hungry. Go on. Just a few more bites, and we'll call it even."

He obeyed. Just like with Eve. He ate one bite, then two, not tasting anything, not seeing anything but Jamie's gaze, Jamie's soft cheeks, Jamie's lips.

He swallowed as she leaned toward him. What was going on? She kept leaning forward until they were only a breath apart. He closed his eyes, ready for her lips on his. Instead, she took her index finger and touched the corner of his mouth. Then she brought that finger to her lips and she sucked the tip. The symbolism wasn't lost on him. She closed her eyes and moaned. He moved, and she sat back in her seat as if she hadn't just come on to him in the most blatant, vivid, obvious maneuver since Marilyn Monroe sang "Happy Birthday."

"What was that?"

"You had some sauce on your mouth."

"In this country, it's traditional to use a napkin for that sort of thing."

"But what fun would that be?"

He sighed, wondering how things had gone so wrong so fast. She had him twisted around her little finger, when just an hour ago he'd had *her* on the edge.

Time for him to do something about it. Now. And the quickest way he knew to get her off balance was to kiss her senseless.

He stood up, went to her side, took hold of her arms and pulled her up. She stared at him in surprise. Good. Then he leaned down to capture her mouth.

Only, she wasn't there.

She'd slipped out, ducking beneath his arm so fast that he had no time to catch her. A moment later, she smiled victoriously, stretched, making sure she pushed out her chest, and yawned.

"How did it get so late? I can't believe how tired I am. It must be the pasta. All those carbs."

"What?"

"Thank you so much for the wonderful dinner." She took hold of his arm by both hands and headed toward the door. "Next time, I'll cook, but I'm not nearly as good as you are. I have a wonderful recipe for Asian chicken, though. Do you like chicken?"

"Uh—"

"Good. Then, that's settled. We'll have dinner."

"Hey—"

When they reached the door, Jamie stood on tiptoes and kissed him briefly on the lips. Then the door was open, her hand was on his shoulder, and he was outside.

"Good night," she said, just barely hiding her amusement. She shut the door, and he listened to her lock all five of her dead bolts.

What in hell had she done to him? He checked his watch. Just after one in the morning. He'd planned to have her in bed by now, and look at him, standing like some schmuck on her doorstep, with nothing to show for the evening but an erection.

He thought of Dale Parker, his roommate at Yale. Thank God Dale couldn't see this mess. Dale used to brag that Chase could charm the panties off every female within five thousand feet without breaking a sweat. Tonight, he couldn't charm a scent from a rose.

It was crazy. The last time he'd been this bewildered by a woman, he'd been in puberty. It was Eve all over again. And while he was supposed to be the serpent, he'd ended up being the goddamn apple.

He thought of knocking, but decided against it. He'd go home, although it would be a few minutes until he could climb on his bike.

No wonder he'd been bamboozled. All the blood that should have been in his brain had migrated south.

JAMIE LEANED AGAINST THE DOOR, her heart slamming against her chest, her breath shaky and unreliable, her thoughts running a hundred miles an hour. She'd done it! She'd actually used some of her techniques and they'd worked.

Of course, what she hadn't anticipated was the backlash. There was a price to be paid for acting wickedly, and she was paying it now. If she looked up *horny* in the dictionary, she'd see her own picture.

Damn, but she'd been cool. She had to hand it to herself, she'd been one savvy babe. He'd panted over her, lusted for her, needed her—and all because she'd taken her own advice.

This was great. Better than great. She should have

done this ages ago. She had so much more to tell her listeners now. Wait till they heard.

Chase Newman seducing her? Not likely. She was *the man!* Wait, that wasn't right. She was *the woman!* Yes, but what she meant was... She knew what she was. Smart. That's what. Smart and in control.

Be that as it may, she still had to deal with the, uh, repercussions. She couldn't possibly just go to sleep. First, she wasn't the least bit tired, and second... The way he'd looked at her. She closed her eyes and remembered. His dark, brooding eyes, his chiseled jaw, his perfect lips. He was a man built for sex, created for making love. If the situation were different, she'd be in his bed so fast she'd make the land speed record.

But it wasn't different. No matter how much her body wanted him, how much her mind kept imagining all the things they could do, she had to keep her distance. Stay one step ahead of him. Too much was at stake.

She pushed herself away from the door. The dishes needed washing. She should do it now, get it over with. She wasn't the kind to leave the place messy. Never had been.

No. Not tonight. Tonight she would say the hell with the dishes. The hell with everything except her fantasies. She might not be able to have sex with Chase, but it didn't mean she couldn't think about him.

Abandoning the kitchen and the remains of dinner, she headed for the bathroom. As she undressed, she closed her eyes, and he came to her in all his gorgeousness. When he smiled, he looked wicked and boyish at the same time. And his cheekbones! He reminded her of Johnny Depp, who was one of the most stunning creatures on the planet. But Johnny didn't have Chase's strong jaw. Or his sexy laugh. Granted, she hadn't kissed Mr. Depp, but she didn't think there was any way he could kiss her more sensually.

Her mind's eye moved down to Chase's chest. Perfectly broad, amazingly muscular, with exactly the right amount of hair. He was her dream date, her fantasy man, her dark stranger.

And he was absolutely, positively not going to be hers.

She brushed her teeth and washed her face in a fury, angry at what the fates had allowed. By the time she got to her bedroom and slipped on her T-shirt, however, her sense of outrage had diminished, replaced by the prospect of climbing between the sheets.

She'd always had a rich fantasy life, and although she might be inexperienced when it came to men, she wasn't a complete sexual novice. She'd learned early that it was perfectly fine to take matters into her own hands, and that, in fact, it was healthy physically and emotionally. More and more studies were touting the virtues of solo sex…

But her focus was far, far away from scientific theories. In fact, what she was feeling was as basic and undignified as it gets. She was going to sleep with Chase, all by herself.

She opened her nightstand drawer. In it were candles (perfect), aromatherapy oils (yummy), a book by Anaïs Nin, which she wouldn't need tonight (thank you, Mr. Newman), and her old standby Bob, her battery-operated boyfriend.

She lit two candles, put lilac scent in the glass diffuser designed to warm the oil, and lit the bottom of that. Then she slipped between her crisp, white sheets and turned the light off.

Sighing into her pillow, she watched the flickering shadows on her walls, just letting herself relax. As her breathing became more rhythmic and even, her eyes fluttered closed and her imagination kicked into gear.

Chase. With his hands on her shoulders. His warm breath on her neck. Her hand went to her panties and slipped inside. No Bob for her tonight—too impersonal. She wanted sensuality, erotica. She wanted to let go and allow her fantasies to carry her away.

She pictured him so clearly, right down to the slightly crooked tooth and the hint of five-o'clock shadow. His hands moved from her shoulders to her breasts, and she imagined with startling clarity his powerful fingers teasing her nipples, making them erect and painfully sensitive.

It was like watching a movie—but there was no plot, no script, just moving pictures and projected sensations. She let her own fingers work their magic as Chase pulled her dress up and off her, letting it drop where they stood. She was naked—no bra, no panties, just naked—and then so was he, and he took her breath away with his flawless physique. Her gaze moved down his chest, in no rush at all. She pictured his nipples, the chest hair that tapered to a V, his rippled abs and his innie belly button. Slim hips and strong, flat tummy.

Her breaths grew faster and more shallow as the sensations in her body shifted from pleasant to intense. It would be over too soon, but she couldn't slow down. The wave had started and there was no turning back.

She let her gaze move down, but before she could see any more, he pulled her into his arms, into a kiss that made her moan. His lips, his tongue, his breath, his taste…it was so real, so perfect, and—

Tensing, she held her breath, letting the wave crest as she shuddered in a glorious climax. A moment later, after she'd gotten most of her equilibrium back, her eyes opened. Staring at the ceiling, at the shadows from the candles, she came to a terrible realization.

He'd ruined this for her. She'd always counted on being able to take care of herself, to exercise her fantasies, to give her sexual side its due. And once she had taken care of business, she could relax and get on with life. Only… tonight she'd climaxed but she didn't feel fulfilled.

Her imagination wasn't enough. She wanted the real thing. She wanted Chase.

She sat up and blew out the candles. As the darkness swallowed her, she laid back down and buried her face in her pillow.

He was ruining everything—her career, her future, and now this, the one thing she'd never questioned or worried about.

It wasn't fair. In fact, it was downright cruel.

CHASE STOOD AT HIS WINDOW, watching the late-night traffic on Fifth Avenue. He should go to bed, get some sleep. He wasn't tired.

Jamie hadn't left him alone. Not even for five minutes. He'd finally been able to climb on his bike and drive back to the hotel, but once he'd parked, he didn't go up. Instead, he walked, block after long block, not seeing the window displays, barely noticing the people he passed, the cars, the sound of the horns.

She'd thrown him a sucker punch tonight.

Jamie had been frightened of him. He hadn't made that up. He distinctly remembered her darting glances, the way she shrank into the walls as he walked by. And when he'd pulled her into that alley, his intent was anything but noble. He liked seeing the shock in her eyes and, more than that, the pounding of her heart as he stood so close. She was frightened, as much of herself as of him. The game had been to awaken her, but now it seemed she'd been awake for years.

He wasn't usually wrong about women. Oh, he might miss the finer details but, on the whole, he knew what he was talking about. He'd given the matter of women almost as high a priority as he gave racing.

Was it the surprise that made him want her this much? She'd certainly pushed the right sexual buttons. He found himself becoming aroused at the very thought of her. The way those big, dark eyes had looked at him so hungrily. Her long, delicate neck. The way her breasts seemed to swell as her dress molded against her chest.

Dammit, he was doing it again. It was ridiculous. He'd left spontaneous erections back in high school, or so he'd thought.

He crossed his room and sat down on the edge of the bed. The phone message he'd scrawled was still on the nightstand. His manager wanted him to do an exhibition race in Paris next week. The offer couldn't have come at a better time. He'd leave New York on Sunday, and forget all about the radio joke and about Dr. Jamie. He loved Paris, and he hadn't seen Anna in almost eight months. Beautiful, blonde Anna, whose estranged husband didn't understand her. Who was very good in bed.

He'd be wise to stick with the Annas of the world. Keep clear of the Jamies.

Not that he was totally giving up. He had till Sunday. Five days to find out if Dr. Jamie's bite was as bad as her bark.

He kicked off his boots, then finished undressing. In his boxers, he went to the bathroom, did his thing, and in short order he was in bed, the do-not-disturb sign anchored on the door.

As his head hit the pillow, an image of Jamie came to

him without his permission. In his mind, she looked at him through half-closed eyes, her lips moist and parted, and she was completely naked.

He hardly knew where to start.

8

"THIS IS DR. JAMIE, and we're talking about sex. Go ahead, Phil."

"I know you've been asked this before, but I don't know what I'm doing wrong. My wife isn't having orgasms—at least, not with me."

"How much time are you spending on foreplay, Phil?"

"I don't know. Five minutes?"

"And what does your foreplay consist of?"

He cleared his throat. "She usually goes down on me, and then I go down on her…"

"And this all takes place in five minutes?"

"Sometimes longer."

"I'm not sure this is going to solve your wife's orgasm deficiency, but I bet it helps. I want you to take notes on this, Phil, and study this. There will be a test."

"On what?"

"On the art of cunnilingus."

"Great."

"First, get comfy. Comfortable enough to hang out a while. Second, use your hands. Tease with your finger-tips. Wet your fingers, then touch everything. Remember, lightly here. You're only revving the engines, not going in for a landing."

Phil laughed, but she could tell this was no joke to him.

"When she moves her hips, you can start with your tongue. Flick the tip of your tongue, or use the flat part like you're licking an ice cream cone. Try everything, and pay attention to her body language. After several minutes of casual exploration, focus in on the clitoris. And be careful about direct stimulation—she might be too sensitive. Again, pay attention to how she moves and what she says."

"Yeah. Okay."

"This would be a good time to use your fingers inside her. Find her G-spot, and if she likes that, keep it up as your tongue focuses on her. Increase your speed and pressure slowly. By this time, she's probably going to be thrashing about, so you'll have to keep up with her. Don't back off. Keep up the pressure as she gets close to her orgasm. Then, as soon as she comes, you move, quick like a bunny, and insert your penis. She's going to be swollen, and she'll love the feel of you inside her. Go for broke. She doesn't have to have another orgasm. She's fine. It's okay to concentrate on your own."

"Whoa. That's a lot of information."

"You sound like a bright guy. I bet you pick it up in two shakes."

"Great, I'll let you know what happens."

"Please do. And Phil? Go for it. Don't be shy. You'll enjoy yourself, too."

Marcy signaled that she had another caller on the line. When Jamie looked at her monitor, she felt a thump in her chest. Chase. He was on the phone. Why? *Why?* What did he want? She wasn't ready. Oh, damn, no. Not yet. "This is Dr. Jamie, and we're talking about—" she swallowed, forcing herself to calm down "—sex."

She pressed the button for line five. "Hello, Chase."

"Hello." His voice was so sexy, she knew they'd just climbed five points in the ratings.

"What's on your mind?"

"You."

She blushed, then willed the heat away. "And why is that?"

"At the moment because I'm staring at your face on the side of a bus. Actually, I'm staring at both our faces."

"Pardon?"

"Step outside on your next break," he said. "You'll see what I mean."

"So, uh, you saw this bus and it made you think of me?"

His laugh did something fluttery to her tummy. "That's not the only reason."

"What else?"

"Last night."

"Oh?" Her pulse was now at a steady clip of about a million beats per second. A part of her wanted to toy with him, to get sexy and intimate and just go with the flow. The other part of her was appalled at the knowledge that they were having this conversation with thousands of strangers listening.

"Did you tell them?"

"Tell them what?"

"About what you did?"

"No. I don't remember doing anything noteworthy."

"That's disappointing. I thought my linguini was quite noteworthy."

Her shoulders drooped. "I apologize. It was outstanding. Perfect."

"Then, why did you send me home?"

"It was late. I was tired."

"No, you weren't."

"You know better than I do when I'm sleepy?"

"I know quite a few things."

"Like?"

"I know how your nipples tighten when you're being kissed. I know the scent of you when you're aroused. I know that you didn't go right to sleep after I left, although I'll bet you went to bed."

The only reason Jamie didn't fall off her chair was that her headphones were attached to the console. "Ex—" She cleared her throat. "Excuse me?"

"Why don't you tell them what you did when you got in bed, Jamie."

"I went to sleep."

"Before that."

"That's personal."

"So you don't talk about that kind of thing on your show, eh?"

"Of course we do. It's perfectly natural. Nothing to be ashamed of."

He chuckled in that low, sexy way of his. "Then, you did satisfy yourself."

Dammit. He'd tricked her. "I didn't say that."

"Yes, you did, honey. You said that to me and about a hundred thousand of your closest friends."

Jamie fought her panic. Looking at Marcy didn't help. Her producer was on two phones at once, the phone bank was lit up like a Christmas tree, and Cujo was laughing his head off.

"So why don't you tell me what you thought about when you were in bed?"

"There's nothing to tell."

"You're lying, Jamie. And you don't do it very well."

"I think it's time for a commercial."

"The commercial can wait." His voice lowered. "Talk to me, baby."

She moaned as she buried her head in her hands. This was impossible, horrible. She was humiliating herself on the air again. The worst part of it was, she didn't know how to extricate herself from the situation with any kind of grace or wit. She felt thick and foolish, and if he called her baby one more time she was simply going to crawl under the console and never come out.

"Jamie?"

"What?"

"Look up."

She lifted her head. Chase, holding a cell phone to his ear, stood right next to Marcy in the production booth.

"Surprise."

"What are you doing here?"

"I thought your audience might like to know what *I* thought about last night when I went to bed."

"No."

"No?"

"Commercial. We must need a commercial now, right? Cujo? Marcy?"

Chase walked over to Cujo's board for a moment. The two men huddled, Cujo nodded, then Chase disappeared for a moment. Fred showed up in the production booth, and then her door swung slowly open. Chase's smile was victorious. He'd gotten her back for last night, all right. And then some.

She had to focus, shift the power. Last night had been so great, so intoxicating. She could do it again. She had to. This was her playground, for heaven's sake. She was never uncomfortable talking about sex. "Come pull up a chair. Put on some headphones. I know my audience would love to hear about your night."

He slid into the chair next to hers, his air cocky, his scent intoxicating. "Where do you want me to start?"

"Why don't you set the scene for us. How do you sleep? Pajamas? Boxers?"

He shook his head. "In the raw."

"That makes things convenient. Do you use any kind of oil? Vaseline, maybe?"

He blinked, swallowed. Jamie had to force herself not to grin. The fly had voluntarily walked into her parlor, and now she had him in her web. No way he could embarrass her on the air.

"Chase?"

"No. No oils. No tricks, no equipment."

"Just your hand?"

"Uh, yeah."

"We've just spent some time giving some oral tips to our male listeners, and now it's time to switch gears. A lot of our female listeners want to understand how to give a really great hand job. It's always better to get that information directly from the horse's mouth, so to speak."

Chase coughed. He turned slightly away, but she'd already seen his blush. This was so great. She couldn't have asked for a more perfect situation.

His shoulders shifted back and he turned toward her. "I lick my palm," he said, slowly and distinctly, "then take hold of my penis at the base. Firmly. Then I move my hand up and down the shaft. I take my time, close my eyes and let my imagination go. Last night, you were the star of my private video. You were naked, and those nipples of yours were like thick pencil erasers, hard and sensitive and very, very pink."

So he'd decided to fight fire with fire, eh? "And I'm

sure you wouldn't mind sharing the dimensions of your penis? So that our listeners can get a visual."

He narrowed his eyes and shook his head, a warning. "A little over eight inches."

"Circumcised?"

"Yes."

"How thick? An inch? Two inches?"

"Closer to three."

"Oh, my. You must be very proud."

"I didn't build it. It came from the manufacturer this way."

She laughed, and then she looked at the window. Cujo was waving both hands at her, signaling for a break. Marcy, Fred and the intern were both on phones, and everyone who was still at the station at this late hour had come in to watch. Ted, of course—but also some of the computer techs, the program manager, his secretary and, if she wasn't mistaken, three of the cleaning staff.

"It seems we're late for a commercial, but I don't want to break right now. Cujo? Can we make this happen?"

Cujo turned to Fred. There was a very brief, very heated discussion, then Cujo pressed his mike button. He said to her and her audience, "It's your show, Jamie. Go for it."

"Wonderful." She turned to Chase. "You were saying?"

"I was saying that the act of masturbating is pretty much the same for all men. What varies is the fantasy. And I've got a rich imagination. Last night, for example, in my mind, you were standing in front of me without a stitch on. And while you may be small, you still have curves in all the right places." He grinned. "I liked your haircut."

She touched the back of her head.

"Not that one." He winked at her. "That Brazilian look. Just that small strip of hair…"

He scored with that one. She hadn't seen it coming and she hadn't prepared her defense. What shocked her, what made it hard to come up with any words at all, was that he was right. She had gotten a Brazilian wax. It had hurt like hell, too.

"Were you peeking when you should have been cooking?" she finally managed to say.

The cocky smile was back. "No. But I knew, nonetheless. Just like I know that when you make love to yourself, you take your time. You like the feel of your own flesh. You don't like to admit it, Jamie, but your sensuality can't be hidden. Not by long, baggy dresses, or your degree. You need sex, baby." He leaned closer to her. "You need it or you'll wither and die."

The flutter in her chest stole her voice for a moment. Why did he have such an effect on her? They were just words. "No one, to my knowledge, has ever died from lack of sex."

"Maybe not physically, but emotionally, spiritually."

"So it's a spiritual experience for you?"

"Oh, yeah. If it's with the right woman."

"We're getting sidetracked here. This is Dr. Jamie, and Chase Newman is here in the studio talking to us about how he masturbates."

Chase's right eye twitched. He turned to look past her, but she kept her eyes on him, forcing him to meet her gaze. He couldn't possibly be as cool as he'd like her to think.

"In Los Angeles, a colleague of mine, Dr. Susie, does her show from her bedroom. She invites guests to come on down, and everyone participates. Her guests get naked, and sometimes they get together right there, on the air."

"Are you suggesting we do that?"

"I was thinking that if you'd like, it would be fine if you wanted to get more comfortable. Maybe take those jeans off. Use all your senses as you explain the process. I'm sure my listeners would love it."

"I'll pass."

"They won't be able to see you, Chase. It is *radio*."

"How about the crew in there?" He nodded to the production booth.

"We can send everyone away except for Cujo and Marcy. Surely that wouldn't bother you."

"Hey, I'm game if you are."

"Oh, no. The host doesn't get naked."

"Why not? Is there something wrong with you? Or are you just embarrassed?"

"I'm perfectly comfortable with my body, thank you. But this show is about you tonight. You and you alone."

"Uh-uh. No go. But nice try."

She thought about taking one more dig, but perhaps she'd done enough. "Hmm. Okay. Sorry, ladies. Maybe next time."

He moved closer. "The next time I take off my pants, it's going to be for you, Doc. All for you."

"Isn't that nice."

He laughed. "Can I go on with my fantasy? Or are you just going to keep interrupting?"

"It's all yours."

"No. But it will be. And when you do give yourself to me, I'm going to teach you a thing or two. I know you have your degree and you've gotten straight As but, honey, there are some things you can't learn from books."

"Such as?"

"Such as what it feels like to come so hard your ears

ring. You know what I'd do to you? I'd put you between my lips and suck you like an ice-cream soda."

Jamie opened her mouth but nothing came out.

"I'd tie you up so you couldn't move a muscle, and I'd put a blindfold on you, and then I'd play like a kid with a new toy. Nothing you could do but moan and come. And, honey, you would *come*."

His eyes let her know this wasn't hypothetical, and it wasn't for the audience. He meant to do those things to her, and her body seemed to be enthusiastic about the idea. She wondered if Howard Stern or Dr. Susie had ever made love to a guest on the air. Maybe she could be the first.

"Jamie?"

From far away, she heard Marcy's voice. Turning slowly toward the window, Jamie saw Marcy point to her computer. It was a caller. A thirty-three-year-old from Soho. Somehow, Jamie managed to punch the right button. "Hi, Alicia. You have something to say?"

"I just wanted Chase to know that if you don't want him, I do."

"Thanks, sweetheart," Chase said, really pouring on the charm, "but Jamie does want me. She wants me more than she dares admit. And soon, very soon, she's going to ask me to make love to her."

"I can't believe she hasn't already," Alicia said. "I mean, come on. Who cares about a bet when she could be rolling in the sheets with you?"

"Why don't you ask her?"

"Okay. Dr. Jamie? Care to comment?"

Jamie stared at her console for a moment as she gathered her wits. She cleared her throat. Then, in what she believed was a very natural tone of voice, she said, "Alicia, I'm glad you asked, because this wager isn't about who gets whom into bed first. It's about women and men, and the right to choose. To own up to our role in the mating dance, and to be cognizant that no one can trick us into doing anything we don't want to do."

"Dr. Jamie?"

"Yes, Alicia?"

"That's such a crock. So what if he seduces you? It's not a crime unless you say no. I don't get the problem."

"And that's why I can't afford to lose this bet. You see, Alicia, the struggle between men and women has been going on for hundreds of years. Since the time when we were nothing but property. We may not be owned by men in the strict sense any longer, but we're still under their thumbs. I talk to young women, women who should be having the time of their lives dating and playing the field, and you know what I hear over and over again?"

"What?"

"The young women are being seduced, but not by a man. By an idea. By the illusion that sex is love. It's not, and there isn't a man alive who doesn't know it. That fantasy is in the feminine domain, and I can't tell you how many women have gone down in flames over it. Shall we talk about teenage pregnancy? Where do you think that starts? With the idea that we're helpless. That if he's trying to get me into bed, he must love me. And if I say yes, I'm saying I love him right back. Only, in the morning, there is no bond, no tie, no love. Just a guy and a girl with completely different agendas."

"So, okay," her caller said, "I get that it can be that way, but isn't it possible that it can be magic, too?"

"Magic?"

"Yeah. Like in the fairy tales. Where it doesn't matter if she was seduced or not because they're meant to be together. They belong together."

Jamie didn't answer right away. "I suppose it could happen like that. It wouldn't be likely, but I'd be lying if I said I didn't think there might be a chance for magic."

"Great. So, um, how do you know?"

Jamie looked at Chase. "To tell you the truth, Alicia. I don't have a clue."

9

CHASE SAW THE CONFUSION on Jamie's face. It lasted a brief second, but it gave him his answer. Dr. Jamie was full of it. He'd suspected before; now he was sure. She talked a good game, but there was a fundamental flaw in her logic. Women weren't like men. They had not only different plumbing, but different wiring. And women, whether they liked it or not, were wired for committed relationships.

It made sense biologically. They needed to count on someone for food and lodging while they tended babies. Survival of the species.

While he did agree that some women could have sex for the hell of it, for the fun, with no strings and no expectations, such women were few and far between, and Jamie was not one of them.

It was a shame, because he'd thought a lot about how this little game was going to end. When he'd said yes, he'd wanted to show the good doctor a thing or two about sex and seduction and everything in between. But now that he was doing just that, the victory was bittersweet.

In the past two days, despite his best intentions, he'd come to like Jamie. Last night had clinched that. She'd be dangerous if she realized her own power. With that quick mind and that sinful body, she could make any man jump through hoops. That's what women in general didn't understand—Jamie, in particular.

Men wanted sex for the release, sure, but being inside a woman was the safest place on earth. No amount of money, power or glory could give a man that sense of security. Hell, men made money and became powerful just so they could get the women.

"Chase?"

He realized Jamie had been trying to get his attention. He'd been so lost in thought that he'd missed the commercials and her station ID. They were on the air. "Yeah?"

"Carly asked an interesting question."

"I'm sorry, I didn't hear it. I was distracted."

"That's all right. Carly, would you like to ask your question again?"

"Sure," came the sultry, low voice from the speaker. "I think women can have sex without love, but they don't want to. I think love is the whole purpose. I wondered what you thought about that?"

"Hmm." He had to be careful about this. The game was still afoot, and even though the outcome was more uncertain than ever, he didn't want to say anything that would mess things up. "I think love means different things to different people. If you're talking about security, then I agree."

"Love isn't security," the caller said, then chuckled softly. "Or, at least, it's a really small part of it."

"Fair enough." Chase leaned forward, closer to the mike. "So what is love?"

"I have no idea," Carly answered. "I've never been in love. Not really. I've been in like, and sometimes in lust, but never in love."

"How do you know?"

There was a pause. Jamie looked at him questioningly. "I think that's a very important question," she said.

"Here's what I think," Carly said. "I think that love is a spiritual, physical and emotional experience, like a three-legged stool. You take one of those aspects away, and the whole thing tips on its side. The secret is to find the balance."

Jamie closed her eyes for a few seconds. Then she smiled. "Carly, are you trying to take my job?"

"No. At least, not right now. I'm just trying to do this life thing well."

"From where I sit, you're doing one hell of a good job. I thank you for sharing with us."

"May I ask Chase one more thing?"

He nodded. "Shoot."

"What is it you know about women that makes you so good at seducing them?"

He opened his mouth to say something clever, but thought better of it. This woman was bright and thoughtful and she deserved an answer. So did Jamie.

"Every woman is unique. They don't get much credit for that. Every woman has a story that's hers alone, but I don't think many people listen to it. Women want to be heard. They want someone to pay attention to them, and I'm not just talking about sexually."

Jamie leaned in, but he put his hand up. He wasn't finished. "I also believe women want to be seduced. They want to pretend they don't have the responsibility. That the choice was taken from them." He looked at Jamie, not surprised to find her expression hardening.

"The thing is, women are responsible for so damn much. They have to take care of the house, of the kids, of the cats, of the groceries, the dry cleaning, the car pools—the list goes on and on. This starts young—real young, from what I can see. Men are out there learning to compete, and women are taking up the slack. They always have. When it comes to love, and even just sex, I think women don't want to have to be the responsible party. For once, they want someone else to do it for them. To make it easy. To take the blame if things get messed up."

"And, believe it or not, I agree with you," said Jamie. "Women don't want the responsibility, so they give it away. Only, it's not that easy. They still get stuck with the consequences of their actions, whether they pretend to choose or not."

"Everybody gets stuck with the consequences, Jamie. That's life."

"So why should women bury their heads in the sand over this one issue?"

"I don't think you give your women friends enough credit. I think they all know what the real story is. They know. But sometimes even the toughest broad needs to be swept away."

"But—"

"You need to be swept away, darlin'. You need it badly."

She opened her mouth but didn't speak, and then Carly spoke up. "Chase?"

"Yes?"

"Fascinating answer. Thank you. Now, can you tell me why you don't have someone in your life? If you know women so well, why aren't you married? Or at least in love?"

"Okay, this is where I stop. I'll tell you all about how I spank the monkey, but I won't tell you about why I'm not married. It's too personal."

Carly laughed. "Fair enough. Thanks, Dr. Jamie and Chase. This was great."

"Thank you, Carly," Jamie said, then nodded at Cujo as she launched into her station ID segment.

While she was still talking, Chase excused himself and went down the hall to the employee lounge. There, he stared at the vending machines until his vision blurred. He wasn't thinking about cocoa or candy bars. His thoughts were with Jamie, and the simple question Carly had asked.

Like her, he'd never been in love, just lust. Or like. But mostly lust. He wasn't allowed the luxury of love, not because he couldn't feel it but because he knew what would happen if he did fall. He'd want what everyone wants—a life, a future, which he couldn't have.

It had never really bothered him. He'd accepted his fate years ago, when he'd discovered the facts about his great-grandfather's death. He could fight lots of things, but heredity wasn't one of them.

So why did he feel uneasy? Because the questioning on the air had come too close to the bone? A long time ago, he'd told a woman friend about his history, and his future, whatever there was going to be of it. She'd laughed and told him he was ridiculous. He'd never brought it up again. People didn't understand. They didn't know about the Newman men.

It wasn't a great tragedy. At least he knew his life wasn't going to go on forever, and he lived accordingly. So what if he'd never know what it was like to love a woman, to have her love him back. It didn't make any difference. Not really.

But as he got out his wallet, retrieved a dollar bill and fed it to the soda machine, a dark, solid fist of regret settled in his gut.

JAMIE ALMOST TOLD CHASE to leave after the show. She was tired in a way that had little to do with sleep. The broadcast had been thoughtful—thanks to Carly and a few others—which should have pleased her. Instead, it just made her more insecure.

Just days ago, she'd been happy. Her show was doing well—her parents thought she was wasting her time and talent, but she believed she was helping people—and she'd made peace with her loneliness.

Now, as she stood in the bathroom of WXNT staring at herself in the mirror, her show was a publicity farce, and the one secret that could destroy everything was threatening in a very real way. Her mother had called this afternoon to ask her if she wanted to talk. Her mother never wanted to talk unless it was to share observations about what Jamie was doing wrong. Of course, the publicity had mortified her parents. They had only been enthusiastic about her radio career after she'd convinced them that her services were of real value. She wasn't sure of that now. Was she helping people? Was it right to tell women they had to take responsibility for every aspect of their lives? What if Chase was right?

The door swung open and Marcy walked in. "I've been looking for you. Chase has a car downstairs."

"I know. I don't think I'm going to go with him."

"How come?" Marcy watched Jamie's reflection as she washed her hands.

"I'm tired. I want to spend some time alone. No one said I had to be with him every day."

"You're right, although you're going to have to explain yourself to your listeners. Are you prepared to do that?"

"They'll understand."

Marcy grabbed a few paper towels and dried her hands.

"Are you sure? They're having fun with this, Jamie. They want you to play."

"They can't want me to play that badly. Surely they'll forgive me for one night."

"You're so young," Marcy said, patting her on the shoulder. "You still think well of the masses. That's sweet."

"Cut it out, Marcy. I'm serious."

Marcy's smile faded. "What's wrong?"

Jamie leaned against the counter and debated her next words. "I'm confused. It's no big deal."

"Confused about what? Chase?"

She nodded. "And how I feel about him."

"Go on."

What the hell. "I have no intention of letting myself be seduced. I don't believe in it, and that's no line—I truly don't."

"But?"

"But every time I see the man, my entire body goes wiggy on me."

"Explain 'wiggy.'"

"This is so embarrassing."

"Talk."

Jamie hopped up on the counter. Her skirt, a pale blue, gauzy number she'd picked up at a flea market, fanned around her knees. Her sandal-clad feet swung back and forth, making her feel about five. "I get butterflies in my stomach. I forget to breathe. I keep touching my hair and blushing and stammering and doing all the stupid adolescent things a girl does when she has a crush on a boy."

"And this surprises you?"

"Yes."

"Why?"

"Marcy, it's me. The one who doesn't believe in seduction, remember?"

"Oh, come on, Jamie. Did you honestly think you wouldn't feel anything for Chase? Any red-blooded, heterosexual woman would…" Marcy raised a brow.

"No. I'm not gay."

"Well, then, what did you expect? He's stunning. He exudes masculinity. He's smart, he's clean, he's rich. He's everything you could want in a man, and, if you haven't noticed yet, he has really big feet."

"Jeez, Marcy."

"It's important."

"That's not what I tell my listeners."

"My point exactly."

"Now you're being obscure."

Marcy jumped up on the counter next to Jamie. "Look, kiddo, I think you're right to help women, especially young women, learn to accept responsibility for their actions. If they're not hearing that message from their parents, they're pretty much SOL. School isn't teaching them. TV isn't teaching them. So you're doing a good and noble thing."

"But?"

"But he's Chase Newman, and you'd have to be jughead-stupid not to want him to seduce the hell out of you."

"Jughead-stupid?"

Marcy grinned. "Okay, so I'm exaggerating, but not by much. The man is the hottest thing since French toast. You've heard the stories about him. Not only is he hot, but he's one of the good guys. He may be playing this out, but, in the end, he'll do the right thing."

"How do you know?"

"You know what Fred told me?"

"What?"

"Chase found out that Fred's daughter had a major crush on one of the Backstreet Boys. A week later, it's her birthday, and who comes to the station?"

"A Backstreet Boy."

"Exactly. It took Fred weeks to finally figure out it was Chase who'd used his father's connections to pull it off. Now tell me, is this not a wonderful guy? Honey, he wants you. And the butterflies in your tummy are saying you want him. What's the problem?"

"Are you suggesting I let him win?"

"It doesn't have to be anyone's business but your own."

"Lie to my listeners? Are you crazy?"

Marcy made a sour face. "Maybe. All I know is, Carly was right. You're not leaving any room for magic."

"I can't have it both ways."

"Let me ask you something. If you win this bet out of sheer willpower, have you really won?"

"What?"

"Seems to me that he has seduced you. You want it. If it weren't for the wager, I think you'd go for it. So, haven't you lost already?"

Jamie climbed down. "No. You're missing the whole point. It's about our actions, not our thoughts. I can wish a hundred times a day to be a jewel thief, but they can't arrest me until I take the diamonds."

"You are, aren't you?"

"What?"

"Thinking about him a hundred times a day. Call me crazy, but I think there's more than just sex and seduction going on between you two."

Jamie wanted to deny the allegation. But she was afraid Marcy was right—not that she would let her friend know that.

Marcy shrugged. "Have it your way."

"I intend to."

"So are you going to go with him?"

"No." She went to the door. "Yes." She pushed it open, then stepped into the hallway. As the door swung shut, she whimpered, "Maybe."

Marcy's droll "You go, girl!" made Jamie whimper one more time as she headed toward her office to get her things so that she could meet Chase.

The thought made her body quiver and her head ache. She was completely screwed.

CHASE HELD THE DOOR to his suite so that Jamie could enter. He'd taken a quick glance, and when he saw the dinner set up, he relaxed. The GM of the hotel had taken care of his requests, as always. It's why he stayed here when he could have picked any hotel in the city. If he wanted a dinner for two from one of the finest chefs in New York at midnight, voilà, it appeared. And they said money couldn't buy happiness.

"Wow. Look at this place." Jamie had zeroed in on the view, naturally. The panorama never failed to thrill. The city looked like something out of a dream from this height. A lesson there—anything can look pretty if you're far enough away.

"Is that dinner? Or breakfast?"

"Dinner. For us." He tossed his keys on the dresser. "Want some champagne?"

"Champagne gives me a headache."

"Not this champagne."

"Why not?"

"Trust me."

"Fine. Pour away."

He lifted the bottle and checked the label. As requested,

it was a 1990 Cristal. Worth every penny of its exorbitant price. He popped the cork, then poured into the flutes. The sound of the bubbles made him sigh. Damn, what a great sound.

He took Jamie her glass and watched her expression as she sipped the chilled liquid. He doubted she realized her forehead was furrowed, probably in anticipation of bitterness. Sure enough, the moment she swallowed, her eyes widened in surprise. "Oh my God."

He nodded. "Welcome to great champagne."

"Very nice." She drank again, a bigger sip.

"Don't chug it. Even if it does taste like heaven it can still make you drunk."

She smiled. "You love this, don't you."

"What?"

"Showing me how sophisticated you are. How worldly."

He nodded. "I suppose I do."

"May I make a conjecture?"

"Why not?"

"Okay." She turned to face him, putting her glass on the coffee table. "I don't fully understand why you wanted to play this game with me, but I'm beginning to get an idea."

"Oh?"

"I think if it's all a game, then it's safe. You don't have to worry. There's an end in sight, and I think that's all that's important to you."

Chase's stomach clenched. She was right, more dead-on correct than she'd ever know. The end was in sight. The end of it all. The end of hearing her laughter. Of watching her eyes widen in surprise. Of touching that smooth, silky skin behind her knees.

He was going to miss that, and so much more. He put down his own glass as he moved to her side. His hand went to her hair and then to her cheek. The softness killed him. The sweet scent of her. The way she sighed.

He pulled her into his arms, wanting to touch her everywhere. To feel everything. He wanted her naked, open, waiting for him. He wanted the safety of being inside her, the immortality of those moments before his climax. All of the important things in life were right here, in this woman and, God forgive him, he couldn't let her go.

He kissed her, and when she trembled he knew she understood what he was asking her to do. The taste of her and the slight hint of champagne went right to his head. He stopped thinking, stopped worrying about anything but this moment.

He lifted her, sweeping his arm under her legs, and he carried her past the dinner under the silver domes, past the bar, through the door and to the bed. He put her down on her knees, so he wouldn't have to stop kissing her. Her tongue darted in his mouth, and when he returned the favor she sucked on him, giving him a sample of what she could do to far more sensitive places on his body.

His hand ran down her back and cupped her buttocks as he climbed on the bed in front of her. Face-to-face, on their knees, he pulled her toward him so she pressed against his jeans. Her soft gasp let him know she'd felt his erection straining for release. Soon, soon.

But first, he moved his mouth to the hollow of her neck, then to the curve below her ear. He licked, nibbled, kissed—lost in sensation, in the softness of her skin.

The world narrowed to a very small space. To a king-size bed and a small woman with too many clothes on.

His hands went to her blouse, pale blue, and her buttons. He undid three, and then he looked down to see she wasn't wearing a bra. The sight of her hard little nipples made him moan in a mixture of pain and pleasure too intense for one man to stand.

Dipping his head, he kissed the top of her breast, then slowly, slowly moved down, his tongue drawing a moist line to her bud. He captured her between his lips, ran his tongue in a tight circle, then sucked deeply.

She mewed as her head fell back. Her hands held his upper arms, her fingers digging in as she fought for balance. He wanted to shake her equilibrium, to make her feel as out of control as he did.

He needed her. He *needed*.

Jamie bit her lip to stop another moan. What he was doing to her! His lips, his tongue—she'd never felt anything like it before. No one had ever... Not even this. Her body was so unschooled, so naive. And under his tender ministrations she was coming alive, blooming as a new flower.

She held on to him as he suckled her right breast, then her left. The sensation was beyond anything she could have predicted. Everything in her was connected. Her nipples and her fingertips and her tummy and, most of all, between her legs. The more he touched her, the more she wanted to be touched. The more she wanted to give herself completely.

He nipped her lightly on the underside of her breast, and then she felt his hand on her leg, his fingers trailing a skittery line up onto her thigh.

She should stop him. She should. And she would, in a minute. In...just a few minutes.

He tickled her inner thigh, and then he moved his mouth from her breast to her lips. His kiss, soul-deep and brazen, ignited another fire inside her. She'd been dry kindling, waiting for a match. And he'd hit her with a blazing torch.

Tongues dueled, fingers grasped, and her heart beat so fast it felt as if she would die from pure pleasure. And then his fingers were on her inner thigh, and while his tongue thrust inside her, his fingers moved to one panty leg, and slipped underneath. She had to stop him. Only, only…

His fingers brushed her sex, just a light, feathery brush that changed everything. But she couldn't…

She pulled away from his kiss, opened her eyes, tried to focus, to pull herself together, but his finger slipped inside her and he rubbed back and forth before settling on the perfect spot. Her mouth refused to do anything but moan as he rubbed tiny circles, making her whole body tremble and sway.

"Chase—"

"Hush."

She shook her head. "No. I can't."

"You can. We can. I feel how much you want it, Jamie. Did you think I couldn't tell? You're wet and hot and swollen and ready, and I'm going to make you scream."

"No."

"Say yes, Jamie. Just that one word. Say yes, and I'll take you straight to heaven."

"I—"

Just as she was about to push herself away, his finger plunged inside her. Not far, though. Her virginity stopped him short.

She shoved him back so hard that she nearly toppled. Instead, she scrambled to her feet and tried to button her blouse with useless hands.

"Jamie?"

She turned around, her face blazing with humiliation.

"My God, Jamie, tell me what that was."

"I have to go."

He was beside her then, and his hands on her shoulders turned her to face him. "Are you a virgin?"

She couldn't say it. She couldn't. All she wanted to do was disappear. Why had she let it get this far? She was stupid! Stupid, and foolish, and now it was all over. Everything. Her life, her career. She'd be the laughingstock of New York.

"Jamie?"

She swallowed hard and nodded. If she could have come up with a lie, she would have, but her brain had stopped functioning.

His head tilted to the side as he gazed at her in utter confusion. "But you're Dr. Jamie, the Sexpert."

"No. I'm Dr. Jamie, the fraud."

10

CHASE FOLLOWED HER OUT of the bedroom, his mind still trying to fold around this startling bit of information. *A virgin.* The thing was, he'd just blurted it out, not really believing he was right. But the look on her face...

Jamie had never had sex.

She grabbed her purse and headed toward the door. He tried to stop her, but she was too quick for him and shut the door in his face. He didn't let that stop him. A second later, he was in the hallway running after her. She couldn't leave. Not yet. Not until he got to the bottom of this.

At the elevator, she pressed the down button a half-dozen times, and as he got closer he saw a tear glisten on her cheek. A pang of something—guilt? compassion?—hit him where it counted.

"Please leave me alone," she said, her voice choked with pregnant sobs.

"I can't. Come back with me. We can talk about this."

"No."

"Jamie, it doesn't—"

She faced him squarely so he could see the pain distort her face. "Go ahead. Say it. I'm a fraud. I am. It's true. So now you know. Now everyone will know. I don't give a damn. I'm tired of pretending. Go call Whittaker. She'll be thrilled. She'll probably get a damn Pulitzer for her exposé."

"I have no intention of calling her."

The elevator door opened, and Jamie slipped inside. "I don't care. Do whatever you like."

He blocked the door with his body. "Just come back."

"No."

"Please."

She squeezed her eyes shut for a moment. When she opened them, the anguish made his chest ache. "I can't talk to you now."

He nodded. Stepped back. "I'll call you," he said as the door closed.

A virgin. He still couldn't quite get it. The most famous sex therapist since Dr. Ruth had never had sex. No, wait. He couldn't be sure about that. She'd never had intercourse. She might have done everything else under the sun. She sure as hell talked like she had. But now he wasn't sure of anything.

As he headed back to his room, he dug his card key out of his pocket. Man, if Darlene got wind of this—

A thought hit him between the eyes. Darlene had suspected. Not necessarily this, but something. Of course she had. That's why she'd been so determined to see this prank through. Why she'd been so convincing when she'd asked him to seduce Jamie. What he didn't understand was what had made Darlene suspect there was a secret. Something had tipped her off, he felt sure of that. A man? A scorned lover? What was the woman trying to prove?

He should have thought of all this before he'd agreed to be Darlene's patsy. He'd never guessed that this might be the outcome, but he should have realized there were ulterior motives at work. He wasn't some rube. He knew people were selfish. Hell, hadn't he agreed to this out of selfishness himself? Sure. He wanted to sleep with Jamie. Who cared what *she* wanted? He had something to prove.

He walked into the suite. Dinner was still warm under the silver domes. Filet mignon with truffles, prepared by one of the best chefs in the country. No need to waste it all, right?

He sat down, removed the dome in front of him and stabbed a baby potato with his fork. Decidedly not hungry, he ate the side dish anyway, then the steak. Despite his lack of enthusiasm about the meal, he had to admit it was incredible. Jamie would have been impressed.

He reached over and grabbed the champagne from the ice bucket, brought the bottle to his lips and tipped his head back.

Not a smart move. He coughed for several minutes and then gasped for breath. Impetuous. That's what he was. Greedy. Selfish.

Everything was always about him, no one else. The excuse he used to justify his behavior had always felt solid: death at thirty-five was a powerful motivator. But it was an excuse—a way to rationalize his actions, no matter how reprehensible.

He'd put Jamie in a terrible position. She'd never be syndicated now, not after this got out. She probably wouldn't work in radio again.

All because he'd wanted to prove he was a stud. It wasn't about boredom, not completely at least. He'd wanted everyone to see he was *the man* in the bedroom. Dammit, his ego was that big.

He lost his appetite for everything but the champagne. He grabbed the bottle in one hand, the glass in the other, then leaned back.

What was he supposed to do now? He didn't have any desire to hurt Jamie, although he already had done so. He didn't want her career to go down the tubes because he was a jerk. Should he lie? Should he just tell Darlene that Jamie had won? That he hadn't been able to seduce the doctor?

He took a drink, and when he didn't choke, he finished the glass and poured himself another, all the while thinking about what it would be like on the circuit once he'd admitted defeat. Oh man, the drivers would have a field day. He'd be the butt of jokes for years to come.

Maybe there was a compromise. A way for both Jamie and him to win. He'd have to think this thing through carefully. And he would, as soon as he had another glass of champagne. Or two.

JAMIE HAD NO IDEA where she was. She'd been walking for hours, barely aware of the traffic or the late-night pedestrians or even of the balmy night air. Her tears had finally slowed to a trickle, and she supposed she should be grateful for that. There was nothing else to be grateful for.

She'd blown it—blown it to smithereens. Her career, her future, her reputation, her credibility—all gone because she'd let herself be seduced. The irony burned like a white-hot brand.

A red light stopped her, and while she waited, she forced herself to tell the truth. There was no such thing as seduction. She had walked into Chase's suite with her eyes wide open. He hadn't done anything she hadn't given him permission to do. She hadn't been hexed or hypnotized or enticed or led astray. Whatever happened—all of what happened—it was her own weakness, her own vulnerability, her own stupidity that had been to blame.

Was it worth it? Was having him touch her worth more than her career?

Her gait slowed as she turned a corner. She thought about the moment he'd put her on the bed. When he'd kissed her and teased her and… She hadn't been thinking about the wager or her job or anything else. Being with Chase had shifted her focus to a very old and basic part of the brain. The place where there were no consequences, where there was no rationale or logic. Just need and supplication, heat and moisture. Primal.

The time for her to have stopped him was way before the bedroom. That's where she should have been strong. Dammit, she never should have gone with him to the hotel. Some part of her had to have known what was going to happen.

A bus rumbled by, and even in the dark she could see the artwork on the side. It was a picture of Chase and a picture of her, superimposed so that they appeared to be gazing into each other's eyes. Her stomach lurched as the bus screeched to a halt about fifty feet in front of her.

Turning abruptly, she headed blindly down the street, the shame so acute that she thought she might throw up. What had she done? How could she possibly face anyone?

She should leave, that's all. Get on a plane heading anywhere, and start again wherever she landed. She could do that. Maybe she could be a secretary. One thing was for sure: she couldn't be a call girl. Not with no experience.

She spied a bench in front of a church, and when she got there, she sank down gratefully. The area registered—she was at St. Mark's Place. Miles from home, but so what? Home, comfort, security—they were all transitory. A moment's indiscretion and, *poof,* they could all be taken away. God, what would her parents say?

Not that they'd be unhappy she was a virgin. They were her parents, after all, but the public humiliation would hit them hard. They'd hated her being on the radio in the first place, and she had a feeling, although neither of them had ever said it, that they would have preferred her using a pseudonym. They didn't want to be associated with the show, or her. She could see it in her mother's eyes.

Now they'd really have something to be ashamed of. Wait until Whittaker's article came out. Oh man. It hurt to think about it.

She could have had sex on several occasions. Okay, that wasn't true; she could have done it twice. Once in high school, when the boy she tutored, a gangly basketball player with unfortunate skin, had groped her at his living room table. And once in college, when Mitch Madden had asked her to go to the midnight performance of *Rocky Horror Picture Show.*

Fool that she was, she'd turned them both down. She should at least have considered her options, especially with Mitch. He'd been really good-looking, and experienced. But, no, she had to run and hide in her books, too scared even to date.

She didn't deserve her show. She didn't deserve her degree. Maybe it was just poetic justice. She'd felt like a fraud all her adult life, and now the rest of the world would agree.

Sighing deeply, she wondered yet again how she'd let things get so out of control. She wasn't a fool, but she certainly had been foolish when it came to Chase. If only his touch hadn't made her shiver, if his voice didn't set off all sorts of wild fantasies. Every time she thought of him, her body reacted, and when she was with him, it got ten—no, a hundred—times worse.

At least now she understood what women meant when they claimed to be victims of seduction. To the unwary, the physical symptoms of attraction could feel overwhelming. But feeling flushed and having butterflies in the tummy did not mean one had to swoon into a man's arms and let him have his way.

It was tempting, though, to abandon all responsibility, to be swept away on an ocean of lust.

She wanted him. She wanted him in a way that was completely foreign to her. It had nothing to do with her intellect, with her rational mind. Her body felt incomplete, yearning to be whole. Her breasts ached, and that was the least of her problems. She squeezed her legs together, trying to ease the discomfort there, but it was useless. There was only one thing that could fix her.

She watched a stretch limo pass by, the darkened windows hiding its secrets. Maybe there were lovers inside, doing naughty things while the driver tried not to look.

Maybe now that Chase knew the truth, she could take that next step. Risk what she'd never been willing to risk before. Maybe it was her turn to live life rather than talk about it.

On the other hand, he probably wanted nothing to do with her. He'd seen her for the phony she was. He and Whittaker were probably having a real good laugh about now.

Jamie sniffed and rubbed her eyes with the palms of her hands. She'd best get used to being laughed at—and staying a virgin. Welcome to the end of the world as she'd known it. Welcome to utter failure.

SHE HADN'T ANSWERED her phone or called him back, even though he'd left a half-dozen messages. So Chase had no choice but to go to the radio station that evening.

His day had been one of unanswered questions, the first of which was why he'd felt compelled to finish the champagne. But after a shower, aspirin and a hot meal, the real quandary surfaced. He had no idea what to do, how to handle things. It wasn't like a race, where there were rules and flags and clear winners and losers. This situation was the kind he always tried to avoid. In truth, he never got close enough to anyone to find himself embroiled in their lives. He was the kind of guy you could completely depend on if everything was going well—which had made a lot of sense to him for a lot of years. Only, last night and today, some strange ideas had popped into his head.

What would his life have been like if he'd gone the other direction? Instead of keeping aloof, guarding himself against making connections, what if he'd put himself out? What if he'd let himself care? Let himself need?

After nodding at the receptionist, a woman he didn't recognize, he headed down the long hallway. With each step, he grew more convinced that he was losing his mind. He'd be gone in a few years—why bother getting involved with Jamie? What did he care what happened to her?

But as he rounded the door into the production booth, he was hit hard, right in the chest. He didn't want to hurt her. He didn't want to blow her secret.

Cujo grinned at him from behind the board. "Hey, lover boy. I heard about you on WGNX this afternoon. They had a whole discussion about the bet. And half the women calling up said they'd do ya. Man, some dudes have all the luck."

Chase smiled even though he didn't feel the least bit lucky. Confused, yes, but lucky?

He turned so he could see Jamie. She was nearly hidden by the big fuzzy microphone and the console, but he could see half of her face. Her pale skin, those huge brown eyes, that tousled hair. Something inside him tensed, and it wasn't just because she was beautiful. There were dark circles under her eyes. She wasn't herself. The pain and defeat of last night had changed her posture and aged her face.

He had a lot to be proud of. He'd hurt her, now held the potential of ruining her whole career—and for what? Because he was such a jackass. He had to prove he could seduce the indomitable Dr. Jamie. But he didn't feel victorious. He felt like crap.

"Hi, Chase."

He turned toward Marcy and managed a smile. "How are you?"

She glanced at Ted, who was standing by the row of tape boxes reading the labels. "I'm fine."

"How's Jamie doing?"

"Okay. Why?"

"No reason."

She gave him a questioning glance, but then Ted walked past her and her attention shifted. Chase watched her stare at the DJ, and it was damn clear that she was attracted to the guy. Chase guessed Ted was at least five years younger than Marcy, but she didn't care. She looked at him like he could fix what ailed her, and give her a smile to boot.

Chase glanced at Jamie, but then Marcy headed toward Ted and Chase had to admit he was curious. She was going to say something, ask Ted a question. But it was none of his business.

Only, it was kind of hard to miss. They were real close, too close for him to get up now without disturbing them. He just wouldn't listen, that's all.

Marcy touched the back of her hair. She looked at the

floor, at the ceiling, then at the floor again. She cleared her throat, and even though Chase refused to look, he was pretty sure she was blushing.

"Come on, girl," he whispered to himself. "Go for it." Oh, hell. He had to look, just a little.

As if his words had spurred her on, she smiled brightly. "Ted?"

Ted turned to her, his face the essence of cluelessness. The man had no idea he was being pursued. Did any man, ever?

"Yeah?" he replied.

"I was thinking about, um... I was, uh, wondering..."

Ted's brows came down as he tried to decipher the conversation.

"Lunch," she finally blurted. "I was thinking about lunch."

Ted's right brow arched. "Yes?"

"Maybe you'd like to, uh, have some."

"Lunch?"

She nodded.

"With you?"

Another nod, this one breathless, from what Chase could see.

"When, tomorrow?"

"Yes."

"Sure. That'd be great."

Marcy's shoulders relaxed as she let her breath out. "Great. Then I'll call you. We can go to Union Pacific, if that's okay."

He nodded, but his face showed none of Marcy's eager infatuation. In fact, Ted looked a little bored. Too bad. Marcy was a nice woman. Attractive, too. And she wanted him so much. She should have asked him for dinner, not lunch. Lunch was business. Lunch was an expense account. Dinner at least had the potential for dessert. For after-dinner drinks.

"I'll make a reservation," she said, but Ted was looking at the door, his attention slipping away with each passing second.

"Great. I'd like that. But, hey, let's talk about it later, okay? I've got to make a phone call."

"Sure," Marcy said with a grin that was as real as Anna Nicole Smith's boobs.

Ted didn't catch it. He just headed toward the door. He stopped, though, just after he stepped into the hallway. "Marcy?"

"Yes?"

"Why don't you make those reservations for dinner?"

Her smile changed completely. In fact, the woman fairly beamed. Ted grinned back, and Chase knew he'd had it all wrong. Ted, the old dog, had just been playing it cool. He knew the score.

Marcy floated across the room, unaware, he assumed, of her silly grin. His own lips curled, and he tried to convince himself that he was just reacting to their situation. That he didn't understand that feeling, that lightness.

Shit, he was in bigger trouble than he'd thought. What in hell was he supposed to do now? How about not taking himself so damn seriously? Come on, this wasn't the end of the world. The girl was a virgin—so what? In some cultures, that was considered a virtue.

A commercial for a local furniture store came on, and he remembered the first night he'd ever seen Jamie. He'd surprised her in the hallway, by the archives. She'd nearly jumped out of her skin. After the initial shock, as they'd stood side by side at the file cabinets, she'd looked him over, and then, as he watched, her cheeks had turned pink, her lush lips had opened and she'd leaned toward him. Not so much that she would have fallen, just enough to tell him she was drawn to him. And the surprise in her gaze turned to fear—and something more. He hadn't thought about it until now, but he remembered feeling as though she wanted to kiss him—that in the next second, she'd be in his arms.

It hadn't happened. A door had slammed somewhere, and she'd bolted like a fawn into the forest.

He leaned to his right so he could see more of her behind her equipment. And it occurred to him why he'd remembered that incident after all this time. Last night, on his bed, she had had that same look in her eyes. That half-frightened, half-hungry stare that made him instantly hard.

She might be a virgin, but she wasn't happy about it. She needed to make love, and it had nothing to do with her radio show.

He was the man for the job. It was going to be fantastic.

11

JAMIE PUSHED THE MUTE BUTTON and turned the show over to Cujo. She couldn't believe she'd made it through the first two hours. Her thoughts were scattered, she had the attention span of a gnat, and she kept expecting Whittaker to burst through the door any second.

Chase had called several times, but she wasn't about to speak to him. He'd done enough to ruin her career, thank you, and she didn't see the need to help him ruin it further.

After the show, she planned to work on her résumé, although hope of getting another radio show wasn't strong. But she might be able to get a job as a therapist. Not in New York, which was okay. She wouldn't mind moving. She'd find herself a nice college town, perhaps, and settle into private practice. Let the scandal burn itself out. She imagined that, in years to come, her humiliation would lessen, and she'd forget about Chase completely.

Her gaze moved to the computer screen, and she saw the next caller up was Dan from Great Neck. He wanted to talk about his girlfriend and her obsession with a celebrity. Cujo gave her the cue, and she leaned in, forcing herself to think about Dan, to give him her full attention.

"This is Dr. Jamie, and we're talking about sex. Up next is Dan from Great Neck. Dan, you there?"

"Yeah."

"Talk to me."

"I've been seeing this girl for almost a year, and everything's been going pretty well."

"But?"

"But ever since you made that bet, she's been going ape over Chase Newman."

Jamie's gaze darted to the production booth. Marcy had her back turned; she was talking to someone Jamie couldn't see. She'd asked Marcy to shy away from any Chase calls. Had Dan told her the celebrity his girlfriend was obsessed with?

"What do you mean, Dan? How is she going ape?"

He sighed. "She's got about a thousand pictures of the guy from every magazine and newspaper she can find. She and her friends talk about him all the time. I mean it. They don't ever talk about anything else. It's enough to make you sick."

"Now, Dan, infatuations are simply that. A dazzling moment when a person assigns all their wildest dreams to someone they don't know. That person becomes everything good and fine and wonderful, but it's only for a short time. Because it's not real. It can't last. It's an illusion. She'll get over it soon, and when she does, she'll look at you again and wonder how she ever thought Chase Newman could have stolen her heart. You stand by her, let her have her moment, don't belittle her or get angry, and, in the end, she'll see she doesn't have to be dazzled to be happy. She can be herself, with all her flaws, and love you for all that you are."

"Seriously?"

"Yes. Trust me."

"But isn't there a way to get her to stop talking about him so much?"

Jamie opened her mouth, but her thoughts were interrupted by the thick, heavy door swinging open. It wasn't Whittaker; it was Chase. All her higher brain functions stopped, and she was left with a great wallop of fear—and, unbelievably, desire. Her insides were dancing with the duel emotions, and she felt completely helpless. Somewhere in the back of her mind she knew she was supposed to be doing something. But she was frozen, panicked. This was it. He was going to tell the world who she was and what she'd done. From this moment on, her whole life would change. Everyone would know that she was a fraud, a phony.

Worse than that was the way her nipples hardened and her chest constricted. Adrenaline surged through her, and she wasn't so naive as to blame it on anything but the truth. She was infatuated with Chase, just the way Dan's girlfriend was. Only, Jamie's problem was infinitely worse. The man held her future in the palm of his hand. She was in so much trouble.

Chase threw her a maddeningly casual smile as he sat down in front of the nearest guest mike, put on a set of headphones, grinned broadly at Cujo—who grinned back—and pressed the button that would put him on the air.

"Dan?"

"Yeah?"

"This is Chase Newman."

"Oh man. Damn. I didn't mean to—"

"It's all right. Is your girl there?"

"You mean you can't hear her screaming?"

Chase nodded. "When she's done, put her on the phone, okay?"

"Are you kidding? It's bad enough now."

"Trust me."

Chase kept his smile as he looked at Jamie. She wondered which would be more newsworthy—Chase exposing her secret, or her having a seizure on the air. Either way, she wouldn't come out smelling like a rose.

"Hello?" A breathless female, her voice quivering in excitement, came over the airwaves.

"What's your name, darlin'?"

"Oh my God. Marie. My name is Marie. Is it really you?"

"Nice to meet you, Marie. I'm Chase."

A squeal that threatened eardrums all over Manhattan made Jamie jerk her headphones off. Chase winced, but that's all.

"Marie?"

"Oh God."

"Marie, listen up. Jamie was right. I'm not anything special. If you knew me at all, you'd understand that."

"Oh, come on."

He shook his head. "It's true. I'm not any different than Dan. In fact, I'm sure you're better off with him than me."

Jamie put her headphones back on and leaned in to the mike. "Why?" Maybe she could put off the inevitable, at least for a little while. Make this about Chase.

He shifted his gaze to her. "Because I don't share well with others."

"Go on." Jamie kept waiting for the other shoe to drop. Any second now—she could just feel it. Her palms sweated, and she felt a trickle of moisture slither down her back.

"The truth is, Marie, I can be a real son of a bitch."

Jamie closed her eyes, braced for the words that would change everything.

"You?" Marie asked. "I don't believe you."

"You should."

Jamie opened one eye. Chase grinned at her, and she realized he was enjoying her torment. "Believe him," she said into the mike.

"Oh, yeah. Take this bet, for example." He scooted closer to Jamie. "I'm not the least bit worried that I'm going to lose. I've already seduced her. She just doesn't know it yet."

"Is that so?" Jamie moved her chair away from him.

"Honey, it's all there in your eyes." He laughed. "Ladies and gentlemen, the woman wants me. In fact, she wants me so badly she can't keep her hands off me. It's a little embarrassing."

Marie giggled. "So why does that make you a son of a bitch?"

"Because not only am I going to win this bet, but I'm going to win it right now, on the air, with a million witnesses."

Jamie's eyes widened in disbelief as he took hold of the chair arm and pulled her to his side. "Are you nuts?"

"Maybe."

"I think we need to go to commercial."

Chase turned toward the window, toward his buddy Cujo. "I don't think so. We're not leaving until you cry uncle."

Cujo bent to his board, his grin broad and a little wicked.

"Hey," she said, not liking any of this one bit. "This is my show. I say what we do."

"Not tonight," Chase said. He looked at Cujo, who nodded and gave him a thumbs-up. Then Chase's gaze moved back to hers, and that's when she clued in. Blackmail. The bastard was holding her secret for ransom and the payoff was just another form of humiliation.

She punched the mute button and faced him, her fury strong enough to shatter glass. "Stop this right now. If you're going to tell, tell. But I won't be played with like this."

He wiggled his eyebrows in a mock-sexy way. "I like it when you get all fired up."

"Chase, I'm not kidding. I'm not going to let you humiliate me."

"So, you want me to tell your audience about last night?"

"Yes." Her heart nearly stopped beating. "No."

"It's your call."

"You *are* a son of a bitch."

He grinned. "I know."

"You seriously want me to have sex with you here? On the air?"

He nodded as if his request wasn't totally outrageous. To make matters worse, if that were possible, her body didn't seem to grasp the situation at all. In fact, she knew enough about the mechanics to realize that her labia had swelled, that the heat on her chest and below was a triggered response. For all intents and purposes, her body thought this was all foreplay.

He reached over, punched the button on her console that put them back on the air, then moved his hand to the back of her neck. "Welcome back, New York," he whispered, his voice gruff and powerful. Different from the voice of a moment ago. "This is the Dr. Jamie show, and we're not talking anymore."

He pulled her toward him, and while she did protest, it wasn't a world-class effort. Then his lips were on hers, and the war between her mind and her body went ballistic.

She moaned as his tongue slipped between her teeth. He worked his magic, sending shock waves through her veins, right to her most vulnerable parts. Then he pulled back, and the first thing she saw was both his hands. When had he let her go? Why had she felt as if she couldn't pull away?

"Stand up," he said, his voice that intimate whisper that had turned her to mush last night.

Her gaze went to the window. Marcy stood next to Fred, and she was arguing with him. Fred didn't seem to care. Cujo still wore that conspiratorial smile. What was going on? Jamie could see every line was flashing, which reminded her...

"Marie," she said. "Are you still there?"

"Yeah. But don't let me interrupt."

"Jamie has to go now, Marie," Chase said. "But don't turn off your radio." He got up from his chair, went to the wall and turned down the lights, darkening the room just enough so that they could see each other, but the folks in the production booth couldn't.

While Jamie was grateful no one could see, she was acutely aware they could hear. All of Manhattan could hear. This was the moment to bolt. To run out of here, and not stop until she was at her apartment. She could be packed and on a plane in a few hours.

No, wait. Maybe it wasn't so bad. It wasn't as if they were on television. Maybe she could play this to her advantage. She could pretend to go along, and then when Chase was all riled up and thinking he was going to win, she could stop everything. Tell her audience that while Chase was very sexy, she hadn't been seduced, and that she'd proved her point. If she could time it right, she'd be able to end the wager, declare victory and turn off the mike so Chase wouldn't have a chance to spill the beans.

It just might work—if she could keep her cool.

Chase settled back into his chair. "Stand up," he said again, his voice commanding, letting her know exactly how seriously he was taking this.

Saying a quick prayer that she knew what the hell she was doing, she obeyed him. She stood, and he pushed her chair away, then moved his so that she was trapped between him and the desk. He parted his knees and moved closer, boxing her in on all sides.

"Look at me."

She felt her cheeks heat. The awareness that her boss, her producer and God knew who else were standing just a few feet away, listening to the sex in his voice, knowing she was doing as he requested, made her want to disappear. But at the same time, it was sort of exciting—which must mean she was as twisted as Chase.

He touched her knees, and she jumped. His cool hands slipped under her dress and slowly inched up her thighs. "Do you like the feel of my hands on your thighs?"

She looked at him quizzically, wishing the light was a hair brighter so she could study his eyes. Oh damn, he was narrating! Giving the whole world a play-by-play. She couldn't do this. Her show wasn't worth it. Nothing was worth it. She turned to escape, but his hands held her steady.

"Where do you think you're going?"

"Out. I can't do this. I won't do this."

"Look at me."

"No."

"Jamie, look at me."

She slowly turned and met his gaze. She barely registered that he'd taken off his headphones. When had that happened?

"It's going to be fine," he said. "Let yourself go. No

one is going to see anything you don't want them to. They'll just hear us—and that's what you do, isn't it? Talk about sex."

"This isn't talk."

"Exactly. It's better than talk." Chase grinned, then leaned toward her mike. "Listen up, all you guys. If you're out there with your girls tonight, join us. Do what we do. Let's make Manhattan into an isle of joy."

"Chase, I can't."

"You can. You are. Just keep looking at me, baby. Just look into my eyes."

The battle continued inside her, but as the seconds ticked by and her heart thudded in her chest, Chase's gaze held her steady. Hypnotized her. Heated her flesh past the edge of comfort.

His hands moved up a few more inches, up to the sides of her underwear. "Hmm. Tell me about your panties, Jamie. What color are they?"

"White."

"They feel like silk."

"I'm not sure what they are."

"They're awfully tiny."

She trembled as his fingers slipped under the elastic and moved inch by inch from her sides to her back. Then his fingers were rubbing at the tender line where her buttocks met the top of her thighs. It was an incredibly intimate gesture. He rubbed her back and forth.

"Jamie."

"Hmm?"

"I want you to lift your dress."

"What?"

"Go on, honey, lift your dress. Let me see those pretty white panties."

She didn't hesitate too long. After all, she'd win in

the end. That's what she had to remember. She gathered the material of her dress in her hands and lifted, slowly, slowly, baring her knees, then her thighs. She hesitated just before her panties would have peeked out.

In response, he moved his hands up so that he cupped her buttocks, and he squeezed her flesh. "Higher," he whispered. "Let me see your panties."

Trembling with an excitement she couldn't have acknowledged, she lifted the material the last few inches. He shifted his gaze to what she'd bared, and moaned his pleasure.

"Jamie, you're so beautiful. Those panties are silk, but your skin is softer." He leaned forward and placed a kiss just below her belly button. "And you smell like vanilla and sex."

Marcy had given her vanilla perfume for her birthday, and Jamie had sprayed some on this afternoon after her shower, so that explained half his observation. But did she really smell like sex? It was true that with foreplay, a woman's body would react with lubrication and a very personal, unique scent. Half of what attracted one man to one woman was scent, and there was no telling who would find one odor sexy and another unpleasant.

She leaned slightly forward and breathed deeply. Chase smelled like sex, too. To her, it was intoxicating. Hypnotizing. Dangerous.

He kissed her again, his mouth moving closer to the top of her panties. Squeezing her buttocks again, he traced his tongue down, not even stopping when he hit the silk of her underwear. She held her breath as he kissed her, each kiss slightly below the last.

Just before he reached her mound, he stopped. "Tell them what I'm doing, Jamie."

"I—"

"You can. Just do it. Tell them."

She opened her mouth, but a wave of self-consciousness made her mute. For the first time since she'd been on the radio, sex had made her embarrassed.

"Honey," he whispered, "go on."

Nodding slightly, she closed her eyes, which made things easier. "He's..."

Chase kissed her again on the same spot.

"He's kissing me...over my underwear."

His mouth moved down, getting perilously close to the top of her sex. "Where?" he whispered.

"Near my..."

"What?"

She couldn't. The scientific term was too clinical, the slang expressions too vulgar. There didn't seem to be the right word. Why was that? Why wasn't there a sexy, slightly naughty, erotic word for a woman's genitals?

He chuckled, and then he threw her off another fifty degrees when he blew a stream of warm air right on the lips of her sex. The sensation made her tremble, made her push against his hands, made her want more.

"Tell them, Jamie."

"He's, uh, blowing air—a thin, hot stream of air—on me..."

"That's right. And now what am I doing?"

She gasped. "He's using his fingers. In back."

"How?"

She squeezed her pelvic muscles to stop the sudden ache between her legs. "Oh my God, he's tracing the line of my bottom."

He laughed again. "The line of your bottom?"

"That's as much as you're going to get from me."

His fingers lifted away from her skin. "And what if I were to tell you that's all you'll get from me?"

She pushed back, but he didn't touch her again. His hands were still inside her panties, but there was no contact. The position, however, had another effect, this one on her front. The silk had been pulled tight, forcing the material to slip inside her lips and rub against her.

"Jamie."

"Don't stop," she whispered.

"Then, tell them the truth."

"I will. But the truth isn't about what to call things. The truth is that your touch makes me breathless. That I'm drowning in an ocean of sensation."

"You're being seduced."

"No. Not seduced. Seduced takes all the responsibility away from me. I'm here. I'm moving my hips so the material of my panties can rub exactly the right way. I'm hoping you'll touch me again, that you'll use your hands and your mouth in every way possible to give me pleasure. I'm not being seduced. I'm saying yes. I'm telling you I want you."

12

CHASE COULD BARELY BREATHE. He'd become so hard that he felt sure one wrong move would cause permanent damage. This level of excitement shocked him. He hadn't known he could feel this way. That he could want someone so badly.

Despite his intention to manipulate the situation, Jamie had managed to take control. That's the thing with women. They could always take control. There were no equal partners when it came to sex. Men were helpless fools the moment the blood rushed south.

What she didn't know was that he'd arranged everything with Cujo. They weren't on the air at all. Cujo was broadcasting the weather and news and whatever else he could come up with until Chase gave him the signal to go back on the air. It was supposed to be his party, his victory. Only, Jamie wasn't surrendering.

"Chase."

"Hmm?"

"Look at me."

He didn't want to. She'd put a spell on him, and he was the one who was helpless now.

"Look at me."

He lifted his gaze. There was just enough light for her gaze to catch his and hold him steady.

"I won't do this," she said, and she let go of her dress. It fluttered on his arms, and he grasped her buttocks again. "No." She reached back and moved his hands, then stepped to the side, escaping from his hold. "You do what you have to do. But I won't play this out, not for you, not for anything. And if that means you need to..." She closed her eyes, unable to say the words, then she looked at him again. "I'll make it easy for you." With that, she put both of her hands on his chest and pushed him back, giving herself an exit. "It's all up to you," she said. Then she took off her headphones, grabbed her purse from beneath the desk and walked to the door.

"Jamie, wait."

She looked back at him, shook her head, and then she was gone.

He stared at the door for a moment, trying to get himself under control. She'd taken him by surprise, turned the tables. He should tell the world what he knew, just to show her who was boss.

Even as the thought entered his head, he realized what a jerk he was. There was no way he was going to hurt her like that. He might be a son of a bitch, but he wasn't a selfish bastard.

This was all supposed to be a laugh. But Jamie had gotten to him. He wasn't sure how. If he'd slept with her, that would explain it—but he hadn't. His physical desire for her wasn't the reason, either.

He cared about what happened to her. And that was something he'd sworn he'd never do.

"Chase?"

He looked up at the speaker mounted on the wall. "What?"

"Chase, what's going on, buddy?"

It was Cujo. He'd forgotten all about him, about the radio show. Hell, he'd forgotten the rest of the world. "Let's do it."

"But she's gone."

"I'll take over the rest of the show." He thought about turning up the lights, but he liked the dark. It was more suitable for a rat like him. He picked up her headphones from the desk and put them on. "This is Chase Newman for Dr. Jamie. And we're talking about sex."

JAMIE WALKED BLINDLY toward the subway, cursing herself, cursing Chase, cursing life. By now, he'd undoubtedly told the world about her virginity, and the uproar was probably in full swing. What troubled her most was that Marcy was finding out this way, instead of hearing it from Jamie.

How could she have let it get so messed up? My God, she'd almost made love to him while the whole world listened in—her mother's friends, her professors, the men and women she'd gone to school with. If it had gone any further, she would have had to resign. Her plan, although desperate, to turn the tables on Chase had failed, just like every other thing in her life. No. That wasn't true. She'd done some things right. She'd found a career she loved. She'd done well academically. She'd made a true friend in Marcy.

None of her accomplishments felt real, though. Nothing mattered except Chase and her job. She'd lose them both tonight, which meant that the only thing she'd have to hold on to was the fact that she'd gotten a bunch of A's.

Terrific. That should be of great comfort on long, cold nights as she circled jobs in the want ads.

She veered off her path when she saw a nice bus stop

bench. Even the subway seemed like too much trouble. She'd sit for a few minutes, then she'd take the bus or hail a cab.

Plunking herself down, she sighed as she watched the traffic speed by, the insanity of the driving somehow making sense to her. Even the cacophony of horns and blaring radios and hydraulic brakes seemed appropriate— a fitting sound track to her pathetic life.

Closing her eyes as she leaned her head back, she let herself be swallowed by the noise. It felt good not to think, not to feel, just to hear.

Only, she kept hearing Chase. His voice got louder and louder, and finally her eyes snapped open. She wasn't nuts. A woman had joined her at the bus stop, and she was listening to the radio. Chase was still on the air.

Jamie checked her watch. A good forty-five minutes had passed since she'd run out of the station. She focused on the woman's radio, wanting to hear what he had to say.

"...empty. I'm serious. There's nothing there."

"That's not true," a female caller said. "You wouldn't be there if you didn't care about anything."

"You misunderstood," Chase said, his voice making Jamie ache all over again. "I said I didn't care about *anyone,* not *anything.*"

"Same difference."

"Not true. I can care about racing with all my energy. But if I should stop racing, the cars wouldn't give a damn. That's not how it is with people."

"Are you trying to tell me you don't care about Dr. Jamie?"

Silence. Jamie's heart stopped, and she crossed her fingers.

"That's right," Chase said finally. His voice was weary and despondent, but the message was clear as crystal.

"I'm not saying she's not great—she is. I'm just not the kind of guy who can love her."

"There's a kind of guy?"

"Sure. You know that. You see them going to work every day, picking up milk at the store. They're the guys at the baseball fields in the summer, watching their kids learn to hit the ball. They're in it for the long haul."

"And you're not?"

"No."

"Why not?"

Silence once again, but Jamie didn't care this time. She had heard all she needed to. His confession had made something very evident—she'd wanted him to want her and not just for sex. Even though she hadn't been aware of her desire, her disappointment underscored how deeply she'd felt.

"I don't stick around," Chase said, "not for anyone."

"Aren't you afraid you're going to end up old and alone?"

"No," he said, and there was something about his voice that made her strain to hear the next words. "I'm not afraid of that at all."

CHASE SLUMPED in the elevator, wrung out from the night. Somehow he'd managed to finish Jamie's show. But that wasn't what had him in knots.

Damn that Fred Holt. The show had never gone off the air. Cujo had given the signal, but Fred had put the kibosh on the plan, and no one had bothered to tell Chase. So all that seduction, all that intimate talk had gone out to a little over a million homes. Great.

If only she'd answered her phone, called him back. He never would have cooked up this crazy scheme.

It had all gone to hell in a handbasket. Instead of the

playful teasing he'd hoped would make her realize he had no intention of blowing the whistle on her, things had spun completely out of control.

For a man with a huge ego, he sure did seem to have a talent for public humiliation. Not Jamie's. His own. Shit, how was he going to convince her that he'd never meant that stuff to be on the air? And that he would never tell anyone her secret.

He had to figure out a way to lose the bet without making himself the laughingstock of New York. If he couldn't, then he deserved what he got.

All he wanted in the immediate future, however, was to go to bed and sleep for about fifteen hours. Damn, but he could almost feel the cool, crisp hotel sheets calling him.

The elevator came to a stop on the ground floor, and the doors slid open. He walked across the lobby, nodding to the night watchman. The heat outside hit him hard. He hated summers in Manhattan. Better to be on the West Coast this time of year—San Diego or San Francisco.

He stopped short when he saw Rupert Davidson leaning against a spit-shined Cadillac. This wasn't good. Rupert was never up this late.

Chase headed toward his manager, his heart beating fast.

"Chase."

"What's wrong?"

"You have a minute?"

"Rupert, what is it? Is my mother all right?"

The older man nodded. "Yes. No one's ill. I just want to talk to you."

"Fine."

Rupert opened the passenger door, and Chase got in.

Once Rupert was inside, the driver took off, not asking where they were going. He already must have known.

"What's going on?"

"I heard your radio show tonight."

"Yeah?"

"All of it."

Chase's defenses went up immediately, although he stopped himself from justifying his actions. He wanted to hear this through.

After a few moments of stony silence, Rupert nodded, cleared his throat and went on. "Your mother heard it, too. She called me. Chase, she was crying."

"Why?"

"Because she hates what you're doing with your life. She feels like she failed you."

"Hey, it was a joke. I wasn't really going to have sex on the air."

"That's not the part that bothered her, although she wasn't thrilled."

"What do you mean?"

"You said some things tonight about not caring, about never sticking around."

"So?"

"So, she wept bitter tears that she'd raised a son with such a narrow vision of life."

Chase inched closer to the door. "You know, of all the people in the world who should understand—"

"Understand what?"

"Why I won't let myself care. Jeez, she was a basket case for years after Dad died. She could hardly function."

"So?"

"Why would I want to do that to someone?"

Rupert sighed. "You're not going to die at thirty-five, Chase."

"How the hell do you know?"

"I just do." Rupert looked him over, then shook his head. "I suppose I should tell you. I've asked your mother to marry me. She's graciously agreed."

The news hit him like a slap. Rupert had finally proposed. Why should it surprise him? He'd been suggesting the very thing for years now. Only, somehow, he never expected... "That's great, Rupert. I mean it. You two should be together."

"Chase, let me ask you something."

"What?" He turned to the window.

"What if—and don't jump all over me—what if you didn't know you were going to die? What would you do differently?"

Chase stared at a billboard with a semi-naked woman swooning over eye shadow. What would he do differently? "I don't know."

"Yes, you do."

He did. He just didn't want to think about it. Because then he'd have to think about everything he'd missed for all these years. Everything he was missing now. Jamie. Loving her. Not fighting his feelings. Watching the seasons go by with her by his side. Children. Dammit, he'd do it *all* differently—but the fact was, he had no future. Sure, he could care about her and be glad of every day. But what about her, after he was gone? What kind of a schmuck would he be to let her love him when he had so little time left?

"I can't tell you what to do," Rupert said, his voice low, tired. "But you don't have to wait until thirty-five to die. You're already dead. By your own hand. You've kept yourself apart from everyone, made yourself an island. That's not what God intended for us, Chase. You have a right to live fully. To love. To care."

Chase leaned forward and tapped the driver on the shoulder. "Pull over."

The driver looked up and checked with Rupert, who nodded. Then they were at the curb, and Chase finally faced his friend. "I miss my father every day," he said.

"Would it be better never to have known him?"

"Maybe."

"Then, I'm sorry for you."

Chase stepped out on the street. He watched the black car disappear into traffic. Rupert had meant well. He just didn't understand. Neither did his mother, which was harder to accept. How many times had she told him that his father was a bastard for dying? That she hated him for leaving?

Chase had learned a lot from his father's death. He understood where his responsibilities lay. But, for the first time ever, he wished things were different. He wished he didn't have to go. He wished he could be like all the other slobs out there, not having a clue when the end was going to come. It was the not knowing that made it possible to love. That underlying awareness of mortality.

But Chase knew what was in store. The goal was to leave with the fewest people getting hurt.

He turned toward home and walked into the shadows of the night.

JAMIE LISTENED TO MARCY'S message twice, but there was no hint that Chase had told her secret. She felt relieved, but not much better. The ache in her chest, planted last night by Chase's brutal admissions, had ruined her sleep.

It wasn't his fault, but her own. She was the one who'd been acting like a fool, who'd taken a stupid publicity stunt and twisted it into something it wasn't. He owed her nothing. She had no business wanting him.

But she did.

And that was about the saddest thing she could think of. Never before had she let herself care about a man. Oh, sure, there was family love, but this was something completely different. This was the kind of romantic attraction she'd read about in her beloved books, from *Pride and Prejudice* to *Gone with the Wind*. Or perhaps it would be more accurate to compare it to a Stephen King novel.

She might still be a virgin, but she was well and truly screwed.

The most horrible part was that Chase had been her last thought before sleep, and her first thought upon awaking. He'd made her dreams wicked and hot, and her body so sensitive that she'd been constantly aroused.

One good thing, if she survived this, was that she understood so much more now. While she didn't regret the basic advice she'd given her listeners in college or more recently, she would have worded things differently. Couched her phrases with more compassion, tried to be more sympathetic.

She'd always known there was such a thing as intuitive knowledge that had very little to do with intellectual knowledge. But she'd always believed that the intellectual was stronger. Now, she wasn't so sure. Despite knowing the truth about her nonexistent relationship with Chase, she continued to want him, to dream of him.

So what did that say about seduction? Was it possible seduction was just the intuitive brain taking over? Was it really not weakness or a wish to give up responsibility?

If that was the case, then she had a lot of apologizing to do. She wasn't quite ready to take a stand one way or the other. All she knew was that last night she'd wanted to make love to Chase, but that she'd stopped before things had gone beyond the point of no return. It had taken all her strength, but she'd done it.

Would she have been able to do the same if they'd been alone? Who knows? Maybe not. And if she had succumbed, would she have been strong enough to accept her own responsibility in the matter?

Sighing heavily, she poured herself another cup of coffee, then sat down at the dining room table. It was her day off, and aside from the nap she so desperately needed, she also had some errands to run. Groceries. The dry cleaner. And perhaps a trip to her favorite secondhand store.

Keeping busy was a good idea. Now, all she had to do was build up enough energy to get dressed.

Another sip, and she was on her feet. But she didn't make it to her bedroom. A knock on the door jump-started her pulse, and she spilled her coffee all over the floor.

She moved slowly toward the door, not at all sure what to do. Let him in? Tell him to leave? Cry? She rose on tiptoe and peeked through the little hole. It wasn't Chase. It was worse.

She unlocked the door and swung it open. "Hello, Mother."

"Jamie."

Her mother, dressed in her usual impeccable suit—blue with a white, starched blouse, navy flats, and a hand-bag to match—walked past her into the apartment. Jamie knew this confrontation was inevitable, but she'd hoped to have it over the phone.

She shut the door behind her. "How are you?"

"I'm fine, so is your father. Although this radio—"

"Want some coffee?" Jamie asked, cutting her off. She wasn't ready yet.

Her mother looked her up and down, and she wished

she'd put on her robe. Her nightgown had a tear on the shoulder. "Sit down, Jamie. We need to talk."

She obeyed. Because she always obeyed. She didn't want to talk to her mother. Didn't want to hear the lecture, to see the look of disappointment on her face. It wasn't as if Jamie didn't know she was making a spectacle of herself.

"Your father and I are concerned over this radio business."

"I know."

"Do you also know that you're becoming a laughing-stock? That my friends have started to makes jokes about you?"

"It's my job, Mother."

"It's not a job. It's a disgrace. You're a PhD, Jamie, and you're throwing your education down the drain. How do you expect to be an equal among your peers? I see you on the side of buses, on billboards, along with that horrible man. What's gotten into you? I thought we'd raised you better than this."

Jamie's gut clenched, and an anger she'd rarely felt bubbled up from somewhere deep inside. "Mother, how old am I?"

"You're twenty-six. What kind of a question is—"

"And when you were twenty-six, you had already married Dad and you were pregnant with Kyle."

"What's your point?"

"I'm a grown woman and what I do is none of your business."

"That's where you're wrong. People know I'm your mother. People assume it's your upbringing that's led you to these ridiculous stunts. How do you think that makes me feel?"

"You know what?" She stood. "I don't care. You'll

just have to find a way to cope. If I embarrass you so much, just lie. Tell people that I've gone mad, that I'm adopted—whatever you like."

"Jamie—"

"I'm in the middle of the worst crisis of my life, and all you can think about is your reputation. I've always done what you said. Until you wanted me to give up the one thing that's totally mine. I love my show, and I love being on the radio. And if I have to do this stupid stunt to keep my show, then I'm willing. This is mine, Mother, all mine. And nothing you can say will change that."

"I see." Her mother rose and picked up her purse. "I was going to make you an offer. Your father and I had wanted you to join us in our practice. But I can see we were once again being too generous. You don't want our help."

"I just want your love, unconditionally. Whether you think I'm being a damn fool or not."

"Love is earned, Jamie."

"No, it's not. Respect is earned. Love is given, freely, no strings."

"Do you respect him? When he lifted your dress up while you were on the air, was it respect you felt?"

"It's complicated."

Her mother nodded. "Think about what you're doing. What this escapade is going to mean to your future. Don't throw it all away, Jamie. You're bright. You can have a great practice. But you can't have it all. Either you're a disk jockey or you're a doctor."

Jamie nodded, even though she disagreed. Nothing she was going to say would change her mother. And if she expected unconditional love from her mother, wasn't it only just that she give the same thing? That she accept her mother for all she was, the good and the bad?

"Mom," she said, as they walked to the door. "I know you want the best for me. And I appreciate that."

"You do?"

"Yes." She kissed the pale cheek, and the scent of lilacs spun her into childhood for a moment. Her mother had always smelled like lilacs. "I love you."

Her mother shook her head, then looked her straight in the eye. "I love you, too, even though you seem to delight in making that difficult."

"Say hi to Dad, okay?"

A wan smile, and then Jamie closed the door. She had no desire to hurt her parents. But she was way past living the life they wanted for her.

This was her crisis, dammit, all of her own making. And it signaled, in a very large way, that she had finally become a woman. She'd slipped out from under her parents' control. How ironic.

_13_

MARCY HEARD TED'S VOICE, but she wasn't certain where he was. Probably behind the big file cabinet, just out of her line of sight. She touched her hair, moistened her lips. Tonight was dinner, their first real date. She couldn't have been more excited. In fact, it was only after she'd been at the station for about an hour that she noticed she'd worn one black pump and one navy. Lucky for her, she'd been able to scoot home and change before anyone else had seen.

Laughter. Ted's rich baritone. And she heard Cal, the morning commute DJ and the biggest gossip since Hedda Hopper. Why Cal was here this time of night, Marcy couldn't fathom, but who could figure out radio personalities. They were all nuts—except Ted, of course. He was perfect.

She listened as she headed around the cabinet, trying to determine if the conversation was private or if she could butt in.

"...a good kid," Ted said.

"Yeah. But between you, me and the lamppost, if I wasn't already married..."

"You old scoundrel."

"That's about the nicest thing anyone's ever called me. What I don't get is why you're not all over her."

"I don't know how smart it is to get involved with someone at work."

Marcy froze. She shouldn't be hearing this. Were they talking about her? Was she the "good kid"? Or maybe it was Jamie. Please let it be about Jamie.

"With those long legs? Are you kidding me? Besides, I heard a rumor that she's been checking you out."

"That's probably because we're going to dinner tonight. But it's not a date, just a friendly meal."

"Friendly meals can sometimes turn into something better."

"That's not going to happen," Ted said. "I'm not interested in her in that way."

Marcy leaned her head against the wall and closed her eyes. She was such a dope. How could she ever have thought Ted would be interested in her. She was so much older. He could have anyone he wanted. Dammit, why had she asked him out?

"I'm going to get some coffee," Ted said. "You want some?"

"Nope. I'm going home. Get myself something decent to drink."

Marcy darted down the hallway and ducked into the first door she saw. It was, unfortunately, the storage closet, and in order to shut the door behind her she had to squash herself between a cleaning cart and several cases of computer paper. Once safely hidden in the dark space, she had plenty of time to think about her folly. She should have known better. Why did she always have to do this to herself? She wasn't unhappy. So what if she was single? This was the twenty-first century, for heaven's sake. Who said she had to be married?

Of course, she didn't honestly think one date with Ted would automatically lead to marriage. Although, dammit, she'd entertained the notion. It would have been nice, really nice. Ted was a decent guy, one of the nicest men she'd ever met. He'd just proved himself by not talking about her lasciviously with Cal when the opportunity presented itself. She should be grateful about that.

But she didn't feel grateful. All she felt was exhausted. She wanted to go home. To crawl into bed and stay there for about two weeks. Instead, she had to go man the phones. If the ratings stayed consistent, tonight should be a killer.

Work would help. It would. She just had to stop thinking about the things she couldn't have. Her life worked, and it would continue to work long after Ted Kagan was a vague memory.

"Jamie, it's Chase."

The words hung in the air in the broadcast booth. Marcy stared at her worriedly, but Jamie just smiled, nodded and hit the button that would connect Chase to her and her audience.

"We have an old friend here," she said, amazed that she sounded so calm, so together. Her insides were doing a tango, and she had to sip some water to wet her suddenly dry mouth. "Hello, Chase."

"You didn't call me back," he said.

Just hearing him started the complex series of bodily reactions she'd given up trying to understand. He changed her, that's all. Altered who she was and what she felt. Her guess was that it happened in her chromosomes, and that it was, in essence, magic. "We're talking now."

"I thought we might do it a little more privately.'

"Why? We've done everything else on the air."

He was quiet for a moment, and she wished she hadn't said that. She should have called him back. But talking to him solo wasn't in her best interest. She'd thought about it for two long days, then decided against it. She'd cry, and she didn't want him to see that. She might do a lot of things she'd regret. This was safer.

"All right. We'll do it your way."

"It's the way we both agreed to do it," she reminded him. "You knew from the start this was going to be public."

"Right. You're right. So, I guess I'll just say it. I give. You won."

"Pardon?"

"I said, I quit. I didn't seduce you. And I know that it's useless to keep on trying. You're right about all of it. No one can be seduced without their permission."

"But—"

"I just wanted your listeners to know, and I won't have another chance to tell them. I'm leaving. I'm going to Paris in a couple of days, then to Budapest."

"You're leaving?"

"Yeah. I wanted to tell you yesterday, but—"

"But I didn't return your call."

"Right."

Jamie refused to cry, even though her eyes filled with hot tears. His respect for her made everything worse. Not only had he kept her secret, but he'd lied about not seducing her—because even though they hadn't had sex, he *had* successfully seduced her. She'd grown used to the idea that he was a selfish son of a bitch—and then he'd gone and done this.

"So, uh, I guess that's all, huh?"

"No. It's not all. It can't be."

"Why?"

"Because…" She tried to think of something that would keep him here, or, if not that, some way to say thanks. "Because there was no default clause. The deal was for two weeks. How do you know you wouldn't be able to seduce me tomorrow? Or in two days?"

"Ah, Jamie," he said, his voice so full of sadness and futility. "Babe, you know that it's not meant to be, right?"

He wasn't talking about the stupid bet. He was talking about them, about a future. Of course she knew it wasn't meant to be. Why would it? Just because he turned her on? Because her stomach did flip-flops whenever he was around? That wasn't love. It was lust. The very thing she told her listeners to watch out for.

"Anyway, I've, uh, got to—"

"Don't," she said, her hand going to the small speaker on her console. "Please."

"It's been fun. I mean it. You're a class act, Jamie, and New York is lucky to have you."

She heard the *click* of his phone, and then in an act of mercy, Cujo took it away to play the news and weather.

"You okay?" asked Marcy over the speaker.

She looked at Marcy in the other room and she nodded, even though she wasn't okay. Far from it. She felt more like a fraud than ever. Chase had been the class act, not her. He'd been willing to make a fool of himself for her, and he'd done it in the most public way.

She hadn't anticipated that he might just up and leave. Not so soon. Not before they—

"Oh God." The words slipped out as she came to grips with the realization that she wanted to sleep with Chase. No, not that she wanted to, but that she'd assumed she would. He was supposed to be the first guy. The one she'd remember forever.

It wasn't possible, not really. She couldn't…

Was that why she'd let him discover the truth about her? Because all along she'd wanted him to be the one? Because…she was falling in love?

Talk about being a hypocrite. She wanted to have sex with him, and she was totally prepared to blame her actions on him. Even after all her degrees, she hadn't seen her own motivation, her own manipulation. She was great when it came to essay questions, but she sucked in the lab. Real life wasn't like the books; it wasn't so black-and-white.

It didn't matter. Who cared about a stupid bet? Let Whittaker write whatever she wanted. The lesson here was a whopper. She had no business telling people what to do with their lives. None at all.

She caught Cujo's hand signal out of the corner of her eye. The show would go on, at least for tonight. Tomorrow, she would tender her resignation.

CHASE LOOKED AT THE PHONE, wondering what he would say if it was Jamie. Who else would be calling? He didn't want to talk to her now, not while he was so busy wallowing in self-pity.

He lifted the phone on the seventh ring, knowing it was a mistake. "Hello."

"What's going on, Chase?"

It wasn't Jamie. "Who is this?"

"Darlene Whittaker. I just heard your noble little speech, and I want to know what's going on."

"If you heard me, then you know. I lost."

"Bull."

"Are you calling me a liar?"

"Yeah. I don't know what went on with you two, but I'll be damned if I believe you couldn't get to her."

"I couldn't."

"A friend of mine saw you two together the other night. According to him, you both looked like you couldn't wait to get to your room. What was that about?"

"Spying on us? Very ethical."

"I didn't send him there to spy. He just happened to see you. So what gives? There's something fishy going on here, and I want to know what it is."

"Darlene, let it go. You have your story. I'm out of here. The end."

"Come on, Chase. I need this. I heard all kinds of rumors about her. Like, for example, that she's not who she claims to be. Her college roommate swore up and down that she never had a date. That she's gay or celibate or both."

"I can't help you."

"You won't."

"Okay."

"I can get the magazine to pay you."

"I don't need money."

"What do you need? I'll get it."

"What is it with you? Why do you want this so badly? What did Jamie ever do to you?"

Darlene was silent for a moment. "I don't like to be snowed, Chase, and neither does the American public."

"Oh, so this is a patriotic effort?"

"A fraud is a fraud is a fraud. Just because she's pretty, she thinks she can get away with anything. God, she's just like the girls I went to school with. As if they're entitled to get everything they want without having to work for it. As if the rest of us should walk ten steps behind—"

"Darlene," Chase said, "this isn't about Jamie. Get help." He hung up, then sat down on the couch. Something clicked about what Darlene had said. That stuff about Jamie's college roommate.

Great. He'd been played like a violin by a woman he didn't even know. She'd set him up, but he'd run with it, and if things had gone Darlene's way, he could have destroyed Jamie's career. All for the sake of his masculine pride.

He didn't feel proud now. In fact, he felt like crap. Leaving was a good idea. He'd go to Paris, get back into his car, get ready for Budapest. That would keep him from thinking about Jamie. About the mess he'd made.

It was odd. He'd left a lot of women in his life. It never ruffled his feathers—even if the sex had been great and the connection strong. But leaving Jamie wasn't like that. He felt strange, conflicted. Probably because he hadn't slept with her. Because she was still a mystery to him.

And because he liked her eyes. The little smile she wore when she listened to him. The way she smelled. The way her hair always looked as if she'd run her fingers through it.

He closed his eyes. Tomorrow he would make his reservations. Make sure his team got packed and moving. But for tonight, all he wanted to do was sleep. His head lolled back against the overstuffed chair.

He thought about Jamie as he drifted away.

HE JERKED AWAKE, DISORIENTED. Unsure of the time, the day, of anything, he pulled it together enough to realize the banging he heard was coming from the door.

Hauling himself up, he glanced at his watch as he went to see who the hell it was. Three-thirty in the morning? Shit.

Pulling the door open, his tirade stopped before it began. Jamie stood in the hallway, her pale skin making her dark eyes seem huge.

"You were sleeping, weren't you."

He nodded.

"I'm sorry. Go on back to bed."

She turned, but he caught her before she got too far. "Hold it."

"No, I shouldn't have come. I'm sorry."

"Jamie, I'm too tired to argue. Just come inside."

She paused and looked at him, then she walked into his suite. She had on a skirt and a blouse, and for once the outfit wasn't several sizes too big. It was particularly nice from the back, the way the skirt hugged her derriere. His libido stirred even before he was fully awake.

"I've been downstairs for an hour," she said, not looking at him, but instead staring out the window.

"Why didn't you come up?"

"Because I'm a big, fat coward."

He smiled. "Hold that thought." Picking up the phone, he dialed room service and ordered a pot of coffee and a bottle of vodka. One would wake him up, the other put him to sleep. He didn't know yet which one he'd need. After the call, he walked over to where Jamie stood. "So talk to me."

"I don't know how."

"Yes, you do. You're a great talker. All of New York knows that."

Her head came up and her gaze met his. "You're right. I'm a hell of a talker. Unfortunately, I don't know what the hell I'm talking about."

"Jamie—"

"I'm quitting."

"What?"

"I'm turning in my resignation tomorrow. I can't do this. I can't continue to lie like this."

"Lie? You haven't lied. Jamie, you're good at what

you do. Damn good. Why throw it away over something stupid like this?"

"Because it isn't stupid. I'm a fraud, and you know it."

"Do you think things would be so different if you'd slept with someone?"

She nodded. "I do."

"You're wrong. Sex doesn't change much of anything. It takes the edge off, but that's about it."

"I can't believe you feel that way."

He shrugged. "It's the truth."

"No. That much I do know. Making love changes everything...if it's with the right person."

He was the one to turn to the window this time. "I don't know about that."

"Chase?"

"Hmm?"

"I didn't come up here to tell you I was quitting."

Something about her voice made him look at her. "Yeah?"

"I came up here to ask you to do me a favor."

He knew what she was going to say. And his whole body prepared to answer her.

"I want to make love to you. Tonight. Now."

He wanted to pick her up and throw her on the bed without another word, but he held himself steady. "I don't think that would be very smart."

She winced, then turned sharply toward the door.

Again, he caught her arm. "Jamie, stop."

She shook her head. "Just let me go. I'm sorry. I shouldn't have asked—"

"Hey. I didn't say I didn't want to."

She stopped tugging, trying to get away. "You didn't?"

"Look at me."

She turned, her cheeks flushed with pink.

"Why?" he asked. "Why do you want to sleep with me?"

"I don't," she said. "I want to make love."

He nodded, somewhat impatient.

She took in a deep breath, let it out slowly. Her gaze steadied, and she faced him squarely. "I want you."

"Why?"

"I don't know. But I do know that every time I hear your voice, I melt. When I'm with you, I feel dizzy and lighter than air. Touching you makes me quiver, and kissing you..." She hid her face behind her hands.

Damn if she wasn't the most adorable creature in the history of the world. "Jamie."

She shook her head, not daring to look at him through her fingers.

He pulled her into his arms, and she snuggled against him. Her heart beat so hard, he could feel it. Her heat warmed him and her scent made him crazy. He kissed the top of her head, and then he leaned down to her ear.

"Me, too," he whispered.

"Really?" Her voice was muffled and tiny, and it made him ache for her.

He put his hands on her shoulders and pushed her back, not away, but so he could see her face. Of course, she was still hiding behind her fingers, but a moment later she dropped her hands. "Really?" she asked again.

He nodded. "I don't want to hurt you."

"You won't."

"You can't know that."

"Let me be responsible for myself," she said. "I'm tired of letting other people make my decisions for me. If you want to make love to me, great. If you don't, I'll get over it. But do whatever because of you, not me."

"See?"

She tilted her head. "What?"

"You can't quit the show. The world needs to hear from you. Your listeners need to hear that."

She smiled, and he felt as if he'd just gotten a great present. Then she rose on her tiptoes, took his cheeks in both her hands and kissed him on the lips. Softly.

Something incredible was about to happen.

14

JAMIE KNEW THE EXACT second he changed his mind. It was all in his kiss, from tentative to bold, from passive to aggressive, from friends to lovers.

His arms went around her as his tongue parted her lips. She wanted to hurry to the bed, but then she would have missed the way his hands moved over her back, down the contours of her hips. She wanted it all, to drown in his arms, to do it all now, even as he took his time.

His lips moved from hers and he nibbled her neck, just below her ear. Goose bumps popped out all over her arms, and she quivered like a bow string. He knew so much, and she knew so little.

No, that wasn't true. She'd read about this over and over again. She'd studied the techniques, and all she had to do was put them to practice.

Kissing. What did she know about kissing? Men liked to mimic sex, to thrust boldly, a prelude, a living illustration. But they also liked to show how they understood a woman's body. Okay, that's why he was nipping her earlobe. She moaned, letting him know he was doing just fine.

Her thoughts sped ahead to the bedroom. Men are

visual. She should undress slowly. Tease him. Make him grow hard watching her.

Actually, that last part wasn't going to be very difficult. She could feel him as she pressed against him. He was already hard. So, what was he waiting for?

Reaching behind, she caught his hands, then pulled away from his kisses. "Come with me," she whispered. She led him past the couch and the TV console into the bedroom. He hadn't disturbed his sheets—yet.

She steered him to the bed and pushed on his shoulders till he sat down. "Wait," she said, trying to think of every seductive trick she'd ever read. She moved back so he could see her whole body, but not too far, because men liked the details. Music. Shouldn't there be music? No. Unnecessary. Think visual. Men like to look.

She stood in front of him and took hold of the bottom of her blouse. Lifting slowly, forcing herself to keep a pace that just about killed her, she bared her tummy, and then the bottom of her bra—which, dammit, was just white, boring and utilitarian, but she hadn't known this afternoon that she was going to sleep with him tonight. It was okay, though. Because men didn't care what kind of underwear women wore, just so long as it was intimate apparel.

She wondered if she should move her hips, even though there was no music. Kim Basinger did that wild striptease for Mickey Rourke in *Nine and a Half Weeks*. But that movie had a score, and Jamie's life didn't.

No, she wouldn't move. Well, she'd move a little. The blouse cleared her breasts and then moved up to her neck. As she lifted farther, the material blocked her view of Chase. Wait. Hold it. She was choking herself. Screw the pace, she had to take the damn shirt off.

Once it had cleared her head, she smiled as seductively

as she could and tossed the blouse behind her. A *thud* on wood reminded her that while tossing clothes was sexy, breaking things was not.

"Jamie—"

"Wait. I'm not done." She went to the back of her skirt and lowered her zipper. Too fast. And she was supposed to let him see her do that. She pulled the zipper up and turned around, then slowly pulled it down once more.

She looked at him over her shoulder. Emotions washed over his face, and his cheeks filled with heat. It was working. Maybe she would give him a little of the old bump and grind. Why not?

She thrust her hips out to the right, then turned her head the other way and pushed her hips to the left. Oh, great. Now all she could think of was the Hokeypokey.

She focused on the task at hand. She was driving him crazy with lust, and she couldn't stop now. The zipper finally came to a stop, and then she hooked her thumbs under the waistband.

Down went her skirt, and after she got it past her hips, she turned to face him again. He was still on the pink side. And he looked as if he was struggling not to take her on the spot.

Bless her textbooks. Bless Nancy Friday and Masters and Johnson and *Yellow Silk*. She let her skirt drop, and just as she was stepping out of it, there was a loud knock on the door that scared her half to death. She dove for cover, and her foot got caught in her skirt. Flailing her arms like two propellers, she managed to keep herself upright, barely. It was Chase who steadied her.

Luckily, he went to the door while she gathered her composure. She'd forgotten about room service. But that was okay. She hadn't gotten to the nitty-gritty of her striptease yet.

While he was gone, she could also retrieve her blouse and skirt. No need for them to be wrinkled. The shirt was on his dresser, and she'd knocked over his cologne bottle. Nothing had spilled, though. Checking to make sure he was still busy, she opened the purple bottle and sniffed. The scent was rich and spicy and masculine, just like Chase. She remembered a hint of it on his skin, a suggestion of something forbidden.

She put it down the second she heard him at the bedroom door. Whirling around, she smiled, preparing herself for Act II.

"Jamie—"

"Wait. Sit down."

"But—"

"Please. I don't want to lose my nerve."

He hesitated, then nodded as he went to his former position on the bed. But the pink had left his cheeks and his expression had become rather stoic. She had her work cut out for her.

Hurrying to center stage, she reached back to unhook her bra. By the second loop she remembered to smile. Of course, she didn't just let the bra fall. Her arms, clamped to her sides, held it on. Seductively and bit by bit, she slipped the first bra strap off her shoulder, then the second.

All that was left was the boob portion. Oh, my. The lights were very bright. But it was Chase, and she wanted him to know everything about her, didn't she?

She lifted her arms and the bra landed at her feet. Chase went into a coughing fit, and she tried to remember if she'd ever read about coughing and libido. Probably. He had to turn away for a moment while he gathered himself together, but she didn't mind the wait.

Looking down, she saw her nipples were hard as

erasers and standing out kind of far. Would he like them? She didn't sag very much, but her boobs weren't going to win any prizes. They were just…boobs.

Anyway, Chase had calmed down and he was looking at her again. It was time for Act III. The panties.

She'd picked a standard pair of blue bikinis this morning, not knowing, of course, that she'd be taking them off so publicly. At least they had no holes.

Thumbs under the waistband, then push down. Slower. This was it, he was going to see her completely naked. He'd be the first man. How she'd dreamed of this moment. But in her dreams, the lights weren't quite so bright.

She felt her own cheeks heat as she pushed her panties down over her butt, and then they were around her thighs, and she just wanted them off so she could get to the bed and climb under the covers. *He* might be visually stimulated, but *she* felt like a fool.

Yeah, yeah, it was all natural and wonderful, and part of the life cycle and all that crap, but she was standing in front of Chase Newman, who was fully clothed, while she was stark naked.

She should turn around. She didn't want to, but he would like it. Okay. Smile. Turn.

When she'd finished the one-hundred-eighty degree turn, the red had come back to Chase's face, and he looked as if he was going to have another coughing fit. Maybe he wasn't feeling well.

She approached him, trying to walk sexy but growing concerned. "Chase? Are you sick?"

He shook his head, then turned to the side.

This wasn't amusing. Now she was worried. She moved to the side of the bed and sat down. "Chase, look at me."

He shook his head again.

Since he wouldn't move, she did. When she was on the other side of him, he tried to hide his face, but she wouldn't let him. She wasn't an MD but she would know if he needed to see someone for his cough.

She tugged at his hands, and they came away from his mouth. His eyes were red-rimmed, and his whole face was hot. This was looking serious, and she was just about to suggest they go to the emergency room when a sound burst out of Chase. Not a cough. A laugh.

Oh my God, he wasn't choking. He was laughing. She bolted off the bed, grabbed a pillow and put it in front of her nakedness.

He let loose with a snort and shook his head, trying like hell to wipe the grin from his face, but it was too late. Her humiliation was total, and all she wanted to do was get the hell out of Dodge.

She moved toward her skirt—the heck with her underpants. Out. She needed to get out.

"Jamie—"

"Please don't say anything," she begged. "I can't take it. I'm sorry. I'm so sorry."

His laughter subsided suddenly, as if a light switch had been turned off. He stood, headed toward her, and if she wasn't fast, he'd be between her and her clothes.

"Honey, don't."

"I asked you not to say anything."

"I have to." He planted himself in front of her, blocking her clothes and her exit. "Please, don't go. I wasn't laughing at you."

"Right. You were just laughing near me. Go away."

He cupped her cheek with his palm. "I don't think I've ever wanted to be with anyone more than I want to be with you right now."

She winced. "Pinocchio, your nose is getting longer."

His low chuckle made her open her eyes. "You're really bad at anatomy."

Her gaze shot down to his pants, and, sure enough, there was a nice-size bulge right where it should be. "Don't tell me you have a fetish for inept strippers."

"I don't. But I think I've got a problem with beautiful radio talk-show hosts."

"Barbara DeAngelis will be glad to hear it."

"Jamie, honey, stop. I think you're wonderful, and delicious, and I loved what you did, and I think I was laughing out of sheer pleasure. You're completely unexpected, you know that?"

"Is that a good thing?"

"Yeah. It's a good thing."

"So there was nothing about my body that put you into hysterics?"

"No." His hand moved from her cheek to the pillow, and he lifted it out of her arms. "You're exquisite. In every detail."

"You don't have to go overboard."

"Would you cut it out? I don't lie."

The joke was over. "Yes, you do. You lied for me on the radio."

"I did not. I didn't seduce you. You won."

"You and I both know that's not true. You seduced me, all right. You made my knees weak and my heart pound, to say nothing of what happened to the, uh, other parts."

His smile turned mischievous. "Is that so?"

She nodded.

"Now, what parts would those be?" He touched her shoulder with the pad of his index finger. "Here?"

She shook her head.

Looking puzzled, he moved the finger to the tip of her nose.

"You're ice cold."

"Hmm." His finger moved to the space between her breasts, and he let it trail slowly downward.

"Warmer," she whispered, and the word described her, too.

Then, looking into her eyes as if she held magic, he circled her breast over and over, the circles becoming smaller and smaller until he was almost touching her nipple. Then his other hand got busy, and, before she even had time to think, she was aching in a way that had everything to do with Chase and being a woman. She was ready.

Her eyes fluttered closed the second he touched her swollen buds. The sensation was unbelievable. Intimate, stirring, thrilling. But, being very greedy, she wanted more.

It didn't seem at all weird to let her hand drift to his pants, to the straining hardness beneath the denim. His moan made her braver, and she found his belt buckle.

Despite her awkward struggles, she got the belt undone, then concentrated on the buttons of his fly, which turned out to be trickier, probably because there was so much strain on the material. He ended up helping her, which didn't matter at all. In fact, he unceremoniously yanked his pants down, then tossed them away, and there he was, in his boxers and his socks. The socks held no interest. The boxers, plenty.

His erection pressed the material out in a tent worthy of an Eagle scout. She had to accept the proof that his laughter wasn't a sign of disinterest. Far from it.

She reached a tentative hand to the front of his shorts and cupped her palm around the bulge. He inhaled sharply, and she felt his penis jerk.

Her previous embarrassment forgotten, she thought of

nothing but his body, her body, and what they were about to do. Twenty-six years she'd waited for this moment. To understand what it felt like to be filled by a man. To feel his lips all over her body. To take him in her mouth.

She pulled his underwear down, pausing briefly to clear the hurdle of his erection. He finished the job, taking off his socks, too. When he straightened up, she held her breath.

He was gorgeous. His broad chest, the light covering of hair over the planes of his muscles. His tummy, flat, rippled, perfect. As for his sex? Spectacular. She wasn't terribly good with measurements, but he hadn't lied about his dimensions.

"Jamie? Are you going to stare at me all night?"

"Oh, no. I want to touch you, too."

He laughed again, but this time she welcomed the sound, recognizing the warmth and affection behind it. "Do you want to stand here or go to the bed?"

"The bed." She reached out, got a firm grip on his shaft, amazed at the softness of his skin and the hardness of what lay beneath, and headed toward the bed.

"Hey, that's attached."

"Well, then, come on."

"Yes, ma'am."

She released him when she got to the bed. Then she sat on the edge and maneuvered him in front of her. Now she was eye-level with his belly button. But she didn't give a hang about that. Her focus was his male parts. She'd seen pictures, movies; read about penises; heard all the different slang names—and yet she'd never seen one in the flesh. Well, that's not true. She'd seen little boys when she baby-sat, but that was comparing apples and oranges. Or cucumbers and... gherkins.

"What's that smile for?"

"Nothing," she said. "Except that I think you've got a beautiful penis."

"Thanks. I like your labia."

She giggled, then took hold of his shaft again.

"Uh, Jamie?"

"Yeah?"

"You do realize you can do more than just hold it, right?"

"Really?"

He nodded. "All sorts of things. It's quite versatile."

"Oh?"

"Well, it doesn't whistle Dixie or anything, but it can make you feel real good."

"I want to try it all," she whispered. "Everything." She touched the very tip of him with her tongue; then, needing more of a proper taste, she licked all around the head.

He groaned and touched the back of her head with his hand. He didn't push, just touched her.

Emboldened, she started teasing him in earnest, licking from head to shaft, all the way down, and then she even teased his testicles with her tongue. His taste was a bit salty, but what she tasted most was…male. Not just any male, but Chase. Distinct, like his scent. Masculine. Intoxicating.

She found herself at the tip again, and this time instead of licking, she took him in her mouth. Although she knew that some women could open their throats all the way, she wasn't nearly that talented. But she could flick her tongue just under the glans, and she could pump his shaft while she sucked him like a lollipop. From his moans, she gathered he had no complaints. And neither did she.

It felt naughty. Scandalous. Incredible.

She wanted nothing more than to please him. To make

him groan with delight. And it wouldn't hurt her feelings if he ravished her until she couldn't walk.

His hand stilled her head, and he pulled away from her. She looked up into his eyes.

"It's my turn," he said.

She didn't argue.

The next moment was something out of her dreams. He picked her up, like Richard Gere had carried Debra Winger, minus the officer's cap. He walked around the bed, and before he put her down he kissed her. It was a doozy, and she sighed with happiness. When he joined her on the bed, he looked at her from head to toe and gave her a sinful smile. A thrum of excitement started in her belly, and even before his hand went to her breast, she was trembling like a leaf.

"You're so beautiful," he whispered. "I want you so badly."

"Take me."

"Are you sure?"

She nodded. "More sure than I've ever been about anything."

"Good," he whispered, and after another brief kiss on her mouth, his lips traveled down to her chin, her neck, her chest, and then those same luscious lips closed over her right nipple. His tongue flicked her, and sensations shot through her, straight to the junction of her thighs. She felt herself moisten, and when he sucked hard, she found her hips moving without any conscious effort.

She was primed, ripe, ready for anything. He'd changed her, right from the beginning. He'd rearranged her molecules, and he'd made her understand what being a woman was all about.

Now, as he suckled her breast, as his hand meandered down her hip and her backside, she understood something else, too. This desire for him was physical, yes, but that was only the symptom, not the cause.

She wanted him to be inside her, to fill her, to complete her. She'd waited a lifetime for this moment, for this man. She ran her hand through his hair, and that brought him away from her breast. He straightened until his gaze and hers locked, and for breathless moments she saw something completely new. She saw herself in her lover's eyes. And she was beautiful.

He slid down her body until she felt his hands on her knees. Gently, he spread her legs, then moved between them. She grabbed the covers with both hands as his head lowered to her sex.

His warm breath made her tense; then his lips were on her and it was all she could do not to cry. And it just kept getting better.

He licked her, slid his tongue inside, found the magic knob and coaxed it from under its hood, and then he sucked her until she thrashed and cried out. His tongue danced, and his finger entered her, teasing, thrusting, unlocking her secrets. Thoughts vanished, the world disappeared as she writhed under him. And then her body tensed, every muscle grew taut trembling, all the feelings she'd ever felt right there where his tongue was—

She exploded.

And, in the next moment, while the fireworks were going off one after another, he was at the gates of her sex, his thick, hot manhood slipping inside.

She moved her hips up, wanting him, needing him. He moved slowly, steadily. When she looked at him, she saw the control, the cords on his neck, the concentration in his eyes. He was holding back so he wouldn't hurt her.

She didn't care. Nothing mattered except having him inside her. All the way.

"Do it," she whispered. "Please. Make love to me, Chase."

"I might hurt you."

"I don't care." She lifted her hips again. "Please, Chase. Now."

He closed his eyes for a moment, opened them again, and as she gazed at his face, he thrust into her. One long, brilliant, unbelievable push until he had stretched her beyond anything she'd known before, until he was fully inside her, until they had become one.

Tears came, but not from pain. From joy. From pleasure. From Chase.

He made slow love to her, and as he did, his gaze never wavered. They connected, not just sexually but spiritually. Something magic passed between them, and she felt as if her fate and his combined to make two new beings. Or was it only one?

She climaxed again, this time in a different way, a softer total body release. And after she finished, he started his climb. Moving faster, his muscles tense and his gaze electric, he thrust harder, harder, and then he gave a cry that was heaven and hell. She wrapped her legs around him, riding his climax, sharing the moment, loving the man.

Loving the man.

Everything changed. In the blink of an eye. On the crest of a wave. In the arms of her man.

15

CHASE STARED UP at the ceiling as Jamie slept, nestled in the crook of his arm. Now, he'd gone and done it. He'd crossed a line he'd avoided all his life. There was no couching it in softer terms, no denying the fact. He'd fallen in love.

It wasn't the sex, and yet it was. It wasn't her little striptease, yet that was when it had first hit him. Then he'd entered her and realized he never wanted to leave. He wanted to be in her, part of her, with her, forever. Only, for him, forever wasn't in the cards.

How could he do this to her? To himself? Never before had he felt so much, so fiercely. He wanted to protect her, to care for her, to give her every gift known to man. He didn't want to go to Paris or Budapest or anywhere that would take him from her side. No one had told him this was what love was like. He'd never suspected. It was consuming, blocking out the sun and the moon and the stars. It made him someone new.

Just feeling her now, her leg curled around his, her hand on his chest, her warm breath against his skin, he wanted to make love to her again. And again.

The way she looked at him, he knew it was true for her,

too. She'd been bewitched, just as he had. Which meant that he was going to hurt her.

Whether today, or next week or in the hour of his death, he was going to crush her with pain. He cursed his father, his genes. For the first time since the truth had come to him, he wanted to change his destiny. He wanted to live.

"Jamie, what have you done?" he whispered, his gaze on her beautiful face. Mesmerized by her pale skin, by the way her eyelashes touched her cheeks, he yearned for something he couldn't have.

The thought of not telling her, of acting as if they had a lifetime ahead of them, was tempting. But it would be a lie, and he'd know it every day. He'd know that it was selfish—and how could he love someone so completely and care nothing for her feelings?

It wasn't fair. In fact, it was a cold, hard bitch—a cruel trick by an uncaring god.

He loved her. It wasn't something he could turn off like a faucet or pretend didn't exist. He had to make some decisions, and he had to make them soon. Before Paris. If there was going to be a Paris.

She stirred, and he wanted to make love to her again. But she was probably sore, and he didn't want to hurt her that way, either. Three times, he'd been inside her. Three times, he'd had mind-blowing climaxes. Three times, he'd watched her shudder with release.

He wanted her again, desperately, but instead he slipped out of bed, careful not to wake her. He went to the bathroom and started a bath. She'd need the warmth and the comfort after such a workout. He even added some bubble bath the hotel had provided.

After a few moments, he went back into the bedroom.

She was awake, and her smile made his insides go crazy. How was it possible to feel so much in such a short time? He'd never believed love could hit him like this, like a truck going sixty miles an hour. But he'd been struck, all right.

"Do I hear a bath?"

He nodded. "For you."

She sighed, and her smile warmed him. "What time is it?"

"Three."

"P.M.?"

"Yep."

"So that's why I'm so hungry."

"While you're in the tub, I'll order food. What do you want?"

"Everything."

He laughed. "I think you need to be a little more specific."

"Eggs. Bacon. Toast. Hash browns. Pancakes. Coffee. Orange juice."

"Is that all?"

"I'll let you know."

Dammit, how was he supposed to leave this? Leave her? She was everything he hadn't known he wanted. All his dreams fulfilled.

She pushed back the covers and got up. On her way to the bathroom she stopped and kissed him. "Thank you."

"My pleasure."

Her grin made her even more exquisite. "I know. I'll be out soon."

"Don't hurry. I'll let you know when breakfast comes."

"Okay."

And then she padded to the bathroom, and he watched

her naked back, entranced by her bottom and her hips and her legs and every part of her—and he wanted her. Again.

"GABBY, SLOW DOWN. Start from the beginning." Jamie sipped some tea as she brought her mind back to Gabby and her problems. It had been a difficult show. All she wanted was to go to Chase. To touch him. To make love to him. But the show must go on. Which, it suddenly occurred to her, was a crock. Who cared about a show when there was love in the air?

No. No, she did care. She loved her job. Just not as much as she loved Chase.

"He ended it," Gabby said through her tears. "He even took his CDs—and the tie I gave him for Christmas."

"Did he say anything before he left?"

Gabby sniffed. "He said he couldn't take it anymore. That I was suffocating him."

Jamie sighed. "I'm so sorry, honey. I know it must hurt like the devil."

"You do?"

"More than you can imagine. I can't think of anything tougher than to love someone with all your heart and not have that love returned."

Gabby's sniffle turned to sobs. For a moment, Jamie just let her weep. Then, softly, she said, "Gabby, there are lessons here. Maybe you can't see them today, but when you're ready, we can talk about them. You're going to find true love, but only if you can learn from this and not make the same mistakes."

"I know. I wanted too much."

"Not too much. Just from the wrong source. You have to be whole before you can share yourself. You have to make yourself happy."

"I'll never be happy again."

"You will. I promise."

"Thanks, Dr. Jamie. And sorry about that thing with Chase."

"No need to be sorry. I won."

"I don't know. You could have made love to him. You could have had the time of your life, but you didn't. That doesn't sound like winning to me."

Jamie wondered if she should tell her listeners the whole truth. No, not now, not tonight. But she knew her show wouldn't be the same after tonight. She wouldn't change the format, but she wouldn't be the same therapist. She saw now how pompous she had been in her posturing. Love wasn't something that could be quantified. Rules were for fools and virgins.

"I'll have to think about that, Gabby. Thanks. This is Dr. Jamie, and we're talking about sex."

MARCY SLIPPED into the booth across from Chase, and a moment later the waitress brought coffee. She was bursting with curiosity. Why had Chase asked to see her, and what was with all the hush-hush business?

He took a sip of coffee, then looked her straight in the eye. "I need to know you won't ever say anything about this conversation to anyone, ever."

"Okay."

"I mean it. I won't talk unless I have your word."

"You do."

He sighed, and Marcy noted how tired he looked. But still gorgeous. Her mind bounced to her man, Ted. Only, he wasn't hers. Not the way she wanted him. They'd had dinner. And after a while, she'd actually had fun. But he hadn't even tried to kiss her good-night. She hated the word *platonic*. It didn't say nearly enough about the ache in her heart.

"Jamie and I—" Chase began. He closed his mouth for a moment, then started again. "Jamie and I have a problem."

"Yes?"

"I can't tell you everything, but there are some things…"

"What?"

"Damn. I don't know how to say this, so I'm just going to talk. Jamie and I—we've, um… I've fallen in love with her."

"That's wonderful."

"No, it isn't."

"Why not?"

"It just shouldn't have happened. That's all."

"Oh, no. That's not enough. Come on, Chase. Spill it."

"You know about my father, right?"

She nodded. "He owned the station."

"And he died at thirty-five."

"I'm sorry. I had no idea he was that young."

"My grandfather died at thirty-five. And his father died at thirty-four. You get the picture?"

"Is it a heart ailment? A congenital defect?"

He shrugged. "The doctors don't know why. They can't see anything wrong, and, believe me, I've had every test in the book."

"But you still think you're going to die, like them."

"Wouldn't you?"

"I don't know."

"I do. Destiny is a hard thing to face when it doesn't hold anything good."

"But you love Jamie, right?"

"Which is the problem. Which is why I'm here. You need to look after her."

"Why?"

"Didn't you hear me?"

"Yeah. You think you're gonna die. I have news for you, Chase. No one gets out of this alive. We're all gonna die."

"Not in the next three years."

"How do you know? I might walk out of here and get hit by a bus."

"Yeah, but—"

"The truth is, you don't know what's going to happen. You might die at thirty-five or a hundred-and-five. You don't know until you go."

"But if I do go in a couple of years, what will that do to Jamie?"

"You're worried about something that might or might not happen in two years? Good God, man, you are gorgeous but you're not very bright."

"Hey—"

"You know what you have? Today. That's all. Yesterday is gone, and there isn't a thing you can do to change it. Tomorrow is a maybe, a complete unknown. So all that matters is now, right now. So you have a couple of choices. You can waste today thinking about a tomorrow you can't see, or you can live right here, right now, for all you're worth."

"You don't get it."

"I do. More than you can know. My mother had Alzheimer's, Chase. I watched a vibrant, lovely, loving woman become a stranger who didn't even know my name. And I thought about all the days I'd wasted with her. When we could have been talking and laughing and just being with each other. I can never get that back. I wasted my todays just like you are doing. I was a fool."

"There's something else."

"Uh-oh."

"It's about Jamie."

She waited, trying not to nudge him into talking faster. "She's... She was... Damn, I don't know if I should tell you. But I really think she needs a friend and, well..."

"If you don't tell me now, I'm going to strangle you."

"Oh, crap. Jamie was...a virgin."

"Pardon me?"

He nodded. "As pure as the driven snow."

"You're lying."

He shook his head, and she knew it was the truth. But how could that be? "She's Dr. Jamie."

He nodded. "Yep. And she was ready to quit because she felt like a fraud. This whole thing, it's been rough on her. I can't help her, but you can."

"Oh man. But it makes some kind of weird sense, you know? Things I couldn't quite put together. Holy— I'm assuming from your use of the past tense that she's no longer?"

"Right."

"So what's the problem?"

"I can't shake the feeling I've done something wrong, something that will hurt her. It wasn't my place—"

"Did you force her?"

"No. Jeez."

"So, she was willing and consenting?"

"Yes."

"So, it's not your problem, unless you totally sucked at it."

His grin said he didn't think so. But then, he was a guy, and sometimes they didn't see so clearly.

"Okay, then. You made love with a beautiful woman who wanted to make love to you. You fell in love with this woman and, from what you say, she fell in love right back. The only fly in the ointment is a future no one can predict. Unlike the rest of us who know every detail of what's going to happen for the rest of our lives."

"All right. I hear you."

"Do you?"

"I watched my mother fall apart after my father died. We nearly didn't make it."

"But you did. And so did your mother. Tell me, have you ever asked her if she'd have been happier if she'd never loved your father?"

He shook his head. "No."

"Ask her. I already know the answer."

He didn't say anything for a long time. Then he got his wallet, left several bills on the table and stood. "Thanks, Marcy."

"You're welcome."

"I'm glad you're Jamie's friend."

She smiled as he walked away, and she wondered if she'd ever be loved by a man like Chase. If she'd ever be loved at all.

JAMIE WALKED OUT of the elevator, and the world shifted one degree to the right. To the perfect. Chase was at her apartment door.

She hurried—hell, she ran—and she didn't even warn him when she jumped into his arms, wrapped her legs around him and kissed him senseless. He staggered, but only for a few seconds. Then he held her tight and kissed her back.

She'd memorized his scent. It was an aphrodisiac, a balm to her soul, a catalyst for her awakening. She'd thought about him all night, and if he hadn't been there, she'd have hunted him down.

He broke the kiss, making her moan, but then he smiled. "You're light as a feather, and normally I could do this for several days, but I have to use the facilities, if you get my drift."

She sighed dramatically. "Oh, okay. I suppose I could let you go. But a real man would have lasted another ten minutes at least."

"No, that would have been a real stupid man."

She slid down until her feet were on the floor, then unlocked her door. Chase scooted past her, and although she knew it was absolutely ridiculous, she felt all warm and fuzzy that they had joked about something so personal, just like a real couple.

But were they? She hadn't asked yet. Maybe because she didn't want to know. He could still leave. He could break her heart this very night. On the other hand...

She went into the kitchen to make some iced tea, and realized she didn't know if Chase liked tea or not. What if he was a beer man? She didn't have beer.

There was so much to learn about him. She didn't know anything about his family, his childhood. Why he'd gotten involved with racing and, for heaven's sake, why he didn't live in an apartment like a normal person. He could certainly afford it.

Who was this man who'd stolen her heart? Tonight, she'd find out.

His boots across her wood floor revved up her engine, and then his arms were around her waist and she leaned against his strong chest.

"Hey, beautiful," he whispered.

"Hey, handsome."

His hands moved to her breasts, and he cupped them possessively. She felt tingly. "What are you making?"

"Tea. Iced tea. Do you like it? I think I have some soda. Or maybe not. There might be a bottle of wine in the back of the fridge. Or I could go to the market—"

He spun her around. "I think I know what went wrong."

"Huh?"

"I should have kissed you immediately."

Her heart melted. "Exactly."

Once more, she was in his arms, but this time she kissed him more leisurely. They weren't going anywhere. And as for finding out about his family? That could wait. Most definitely.

Chase couldn't believe how good she felt, how she excited him so quickly. He'd meant to talk to her, to figure out together what they were going to do next. But there was no talking possible, not until he'd sunk deep inside her, until he'd made her thrash and scream, until they'd both come. And come again.

He led her toward her bedroom. Even holding her hand made him crazy. Damn, he'd thought he understood sex, but he hadn't. Sure, he knew what part went where, but he'd never guessed that it could be this fine, this important. Who knew that caring more about her than himself would lead to the most intense release he'd ever known?

"Chase?"

"Hmm?"

"Am I supposed to undress you?"

He grinned. "Not unless you want to."

"I'd rather we just hurried."

"Really, now," he said, drawing the words out slowly. He sat down on the edge of her bed, stuck his hands in his pockets, which wasn't all that easy considering his raging hard-on, and gave her a puzzled look. "You want us to hurry? Is that what you're saying?"

"Yes."

"Hmm."

"Chase!"

"Yeah?" he drawled.

"What are you doing?"

"Making you nuts."

She shook her head. "And you're doing a terrific job. I'm taking off all my clothes right now, and then I'm getting in the bed and I'm going to have sex. If you want to join me, that's fine."

"And if I don't?"

"Then, honey, it would be your loss."

He reached up, grabbed his shirt in his fists and ripped it open, sending buttons flying across the room.

Jamie laughed, really laughed, and it turned out that he got naked before she did. Then he had to help her unhook her bra and slip off her panties. He didn't mind.

And when she trailed kisses down his chest and took him in her mouth, he had to use all his control not to come in seconds. When he couldn't stand the pleasure anymore, he lifted her by the shoulders and spread her on the bed. He kissed her over and over as his hands slid down to her sex, and then he explored her like a blind man reading braille, every wrinkle and fold and crevice, and her pleasure became his pleasure.

After a long, long time, she took the lead, and she had him flat on his back. She straddled him, and their eyes met. She lowered herself inch by slow inch, then she did the most amazing thing. She moved her body like a belly dancer would, undulating, squeezing, swaying over him in a way designed to make him mad with lust.

He felt the wave build, and she somehow knew, and her

rhythm changed. No more tricks or teasing. She balanced herself on her feet, braced her arms on his chest, and she rode him until he wanted to yell. Full strokes, until only the tip was inside her, then down to the base, over and over, so tight, so hot, he couldn't think, couldn't see. But he could feel.

He thrust his hips up to meet her, and then he came so hard he almost blacked out. He heard his own cry as if from a distance, his whole focus, every part of him, centered on their connection.

When he came back to earth, she was still on top, and he was still inside her. She smiled a woman's smile, knowing exactly what she'd done to him.

"So you say you've never done this before?" he asked.

She shook her head. "Well, except for last night."

"Fair enough."

"What's that smile for?"

"I was just wondering what you'll be like when you get good at this."

She smiled as she leaned forward, then she kissed him. He never wanted the moment to end. He had had enough of reality. Now he wanted ecstasy, and he wanted it forever.

His intention was to tell her everything. But, coward that he was, he didn't.

Tomorrow. Tomorrow would be for hard truth. Tonight would be for magic.

SHE TIPTOED OUT of the bedroom and closed the door. He needed to sleep some more. So did she, but that wasn't going to happen. Since she'd already grabbed a shower, she might as well get something to eat. It made sense to her that lovers died in each other's arms—they probably just screwed each other to death. That wasn't going to happen to them. She figured she'd wake up Chase with a big old omelette and some toast, and if she wasn't mistaken, there was some bacon in the crisper.

But first she'd grab the paper. She undid the locks as quietly as she could, then opened the door a smidge. As always, the *Times* and the *Post* were side by side at her door. She grabbed them, hoping no one would walk by; she had on Chase's shirt, and it had no buttons. Once inside, she locked the door again and headed for the kitchen.

She didn't open the paper until the eggs were in the pan and the bacon was cooking in the microwave. Why she chose to look at the *Post* first was a mystery. It wasn't her usual habit. In fact, she always looked at the *Times*. But not this afternoon.

She stood by the table, juice in one hand, and unfolded the paper. For a moment, she didn't understand the headline. She certainly didn't think it was about her. Not until she saw the picture of Chase, the picture of her.

Her gaze moved back to the bold words, "Sex Doctor a Virgin!" And then the byline, "Darlene Whittaker."

The juice glass slipped from her hand and broke into a million pieces, right along with her heart.

16

JAMIE HAD TO SIT DOWN, or else she would fall down. God, how could he? She'd thought she knew him, but it was all a charade. The betrayal was like a fatal knife wound killing her over and over again.

Chase had never loved her. She didn't even know if he liked her. And she would have given up the world for him.

Burying her head in her hands, the tears came, her grief made tangible. It wasn't enough. She needed to do something, hurt someone, rail at God. But she couldn't, not with him in the other room.

How could she have been so stupid, so wrong? Dear God, she had no business telling anyone on earth what to do. How could she give advice when she was such an unbelievable moron?

She thought back to the way he'd laughed at her impromptu striptease. To know the laughter had been real, that it wasn't affectionate or loving in any way, made her want to crawl under a rock and die. Why had he come to see her last night—after his mission had been accomplished?

Was it to rub salt in the wound? To dig up more of her

secret past? Or was she just a convenient hole before he went off to Paris?

She stood up, rage filling her with the need for revenge. She'd go in the bedroom. Confront him with his lies. Tell him... Tell him what? That he had crippled her? That she'd fallen for all of his honeyed words? That she was the biggest fool in America?

It was too much, too new for her to speak with any clarity. She wanted him out of here so she could curl up in the fetal position and weep until there were no more tears. Maybe later, maybe after she'd cried herself a river, she'd be able to ask him why. How he could be so evil. What he got for making such a fool of her.

To think he and Whittaker were in cahoots the whole time. She moaned with the humiliation. Of course she'd lose her job, but she'd also lose the respect of her peers, her listeners and everyone else that mattered to her.

If only she'd been strong. If she'd stuck to her guns. If she hadn't been duped by his smile, his voice, the way he looked at her.

Her world had crashed around her, and the only thing she could blame was her own naiveté.

She sprang from her chair, a wave of panic sending her into the living room and to her bedroom door. She must get out. Now. God forbid he should wake up. But where could she go?

Marcy. She'd talk to Marcy, and her friend would help her see. What time was it? Two in the afternoon. Wherever Marcy was, she'd have her cell phone with her. The only thing Jamie had to do was somehow get her clothes without waking Chase, and get the hell out of here.

Opening the door slowly, she saw that he was still sleeping the sleep of the innocent. The bastard. On tiptoes, she walked in, gathered up her clothes, her shoes, her purse. Then, without disturbing him, she walked away and closed the door behind her. With luck, it would be the last time she'd ever see him.

Five minutes later, she was dressed. Her hair was a nightmare and she wasn't wearing makeup, but she didn't care. She couldn't be here, not another second.

When she reached the front door, her gaze went back to the bedroom. Half an hour ago, she'd been walking ten feet off the ground. Her world had been shiny and perfect. Now, she felt like she'd been hit by a speeding train. Thanks, Chase.

"CALM DOWN, I can't understand you," said Marcy.

Chase rubbed the sleep out of his eyes and stared at the newspaper headline again. It still turned his stomach. "Darlene Whittaker wrote a front page story for the *Post*. Want to hear the headline? 'Sex Doctor a Virgin.' Want to hear the line after that? 'How her hoax will change radio forever.'"

"My God."

"Is that all you can say?" He crumpled the paper in his hand, wishing it were Darlene's neck. Or Marcy's.

"What do you want me to say? It's devastating."

"Then, why did you do it?"

"What?"

"Marcy, I didn't tell Darlene. That leaves you and Jamie. Considering she ran out of her own apartment, I don't think she's the main suspect."

"Chase, watch it. You don't want to say something you'll regret."

"You're telling me you didn't call Darlene?"

"I'm telling you exactly that. I haven't opened my mouth, not to a living soul."

Something told him she was telling the truth, which meant that somehow, someone else had found out about Jamie. "Do you think Jamie could have told someone?"

"She wouldn't have called Darlene Whittaker if the reporter was the last person on earth."

"I don't mean Darlene. I mean anyone. An old friend. Someone at the station. Someone she thought she could trust."

"I can't tell you that. But for what it's worth, I'm probably her closest friend and I knew nothing. I was stunned when you told me."

"You were?"

"Well, of course. What did you think?"

"I don't know. You were pretty cool."

"I get paid to be pretty cool."

"Shit." He sat down hard. "She must think it was me."

"Probably."

"So how do I clear myself? She'll never believe me."

"She will, Chase, if what you told me was true. If you love her, she'll know it. Maybe not immediately, but she'll come around."

"Are you sure?"

"I hope so. Damn, I hated that bitch Whittaker from the moment I saw her."

Chase stood, his thoughts tumbling on top of each other. "Marcy, find her. Take care of her. I've got something to do. But whatever you do, make her do her show tonight."

"Wait—"

He didn't. He was going to make sure Jamie knew he hadn't told about her. And he was going to get a retraction in the paper. No one messed with someone he cared about. Not if they expected to keep breathing.

JAMIE AVOIDED almost everyone on her trek to the office. Everyone except the news vendor on the corner. He grinned at her as if they'd shared a joke. "Hey, is what they say in the paper true? You still a virgin, Doc?"

She didn't answer him, afraid she'd burst into hysterics right there on 57th Street. Instead, she walked as quickly as she could inside the building, went right to the emporium on the ground floor and bought a rather ugly, old-fashioned men's rain hat. It cost almost forty dollars, but Jamie didn't care. If she could have, she would have bought a tent to hide under.

The thing she'd feared most had come to pass. To make matters worse, the truth being revealed turned out not to be the most devastating event in her life. That honor went to Chase Newman's deception. She'd finally dared to love, to trust. And he'd squished her under his boot heel like an ant.

Shoving her change in her pocket, she plopped the hat on her head and brought it down over her eyes so that she could barely see. But then, people could barely see her, so that was fine.

Her disguise worked all the way to her office. Of course, it helped that no one was in the reception area. She prayed for Marcy, who hadn't answered her phone, to be in her office. And for a change, her prayer was answered.

Marcy rose from her desk, and from the look on her face, Jamie knew she'd read the story.

She flew into the older woman's arms, and for a long time, she had no idea how long, she wept, bawled like a baby. Wave after wave of pain washed over her, and she was helpless to stop it.

Marcy rocked her back and forth, calming her with quiet compassion until Jamie could breathe again.

"I don't understand," she said, her voice laden with tears. "How could he? I fell in love with him and he—"

"You don't know that," Marcy said. "He might not have had anything to do with it."

"No one else knew. No one on the planet."

"Honey, there could be another explanation. Even if you can't see it right now. What you have to look at is what you know about Chase. Did he ever behave in a way that would even suggest he could do something this heinous?"

"Marcy, I've only known him a week. He could be Jack the Ripper, for all I know."

Marcy pushed her back to arm's length and forced Jamie to meet her gaze. "That's a lie, and you know it."

"How is it a lie?"

"Because you're incredibly intuitive. Why do you think you're so brilliant at what you do? You read people, Jamie, like I read a book. You see where they need confidence, or where they've been wounded. You can't fake that. Radio audiences are too smart for that."

"Radio audiences? I don't have any, not anymore. Everything I love was wiped out with a headline. I'm a fraud, Marcy, and it's time you knew it. I have no business trying to help people. What the hell do I know? I believed in Chase."

"I still believe in Chase."

"Why?"

"Because I'm pretty damn intuitive myself. And I think he loves you and he wouldn't ever hurt you."

"No? Okay, aside from the whole life-altering-betrayal thing, what about Paris? Budapest? He's out of here. On the next plane. What does that say about his love for me?"

"You don't know that, either."

"Marcy, who's your friend, him or me? Why are you trying to protect him?"

"Because you're my friend. And I think you care a great deal about Chase, and the same is true for him."

"Right. He cares for Chase, too."

"Stop it."

"Why? He told Darlene Whittaker the most awful secret of my life!"

"Why is it so awful?"

Jamie stopped. "What?"

"Why is your being a virgin so awful? Lots of people are. It's not that big a deal."

"Tell that to Lorraine or Gabby. These people trusted me."

"So? They still do."

"That's not possible. I betrayed them. How can they get advice on sex from someone who's never had sex?"

"Jamie, honey, what you talk to them about isn't sex. It's about being a person. Feelings. Emotions. How to handle the scary business of life."

"Exactly. And I don't have any idea how to handle life."

"Yes, you do. Your gift hasn't been diminished. In fact, I bet there are hundreds and hundreds of women who'll applaud your decision to wait."

Jamie shook her head. "Yeah, I wasn't satisfied with sleeping with any son of a bitch. I waited until I found *the* son of a bitch."

"Will you at least give him a chance? Let him tell you his side of the story?"

"No. The evidence is in black and white. He did this thing to me, and I'm sorry, Marcy, but it's unforgivable."

"I think you're making a mistake."

"It wouldn't be the first time."

CHASE RODE UP to Darlene's apartment building and stepped off his bike. She was home, he knew that. He also knew quite a number of other things about her. The past few hours had been hectic but fascinating. He'd never dreamed so many of his father's old friends would help. And each one had a story to tell, a memory to share. His father, even in his short life, had touched a hell of a lot of people.

But that wasn't the central issue. Darlene needed a lesson in ethics, and he was just the man to teach her.

JAMIE SIPPED HER TEA curled up in Marcy's leather chair, hiding from the rest of the world. She was supposed to go on the air in a few hours, but she didn't see how. She was a wreck.

Her mind kept slinking over to Marcy's side, trying to conceive of some way Chase could be innocent. But it was dangerous ground, like walking in quicksand. If she continued to harbor the slightest doubt about his guilt, then she was likely to let down her defenses—and then she was done for. Chase was too slick, too charming. And the truth was, she wanted to believe him. She wanted everything to be the way it was this morning. When he'd made slow love to her. The look in his eyes—

No, no, no. She couldn't go there. It would just start her crying again, and she didn't have the strength.

The sound of someone entering Marcy's outer office distracted her, and she sighed, staring at the slightly open door, waiting for her friend to come in. Only, she didn't. Just as Jamie was going to get up to investigate, she heard someone else come through the outer door.

"Hey, Marcy."

That was Ted's voice.

"Hello."

"You wanted to see me?"

Marcy cleared her throat. "I did."

"Here I am. Want to—"

"No. I want to stay right here, because if I don't spit this out this second, I never will."

"What?"

Jamie leaned forward, straining to hear, even though she knew it was none of her business. Marcy's voice sounded so...odd.

"I wanted you to know that when I asked you out to dinner, it wasn't as a friend."

"No?"

"Uh-uh."

"What did you ask me out for?"

"Damn. I'm sorry, I'm probably going to embarrass the hell out of you. I never dreamed I'd say anything like this, but my friend, she's going through a lot right now because she doesn't know the real story, and I don't want to miss out on something that could be totally terrific because I was a chicken, so I'm just going to say it, and you don't have to worry, if it's no, I'll under—"

Marcy's voice stopped mid-word. But, if Jamie wasn't mistaken, there were still signs of life coming from the other room. Kissing sounds. Scratch that. *Major* kissing sounds.

After an embarrassingly long time, she heard a deep intake of breath and a nervous cough.

"Why didn't you tell me?" Marcy asked.

"I wasn't sure how you felt."

"Me? Are you kidding?"

He shook his head. "I haven't done this in a while. I wasn't sure I was reading the signals correctly. I've been trying to get up my nerve to talk to you."

"Oh."

He laughed softly. "Thank you."

"Me? For what?"

"For being so brave. Imagine all the time and misery we've saved because you were willing to put yourself out there. No wonder I'm crazy about you."

"Really?"

Marcy's voice was high-pitched, breathy, and so full of happiness that Jamie wanted to cry. For her friend. Okay, so some of it was jealousy, but the lion's share wasn't. She just kinda wished she couldn't hear all the smooching. She loved Marcy, but not that much.

There was no way to sneak out. She'd have to wait until they finished. She might as well use the time to think. About Ted and Marcy. About bravery. About missed connections.

"Is it true?"

Jamie inhaled, closed her eyes and prayed for the right words. "It was true, Lorraine. It's not true any longer."

"You mean, you lost the bet?"

The bet? Who cared about that? She'd just admitted that she'd had no personal sexual experience while she was counseling on the air, and her listeners were concerned about the bet?

"Dr. Jamie?"

"No, Lorraine. I didn't lose. Because I walked into the situation with my eyes open. There was no seduction, no trickery. I'm fully responsible for my own actions."

"Wow. So, uh, was he, you know, as good as he looks?"

Jamie felt as if she'd been punched. But she'd made the decision to answer any questions honestly. To speak only the truth, whatever the repercussions. "He was."

"Man, that is so cool."

"Are you telling me you're not upset about my, uh, situation?"

"You mean the article?"

"Yes."

"I can't believe you got to be as old as you did without doing the deed, but, no, why should it bother me?"

"Because I've given you advice."

"So has my priest. Your advice is better."

"Oh."

"You sound disappointed. Did you want me to be upset?"

"No," she said, but she had to wonder if that was the absolute truth. "I just felt so guilty. Now, I'm feeling pretty foolish."

"I have someone you can call," Lorraine said. "Her name is Dr. Jamie, and she's the best. She helped me see that I'm doing the best I can with what I've got, as long as I'm taking responsibility for my actions. That I need to be true to my heart, and that I need balance in my life."

Jamie's eyes burned with tears that she struggled to hold back. "Thank you," she whispered. "More than you'll ever know. This is Dr. Jamie, and we're talking about life."

Cujo took his cue, and Jamie leaned back in her chair, trying to figure out what had just happened. She'd been on the air for almost an hour with three different women. Not one had cared a whit about her virginity. They were curious about her reactions to her first time, and, despite her vow to be honest, she wasn't able to talk about that. Not that she lied. She just explained that she wasn't ready for the discussion yet.

The pain was so acute, maybe she'd never be ready. But then, how else could she turn this fiasco into something positive? There was a lesson here. She just wondered what it was.

At least she still had her show. Which was a bloody miracle. Marcy had clocked in a record number of calls, and Fred had been using the *Post* article to generate more publicity. So, was she nuts for feeling as if she'd been a fraud? That she owed everyone an apology?

The commercials were almost over, and for that she was grateful. Too much time to think led her straight down the tubes. She'd heard so many good things about Chase from people who'd known him for years. How could that be? Was it possible Marcy was right?

Four, three, two... "We're back." She scooted closer to the mike. "Our next caller is—"

"Dr. Jamie?"

At Marcy's voice, Jamie looked up at the window. Her producer rarely interrupted her show, especially not seconds after a commercial break. "Yes?"

"Why don't we talk to our next caller after we visit with our guest?"

Even before the door to her booth opened, Jamie knew it was Chase. She stood, wanting to run and hide, but there was only the one door. How could Marcy betray her, too?

Astonishingly, it wasn't Chase who walked in. Her old nemesis Darlene Whittaker had come back to the scene of the crime. *Oh, perfect.* Jamie would have given just about anything to disappear from the face of the earth right now. Her anger felt like a burning coal in her stomach, and if she'd known the first thing about martial arts, Whittaker would be on her butt by now.

"Jamie?"

Marcy's voice reminded her she was on the air. "Our guest is none other than Darlene Whittaker. Normally,

Darlene writes magazine articles, but lately she's been moonlighting for the *New York Post*. How nice to see you, Darlene."

The woman of the moment didn't seem very happy to be there. Where Jamie had expected gloating, she saw only discomfort. Jamie felt no sympathy.

"I'm, uh, sorry about all this."

"Right. So, tell me, did you and Chase have this all planned out before you came to the station that night? Or was it an impromptu deal?"

"Chase didn't know."

"Uh-huh."

Whittaker, pale in another black dress, this one boxier than the last, her hair pulled back in a tortoiseshell clip, swallowed, then turned for a quick glance at the door behind her. "He didn't."

"Want to tell me how you got this little tidbit of a headline?"

"I had someone planted in the coffee shop across the street."

"Someone?"

She nodded miserably. "He was there in case anyone from the station came in. He was supposed to eavesdrop. See if he could get any dirt."

"He must have gotten pretty sick of their apple pie."

"He wasn't there all the time. He knew when anyone from your show had a break. He timed it well, and he had one of the waitresses call. One of those times, he hit pay dirt."

"All for little ol' me?"

"Look, I'm sorry, okay?"

"Why?"

She didn't answer for a long while. Jamie just sat still and waited.

"You want the truth?"

Jamie nodded.

"Not because I ran the story, but because it backfired. No one cares. The paper has gotten hundreds of calls. *Vanity Fair* wants to pull me and assign another writer to do the article on you."

"I see."

"Can I go now?"

"No. Why are you here, Darlene? You don't want to be."

"You know."

"Tell me."

"Chase. He brought me down here. He wanted you to know he didn't spill the beans intentionally."

Jamie's relief should have been complete, but there was still one piece missing. She looked at Marcy. "Send him in, okay?"

Marcy nodded.

"You can go," Jamie told Whittaker.

The woman didn't need a second invitation. The door swung open, she dashed out, and Chase walked in. God, her heart went crazy, beating as if it wanted to hop out of her chest. She could hardly gather a breath, and dammit if she didn't start crying again. He hadn't told, at least not directly.

He held out his arms to her, but she stepped back. "Wait."

He let his arms drop. "What is it?"

"I need to know. Someone overheard you in the coffee shop. Who were you talking to, and why on earth would my virginity be part of the discussion?"

Chase stole a glance at Marcy, then his gaze came back to Jamie. "I was talking to your producer," he said.

"And, even though it was a confidence, I needed her to know all the facts before I made my final decision."

"What decision?"

"In a minute. Marcy and I talked a lot that afternoon, and all either of us wanted was your happiness. My God, you have to believe that."

"I'd like to." He stepped closer, and this time she didn't back away. His dark, soulful eyes made her want to run to his arms. But she couldn't, not until this was all cleared up.

"Marcy was helping me decide whether I should stay or go. Leaving was pretty much the only option I could see. I never meant to care for you."

"Remarkably, this isn't making me feel better."

"Give it another minute. See, there was something I hadn't told you, something big."

"Do I really need to hear this?"

"Yeah, you do. Jamie, my father died at thirty-five. My grandfather, my great-grandfather, they all died around that age."

"Is it a medical syndrome?"

"Not that they're aware of. But my mother, she called it the Newman curse. She's always been pretty convinced I would go the way of the rest of the men in my family."

"And?"

"And I'd seen what happened to her, to me, when my father died. I didn't want to put you through it."

"Is it a sure thing? No question, you're gonna go in three years?"

He shook his head. "But it's a damn strong possibility."

"And you weren't sure I'd want you under the circumstances."

"That's about right."

"You should have asked me."

"I know."

She made the move this time. Right up to him, so she had to lean her head back to make eye contact. "Chase, I love you."

"I know."

"And I think you feel the same way about me."

"I do."

"So what the hell is the problem? If I lose you, it'll be horrible, but infinitely better than if I'd never had you at all."

"Are you sure?"

She sighed. "You love me, right?"

He nodded.

"So reverse the situation. If I were the one with the supposed curse, would you want me to leave today?"

His arms went around her back and he pulled her close. "Not on your life."

"Yours, either."

"It might really happen, you know. This isn't a joke."

"I'll deal with it, either way, any way. But I'm still not sure why you told Marcy—"

"I told her because I wasn't sure of the right thing to do. Marcy is your closest friend. I trusted her judgment. And I wanted her to look out for you."

"What did she say?"

"She said I should stop being a damn fool. That if we love each other, that's all that matters."

"Smart cookie, that Marcy."

He nodded. "I wonder if she's smart enough to find a replacement for you."

"What?"

"Because I'm stealing you right here and right now. You're coming with me, and I'll tell you what we're gonna do."

"Yes?"

"We're gonna talk about love."

"Okay."

"And then we're gonna do something about sex."

"Okay."

"And then—"

"Wait," she said, putting her finger to his lips. "Let's save the rest for just us."

"Deal." Then he leaned down and kissed her. The man who'd lied for her, fought for her honor, been so concerned about her well-being that he was willing to walk away, kissed her.

She kissed him back with all her heart and all her happiness. Just as she'd known in some deep, secret place that he was going to be the one, she also knew she'd have him for a long, long time.

Forever, no matter what.

He pulled back, took her hand and tugged her toward the door. She just had enough time to toss her headphones to Ted before she was swept down the hall and into the elevator. When the doors hissed shut, Chase did something *very* naughty and *very* wonderful.

She was the one to press the emergency stop.

Epilogue

Seven years later...

"Hello, everyone. Good morning. It's Dr. Jamie, and we're talking about life. My first guest this morning is none other than my incredible husband, Chase. Are you there?"

"Yep."

"Happy birthday, sweetie. For those who don't know, today is Chase's thirty-eighth birthday."

"Thanks."

"Why don't you tell the listeners what we did to celebrate?"

He laughed and, as always, even after all these years, it made her stomach do flip-flops. "We went to the doctor."

"And?"

"We got me a complete physical."

"Right. And what was the outcome?"

"I'm healthy as a horse."

She grinned. "Now I'll tell you about your other present."

"What would that be?"

"Tonight, Marcy and Ted are going to pick up the kids

for dinner, and they're going to watch them all night long."

"Oh?"

"And I'm going to…"

"What?"

She laughed. "Sorry. I'll just have to show you. But I will give you a hint. The last time you saw me do this thing, you couldn't stop laughing."

He was quiet for several seconds. "Oh, really?"

"This time, I don't think you'll be laughing so hard."

"Jamie, have you had lessons?"

"You'll have to find out. And, my dear listeners, I just want you to know that while sex is wonderful, healthy, normal and exciting, it's love that makes the world go round. This is Dr. Jamie, encouraging you all to go for it…"

* * * * *

Harlequin Blaze

COMING NEXT MONTH

Available August 30, 2011

#633 TOO WILD TO HOLD
Legendary Lovers
Julie Leto

#634 NIGHT MANEUVERS
Uniformly Hot!
Jillian Burns

#635 JUST GIVE IN…
Harts of Texas
Kathleen O'Reilly

#636 MAKING A SPLASH
The Wrong Bed: Again and Again
Joanne Rock

#637 WITNESS SEDUCTION
Elle Kennedy

#638 ROYALLY ROMANCED
A Real Prince
Marie Donovan

You can find more information on upcoming
Harlequin® titles, free excerpts and more at
www.HarlequinInsideRomance.com.

HBCNM0811

REQUEST YOUR FREE BOOKS!
2 FREE NOVELS PLUS 2 FREE GIFTS!

red-hot reads!

Rafael de Luca had been in bad situations before. A crowded ballroom could never make him sweat.

These people would never know that he had no memory of any of them.

He surveyed the party with grim tolerance, searching for the source of his unease.

At first his gaze flickered past her, but he yanked his attention back to a woman across the room. Her stare bored holes through him. Unflinching and steady, even when his eyes locked with hers.

Petite, even in heels, she had a creamy olive complexion. A wealth of inky-black curls cascaded over her shoulders and her eyes were equally dark.

She looked at him as if she'd already judged him and found him lacking. He'd never seen her before in his life. Or had he?

He cursed the gaping hole in his memory. He'd been diagnosed with selective amnesia after his accident four months ago. Which seemed like complete and utter bull. No one got amnesia except hysterical women in bad soap operas.

With a smile, he disengaged himself from the group

around him and made his way to the mystery woman.

She wasn't coy. She stared straight at him as he approached, her chin thrust upward in defiance.

"Excuse me, but have we met?" he asked in his smoothest voice.

His gaze moved over the generous swell of her breasts pushed up by the empire waist of her black cocktail dress.

When he glanced back up at her face, he saw fury in her eyes.

"Have we *met?*" Her voice was barely a whisper, but he felt each word like the crack of a whip.

Before he could process her response, she nailed him with a right hook. He stumbled back, holding his nose.

One of his guards stepped between Rafe and the woman, accidentally sending her to one knee. Her hand flew to the folds of her dress.

It was then, as she cupped her belly, that the realization hit him. She was pregnant.

Her eyes flashing, she turned and ran down the marble hallway.

Rafael ran after her. He burst from the hotel lobby, and saw two shoes sparkling in the moonlight, twinkling at him.

He blew out his breath in frustration and then shoved the pair of sparkly, ultrafeminine heels at his head of security.

"Find the woman who wore these shoes."

Will Rafael find his mystery woman?
Find out in Maya Banks's passionate new novel
ENTICED BY HIS FORGOTTEN LOVER
Available September 2011 from Harlequin® Desire®!

HDEXP0911

ALWAYS POWERFUL, PASSIONATE AND PROVOCATIVE.

**NEW YORK TIMES AND USA TODAY
BESTSELLING AUTHOR**

MAYA BANKS

**BRINGS YOU THE FIRST STORY
IN A BRAND-NEW MINISERIES**

PASSION & PREGNANCY

*When irresistible tycoons
face the consequences of temptation.*

ENTICED BY HIS
FORGOTTEN LOVER

A bout of amnesia…a mysterious woman
he can't resist…a pregnancy shocker.

When Rafael de Luca's memory comes
crashing back, it will change everything.

*Available September
wherever books are sold.*